Ariel Ellman

WitchBound

Book One

The Northwoods Pack Series

This is a work of fiction. Names, characters, places, and incidents are either the product of the author's imagination or are used fictitiously, and any resemblance to actual persons living or dead, business establishments, events, or locales, is entirely coincidental.

WitchBound

© Copyright 2023 by Ariel Ellman

All rights reserved. No part of this book may be used or reproduced in any manner whatsoever without written permission of the author except in the case of brief quotations embodied in critical articles or reviews.

Cover Art by Daniel Hertzberg

Publishing History: First Edition

Published by Ariel Ellman

To my Writers Circle workshop group.

1

I almost passed out in relief when I pulled up the long dirt drive and spotted my newly inherited log cabin I'd abandoned my New York City apartment for. Its light-golden log frame and wide glass picture windows overlooking the lake, sparkled in the Maine late spring sunshine, giving off Hallmark movie vibes, right down to the forest green Adirondack chairs arranged cozily on the wrap-around porch. Add a pine wreath to the door and some snow dusting the welcome mat in the winter, and I could be living in a real-life holiday special, *Christmas in the Maine Northwoods*.

That was the first thought that flashed through my mind when I came to a stop. Then I wondered who the scary looking welcoming party was, as a trio of three, seriously buff, huntsmen looking guys stepped out of the woods.

"What's he doing?" one of the guys called out as I sat unmoving in my ancient, dark red, GMC pickup truck, staring at them, lining up in front of the cabin.

They were probably early 20's, just a few years younger than me. One had dark skin and a cool, messy afro, the other two were white, with a dark brown man-bun, and tangle of deep red curls. They had on dark T-shirts and ripstop pants, and man-bun had a knife strapped on his waist. They were either going rock climbing or about to kill me.

"What do you think I'm doing?" I muttered under my breath, checking to make sure my truck door was locked. "Not getting out of the truck in the middle of the woods to be murdered by the evil queen's huntsmen, obviously."

"Huntsmen? Do you think that was an insult or a compliment?" the tallest of the three guys asked his companions.

Oh, this was great. There was only one reason I could think of that the evil huntsman guy could have heard my muttered commentary inside the truck from across the driveway. They must be fucking werewolves. My new werewolf friend Cian, the guy who left me this cabin and truck, totally had supersonic hearing. That guy could hear me breathing when I was a block away from him.

Of course, he conveniently left out the part about the other werewolves lurking in the woods around his cabin when he sent me here. With my luck, I'd just stumbled onto an entire werewolf pack and was probably trespassing on their territory.

"You idiots weren't supposed to come here," a deep voice called out in exasperation, and the most beautiful guy I'd ever seen stepped out of the forest and in front of my truck.

If the other guys were the evil queen's huntsmen, this guy was definitely their leader. He radiated authority and power. He was all raw masculinity and hear me roar, several inches taller than my own six-foot frame, with short dark hair, just long enough to run your fingers through, long legs tucked into jeans and work boots, with an open flannel over a T-shirt that did little to hide his rippling chest muscles and perfect abs.

He looked scary, and from the way the guys behind him were shrinking back, he must be dangerous, but instead of fear, I instantly thought, safe and warm, and yum. If he was the leader of the huntsmen, he was the one who helped Snow White get away.

I had the strangest desire to jump out of the truck and lick him, and I don't just mean in a sexual way. He made me want to curl up in his lap and nuzzle his chest by a fire, and I'm not a nuzzler. I'm more of a bend-you-over-in-a-dark-alley kind of a guy, who tosses your number in the dumpster after I walk away. It's not that I'm an asshole, exactly, I just don't cuddle, nuzzle, or do attachment.

"Get out of the truck, we're not going to hurt you," the super-hot, guy-in-charge commanded. At least, it felt like a command, and that's what broke the dreamy, I want to curl up in your lap and lick you all over spell for me. You could say I'm a little prickly about being ordered around. Comes with the territory of having to fend for myself my whole life. I don't let anyone push me around, and I have plenty of my own rippling muscles under my shirt to back me up.

"Fuck off," I shot back, reaching below my seat for my trusty K-bar knife. If these fuckers wanted to rumble, they weren't getting me out of my truck without a fight.

"Did he just tell Griffin to fuck off?" huntsman number two exhaled in shock. The other guys gaped in disbelief.

Hottie lumberjack centerfold cocked his head to the side and stared at me curiously, his nostrils flaring as my heart rate sped up and he seemed to smell the adrenaline running through my body as I tensed, readying myself for the fight. Enhanced hearing and smell were definitely signs of a werewolf. This was perfect, things were looking worse for me by the minute.

But instead of dragging me out of the truck, he sniffed the air between us again, his eyes going carefully blank.

"Get out of here," he growled at the guys behind him, and as they turned and ran into the woods, he stepped away from the truck, raising his hands up in a non-threatening way.

"They weren't supposed to come here. They were just being stupid, nosy kids because they heard you pull up. I'm sorry if they scared you," he said, continuing to back away until there was a healthy distance between us, and my heart rate started to regulate. It was almost like he could hear it beating in my chest, because he stopped backing away as soon as it slowed down.

He called those burly wolves, kids? I mean, I guess they could have been teenagers, but they looked pretty scary to me.

"What do you want?" I finally asked, manually rolling the truck window down now that he was standing a respectable distance away. He might have enhanced hearing, but I didn't, and I was sick of straining to hear him.

"This is my brother's house, and that's his truck," he replied, inhaling deeply, sniffing the air between us when I rolled the window down. His eyes flickered with something unidentifiable, and I caught a sudden flash of heat before they went blank again.

"Cian's your brother?" I exclaimed, tired of hiding in my truck, waiting to be attacked. I shut the engine off and hopped out, tucking the K-bar into the back of my pants, because, duh, not a complete idiot.

"Yes," my huntsman/werewolf replied quietly, his eyes drinking me in as I walked over.

He smelled like the forest, and a shiver brushed across my skin as I stopped in front of him. Jesus, what was it with this guy? It wasn't like I hadn't been around a hot guy before. I had plenty to drool over on a daily basis, bartending at a gay bar in the city, and it was a rare night someone didn't take me up on my well-practiced under-the-eyelashes, come-hither invitation. And I don't think it was the werewolf thing that had me sweating him, because I'd lived with the guy's brother for the last four months and never once considered mounting him.

"Finn." I held out my hand.

"Griffin." He clasped my hand in his roughly. Up close, he was even bigger than I'd thought. He had at least four inches on me, and his hand was almost double the size of mine as he swallowed up my palm in his tight grip.

"I didn't know Cian had any family," I admitted, regretting my words as a flash of pain shot through Griffin's dark eyes.

"Are you together? Are you his boyfriend?" Griffin asked, the words coming out in an almost strangled growl.

"Me and Cian? God, no," I laughed, and something like relief flashed in Griffin's eyes before he looked toward the lake, visible through the trees behind us.

"But he gave you his house and truck?" Griffin brought his dark, searching eyes back to meet my gaze.

"Yes," I sighed, running a hand through my rumpled hair. "He gave me his house and truck, and I quit my job and gave up my apartment, so unless you're about to tell me this was a whole twisted joke, and the place is actually yours, I'd like to go inside. You're welcome to join me. It's just that I've been driving for the last eight hours, and I desperately need to take a piss and eat something, I feel like I'm about to pass out."

"Of course, go ahead," Griffin murmured, stiffening in what looked like concern. "Here." He yanked a rumpled looking protein bar out of his jeans' pocket and thrust it into my hand. It was warm and slightly squashed.

"Uh, thanks, I guess." I tore the wrapper open and sniffed it before biting into it as we walked up the porch steps to the house.

"Better?" Griffin eyed me as I scarfed down the bar while digging into my pocket for the key to the cabin.

"Unmf," I replied over a mouthful of the protein bar, pulling the crumpled envelope with the letter and the key Cian had sent me out of my pocket.

Griffin stepped away from me as I pulled the key out, his eyes sweeping over his brother's scrawling handwriting on the envelope.

"You can read it if you want," I offered, holding out the letter.

I was suddenly struck by how similar the brothers looked. I don't know why I hadn't seen it when Griffin first jumped in front of the truck. They had the same soulful dark eyes and playful, questioning slant to their brows. I guess it was just that Cian had never felt sexual to me, and the pheromones his brother was giving off were so distracting, I could barely remember my own name.

Griffin took the envelope silently, following me inside and flipping on light switches with an easy familiarity as we walked through the house. The cabin was as charming inside, as it was on the outside, small, but cozy and obviously well-loved.

The wide-planked hardwood floor of the large living room overlooking the lake, was covered in a braided, well-worn rug, its colors muted with age. A set of wooden canoe paddles hung on the wall above a massive stone fireplace, giving off a laid-back vibe, and there were signs of Cian and his mate Nate everywhere.

I instantly understood why Cian never wanted to come back here, why he gave me his cabin and truck and took off. Everywhere I looked, there was a reminder of the life Cian had lost with his mate. A set of fishing poles and a tackle box leaned against the wall by the porch door, two rain jackets hung on a wrought iron wolf hook in the entryway, and a massive jigsaw puzzle of a forest landscape lay incomplete on the rustic, log coffee table.

"We didn't want to touch anything after Nate died and Cian left, we didn't know if it was better to leave things as they were or pack them away," Griffin said, watching me take everything in.

"I don't know if Cian will ever be able come back here," I sighed, and Griffin raised an eyebrow at me in response, settling into an overstuffed leather chair by the fireplace with his brother's letter still clenched in his hand.

"When Cian wrote me that letter, giving me his cabin, he said he needed to learn to live in a world without Nate," I tried to explain. "He said he felt deaf and blind without him, his limbs dead. There were days I didn't think Cian would lift his head up from the pillow at all. But maybe once he learns to live without Nate, he'll come back here and want the reminders of him that are left behind."

"Bathroom is down the hall," Griffin replied, his face blank as he turned on the rustic wrought iron lamp on the table beside him, and I slipped into the bathroom to leave him to read in peace.

It had never occurred to me Cian had any family. He was so obviously, heart wrenchingly alone when I found him passed out in the alley behind the bar while taking the trash out. He was skin and bones, covered in piss and vomit, and I'd just assumed he was like me, a street kid, runaway, or orphan, who grew up in shitty foster homes and on the streets.

When Cian shifted into a huge, reddish-brown wolf, bone crunching sounds and all, right in front of me while waking up one morning, I didn't completely freak out. Unless you count diving off the bed and grabbing my baseball bat as freaking out.

I'd read enough stolen comic books from the newsstand and seen every episode of *Teen Wolf* and *Vampire Diaries*, the idea of a werewolf was more intriguing than terrifying, and once Cian made no move to attack me, I tried to get his origin story out of him.

Sadly, the skinny, 20-year-old kid was wired tighter than I was. I only got bits and pieces out of Cian over the four months he lived with me, and he never mentioned he had a family or brother he'd left behind somewhere.

"You took care of him," Griffin said quietly, when I stepped out of the bathroom. He was standing by the sliding glass doors that led to the wraparound porch overlooking the lake, holding his brother's letter in his hand.

"Yes."

"Why?" Griffin asked so softly I almost missed the question.

"He was all alone," I shrugged uncomfortably. The truth hitting a little too close to home for me.

"But you weren't together?" He clenched the letter tightly, staring at me with dark, unreadable eyes. I could tell the question was important to him, like it held a deeper meaning.

"No."

"Never?" Griffin closed the space between us in a few quick strides.

"Never," I snapped back, annoyed he was pressing the issue.

"Why did you come here?" Griffin crowded me as I backed up against the thick log wall, the ridges digging into my back and neck as he braced his hands against the wall on either side of me, holding my body in place.

"To see the sunshine on the lake and the snow covering the pine trees."

"Sunshine and snow, that's why you're here?" Griffin asked, his gaze hot and possessive, as his eyes swept over me.

"Bro, I am so not fucking you right now, no matter how hot you are," I snorted, twisting out from under him. "You're Cian's big brother, for fuck's sake, and I don't even know why I'm here or he never told me about you."

"You said you weren't together," Griffin growled low in his throat, pushing me back against the wall.

"We're not. We weren't. It wasn't like that, okay? He was like my little brother, and every time you say it, it makes me want to throw up."

"I'm sorry," Griffin blew the words out in a rush, stepping away from me and running his hands through his dark, rumpled hair. "Your smell is driving me crazy," he confessed, staring at me helplessly. "It's like the earthy scent of the forest floor after a rainstorm."

"I smell like dirt?" I stared at Griffin, shaking my head at him wearily. "Good-bye, Griffin. It was swell meeting you, really, just the best, but I need a hot meal, a warm shower, and a soft bed in that order, and I don't want you in any of it. So please, get the fuck out of my cabin."

Griffin growled low in his throat, staring back at me with a mixture of amusement and disbelief in his eyes. "That's twice you've told me to fuck off."

"Yeah well, don't make me tell you a third time. I'm hungry and cranky and you don't want to see me pissed off. And for fuck's sake, stop smelling me," I snapped, as Griffin followed me into the kitchen, breathing in my scent. "I smell like dirt, remember?"

"I said you smell like the earthy scent of the forest floor after a rainstorm," Griffin corrected, brushing up against me and rubbing his face across the top of my head. "It's a beautiful scent," he growled, all serious. "But I like our scents mixed together even better." He stepped back from me, inhaling me in satisfaction.

"Did you just mark me up? Hello, boundaries?" I quirked my brow at Griffin. "We just met; we haven't even hooked up. Don't you think it's a little premature to go all wolfy possessive on me at this point?"

"What did you say?" Griffin went completely still as I walked away.

"Which part?" I huffed, opening the freezer, relieved to find it stocked with frozen pizza and waffles.

"The wolfy possessive part." Griffin stalked over, as I popped two waffles in the toaster and turned the oven on for the pizza. "How much did Cian tell you about himself, exactly?" he asked, leaning against the counter in a deceptively casual stance, his eyes tracking my every movement.

"I know he's a werewolf, and I'm assuming you are too, so let's just get that out of the way, okay?" I grabbed my waffles out of the toaster, still half-frozen, and shoved one in my mouth. "I'm usually a much more dignified eater, but I'm literally about to pass out." I swayed lightly on my feet.

"Sit down," Griffin commanded gruffly, yanking me over to a stool at the large island in the center of the kitchen. He grabbed a pizza pan out of a cabinet next to the oven and slid the pizza in before coming to sit beside me.

"Thanks." I lowered my head to the island as another wave of dizziness washed over me. I stuffed the second waffle I'd been clenching in my hand into my mouth, and sighed in relief as I chewed, feeling a little steadier. "A soda would be good too, if you know where one is around here," I told Griffin, keeping my head down as the blood flow started to return to my brain.

Griffin jumped up and returned a minute later with a can of cola and a bag of chocolate chip cookies, cracking the tab on the soda and sliding it over to me.

"I figured Cian would be good for junk food; it's all he ate when he lived with me." I smiled weakly at Griffin, lifting my head up to take a sip from the cola.

"I kept the place stocked for him with his favorites, in case he came back," Griffin said quietly, his eyes watchful.

"I'm fine now. Sorry to be so dramatic. It was a long trip and I wanted to get here during daylight so I didn't stop to eat when I should have. Although, thank god I didn't. Your goon squad would have freaked me the hell out a lot more if it had been completely dark out." I shuddered, ripping into the bag of cookies.

"A couple of seventeen-year-old boys scared you, but I didn't?" Griffin choked on a laugh of disbelief, shaking his head in wonder.

"You?" I cocked my head at Griffin, sweeping my gaze over his deep-set black eyes, flashing honey gold, like they couldn't make up their mind, scruff-covered face, and rumpled dark hair. "Nah, you didn't scare me at all. You, I wanted to lick," I admitted with a laugh.

Griffin's eyes blazed with a predatory satisfaction, and he leaned forward, his gaze darkening with heat. "Oh, there will be plenty of licking," he promised. "Eat your pizza and get some sleep. We'll talk about everything in the morning."

"Stop ordering me around," I muttered in annoyance. "I told you to fuck off twice already, and I warned you, you won't like it if I have to tell you a third time. I'll eat and sleep when I want to and I'll talk to you when I'm good and ready, not when you dictate to me."

"You don't like when I order you around?" Griffin threw back his head and laughed so loudly, it shook the cabin walls. "You're going to talk to me tomorrow after you've eaten and had a full night's sleep, and I promise you, you're going to love when I order you around." Griffin's eyes swept over my body with a possessiveness that sent a bolt of heat to my groin and sucked the breath out of me.

2

Bacon. That was the first thing I smelled when I woke up the next morning to the sun bouncing off the lake and streaming in through the bedroom windows. I don't think I'd ever seen so much sunshine filling a room before. My homes tended to be dark and dingy, in basements, or single rooms with a tiny window looking out into an alley, another building blocking the sun. That was one of the things Cian had promised me in his letter, sunshine in the spring and summer, and snow-covered pine trees in the winter.

"Okay, Cian, you were right about the sunshine, but did you have to leave out the part about your insanely hot older brother and the werewolf pack that came with the house? I know you had epic sex and an amazing love story with your wolf-mate, but if this is your idea of a blind date, I'm not amused," I grumbled, stretching, and throwing off the blankets.

I was starving again, and the smell of bacon, coffee, and possibly pancakes was too much to ignore, even if I did have the sinking suspicion it was going to be accompanied by a super-hot, bossy werewolf. Griffin had refused to leave last night, stretching out on the couch like a sentry, while I stormed off to bed, tossing and turning with visions of licking him like an ice cream cone keeping me up all night.

"Hungry?" Griffin called from the kitchen as I padded barefoot through the house. He'd obviously heard me rustling around with his super-wolf ears, and he turned to greet me, sucking in his breath. Well, what did he expect? I wasn't showing off, but I wasn't getting dressed for breakfast either. It served him right, getting an eyeful of me all rumpled and sexy, bare-chested, with my low-slung boxers resting just below my hipbone, skin still warm from sleep.

"I could eat." I stretched my arms over my head innocently, my boxers slipping down further on my hips.

"You really think you'll win this game?" Griffin rasped, his eyes flashing a deep golden yellow as he stalked toward me.

"What game?" I taunted, stepping around him and snagging a piece of bacon from the plate on the stove.

"The one where you end up bent over this counter, screaming my name," Griffin growled, shoving me over to a chair at the island.

"Like that's gonna happen," I snorted, as Griffin slid a plate of pancakes and bacon in front of me.

"Oh, it's happening," Griffin promised, adjusting himself with a sigh as he stared at me with a mixture of lust, tenderness, and frustration.

The pancakes and bacon were delicious, and I polished everything off while Griffin silently watched me eat. After, I walked out onto the porch with my coffee to see the promised spring sunshine in full effect.

"It is beautiful," I murmured when Griffin stepped out beside me. "But Cian left out the part about it being cold in the morning."

"What was he like when you found him?" Griffin asked, pulling his hoody off, and dropping it over my head.

"Quiet," I sighed, sinking into the warmth of Griffin's sweatshirt, inhaling his scent as it drifted over me, settling into my pores like it belonged. "He didn't say anything for a few days, just watched me to see what I'd do, but not with any real sense of self-preservation. That was what got me, you know? He seemed to have just given up. I'd been there before myself, only no one was there to pick me up out of the alley, so I wanted to do it for him."

"What happened to you? Where's your family?" Griffin asked.

I lifted my mug of coffee up to shield my face. "Oh, you know, around somewhere, I guess."

Griffin reached out a hand to brush away a lock of my hair as it fell over my face, and I flinched, jerking away.

"I don't love being touched when it's not sexual, when I'm not expecting it," I tried to explain awkwardly.

"Good to know." Griffin eyed me thoughtfully as I brought my coffee mug back up to my lips.

"Anyway, he was quiet, Cian, when I first carried him home with me." I was conscious of Griffin's contemplating eyes on me. "Then I caught him shifting one morning, and it kind of broke the ice between us," I laughed.

"So, you know about what he is?" Griffin asked carefully.

"I told you last night; I know what he is, I know what you are." I set my mug down on the porch rail and turned to face the tense werewolf beside me.

Griffin held his arms stiffly at his side, his eyes guarded.

"I don't care, if that's what you're worried about," I sighed. "I mean, I didn't know there would be a whole werewolf pack lurking in the woods here or I might not have come, but if it's a secret, you don't have to worry about me. I'm not going to tell anyone or anything. Cian is my friend, and he gave me his place, that's why I'm here, plain and simple. I didn't know he had any family, so if this is like, going to be a problem or something, I'll just go and you can have his cabin back, okay? I don't have the money for a lawyer or anything and I don't even know if it's legal Cian gave me his house. All I have is a letter and a key. But I can't give you back the truck, because I need it to get out of here and back to civilization."

"It's legal," Griffin said softly, swinging his gaze away from my face to stare out at the lake. "Cian made it legal. He sent us a letter too, telling us he gave you his house, and the 10 acres of forest and lake it sits on."

"Oh," I said, trying to take it in now that it was real. I was 25 and I owned a house and 10 acres of land in the Northwoods of Maine. I'd never owned anything before in my life and was usually one-month shy of getting kicked out of whatever shithole room I was renting, and a 20-year-old werewolf kid gave me his house and 10 acres of land on a lake. I wasn't really sure what to do with that.

"Have you heard from him at all? I mean, do you know where he is, if he's okay?"

"He severed his pack ties when he left." Griffin's voice was raw with unchecked emotion. "He blamed me, that's why he cut ties with the pack after Nate was killed. It's why we haven't been able to find him since he left. One day he was there, in our heads and hearts, and then he was gone, like a piece of us had been ripped away."

"Why did he blame you?" I asked, wanting to touch Griffin, but not sure if I should.

"Because it was my fault. I'm the Alpha. I'm responsible for the pack, so Nate's death was on me, is on me. It happened three years ago, our father had died a few months before and I had just become Alpha. I was only twenty-three." Griffin held up his hand before I could respond. "I'm not making any excuses for myself; I'm just trying to explain. There was another pack, across the border in Canada, and they wanted to take over our territory for years. When my father died, I guess they saw a young, inexperienced Alpha taking over, and figured they should strike. They attacked us, we held them off and won, but there were casualties on our side too, and Nate, Cian's mate was one of them. Nate and Cian were just teenagers, had discovered each other the year before, and were so in love it was nauseating to be around them," Griffin murmured with a ghost of a smile. "And they stunk of sex, literally reeked of it." Griffin laughed weakly. "My parents hadn't expected Cian to find his mate so young, but they were happy for them. They gave Cian this house and land as a mating present, on the condition he wait until he was eighteen to move out of the pack lodge. Nate was a great kid, gentle, mischievous, full of heart, everyone loved seeing them together. It was impossible not to. Two horny teenage boys in love who were mates and had found each other at such a young age, you couldn't not smile when you were around them. They used this place like a clubhouse/lover's retreat, and they were excited about moving in when they turned eighteen. Cian wanted to adopt a million stray werewolf cubs. They were going to build a family here, a life together, and it was stolen from them for something so stupid, for the pursuit of power." Griffin kicked at the porch rail; his hands clenched into helpless fists.

"Did Cian run away right after it happened?" I asked. "Has he been on his own for the last three years?"

"Yes, until you found him." Griffin turned to face me again. "Because of you, maybe Cian will come back home to us one day, when he's ready."

"But I didn't do anything," I protested, my face heating with shame. "I didn't even know Cian had a family. He only really talked about Nate."

"You gave him a family when you picked him up from the ground and carried him home with you. You saved his life and gave him back the strength to live. We thought he was dead," Griffin choked. "The majority of wolves don't survive the loss of their mate."

"I feel like maybe I shouldn't live here, like it isn't right."

"He wanted you to have the cabin, but you don't have to decide what to do with it right away." Griffin paused, like he wanted to say something else, but then he stopped, just staring at me silently.

"Well, actually, I kind of do have to decide," I sighed. "I didn't have anything keeping me in New York, so when Cian gave me his cabin and truck, I gave up my apartment and job and came straight here. So, I either have to move into the cabin and get a new job or go back to the city and find a new place to live and another bar to tend."

"Or you could move into the pack lodge," Griffin said gruffly, closing the space between us and backing me against the porch rail.

"Why would I do that? I'm not a wolf or part of your pack." My heart sped up and my dick sprang to attention against his leg. God, it was annoying the way my body reacted to him.

"Because." Griffin began, his eyes darkening with heat. "Because it's a good idea." He leaned into me, brushing his nose against mine.

"It's the dumbest idea I've ever heard." I closed my eyes as Griffin scraped his teeth against my jawline, tracing the outline of my face with his. It was the most intimate thing anyone had ever done to me, tracing my face with their own. He smelled so good, like the home I always wished for, but never had, and my whole body tingled as I was filled with a deep yearning I didn't understand.

I opened my eyes to Griffin's gleaming, dark gold gaze, needing to break the intimacy between us before things got too intense.

"I appreciate the effort and all, but the wolf foreplay isn't really necessary, I'm down for the hookup." I flashed him a teasing grin, one I used all the time at the bar to keep things light and easy.

"Wolf foreplay?" Griffin grinned back wickedly. "Move into the lodge and I'll show you wolf foreplay." He trailed his fingers down to my waist and slipped them into my boxers, wrapping his strong hand around my dick.

"If I don't stay here, I'm going back to New York, not moving into a werewolf lodge with my friend's brother." I gasped, staring into Griffin's honey gold gaze, as I came in his hand in an embarrassingly quick, hot burst. "Even if he can make me come in ten seconds flat."

"I think that was more like 30 seconds," Griffin teased, licking my sticky semen off his fingers.

"I usually last way longer than that," I blushed, as Griffin grinned at me with dark, heat-filled eyes.

"Oh yeah?" Griffin breathed, capturing my lower lip between his teeth "How much longer do you usually last?"

"Much longer," I moaned, as Griffin trailed his lips across my jawbone and down my neck.

I'd had a million random hookups with guys I'd just met. In the bar where I worked, on the streets where I'd lived, in clubs after a long sweaty night of dancing, but this was completely different. Griffin's lips on my body felt like they belonged there. His hands on my skin, pulling his hoody off me, were tender and rough at the same time. There was an urgency to his touch, but it was also gentle and intimate, and when Griffin flipped me around and leaned me over the porch rail, all I could think was yes and more.

Griffin's breath was so hot against my skin, I didn't even realize he'd pulled my boxers down until he was kneeling on the porch behind me, his lips on the hollow of my spine, right where it dipped into the curve of my ass. And when he spread my cheeks and buried his face inside me, I was lost. All I could smell was Griffin, pine needles-sunshine-snow-in-the-forest, and I just wanted to curl up in his lap and lick his face, his chest, his fingers, taste him, breathe him in, burrow inside him.

"You're so fucking beautiful; you smell like the dirt on the forest floor, but it's the good dirt," Griffin moaned, pulling his head out of my ass. "You don't understand, it's the earth after a rainstorm, Finn. It's the fertile ground that calls out to the wolf in me." Griffin stood up, pressing his body into mine, his breath hot on my neck, his lips in my hair as he bent me over the porch rail. "You are mine and home and no one else will ever have you."

He was so warm and safe against my skin, I never wanted him to let me go. My body ached for him to lean me all the way over the railing and push deep inside me, and when he said I called out to the wolf in him, I thought yes, and fuck me, please.

But when Griffin eased the tip of his dick gently into my entrance, the part of my brain that wasn't mush, started screaming no, and stop, and get off. Suddenly I couldn't breathe, and I pushed off the railing and shoved Griffin back, running down the porch steps, naked, to his brother's truck.

"Finn, wait, it's okay. Don't go. I'm sorry," Griffin called after me.

The keys were still in the ignition from the day before, and I started the truck and backed out of the driveway, my naked ass sticking to the seat. And I was crying because even though I was twenty-five, I felt twelve again and scared, so scared, and I had to get away.

3

I never unpacked the truck the night before, so my stuff was still piled on the seat next to me, and I pulled over a few miles down the road and fished a pair of shorts and a sweatshirt out of my duffel bag. The late spring Maine morning was already starting to warm up, and I rolled down the window letting the fresh air dry the tears on my face.

I couldn't believe what had just happened. I couldn't believe I had cried. I hadn't let a guy get that close to fucking me since I was sixteen and in love with a street hustler named Luke, who was even more fucked up than I was. That was back when I was young and naïve, and thought I could fix broken boys even though I was a broken boy myself.

I felt ancient now, at 25, remembering the kid I was back then, remembering the feel of Luke's dirty fingers spreading me open, his sour breath against my face while he begged me to let him fuck me just once. The feel of his bony, teenage body pressing into mine, my face squashed against the bathroom stall in Grand Central Station. My desire to please him, to tame him, to quiet the demons that plagued him, wrestling with my need to protect myself, to not give in to what I knew would break me into so many pieces I was afraid I'd never be able to put myself back together again.

In the end, I'd sucked Luke off instead, and afterward, he left me on my knees in the stall, alone, like I'd known he would. But at least I could still get up and walk away, only a little bit broken, like a piece of paper hanging half off where it was torn, nothing I couldn't tape back together, even if the crack showed through the clear film.

But just now, with Griffin, god, what had even happened? He'd felt so good against my skin, so sweet, and warm, and right. He was everything Cian had promised me I'd find at his cabin, warm sunshine on my skin and snow-covered trees in the forest. I wanted Griffin to spread me open and bury himself inside me. I wanted to feel claimed by him, to be owned in a way that said I was his.

But then the fog cleared for a second, and I was twelve years old again, back in the shed behind my foster house. And my foster father, Frank, was pushing me over the lawn mower handle, and it was digging into my belly, and the blood was rushing to my head as my face hung down, and it hurt so much when he pushed inside me, but I didn't say no because I was scared, and I had seen him eyeing the new kid, and he was only nine.

And when Griffin yelled, "Wait," and "it's okay." I remembered the social worker in the hospital with the sad eyes, and the doctor, who told me I would be okay afterward. But I wasn't, and I'm not, and I shouldn't have come here to this cabin in the woods where the sun shines so brightly it hurts my heart, and the pine trees' promise of snow-heavy branches in the winter fill me with longing.

I didn't even realize I'd driven into town until I came to a stoplight on the main street. Cian's property was pretty far out, so I must have been driving for half an hour, thinking of the way Griffin felt and smelled against my skin, remembering his soft words in my ear, the way my heart swelled until it didn't anymore, and I was running away like a crazy person, driving off naked in his brother's truck.

"Kill me now," I groaned in mortification, wishing the whole encounter with Griffin on the porch was just a bad dream I'd wake up from when I got back to the cabin.

I slowed to a stop in front of a bar, when I noticed a *help wanted* sign taped to the front door. The sign had seen better days and looked like it was scrawled in black sharpie on the back of a bar napkin, hanging half off the door under a rickety sign that said Molly's. It was only 10:30, but it looked like someone was in there, taking bar stools down and getting ready for the day, so I decided to check it out.

I was a hot mess, but from the looks of Molly's sign, there was a chance the owner didn't have very high standards. If she hired me in the state I was in right now, it was probably meant to be, and I should just stay here in my cabin in the woods and try to figure my life out. Somehow, I felt like I owed it to Cian to bring happiness, love, and hot, dirty sex to his cabin again, even it took me a lifetime to figure out how to get there.

"Hey there, anyone home?" I called, pushing open the door to the dark bar and stepping inside.

The inside screamed roadside biker bar, with its beat-up wood plank floors, dartboard on the wall next to an ancient Budweiser sign, and pool table in the corner with a broken cue, probably a remnant of last night's bar fight lying on the felt top.

"We open at twelve," a woman called out, wrinkling her nose when she popped her head up from behind the long wooden bar where she was bent over stocking glasses. She was beautiful, in a tough, don't even think about fucking with me, ever, way. Old enough to be my mother, probably late 40's, early 50's, but in better shape than most 20-year-olds.

She totally rocked the cut-off jean shorts and plain white tank top she was wearing, and the Celtic symbols tattooed on her arms rippled across ropy muscles, as she twisted a towel inside a glass, giving it a final polish. Her hair was dark, almost jet black, pulled back in a simple ponytail, framing a pale, freckled face that was staring at me curiously.

"Uh, I'm just here about the job. I saw the sign out front. Are you Molly?" My voice trailed off as she stared at me like I had three heads.

The woman nodded, her head cocked to the side, eyeing me like a foreign species in a zoo. Okay, so maybe this wasn't the best idea I'd ever had, I suddenly realized, catching sight of myself in the mirror above the bar.

Gak! I literally looked like I had just been bent over my porch railing about to get the shit fucked out of me. My normally chin length, unruly blond hair was tousled in a total I just got fucked way. I had beard burn on the sides of my face where Griffin must have been nuzzling me from behind, trying to rub his scent all over me. I was wearing purple board shorts and a lemon-yellow sweatshirt that read *Shout Out to Sidewalks for Keeping Me Off the Streets*, and holy shit, I'd forgotten to put shoes on, so I was applying for a job in bare feet. Just when I thought things couldn't possibly get any worse, I also realized Molly was sniffing me with a look of fascination.

"Shit," I muttered. "Of all the gin joints in town, I have to wander into the werewolf bar looking for a job, reeking of sex with their Alpha."

Molly raised her eyebrow. "You said it, not me."

"Forget I was ever here," I groaned, turning to walk away.

"You got any bartending experience? Own any shoes?" she called as I was heading out the door.

"Um, yes and yes."

"Put 'em on, take a shower before you come to work, and you've got the job."

"Really?" I gaped. "I mean, that's great, okay. You must be really hard up if you're hiring the barefoot walk of shame guy, but good for me, right?" I yanked open the door and ran out before she could take back her offer.

"You start tonight," Molly called after me. "6:00-2:00, don't be late, and don't forget to shower, unless you want a lot of curious wolves in your business."

"Got it. 6:00-2:00, and shower," I reminded myself, hopping back into my truck. "And shoes."

Griffin was gone when I got back to the cabin, and he'd cleaned up the breakfast dishes and even made my bed and folded the clothes I'd left strewn across the bedroom floor. God, who was this guy? Super-hot, Alpha in charge, and he cooked and cleaned? Of course, I had to blow it with him.

I had no idea what I was going to say to Griffin if I saw him again. Who was I kidding, *when* I saw him again. But it was probably all for the best anyway. I mean, look what happened to Cian after he lost his guy. Werewolves were way too intense for me. I couldn't even cuddle after sex, or before it for that matter.

The farthest I'd ever gotten in a relationship was buying a guy a cup of coffee and a donut the morning after he blew me, and that was only because he'd passed out on my couch afterward and I didn't know how to get rid of him without offering to buy him breakfast. Of course, I think he thought we were going to breakfast together, not that I was going to shove a paper cup of black coffee and a glazed donut from the corner bodega in his hand and wave good-bye.

Fuck, I was messed up. Fuck my parents for abandoning me and fuck my foster father Frank for making me hate being touched. Fuck that I wanted Griffin to touch me even though I couldn't handle it, and fuck Cian for sending me here to his perfect little love nest in the forest where the sun shines in the summer and the trees drip with snow in the winter, and his Alpha werewolf brother smells impossibly like both seasons mixed together.

I unpacked my truck, not totally sure if I was staying for good, but figuring I'd at least better move my stuff in for the time being and take a good look around now that I was finally alone here.

There was plenty of room in the cabin for what little I had. It was obvious Cian and Nate hadn't moved in yet and were just using the place as a hangout.

The loft above the living room was totally calling my name, and after I finished unpacking, I climbed the ladder to check it out. It felt like a treehouse fort, tucked under the eaves of the cabin. There were plaid floor cushions and bean bag chairs arranged cozily against the wall next to a giant basket with folded quilts and knitted throws. Books on nature, rock climbing, boating, and fishing, local folklore, and poetry lined the shelves of a built-in bookcase in the corner. A telescope stood facing a window overlooking the lake, and a sketch pad and set of charcoals lay abandoned on the floor by a lamp.

I leafed through the sketchbook, knowing instantly it was Cian's. He drew on everything in my apartment when he lived with me, and he was an incredible artist. Most of these sketches were of Nate, his head tilted to the side, mouth curved upward in a teasing smile, Nate sunning himself on the dock, jumping into the water mid-air.

I closed the book on a sketch of Nate sleeping, sprawled out nude in a pile of rumbled blankets on their bed, and picked up a book on local plant life instead. It suddenly felt like a violation, looking through Cian's collection of such intimate moments.

Someone was keeping the loft clean and dust-free, and it was so inviting, I couldn't help curling up on the floor cushions with the plant book. It must have been Nate's, Cian told me he was obsessed with plants and wanted to be a botanist. Unfortunately, the subject wasn't as stimulating for me, and the loft was so cozy, I fell asleep and didn't wake up until 5:30, which left me zero time to shower and get ready for my new job.

―――――――――•―――――――――

The bar was already hopping when I arrived for my shift five minutes late, in a full panic, and I had to circle the block twice to find a parking spot on the street because the small lot was full, which made me ten minutes late before I actually ran through the door.

I'd at least changed out of my shorts and hoody, into a pair of faded, ripped jeans and an old *Selena* T-shirt, and stuffed my feet into my lemon-yellow, high-top Converse sneakers, but I still wasn't wearing any underwear since Griffin had pulled mine off me this morning.

"You didn't shower," Molly sighed, walking by me with a tray of drinks. "And your shoes aren't tied."

"Working on it, I promise," I mumbled over my truck keys, which I'd stuffed in my mouth to free up my hands, to tie my sneakers.

"Gonna be an interesting night." Molly shook her head as she walked away.

I'd been tending bar since I was fifteen and scored a halfway decent fake I.D. that put me right at my 18th birthday. Legal to serve, just not to buy in the state of New York, not that it really mattered in the types of bars I started in anyway. But it meant after ten years of bartending, I knew my way around a bar on a busy night, even one with snowshoes and moose antlers mounted on the walls, and I didn't have to be told twice to jump in and get to work.

The first half of the night flew by in a blur until around 10:00, when the werewolves started piling in. I don't know I would have instantly known they were wolves, although I was starting to notice subtle differences in the way the wolves carried themselves, and the extra muscle they all seemed to have. Even the women were ripped. I was 6 foot in bare feet with 180 lbs. of muscle, and I was pretty sure most of them could kick my ass. But whether or not I would have noticed them initially, they all noticed me.

"I told you to shower," Molly laughed, when the first guy leaned over the bar and sniffed me with a shocked expression. Then the rumbling started, and I heard, "Who's the hot blond guy who smells like Griff?" And, "God, he reeks, what the fuck?" Then there was, "I'd mark him up too, if I was fucking him. He's hot as shit. But why does he smell like Griffin?" And that was just the comments I overheard; the up-close conversation was even worse. The wolves were super polite, but unsure, like they didn't know if they should show me respect because I smelled like I'd just come from rolling in the hay with their Alpha, or if it was just a one off in the back, and I didn't mean anything, in which case they were free to hit on me or ignore me completely.

It was exhausting dancing around the questions in their eyes all night, and I was starving since I'd slept through dinner, so I didn't hear the customer call out to me from across the bar the first time, but everyone heard him the second.

"Hey Blondielocks, how about another shot of tequila?" he called flirtatiously, sliding his shot glass down the bar to me, and holy shit was he hot. Molly must have served him his first shot because I definitely wouldn't have missed this guy even with all the eye-contact I'd been avoiding since the wolves had shown up.

He was all loose-limbed and teasing eyes, his voice a drawn-out drawl with a hint of south in it, more Texas than Mississippi, with a buzzed head and an eagle tattoo stretching across his thick bicep. I put him close to my own age, maybe a year or two older, just out of the military or finishing up his eight years.

I was a sucker for a military guy, especially the ones with all the repressed gay feelings; they literally fell apart under my tongue as soon as I parted their ass cheeks. This guy was definitely not repressed or in the closet though, and his eyes played with me as he worked his way down the bar to meet me halfway. Not a wolf either, since his playful attitude didn't shift away once he got closer to me and caught my scent.

He was just a regular guy, and exactly what I needed after an emotional breakdown this morning, a long shift, and the tension of dancing around the wolves all night.

"Texas, I knew it," I grinned back at my guy as he reached for his shot, and I caught sight of the Texas flag tattooed on his other bicep.

"That obvious, huh?" he drawled, brushing his fingers across mine as he pulled his shot glass away.

"It was either Texas or Tennessee. You've got a little Nashville vibe, but I was leaning toward Texas."

"How about you? Let me guess, Venice Beach? You definitely don't look like you tend bar in the woods, on the regular." Texas held my gaze, reaching for my hand and turning it over to run his finger across my pulse in a slow circle.

It was hypnotic, and for a long slow moment everyone in the bar faded away, and all that I could feel were his fingers on my wrist and the promise of his hot mouth on my dick.

"Take a break," he whispered huskily.

"I only get ten minutes," I murmured back, lost in the heat of his gaze.

"I only need five to get you off, baby," he promised.

I ducked under the bar, the wolves forgotten, as my Texas Ranger pulled me down the hall.

"It's a mistake, handsome," Molly called as I passed her by.

"Probably," I agreed, my voice thick with lust and the need to release all the pent-up emotion of the day.

"Ah, fuck it. Here's to mistakes. I'd go in the back room with him too, Blondielocks," Molly laughed. She tossed back a shot and saluted me with her glass as Texas pulled me into the bathroom and tugged down my jeans.

"I wanted to suck you off the second I walked into the bar," he moaned, slipping me into his mouth. And then he was circling my dick with his tongue like he circled my palm with his finger, and his mouth was so hot and wet, and he didn't want anything from me but this, my dick in his mouth for five minutes and he didn't offer me any sweet words or make any promises he wouldn't keep.

He just sucked me down until I came in his mouth in a hot burst, and it was perfect. It was perfect, until I suddenly smelled pine forests, sunshine, and wet snow on thick fur branches. I opened my eyes in dazed confusion to Griffin yanking Texas up off the floor with a roar. His eyes gleamed a dark, wolfen gold, and he looked like he was struggling to keep his wolf under control, as he pinned Texas against the wall, his hands around his throat.

"Stop! You don't get to do this," I screamed at Griffin, my jeans still down around my ankles and my dick out, dangling between my legs. "I don't even know you; I don't owe you anything. Fuck off, wolfie."

Griffin dropped Texas to the ground and turned to me, pinning me against the bathroom wall with a low growl.

"Why?" he demanded, holding my gaze with wild eyes.

"Because I almost let you fuck me this morning!" I yelled back, as Texas slipped out the bathroom door, my semen still on his lips. I shoved Griffin away, yanking my jeans up. "I stopped thinking when you started touching me on the porch, and I just smelled you, all pine needles and sunshine and warmth, and you felt so good and safe, and I wanted you to fuck me, until I didn't, because I don't let anyone fuck me!"

Griffin pulled me out of the bathroom and through the bar, which was empty, because I guess everyone took off when the Alpha werewolf started fighting with his maybe boyfriend, who was in the bathroom getting a blowjob from a hot stranger.

When we reached the street, Griffin stopped in front of my truck, yanking the door open and shoving me inside, before climbing in beside me.

"Of course you have a set of keys to your brother's truck," I grumbled, as Griffin started the truck without a word and pulled into the road. "Just wondering, is this the part where you take me somewhere to kill me?" I asked, as a wave of dizziness swept over me and my stomach started to rumble, reminding me I'd forgotten to eat again.

"Yes." Griffin shoved another one of his protein bars at me. "So, you better eat, you want to have the strength to fight back."

"I could take you," I mumbled over a mouthful of the protein bar.

"You could, I'd never fight back. I'd never hurt you."

We didn't talk after that. I finished the protein bar and rested my head against the truck window the rest of the ride back to the cabin, breathing in Griffin's warm, comforting scent.

4

When we got back to the cabin, Griffin followed me inside, marching straight into the bathroom, turning the shower on, and walking back out to glower at me.

"I'm sorry, I don't speak werewolf, is the running water code for something, or do you just feel like freshening up?" I kicked off my sneakers.

"You reek," Griffin growled. "I can't talk to you, covered in that guy's scent."

His eyes flashed black and gold, and I could feel his wolf straining to break free as he snapped at me through clenched teeth.

"Were you planning on talking to my dick? Because that's the only part of my body he had his mouth on." I snapped back, sick and tired of this Alpha werewolf, who I'd only met yesterday, trying to dictate to me.

It was probably the wrong thing to say though, because the next thing I knew, Griffin was in front of me, and god, how was he that fast? And strong. He scooped me up like I weighed nothing, like I wasn't a built as fuck, grown ass man. He had me upside down in a fireman's hold, and it was sexy as shit, hanging over his shoulder, until he dumped me fully clothed into the shower.

"What the hell?" I sputtered, pulling my sopping wet T-shirt off, and throwing it at Griffin.

"You seem to be under the impression I'm not scary," Griffin bit out, yanking my wet jeans down and dumping half a bottle of bodywash over my head. "Trust me when I say, you are very wrong about that."

"Hey, you said you'd never hurt me," I reminded Griffin, as his eyes gleamed dark gold, and his body thrummed with barely contained fury. "Remember all that stuff you said in the car about how I could take you because you'd never fight back?" I kicked my wet jeans the rest of the way off and backed up against the shower wall as he advanced on me.

"I said I'd never hurt you. I never promised I wouldn't scrub the stink of another guy from your body," Griffin rasped, grabbing my wrist, and pulling me back under the shower spray.

He rubbed the bodywash into my skin roughly, scrubbing every inch of me from the top of my head to my toes, and I let him because of the way he looked at me, with a mixture of tenderness and longing, and the way his hands felt on my body, warm and safe, rough, but gentle at the same time.

"I don't even know you," I complained, as Griffin soaped my dick, washing it three times, like he could erase the lips that had been wrapped around it just an hour ago.

"Yes, you do," Griffin sighed, turning off the water and handing me a towel. His T-shirt was soaked from leaning into the shower to scrub me down, and it was hard not to stare at his broad, muscled chest, as he pulled his wet shirt over his head and dropped it into the hamper against the wall.

"No, I really don't." I wrapped the towel around my waist and stepped out of the shower. "And you don't know me. If you did, you would know my dick's been in way too many mouths for you to wash off. I'm dirty as fuck, and if one blowjob in a bar bathroom made you throw me over your shoulder and scrub my dick three times, you'll want to drown me in a bucket of bleach after you really get to know me."

"I don't think you're dirty. I don't see you that way." Griffin followed me out of the bathroom and into the bedroom. "I don't have a problem with how many guys have sucked you off in the past, I just don't want to smell any new ones on you now."

Griffin plopped down on my bed, lowering his head into his hands as I stood in my towel, dripping on the floor in front of him.

"I didn't expect this, okay? I'm not ready for it. I have a pack to lead and a lot of territorial shit to deal with right now, but you're here, so there it is." Griffin lifted his head to stare into my eyes, his dark gaze hot and miserable. "You pulled up in my missing little brother's truck yesterday, scared, but ready to fight us all. Tough, defiant, and so hot, your hair falling over your eyes. You smelled like rain-soaked earth, and I just wanted to howl and sing and chase you through the woods, until I caught you and buried my teeth into your neck just above your collarbone, marking you as mine. And then you told me to fuck off, and it was so funny because you didn't care who I was, and you weren't afraid of me. Wolves run at the sound of my name, but you just sat there, ready to take me on."

"I don't understand." Though I was afraid I did.

"You're my mate," Griffin groaned miserably, leaning his head forward and pressing his face into my stomach.

"I'm not." I stood stock still, absorbing Griffin's words as he sat silently with his head pressed against my bare skin, his chin grazing the top of the towel wrapped around my hips. "I'm not a wolf, I can't be your mate," I protested, dropping down to the floor in front of Griffin. "I don't think that's a thing."

"It's a thing." Griffin's mouth quirked, as he raised his head back up to meet my panicked gaze.

"No, I don't think it is," I argued. "I don't think you understand.

If anyone was going to be a wolf's mate, it wouldn't be me. I'm like the anti-mate. I don't even do overnights, or like any post-cuddling at all. I don't return phone calls or texts. I barely even give out my real number to guys. That whole bathroom blowjob thing you interrupted earlier, that's as intimate as I get, so trust me, you must have gotten your wolf signals crossed or something, because there is no fucking way I'm your mate."

"It's not a signal that can get crossed, or a thing you can mess up or be confused about. Believe me, I don't like this anymore than you do. You're a huge pain in the ass," Griffin exhaled, leaning down, and rubbing his face across the top of my head and into the curve of my neck.

"You're doing it again, aren't you?" I tensed up. "Marking me with your wolf scent."

"Hmmm..." Griffin mumbled noncommittedly, working his way around to my shoulders and then down to my chest, his teeth grazing the skin above my collarbone with a soft groan of longing as he passed it by.

"You're not going to pee on me, are you?" I asked drily, when Griffin pushed me down onto my back and lifted his leg over my body.

"Would you like me to?" he grinned wolfishly, his eyes flashing with mischief.

"No!" I swatted Griffin in annoyance as he covered me with his body, burying his face into the soft folds of my neck, inhaling deeply in satisfaction.

"So, remember how I told you I don't love to be touched?" I wheezed underneath Griffin, as he pressed his full weight down onto me. "This definitely falls under the touching category. I'm suffocating here."

"When you're not expecting it, unless it's sexual," Griffin echoed my earlier words from this morning on the porch, rolling off me, and sliding to the side, widening the space between us.

"Yes, not a huge fan of surprise touches."

"No surprises," Griffin agreed, reaching out his hand slowly, holding it out in front of my face.

It was strangely comforting, his hand just hovering in the air where I could see it. He waited, giving me a chance to anticipate his touch, before gently brushing his hand across the side of my face. It was almost like he was petting me, and I closed my eyes, breathing him in as he trailed his fingers down the side of my cheek, bringing them under my nose, and down across my jawbone.

"Don't even think of scratching under my chin."

"I wouldn't dare," Griffin laughed huskily, trailing his fingers back up my face and into the tangle of my hair.

"Or behind my ears," I warned, as Griffin ran his fingers down the side of my head and into the curve of my neck.

"No scratching," Griffin agreed in mock seriousness. "Unless you want to scratch me, I love a good scratch behind the ears."

"Just behind the ears?" I opened my eyes and met Griffin's gaze, dark and slitted with need. Even without special werewolf hearing, I could make out the rapid beat of his heart as I trailed my fingers down his chest, scratching my nails lightly above the waistband of his jeans. Griffin watched me under his eyelashes, biting down on his lip in strangled anticipation, as I slid closer, unbuttoning his jeans, and slowly teasing his zipper down. He was so insanely hot, when I wasn't freaking out about him being all over me, I wanted every inch of his bare skin against mine, his sweat on my tongue, his muscles contracting under my touch, the sound of his voice, moaning in my ear.

"I warned you once, you'll never win this game," Griffin rasped, as I lightly scratched my fingers across his bare stomach, just above his pubic bone.

"You think I can't run with the big bad wolf?" I grinned wickedly, pushing Griffin onto his back.

"You can play with me all you want, little pup, but when I'm done with you, you'll wish you stayed on the porch," Griffin growled warningly.

"I'm no little pup, I never stay on the porch, and I will win this game," I promised, climbing on top of Griffin, straddling his waist.

"You won't." Griffin unwound the towel from my hips, tracing my hipbone with his fingers.

"I will." I slid my hand lower, scratching my fingers through his tangle of pubic hair.

"Oh Finn," Griffin laughed, his eyes sparkling with heat and mischief as he reached between us, palming my dick. "You don't even know the rules, my little pup."

"Rules?" I gasped, as Griffin closed his warm, strong hand around me.

"Never go into battle without knowing the rules of engagement," Griffin tskd, his hand gliding over my dick with slow, tortuous strokes.

"Are we in a battle?" I closed my eyes as Griffin traced the line between my sack and my ass.

"Not anymore. Now the victor is enjoying the spoils," Griffin growled, keeping one hand wrapped around my dick, while he fisted another in my hair, pulling me down and capturing my mouth in a kiss.

I rarely kissed any guys, their mouth usually on my dick instead of my lips, but Griffin's tongue in my mouth was hotter than any blowjob I'd ever had. I felt marked, claimed, owned, as his rough face scraped my cheek, his lips everywhere, on my mouth, my jaw, my ear. His tongue traced my Adam's Apple, his teeth scraped my collarbone, and I never wanted it to end, until he suddenly tried to roll me over onto my back.

"Rule number one, know your enemy's weakness," I breathed, pulling out of Griffin's grasp, and sitting back up across his lap. "I told you, I'm no little pup," I challenged, palming Griffin's dick as he gazed up at me through dark, slitted eyes. "And you're not the victor here."

"You are my weakness," Griffin conceded, wrapping his hands

around me and matching me stroke for stroke. "But not my enemy, never my enemy," he groaned, as we came together in a hot, sticky, rush.

"Checkmate." I exhaled, rolling off Griffin and grabbing my discarded towel to clean us up.

"It's a draw," Griffin laughed, reaching out blindly for my hand, as I wiped his chest off, his eyes closed in post orgasm bliss.

"Whatever," I snorted, neatly avoiding Griffin's outstretched hand as I climbed over him and stood up. "And FYI, I'm gonna be really pissed if you got me fired tonight, clearing out the bar with your little wolfout."

"You're not fired. Molly's pack, and you're my mate. She wouldn't dare."

"First of all, I thought we already cleared up the whole mate confusion thing."

"Oh, we cleared it up alright," Griffin agreed with a lazy grin, opening one eye, and staring up at me. "You're my mate and you admitted it."

"I did not," I gasped in outrage, as Griffin reached up a hand and yanked me back down on top of him.

"Oh yes you did, my little wolf," Griffin growled against my neck, flipping us over onto my back. "You said mine and home," he rasped against my neck, grazing his teeth across my collarbone.

"I said that out loud?" I groaned, closing my eyes as Griffin trailed his tongue across my neck, breathing me in.

"Home and mine, and Griffin, you smell like the forest and sunshine and snow all mixed together, and Griffin, you're so warm and you make me feel so safe."

I opened my eyes to Griffin's dark, wolfen gaze, gleaming with possessive glee.

"I didn't know I said all that out loud," I moaned in dismay, vaguely recalling thinking those things when Griffin had his lips all over me.

"Those are mating words, little wolf pup," Griffin growled against my neck, scraping his teeth across my collarbone with a soft moan of restraint.

"I'm not your little wolf, I'm not a wolf at all," I gasped, as Griffin trailed his tongue in a slow circle above my collarbone, where I knew, he was dying to sink his teeth in and mark me permanently as his.

"Ah, but you're my mate, so that makes you my little wolf," Griffin breathed in my ear.

"I think you just heard me wrong." I squirmed underneath Griffin and pushed at his chest to get free. "I was talking about the cabin, saying this is my home and it smells like the forest, and sunshine, and snow." I stuck my tongue out at Griffin as I wriggled out from beneath him.

"You are home, and mine, and safe, and Griffin, you feel like warm sunshine on my skin, and you smell like snow-covered pine needles." Griffin practically sang my words back to me, his eyes flashing with heat, satisfaction, and something deeper and primal that called out to me. "You claimed me with your mating words, and you can't take them back, little wolf of mine," Griffin called after me as I took off out of the room.

"Everyone knows nothing you say in the heat of the moment counts!" I shot back.

5

"So, about last night," I began, walking into Molly's bar with a bouquet of wildflowers, a bushel of blueberries, and an apple pie I'd bought off a farm stand on the side of the road.

"Still no shower," Molly sighed, shaking her head at me in disappointment.

"I showered twice," I protested, my face heating up.

"Huh, that's interesting." Molly studied me from across the bar, setting the last glass from her tray down on the shelf. "You reek worse than yesterday."

"That's because Griffin is crazy clingy and possessive, not because I didn't shower this time," I sighed, walking over, and setting my apology gifts on the bar.

"Griffin? My Alpha? Clingy and possessive?" Molly threw her head back and laughed so loudly, the bar shook with her mirth.

"Yeah, your Alpha is the touchiest-feeliest guy I've ever been with in my life. It's not my fault he won't stop rubbing up against me and licking my neck and shoulders. I could barely sleep last night with him wrapped around me like a pretzel. Plus, he sat in every piece of furniture in my house and rubbed himself all over the inside of my truck. I'm pretty sure he peed on the tires too, even though he won't admit it. And I caught him using my fucking toothbrush this morning, so you can't blame me this time if I smell like him."

Blank-faced, Molly gathered up the flowers I'd brought her and walked over to the sink to fill a pitcher of water for them.

"Can't say I've ever heard touchy-feely used to describe my Alpha before," she snorted, filling the pitcher, and arranging the flowers so they fluffed out and spilled over the sides. "I've heard, coldest bastard to roam the earth, terrifying as all fuck, and my personal favorite, Balor, the Celtic God of Death." Molly turned around, grinning at me. "But I've never heard anyone accuse Griffin of being too touchy-feely, and he never spends the night."

"Well, maybe you've just never met anyone he's slept with before or dated..." my voice trailed off awkwardly as Molly continued to stare at me in amusement. "You probably only know Griffin as the Alpha of your pack and I'm sure he has to pretend to be scary for that."

"Pretend to be scary?" Molly gawked at me. "Griffin is the most feared Alpha in the northeast. He single-handedly wiped out the entire Sinclair pack when they attacked us and killed his brother's mate, three years ago. He lined the fence posts of their pack border with their heads and burned their lodge to the ground with the few wolves who were left inside. He showed no mercy, no quarter. He slaughtered them all. And I know wolves he's fucked, and trust me, touchy-feely and possessive, are not words they'd use to describe him."

"What do you mean?" I plopped down at the bar in front of Molly, trying to sift through everything she'd just said.

"The word is, it's one cold ride," Molly shrugged. "I've heard the fuck is rough and intense, but the only thing you feel is his dick in your ass, he holds himself so far back, barely keeping a hand on your shoulder to keep himself in place. And Griffin's never marked another wolf or human before. If anything, he makes sure no one ever walks away from a fuck smelling like him."

"Are you sure we're talking about the same guy?" I tried to remember if there had been a single time since I'd met Griffin that he hadn't touched me or rubbed up against me in some way. And the way he wrapped his body around mine last night, his arms curled around my waist and his face buried in the crook of my neck, like he never wanted to let me go, touchy-feely was putting it mildly.

"Oh, I'm sure. I held the brat when he was born. I was the pack midwife until I finally trained my replacement and retired last year and bought this place. Speaking of which, I don't usually hire bartenders to clear the place out, it's a little hard to make money if the help chases the customers away."

"About that," I flashed Molly my best puppy dog eyes, sliding the bushel of blueberries and pie across the bar toward her. "I promise I'll always come to work on time, take multiple showers before my shift, wear shoes, and not hook up with any more Texans in the bathroom, if you'll give me one more chance." I batted my eyes at her.

"Hmmmm, you need to work on your charm a little more," Molly snorted, taking the pie and pushing the blueberries back across the bar to me. "Batting those innocent green eyes might work on all the boys lusting after your dick, but it takes a lot more than a pretty face to win me over, Blondielocks. Why don't you take those blueberries back home with you and bake me up a couple dozen muffins, then come back tonight, showered, in shoes, and on time with my muffins, and we'll talk."

"Done."

I grabbed the blueberries and hopped off the bar stool. I had thirty dollars left in my wallet and did not need to be told twice when I was given a second chance at a job. At this point, I would have sucked off the grizzled old dishwasher Molly had working in the back of the bar if she'd asked me to. Bake her a few dozen muffins? I'd go all Paul Hollywood on her ass and bake her the best fucking muffins she'd ever had if she didn't fire me. At least, that was the plan, after I googled *The British Baking Show* muffin recipes. Cian had to have Wi-Fi at the cabin, right? I mean, even werewolves must use the internet.

I stopped at the store before heading back, googling muffin recipes on my phone while I roamed the aisles, in case werewolves didn't use the internet and there was no Wi-Fi at the cabin, because I'd already discovered my cell service was practically non-existent there.

Standing in the baking aisle, wondering if I needed to buy a muffin pan, I saw her. It was like seeing a ghost. She was a grown up, female blend of Cian and Griffin, with midnight eyes and thick, dark hair. She looked early 50's, kind of laid back, country rocker, with her loose side braid, bootcut jeans, dark red leather cowboy boots, and green embroidered tank top.

"You're Cian's mother," I said, before I could stop myself.

"Yes, Lillian Walsh. I'm Griffin's mother too," she smiled gently, wrinkling her nose, and quirking a questioning brow at me.

"Of course," I stuttered awkwardly. "It's just, you look just like him, like Cian, and I didn't realize how much I missed him until I saw you." I stumbled over my words, wishing I could take them back as Lillian's eyes filled with a deep sorrow.

"You're Finn." She reached out a hand toward my face, and I startled at her touch, trying not to flinch, as she brushed her hand across my cheek gently. "Cian told me about you in the letter he sent, saying good-bye. He even mentioned your shaggy blond hair," she smiled. "Told me I should give you a haircut. I didn't know if you'd come, but I'm so glad you're here. I wanted the chance to thank you for everything you did for him."

"I didn't do anything, really. At least, not enough. I didn't do enough, obviously. I didn't bring him home." I was suddenly filled with a deep sense of shame and failure, standing in front of my missing friend's mother.

"It was not your burden to carry," Lillian murmured, squeezing my hand. "I'd love to hear about his time with you, even if it was mostly filled with grief. You probably didn't get to see much joy in Cian, but he was so full of life before he lost Nate. We all miss him so much."

"No, the Cian I knew wasn't interested in joy," I agreed. "But we became great friends anyway. He's the stubbornest kid I've ever met. I had to force milkshakes down his throat when I first brought him home with me, because he wouldn't eat, but after I told him how much they cost, he stopped spitting them out and started bringing me shakes to the bar in the middle of my shift. Even at his lowest point, Cian would notice little things about me, like how I would get hungry easily, and he'd stuff a fry in my mouth when I was trying to get him to eat. He looked out for me as much as I looked out for him. He was just like that, you know?"

"Yes," Lillian choked, her eyes filling with tears.

"Do you know how to make muffins?" I asked, squeezing Lillian's hand.

"Muffins?" she laughed, blinking back her tears, and glancing down into my overflowing basket of random baking supplies.

"My new boss, Molly, is making me bake her blueberry muffins by tonight if I want to keep my job, and I've never baked anything in my life. I've never even had a full, functioning kitchen before now. Do you know if there's a muffin pan at the cabin?"

"Molly's making you bake her muffins? God, she's such a bitch," Lillian laughed, taking my basket from me, and linking her arm through mine. "You must have really pissed her off, she doesn't even like muffins."

"She doesn't like them?" I gaped, as we walked over to the checkout counter.

"Hates 'em," Lillian laughed cheerfully, lifting my basket onto the counter, and smiling hello to the cashier.

"Are you sure?" I bit my lip as my grocery total flashed across the screen, exactly the amount I had left in my wallet. "Maybe it's a different Molly."

"There's only one Molly in town capable of employing anyone," Lillian grinned as she waved me away from the cashier, sticking her own credit card in the machine. "I've known her my whole life, so I'm positive she doesn't like muffins. But if she told you to bake them for her, they better be the best damn muffins you'll ever bake."

"Great," I groaned.

"Don't worry, I'll help you," Lillian laughed, following me outside to Cian's truck.

"So, what's the deal with this town, anyway?" I asked Lillian, as she waved to someone in the parking lot while we walked over to the truck. "Does everyone here know about your pack, or is it a secret? Cause, I definitely felt like some of the customers at the bar seemed like they knew about the wolves and others maybe didn't."

"Hmmm... that's a complicated question." Lillian opened the passenger door to the truck, climbing in after me. "Wolves have been living in these woods for centuries, so we're woven into the fabric of the area, but Colm, Griffin and Cian's father, only established our pack 30 years ago when he came here, answering the call of the Alpha."

"Soooo...The townspeople do know about your pack, or they don't?" I asked, starting the truck.

"We're not officially out to the world, but there's always been myth and lore surrounding our presence here, and after Colm established the pack and absorbed the town into pack territory, people noticed certain benefits, and just accept our presence here without too many questions."

"Huh." That was the most non-answer, answer, I think I'd ever gotten to a question, and I was debating pushing it further, when Lillian suddenly shifted in her seat, sniffing the interior of Cian's truck, and studying me with an unidentifiable expression on her face.

"When did you get here?" she asked.

"Three days ago." My face heated up in embarrassment at the contemplative look Lillian cast me. "I know the truck smells like Griffin, and it's weird, because I only got here a few days ago, and Cian left me his house and land after only knowing me for four months, but I don't really know what to say about it all, okay? I've just been chalking it up to a weird werewolf thing, but you're a wolf, so if you start acting like it's weird, then I'm going to start freaking out. So, can we just pretend it's normal one of your sons left me everything before he disappeared, and the other one won't stop marking me and all my stuff with his obnoxious, overpowering, Alpha, hear me roar, wolf scent?"

"Absolutely," Lillian murmured, turning away to hide the small smile that crept into the corner of her mouth.

6

"Oh my god, you totally saved my ass. These are amazing. Even if she hates muffins, Molly can't find fault with these," I moaned blissfully around a mouthful of warm, buttery muffin crumbs and blueberry juices.

"So, what'd you do to get on her bad side, anyway?" Lillian asked, arranging the last of the two dozen muffins in a cloth lined basket.

"Ahhhh, I'd rather not say," I laughed awkwardly, my face heating up.

"That bad, huh?" Lillian grinned. "You've only been here a few days and you've already managed to cause quite a stir, no wonder Cian sent you here. He always loved to shake things up," she sighed wistfully, looking out into the wide-open living room. "He had such plans for this place, you know, him and Nate. It was my parents' house. I grew up here."

"I had no idea," my voice caught. "You can have it back, really. I mean, I don't think Cian was in the kind of place to be making big decisions like this. It's your family cabin, it should stay in the family, especially in case Cian comes back one day."

"Oh, I think Cian knew exactly what he was doing," Lillian smiled softly, walking over to me, and taking my hand. "Welcome to the family, my sweet boy." She kissed my cheek gently.

"I appreciate the welcome and everything, but I'm sorry if I gave you the wrong impression. If this is about Griffin and the smell thing, I can explain." I backed away from Lillian nervously. "That's not, like a thing. The thing between me and Griffin. It's not an actual thing, the whole I smell like him thing."

"Uh huh," Lillian smiled gently as I continued to back farther and farther away until I was almost at the door of the cabin.

"It's more like an awkward misunderstanding," I tried to explain as Griffin's mother stared at me with her heart in her eyes.

"I felt that way too, at first, with Griffin's father." Lillian stared past me out at the lake. "It just felt so big, too big for me, and he was the Alpha, so there was so much weight and responsibility. I didn't know if I was ready for it. But now, I would give anything to go back and grab every minute, every extra minute with him," she choked. "We were like one soul intertwined. It's so hard to breathe without him. I don't know how Cian is bearing the loss of his mate alone, without the support of Griffin and the pack. It's hard enough with the pack in my head and heart, keeping me going. But Cian, he cut us off and he's all alone out there."

"He wasn't all alone. I was with him part of the time and he might have someone else with him now," I soothed, taking Lillian's hand, and walking over to the couch with her.

"Griffin is so angry at him for leaving, you know. But he doesn't understand what it's like. Losing your mate, it's an unbearable weight that pulls at you, dragging you down to the ocean floor. Your lungs scream for breath, but only water fills them. It's like drowning over and over again," Lillian choked, lowering her head into her hands. "It's my fault Cian left. I wasn't strong enough to pull myself up from the ocean floor when he needed me. I wasn't strong enough to breathe for him because I could barely breathe myself."

"Griffin's a bossy, know-it-all. Of course, he doesn't understand." I placed my hand on Lillian's shoulder. "I didn't know Cian before he lost Nate, but I knew him after, and his lungs were so full of water, he was drowning every second of every day. But I breathed for him, I swear I did. I breathed for him until he was able to breathe again himself and he was strong when he left," I promised Lillian. "He just wasn't strong enough to come back home to his pack. I think he just has to do this his way. He has to find a way to heal on his own, but I have faith in him, and I believe we'll see him again when he's ready to see us."

"Thank you," Lillian wept, burying her wet face against my chest, and wrapping her arms around me tightly. "Thank you so much."

"Now we're even for the help you gave me with the muffins," I mumbled awkwardly, untangling myself from Lillian's arms.

"Oh my god, it's 5:30. Don't you have to be at the bar at 6:00?" Lillian swiped at her wet eyes, looking down at her watch.

"Fuck! Not again. This is so not happening again," I yelled, grabbing the basket of muffins off the counter, and running out the door. "Can you get home from here?" I called to Lillian as I yanked open the door to my truck.

"Yes," she laughed, waving me away.

I had shoes on at least, I felt them on my feet on the gas pedal. I couldn't remember what shoes I was wearing, and I was afraid to look down at my clothes, pretty sure I hadn't changed since I'd thrown on a pair of pastel pink, low riding board shorts and a lime green tank top earlier, but I was on time, almost. The truck clock said 6:01 when I screeched into the lot, wedging myself into what was sort of a space near the front entrance.

"I have the muffins," I chanted to myself, grabbing the basket off the front seat, and running into the bar.

"Wow," Molly whistled when I burst through the door, almost knocking her over. "Just when I thought things couldn't possibly get any worse, Malibu Ken shows up, covered in blueberry juice, and wait, what's this?" she leaned in, inhaling deeply. "Reeking of the mother now, too? I swear to god, if you clear my bar out again tonight, Blondielocks, I'm gonna kick the shit out of you."

"I won't," I promised, thrusting the basket of muffins into Molly's hand, and running for the bar before she could tell me I was fired.

I was walking out of the bathroom an hour later when I heard Griffin's voice in my ear.

"I'm about to touch you," he whispered against my neck, sneaking up behind me and slipping an arm around my waist.

"Just because you warned me first, doesn't mean you can still grab me whenever you want," I huffed, annoyed at the way my body seemed to almost sigh in satisfaction at Griffin's touch, settling against him like it belonged.

Griffin ignored my complaint, nipping my ear playfully, as he held me against his chest. "Why do you smell like my mother?"

"We were baking muffins together, and then she cried on me. But it was a good cry. I mean, I didn't make her cry. Well, maybe I did, but not intentionally. Not because I was mean to her or anything," I tripped over my words, twisting out of Griffin's arms. "What are you doing here anyway?"

"I came to make sure Molly didn't fire you," Griffin teased, pulling me back into his arms and capturing my lower lip between his teeth.

"You came to mark me back up," I exhaled in exasperation when Griffin started rubbing his face all over me in what was becoming a very familiar manner.

"That too." He squeezed my ass as I pulled away.

"Well, fuck off, I'm working, and Molly already warned me she's going to kick my ass if I cause any disruptions to her business tonight."

"So, don't cause any disruptions," Griffin grinned, pulling out a bar stool and sprawling out lazily against the bar.

"I'm not the one who causes the problems! You're the one who can't stop marking me up like a big statement to the whole world."

"And yet, you're the one who wore my slippers to work," Griffin grinned, as I turned to duck behind the bar. "Quite a statement you're making, little wolf, wearing your mate's slippers to work," he choked on his laugh as I groaned, looking down at my feet stuffed into his moccasins.

Griffin stayed my whole shift, lounging at the bar and scowling at the rare human who came too close to me, then moving into a corner table to hold court when the wolves started pouring in. Whatever questions the wolves had yesterday, Griffin put to bed the first time he grabbed me when I passed him by, rubbing his head against mine, while clamping a possessive hand on my shoulder. The second and third time were overkill, and when Griffin pulled me into his lap and licked my cheek, I'd finally had enough.

"Will you fuck off?" I exhaled, pushing Griffin away and swiping at my cheek in exasperation. I'd been on my feet for seven hours, and even though Griffin had shoved a burger in my hand three hours ago, and stood over me, glowering, while I'd chewed every bite, I was hungry again, cranky, and suddenly so tired, I could barely think. It had definitely been a whirlwind few days, and I realized with all the wolf-mate drama, I hadn't had time to process anything since I'd jumped in my truck and drove up to Maine three days ago, even though it felt like I'd been here for a month already.

"You're exhausted." Griffin narrowed his eyes at me, taking me in.

"Don't even think about dragging me out of here in the middle of my shift and tucking me into bed like a fucking wolf pup," I snarled, ignoring the wide eyes of the wolves sitting next to Griffin.

I could care less what Griffin's packmates thought of me at this point, and I was as fed up with their appraising looks and whispered comments all night as I was with Griffin's outrageous display of possessiveness. I'd fucking had it with all of them, and what I really needed, I decided, was a drink and a dance. It was time to get this party started. If Griffin wanted to claim me publicly as his mate without even bothering to get to know me first, then he deserved to see what I was all about on a Friday night at the tail end of a long shift.

"Who's buying me a drink?" I yelled into the crowded bar, plugging my phone into the speaker in the corner. I cranked the volume up as Nicki Minaj's, *Super Bass* filled the room, kicking Griffin's slippers off and climbing up on the bar.

"I knew there was no way this night was going to end smoothly," Molly groaned behind me.

"I'll buy you a whole bottle," Anya, a wolf I'd met earlier in the night at Griffin's table, called out over the loud thrumming beat of the music.

As I dipped my head back and Molly poured Fireball down my throat, the 20-something wolf climbed onto the bar next to me, and we shook our asses and grinded to the beat while everyone in the bar yelled and cheered and ordered more drinks.

Anya was definitely my new best friend, and I told her so at least five times as we passed the bottle of Fireball back and forth, twerking our asses in sync. She was everything a 25-year-old gay man loves in a girlfriend. Outrageously beautiful, with dark black skin, the color of the most perfect night sky, and a mass of beaded braids she draped over my face as we grinded our hearts out together, singing along to Nikki, Cardi, Kylie, and all the bad ass bitches on my playlist. Anya egged me on and on until Molly finally yanked my phone out of the speaker and yelled last call out into the bar.

"I'd yell at you for getting wasted on the job, but your shift was almost over when you started your boy-gone-wild routine with your little friend here. Plus, you tripled my profits with the second wind you kicked up in the customers, so you can come back tomorrow night, if you're wearing fucking shoes," Molly called, as Griffin scooped me up off the bar and threw me over his shoulder.

"What are you doing?" I mumbled. "Where's my new friend? Who turned the music off?"

"Time to go home, Disco Queen," Griffin laughed, carrying me out of the bar and gently depositing me in my truck.

"But I want to keep dancing, and I want more of that yummy cinnamon stuff, and I want to fuuuuck....." I pulled Griffin into the truck with me, falling back on the seat and staring up at him from under my eyelashes.

"Hello, have you always been this hot?" I reached up, winding my arms around Griffin's neck. "Why are you upside down? And why is your dick not in my mouth?" I complained, sucking Griffin's bottom lip between my teeth.

"Finn," Griffin growled against my mouth, his eyes flashing with warning as he scraped his teeth against my jaw.

"You taste so good, why do I want to bite you and why do I want you to bite me?" I moaned, my tongue loose with the taste of the warm, sweet, cinnamon Fireball Anya had poured down my throat for the last hour.

"You can bite me all you want when I get you home," Griffin promised, pulling me up and buckling me into the seat.

"What are you doing?" I licked a line down Griffin's face, nipping at his jaw.

"Not fucking you, drunk off your ass, in the parking lot of Molly's bar with half my pack still loitering around," Griffin groaned, as I tugged at the zipper on his jeans and reached my hand into his underwear, pulling him out.

"But you smell so good," I protested, kissing my way down Griffin's chest as I palmed his rock-hard dick in my hand. "I want to taste you, all salty and sweet."

"I'll let you do whatever you want to me after I get you home, little wolf, I promise. I'll take care of you," Griffin rasped with restraint as he pulled away from me and tucked himself back into his pants, closing the door to the truck and walking around to the driver's side.

"Fuck waiting till we get home," I moaned, trying to wriggle out of my seatbelt and climb into Griffin's lap.

"Jesus, you're a hot little slut after a couple of drinks," Griffin exhaled, his voice thick with heat and tenderness as he started the truck.

"I told you, you wouldn't like me after you got to know me," I groaned. "You're probably wishing for that bucket of bleach now, huh?"

"Baby, I'm going to show you how much I love what a dirty little wolf you are as soon as I get you home," Griffin promised.

"Will you let me bite you then?" I asked Griffin dreamily, closing my eyes to blissful sleep.

7

"Please tell me last night was a dream?" I moaned the next morning, opening my eyes to Griffin sprawled in bed beside me, running his fingers lightly through my tangled hair.

"It was a dream," he grinned, leaning forward, and brushing his nose across mine tenderly.

"Oh, god. The last thing I remember is 'Hollaback Girl' playing, and that wild girl with the beautiful dark skin and crazy mess of braids on the bar, dancing with me. I knew she was trouble, the minute she winked at me when you first pulled me into your lap at the beginning of the night."

"Yes, it was Anya's fault you climbed up on the bar, drank half a bottle of Fireball and danced the night away, screaming 'B-A-N-A-N-A-S' in time with Gwen Stefani, before trying to blow me in the parking lot, and begging me to fuck you halfway to Texas in front of my pack," Griffin snorted, his mouth quirking at the sides as I stared back at him in horror.

"You said it was a dream," I wailed, pulling the blankets up over my face.

"Oh, it was a dream alright," Griffin laughed, pulling the

blankets down and pressing his lips to my forehead. "An X-rated one."

"Fuck off. Friends don't let friends try to blow them in the parking lot when they're drunk off their ass on half a bottle of Fireball!"

"Baby, you're lucky I didn't drill you into the seat of the truck and claim you with my mating bite, the way you were climbing all over me and moaning, Griffin, you're so beautiful, and you're mine, and I want to bite you and why aren't you biting me?" Griffin growled low in his throat, his eyes flashing deep honey gold.

"You wouldn't dare," I gasped, backing away from the predatory glint in Griffin's eye as he climbed over me.

"The only reason I didn't, little wolf, is because I want you fully sober and aware of every sensation when I bury myself in your sweet ass and sink my teeth into your skin. I'm going to fuck you and mark you and make you mine, the way I know you want me to, deep inside, not when you're drunk off your ass across the seat of my brother's truck in a bar parking lot."

"Ok, enough, I get it. I was an asshole last night," I groaned, rolling out of bed.

"Not an asshole, a very sexy, cute, drunk, little wolf pup." Griffin slapped me on the ass as I stood up.

"Not a wolf," I grumbled, flipping Griffin the bird as I made my way to the bathroom to down half a bottle of Advil and soak my head in the sink.

Griffin stuck his head in the bathroom door as I turned on the shower. "I have to go back to the lodge today. I've been neglecting things these last couple of days."

"I never told you to camp out here. You're the one who hasn't left my side since I arrived," I shot back, cranky, and annoyed, and not sure why I suddenly couldn't breathe at the thought of Griffin leaving.

"I'll be back tonight," Griffin laughed softly, and I could tell from the smug tone of his voice he could hear the way my chest tightened, and my heart started racing when he said he was leaving. Fuck his whole supersonic wolf sense, it was really starting to get on my nerves.

"Get some rest today. I told Molly you're taking the night off."

"You can't do that," I sputtered, sticking my head out of the shower to glare at him. "You can't order people around on my behalf."

"Of course I can; I'm her Alpha. I can order her around all I want." Griffin called back as he walked away.

"That's not a thing you can do," I yelled.

"Oh, it's definitely a thing," Griffin laughed, as I heard the door close behind him.

After a hot shower, a handful of Advil, two cups of coffee, and a peanut butter and honey, frozen waffle sandwich, I started to feel human again. I was standing on my porch in my bathing suit, contemplating jumping in the lake, wondering if it mattered I didn't know how to swim, when my new best friend pulled up in my driveway on an ATV.

"Hey Blondielocks," Anya called, pulling her helmet off, and shaking out her braids.

"There's got to be a better nickname you can give me."

"I don't think so. It's what the whole pack is calling you now, and it's awesome because Griffin has no idea it started with the Texan who blew you in the bathroom," she crowed.

"Wow, there's no way this isn't going to end badly."

"Yup, but we might as well have our fun while we can, before Griffin finds out and beats the shit out of us," Anya chirped.

"Griffin being able to order you guys around, isn't really a thing, right?"

"Oh, it's a thing." Anya laughed, walking up the porch steps.

"But like, what does it mean exactly?" I asked, biting my lip nervously.

"Are you asking what's it like to have an Alpha?" Anya cocked her head.

"I guess... I mean, what's all of it like? Being a wolf, being in a pack, having an Alpha, having Griffin specifically as an Alpha..." my voice trailed off as I continued to gnaw at my lip.

"Your heart is about to jump out of your chest." Anya walked over and placed her hand on my shoulder. "Are you having a panic attack?"

"No, I'm not having a fucking panic attack." I shoved Anya's hand off my shoulder and stared out at the lake as I willed my heartbeat to slow down. "I just have a problem with authority figures."

"Huh, that's awkward," Anya clucked her tongue in sympathy. "You, being the Alpha's mate and all."

"I am not Griffin's mate," I bit out through clenched teeth, as my heart rate started to speed up again.

"Um, okay, but, pretty sure he disagrees with you on that," Anya quirked her mouth to the side.

"Well, that's his problem, not mine." I swung my legs over the porch rail and stalked down to the lake.

"Are we going swimming?" Anya called after me, shedding her clothes. She caught up, standing naked beside me on the dock.

"Go away, I'm sick of bossy wolves," I sulked.

"Me too," Anya laughed. "Why do you think I want to be friends with you? I'm the second youngest of seven in a family of wolves, all everyone in my life does is boss me around all day."

"I'm going in," I announced. I was going for it, whether I knew how to swim or not, and I ran off the dock with a wild war cry.

Cold, so cold, was the first thought I had, before I started sinking and gasping for breath, struggling to push my body back up and keep my head above water. I choked and sputtered on the water filling my lungs, thrashing wildly, until Anya dove into the lake and pulled me out.

Is this what it felt like for Cian and Lillian all the time? I wondered in a half-drowned daze as Anya dumped me on the dock.

"You idiot! You complete and total moron!" Anya yelled,

kicking me. "Why would you jump in the lake if you can't swim?"

"Ow! I almost drowned, and you're kicking me?" I yelled back, sputtering on the lake water, I was still coughing up.

"Do you know what Griffin would have done to me if you'd drowned?" Anya shrieked, kicking me a second time. "He would have burned me alive and hung me from a spit in front of the lodge!"

"Jesus, I feel like there are so many things we need to talk about right now," I sighed, lacing my hands behind my neck, and closing my eyes to the warmth of the sun on my face.

"Can we start with why you tried to drown yourself? I mean, I've heard Griffin is an ice-cold fuck, but it can't be worth killing yourself over."

"I wouldn't know, I haven't fucked him."

"That's not what it looked like last night in the bar parking lot," Anya snorted.

"I haven't fucked him, fucked him, like, my dick's never been in his ass, and his has never been in mine." My body tingled at the memory of Griffin's hot mouth against my skin. "But he feels like warm sunshine and smells like snow-covered-pine-trees in the forest. There's definitely nothing cold about his touch. His mouth is so hot against my skin, I literally burn when he touches me."

"Oh my god, those are such mating words; ewww, gross. When my sister, Nahla, found her mate, she was all, he makes my wolf sing, and he smells like the fresh dew on morning grass- and lights a fire deep inside me-gag. You are so Griffin's mate; I can't believe you're even trying to deny it."

"I can't even deal with that thought right now. Can we talk about the whole Alpha thing and everyone being afraid of Griffin, for a minute?"

"If you tell me why you jumped in the lake without knowing how to swim."

"Oh my god, you're like a dog with a bone; it's so not even a big deal."

"Um, wolf, not dog, you know that's like, really insulting, right? Almost racist, kind of."

"Don't be an asshole, you know what I meant," I shoved Anya in exasperation. "I didn't jump in the lake in some grand suicide attempt. I've just never been in a lake before, in any water, actually. The only reason I even have this bathing suit, is because I bought it for a luau night at the bar I used to work in. I didn't realize it was so easy to drown, I thought I'd just figure out how to swim or something."

"You've never been in the water?" Anya gaped at me.

"I grew up mostly alone on the streets of the Bronx, and no one ever took me to a beach or pool, or lake, or taught me to swim, okay? The lake just looked so cool, calm, and inviting, calling out to me from the porch, and I thought, fuck it, I want to see what it feels like against my skin."

"Okay," Anya murmured, stretching out beside me on the dock and lacing her hands behind her head to match mine. "Griffin is an amazing Alpha. When we say he's scary, we don't mean to us. He lives to protect us and keep us safe. That's what being an Alpha is. It's not about authority, it's about leadership."

"But Molly said some things the other day, about the Sinclair pack who attacked you guys and killed Cian's mate three years ago."

"What about them?" Anya growled.

"That Griffin slaughtered them all and didn't show any mercy."

"He couldn't show mercy. That was his moment as a new Alpha. He had to show absolute dominance to the rest of the shifter world, or we would be vulnerable forever after. It's not like it is in Europe, here. We don't have a governing Wolf Council, it's kind of a wild west, every pack for themselves environment, but the U.S. packs usually honor an Alpha's claim, unless they show weakness or an inability to hold onto their territory."

"What about in Canada? Do they have a governing Wolf Council? I mean, did someone like, officially sanction the attack on your pack?"

"They're kind of in a weird in-between state there. They pretend they're independent, but they're definitely influenced by Europe. So, we're still trying to figure out who was really behind the attack on us. It was so bad, Finn." Anya's eyes clouded over at the memory. "We were still recovering from losing Colm, Griffin's father, our Alpha before him, and everyone was such a mess. Griffin was trying to keep the pack together and be strong for his mother, and we were all so raw, vulnerable, and aching. The Sinclair pack came in out of nowhere like vultures and ravaged us. They ripped Nate apart right in front of Cian and there was nothing he could do. It happened so fast; they were so fast. They must have been preparing for it as soon as they heard Colm was sick, and they were ruthless. They were determined to wipe us out and take over our territory, and Griffin just came into himself as an Alpha in that moment and completely took over. He saved us, but he also helped us heal afterward. That's the strength of a true Alpha, when they bind the pack together. He's a legend now, and other packs have been traveling across the country to come and meet with him for his counsel."

"But Molly made it sound like everyone's afraid of him, like he's this really scary guy."

"Molly's in love with Griffin's mother and she's a bitch and resents Griffin because she hated his father for taking Lillian from her," Anya snorted.

"Woah, wait, say that again?" I exclaimed, rolling over to gawk at Anya. "Molly's in love with Lillian?"

"Yup," Anya grinned. "Pack life is like one huge soap opera. You'll get used to it."

"More like a telenovela!" I exclaimed.

"Molly's not bad, and she probably didn't mean to make Griffin sound all scary. She thinks he's a good Alpha too, even if she'll never admit it. A lot of the other packs are afraid of Griffin now, but they respect him too. He's so young, but he did what he had to do, and he had only just become Alpha. He stepped up. It was badass, truly."

"Huh," I murmured, rolling back over, and closing my eyes to the sun again while I digested Anya's words. Everything she'd said I kind of already felt about Griffin. He just had this overall fierce but honorable vibe to him.

"Anything else you want to talk about?" Anya asked, dipping her fingers into the lake, and flicking me with the cold water.

"Lillian said losing your mate is like drowning every minute of the day, and I saw what it did to Cian. He had no will to live when I found him, and that was two and a half years after losing Nate."

"Wolves mate for life. Losing a mate is like losing half your soul, and most wolves don't survive it," Anya admitted. "But everyone handles it differently and some are stronger than others. I think it's almost harder when you're really young, like Cian and Nate were, because you don't have anything else to pull yourself up for, like children or big pack responsibilities. Then in other ways, I think it's harder for the older ones, who have been together for so long. The bond is so tight between them, they become like one. My parents are like that. They're centuries old and they've been together forever. They can sense everything about each other almost instantly, even when they're far away. Their mating bond is so strong, they're completely in sync. A mate is a gift, they're the other half of your soul. It's scary to think about losing them, but it's amazing if you're lucky enough to find them in the first place."

"What do you mean, they're centuries old? Like, literally?"

"Yeah, werewolves aren't immortal, but we live for a really long time. The aging process starts to slow down after we reach full adulthood in our late 20's."

"Perfect, so if Griff and I stay together for a while, I'll get grey hair and a saggy ass, while he remains a stud?"

"I think you're a long way from grey hair and a saggy ass," Anya rolled her eyes. "And he could always turn you... If you wanted him to."

"Turn me? Like into a werewolf?" I gawked at Anya.

"Yeah, I mean, I know a few wolves whose mates were human, and one of them opted to turn, not like right away, or anything," Anya added hastily as I continued to gawk at her in shock.

"When you say turn... You mean like actually turn into a werewolf? Like Griffin would bite me or something?"

"I mean, it's more complicated than that, but yeah... and not to jump ahead, but a turning bite is different than a mate bite, so I just don't want to like, confuse or totally freak you out or anything."

"Okay, totally not ready for this conversation!" I made a face at Anya. "Let's just focus on one werewolf thing at a time. Back to the whole mate thing. Does it like, hurt your parents when they're apart?"

"I don't think so. I mean, I'm not mated, so I don't know exactly what it feels like, but they just seem edgier, restless, wired a little tighter when they're apart. Listening internally and checking up on each other. They're definitely a lot more peaceful when they're together. My father hates when my mother has to go away. He'd much rather she was glued to his side, 24/7," Anya laughed.

"What does your mom do, I mean, what's her job? Why does she have to go away?"

"She's Griffin's second in command. She was second to Griffin's father and now she's second in command to Griffin. So, she travels with him when he has to go to Alpha meetings with other packs and stuff, and my dad's the pack enforcer, so he often has to go away to deal with problems too."

"Woah, back up, you need to break things down a little for me here. I don't know what this shit all means, or even what Griffin's job really is. I've seen a lot of T.V. shows, but werewolf life is different in all of them. And I probably should have asked this earlier, but are there vampires too? There are vampires too, aren't there?" I glanced across the lake at the surrounding forest, nervously.

"Yup! Vampires, witches, shifters, they're all real, and the three sides are kind of at odds, although it wasn't always like that. Supposedly there's some ancient prophecy involving a witch and wolf who are supposed to unite the three sides and bring us all together, but no one believes it, it's just a fairytale we all grew up on."

"I knew there were vampires! Witches too? Fuck this shit! Cian had to send me that letter about his sunshine filled cabin and leave out all the details about his werewolf pack and the vampires that are probably lurking around in the woods he gave me."

"Relax, Blondielocks, your land is in pack territory. There are no vampires here. Their lair is in the outskirts of Portland, a few hours from here, and they stopped hunting in these woods when Griffin's dad formed the pack and took over the whole territory. They stick to their turf, like we stick to ours, and the vampire in charge of the Portland Lair owes Griffin big time anyway. Griff rescued his missing brother when he discovered him imprisoned at the Sinclair lodge." Anya grabbed my arm and yanked me up. "C'mon, let's go to town. I'm starving. I'll buy you a crepe from the crepe truck and you can help me scout out the hot tourists and find someone for me to hit on."

"What about my werewolf history lesson?" I complained, following Anya back up the hill to the cabin as she gathered her discarded clothes and slipped them back on.

"It can wait, there's nothing pressing you need to know about right now, and I need to eat and get laid. We don't all have super-hot Alphas we can suck off in bar parking lots when we're horny and drunk, you know. I went home alone last night, and it sucked."

"Again, with the slut shaming!" I shoved Anya roughly with my shoulder. "I don't have any issues with my sexuality or who I am. I'm not ashamed of my drunken bar top dancing last night, or that I tried to get my man off in the parking lot, thank you very much."

"Chill out, I'm just teasing you. We don't care either. Wolves are very free with our bodies, and the whole pack enjoyed your bar top striptease."

"My what?" I gawked at Anya as she threw me a helmet and hopped on her ATV. "Please tell me I didn't strip in front of my maybe boyfriend's entire pack."

"Just your shirt, but you did pull your shorts down low a few times and gyrate around, giving us an awesome view of what you're working with down there. Let's just say there were some jealous looks being thrown Griff's way last night," Anya laughed, starting up her ATV as I climbed on behind her.

8

"What is it with you and the no shoes?" Molly shook her head, walking up to me and Anya as we messily devoured our Nutella and banana crepes, while balancing our ass cheeks on the edge of a fence overlooking the lake behind the crepe truck.

"I was swimming?" I mumbled in a half question over a mouthful of chocolate covered bananas.

"Is that why you're not wearing a shirt either?" Molly raised her brow at me: sitting in the center of town, perched on the edge of a fence in nothing but my bathing suit. "Or are you just getting ready to hop up on the fence and give us another show?"

"Give him a break, Moll, I dragged Finn into town in his bathing suit because I wanted a crepe, so fuck off, and leave us alone," Anya replied for me.

"You're not Griffin's second, yet, little girl," Molly snorted at Anya, clearly unimpressed by her mouthing off. "Try telling me what to do again and I'll wrap those pretty little braids around your neck."

"You're going to be Griffin's second?" I gawked at Anya, swiping at my Nutella smeared face with the back of my hand.

"That's disgusting," Molly shook her head at me. "You better wash your hands before you come to work tonight, since we both know you're not going to shower."

"Uh, okay, I thought Griffin said I had the night off though..." I stuttered, shrinking back under Molly's penetrating stare.

"Are you sick?" Molly raised her eyebrows at me. "Because it looks to me like you're living it up with your gal pal here, stuffing your face with chocolate and bananas and going for swims in the lake. If you don't want the job, I'm happy to replace you," she offered, her face expressionless as she stared me down.

"No, that's okay. I definitely want the job. I'll be there," I mumbled, jabbing my elbow into Anya when she started making chicken squawking sounds at me.

"I literally can't think of a single worse combination than the two of you," Molly muttered as she turned to walk away.

"Yeah well, we all know no one else would work for you since you're such a fucking bitch, so you better be grateful you've got Finn," Anya called after Molly, throwing a piece of crepe at her back.

"I feel like you're really lucky that missed," I winced, as the crepe sailed over Molly's shoulder, and she shot Anya a death stare before continuing on her way.

"Whatever, that bitch so needs Lillian to get over losing Griffin's dad and hop back in bed with her."

"Lillian and Molly were a couple?" I yelled, planting my Nutella smeared hands on Anya's shoulders and shaking her. "How could you causally slip that into conversation? You said Molly had the hots for Lillian, you never told me they used to be together! And how do you know so much about everyone's history? Aren't you like, 14?"

"I'm 23, fuck you very much," Anya stuck her tongue out. "And my mother tells me everything because I'll be Griffin's second soon. She's training me to take over for her."

"You could have led with that, you know," I made a face at Anya.

"Like, hi, I'm going to be your Alpha fuckbuddy's second one day, so you might not want to confide in me and like, be my best friend, because my loyalty will be to him and not you."

"That's not how it works, idiot," Anya smacked me across the head. "My loyalty is to my Alpha, yes, but it's also to the pack. It's not a separate thing, which you'll realize once you officially become pack. Also," Anya covered my mouth with her sticky Nutella hand when I tried to interrupt. "As Griffin's mate, you are the single most important person to him, so I will like, be your bodyguard on top of being your most loyal friend and packmate."

"I'm never going to be pack. I haven't even decided if I'm going to fuck Griffin or hang out with him on the regular. I don't do relationships and I definitely don't 'mate' with people."

"It doesn't really work that way, you know." Anya twisted her mouth in a sympathetic grimace. "When you find your mate, you can't resist the call. It's not like something you choose to accept or not. You just belong together and that's it. My mom said Lillian tried to resist it at first when Griffin's dad showed up. She and Molly had been together since they were teenagers and even though they weren't mates, their bond was really strong. Molly even tried to get Lillian to run off with her, but she wouldn't. I can't really blame Molly for being such a bitch, it must have been excruciating to feel the love and connection between Lillian and Colm through the pack bonds. Not to mention, she was the midwife, so she delivered Griff and Cian too."

"Is that why she gave up midwifing and bought the bar? So she wouldn't have to deliver any more of Lillian's pups?"

"No, she bought the bar after Colm died. She wouldn't have stopped being the pack midwife while Lillian was still having pups. She never left her side during both pregnancies. She slept on the floor beside Lillian during every full moon, making sure she didn't shift. Werewolf pregnancies are very dangerous, its why some couples are mated for 200 years without producing any live pups. We've come a long way with what we've learned, and it's gotten much less dangerous for werewolves to have children now, but I think Molly just needed to do something else. She saw so much loss in her time as a midwife, so much she couldn't prevent, she was ready for a little peace and simplicity."

"I'm so confused," I moaned, leaning my head against Anya's shoulder. "Can you like, give me the short movie version of the werewolf world, so I know what the fuck I'm dealing with?"

"Yes, but not here. If I'm going to tell you werewolf/vampire bedtime stories, let's at least go back to your cabin and curl up on your couch with a bowl of popcorn."

When I walked into the bar several hours later, 30 minutes early for my shift, showered, fully dressed, and wearing shoes, Molly mock-fainted, reaching up a hand to feel her brow.

"Am I delirious? Is this a fever dream?"

"Ha, ha." I rolled my eyes, slipping behind the bar to check if anything needed to be re-stocked before the bar started filling up for the night. I was in a fog, still trying to absorb everything Anya had told me that afternoon.

"You still don't seem to own any clothes that didn't come out of Malibu Ken's surf shack, but it's a shocking improvement to see you fully dressed, wearing shoes, and not stinking like the Alpha just shot his load all over you." Molly's eyes drifted over my faded ripped jeans, worn so bare they were almost white, vintage *Marry Me Jane* T-shirt, and hot pink checkerboard Vans.

"Thanks. I have my moments." I grabbed a handful of pretzels as my stomach grumbled, reminding me why I was half an hour early for my shift tonight. I had forgotten to grab dinner on the way to work. "You should really serve food here."

"You gonna cook it?" Molly snorted, raising her eyebrow at me.

"I know Lillian baked those muffins for you, Blondielocks."

"Who the fuck cares who baked them, it's not like you ate any of them! Lillian told me you hate muffins. You just made me bake them to torture me."

"The customers liked them," Molly shrugged. "You could bake more muffins and I'll serve those."

"How about dividing up your pretzels into a few bowls so everyone doesn't have to fight over the one bucket, at least?"

"You want to add cooking to your list of duties, Malibu Ken, go right ahead. All they're getting from me is a bucket of pretzels."

"I'm from New York, not California," I stuck my tongue out at Molly as Anya walked into the bar.

"Sure you are," Molly laughed.

"What the fuck is her problem?" I exhaled, as Anya plopped down in front of me.

"I told you, she's sexually frustrated," Anya grinned, grabbing a pretzel from the bucket.

"She could at least have a few flavors of pretzels, or some chocolate covered ones."

"You PMSing?" Anya clucked her tongue in mock sympathy. "Poor baby wants some chocolate covered pretzels?"

"Fuck off, you completely traumatized me today me with your six seasons worth of werewolf history I'm still trying to digest, and I forgot to eat dinner before I came to work."

"No sweat, I'll get you a pizza from across the street. And chill out about the werewolf stuff." Anya scanned the bar, dropping her voice. "You're way over-dramatizing everything, it's really not that big of a deal."

"Not that big of a deal?" I rolled my eyes at Anya.

I needed another bottle of Fireball to drown out the buzzing in my head from all the stuff Anya had told me today, and she hadn't even gotten to the vampire/werewolf relations before I kicked her out to get ready for work.

"I told you, the most important thing you have to remember is Griff has become fucking legendary since we defeated the Sinclair Pack, and you're his mate, so you're going to be right in the thick of everything with him, leading the whole werewolf world! Now, stop overthinking things, Blondielocks. I'm going to get your pizza before you faint, and Griffin finds out I didn't feed you." Anya planted a wet, sloppy kiss on my forehead.

"I am not Griffin's mate and I'm definitely not leading the werewolf world with him," I hissed, turning to serve the impatient lumberjack looking guy who was walking over.

I was already comfortable at Molly's, the rhythm here wasn't that different from bars in the city, even though it was a small, rural town. The weeknight crowd was mostly people stopping in for a drink after work, they were just coming from the lumberyard and tackle shop instead of an office downtown, and the weekend customers wanted the same thing they wanted everywhere, conversation, a nice buzz, and a good fuck.

Probably wasn't a good idea to help them with the fuck, after my disastrous experience with the Texan in the bathroom, but I had the conversation and buzz hookup in the bag, leaning over the bar, laughing at bad jokes, and refilling shots.

I could sort out the wolves from everyone else pretty easily now, even though there seemed to be one uniform for all. Wolf or human, male or female, everyone around here basically dressed the same. Either L.L. Bean, or Yeti and Filson T-shirts, Patagonia and Northface hoodies, Merrell boots, Carhartt pants and jeans, and flannel or fleece at night.

Anya had tried to explain the town dynamic to me, but all I really got was that some of the people in town knew about the pack and the ones who didn't, kept their distance because they either suspected something wasn't kosher with the wolves or they just didn't give a shit. It was hard to tell with rural Mainers.

There was definitely an unspoken divide in the bar though,

almost an invisible line that divided most of the wolves and non-wolves, with a few locals mixed in with the pack who were obviously in the know. Everyone but me seemed to get it, so I just followed their lead. Cian was the only wolf I'd ever met before coming here, and they all seemed to have the same chill vibe, although I imagined they were pretty scary if you fucked with them.

"If you're not going to dance for us again, will you at least share your dinner?" a wolf teased me as Anya returned with my pizza, plopping it down in front of me on the bar.

"You guys should definitely serve food here," someone else chimed in, sniffing the air in front of me longingly.

"Right?" I opened the box, offering the guy sniffing my food a slice.

"Totally," another wolf agreed, tossing back the rest of his beer. "These pretzels suck. Molly should at least have some wings and shit."

"How about those muffins? Are there any of those muffins left from last night?" someone else yelled, reaching an arm out to yank the bucket of pretzels down the bar.

"Nah, those were gone in 5 minutes. Lillian made those. They were fucking awesome," a young, hot wolf named Grant called out. I was slowly beginning to pick up on the names of the regulars, although most of the wolves I'd met last night were a drunken blur.

"How could you tell Lillian made them?" I asked over a mouthful of pizza.

"Everything Lillian makes is amazing." Anya pushed a wolf's hand away from my pizza box. "Fuck off, Ry, Blondielocks needs the fuel. Go get your own pizza across the street."

"We should get Lillian to cook for the bar." I passed the forlorn looking wolf next to Anya a slice of my pizza.

"Stop giving away your food!" Anya ripped the slice of pizza out of the wolf's hand. "No begging! Bad wolf," she smacked him on the nose. "Getting Lillian to cook for the bar would be a genius idea if we could get her out of the lodge, but she rarely leaves since Colm died, and when she does do anything, it's usually in spurts, like the energy it takes her to engage for an hour leaves her drained for a week afterward. She hasn't gotten out of bed since she baked muffins with you yesterday."

"Really?"

"Yeah, we all felt her through the pack bonds when she was with you, and it was nice to see her sparkle again, but she faded after she got back."

"What do you mean, you could feel her with me?" I dropped my pizza crust down and shoved the box under the bar when Molly glared at me across the room.

"That was your break for the night," she called.

"Everyone in the pack has a color of their own you see through the bonds," Anya explained. "Before Colm died, Lillian's was a bright pink that shimmered like it was laced with gold and silver. But after she lost Colm, it faded to an almost pinkish grey, and it stopped sparkling completely after Cian left, except the other day, when she baked the muffins with you. It deepened to a dusty rose and there was a hint of silver again for a little while."

"Okay, this is way too much to absorb sober. You and I are stealing a bottle after my shift and going back to my place to finish the werewolf history lesson you started. I feel like we only got halfway through the second season, and you keep fast forwarding to the last one, even though I've missed everything in the middle."

"Probably not gonna happen tonight," Anya laughed, as Griffin stalked toward the bar, a dark look in his eye. "Pretty sure your mate has other plans for you."

"Not my mate," I muttered under my breath as Griffin sat down in front of me.

"I distinctly remember telling you to rest up and not come to work tonight," Griffin glowered.

"And I distinctly remember telling you, you can't order people around to give me the night off," I hissed back.

"Molly," Griffin yelled loudly across the bar. "You have a problem with Finn taking the night off tonight?"

"No problem here," she replied sweetly, turning back to her customer.

"Let's go." Griffin reached across the bar, grabbing my arm.

"You can't just do this," I exclaimed, as Griffin lifted me up, pulling me over the bar and sliding me down his body.

"I should be throwing you over my shoulder and carrying you out of here right now," Griffin growled in my ear.

"Try it, and I'll bite a chunk out of your ass." I pulled away.

"I brought dinner for you, and you weren't there," Griffin scowled accusingly.

"You brought me dinner?" I melted a little.

"I came back early to feed you because I know how you get when you don't eat," Griffin grumbled.

"I'm still hungry. I only got to eat one slice of pizza before Molly scared me into hiding the rest of the pie under the bar."

"Does this mean you're coming with me? Or are you still going to make a big thing of it and argue about staying?"

"I mean, it's not really cool you barged in here and wolfed out on me, dragging me over the bar like a ragdoll."

"So, you're not coming?" Griffin stared at me with a mixture of weariness and frustration.

"You have serious boundary issues." I glared at Griffin, not wanting to give in too easily, although I did think it was really sweet he'd brought me dinner.

"Boundary issues." Griffin stared at me blankly.

"Yes, you know, personal boundaries? Like, it's not normal to barge into someone's job and drag them across the bar because you want to have dinner with them."

"You were supposed to stay home today."

"Like a dog?" I raised an eyebrow. "I don't stay put."

"I literally have no idea what you're talking about right now." Griffin stared at me like I had three heads.

"Oh my god, you're impossible! We'll talk about your issues while we eat." I followed Griffin out of the bar and over to my truck, which he seemed to take ownership of whenever we were together.

Griffin yanked open the driver side door, and my body tightened and started to itch in response to his tension. Misery poured off his body in waves, and I wanted to touch him, but I didn't, suddenly feeling unsure and vulnerable as we drove down the road in silence.

"Did you get some work done today?" I finally asked awkwardly.

"Yes." Griffin opened his mouth like he was going to say something else, but then closed it again, staring straight ahead with dark, brooding eyes.

"Anya and I hung out today."

"I know, you were supposed to rest."

"Yeah, about that, not really okay with being treated like a two-year-old. 25-year-old, grown ass man here. Been on my own since I was 13, pretty sure I know when to rest or not."

"You've been on your own since you were 13?" Griffin's eyes flashed yellow gold with anger. "What happened to your parents, your family?"

"I don't know. I can't remember my parents at all. I was found curled up in a dumpster in the Bronx when I was ten, and I don't have any memories from before then. The state put me in foster care and said I probably experienced some kind of trauma that blocked my memory."

"What about your other family, could the state not find anyone else to step in and care for you?" Griffin asked quietly.

"There was no pack," I snapped, pulling away when Griffin reached for my hand. "The human world isn't like your little wolfdom here. We don't have packs and packmates. If your parents are deadbeats, you're usually fucked. I was fucked, but I figured it out. I got by, and I certainly know how to take care of myself."

"Yes," Griffin agreed quietly. "You've made that really clear."

9

I practically ripped the truck door off its hinges when Griffin finally slowed to a stop in the driveway of the cabin. I didn't know what the fuck was going on with him, but his werewolf tantrum was really pissing me off. I couldn't believe he dragged me out of the bar to bring me back here for dinner, then spent the whole half hour truck ride barely speaking to me.

When I walked into the cabin, I stopped short in shock. Classical piano music was playing softly in the background, and a red plaid blanket was spread out on the floor in the center of the living room with a picnic laid out on top. There was a rustic looking platter with cheese, olives, salami, and French bread, and a bottle of wine, two glasses, and a box of chocolates. It looked like a photo shoot for *CountryLiving* magazine.

"You made me a picnic with wine and chocolate?" I gulped, as Griffin walked up behind me.

"Yes," he sighed.

"I've never had a picnic before."

"I don't know what you like." Griffin rested his chin on the back of my head, holding his body back, not crowding me.

"I'm pretty sure I like picnics. I mean, I've never had one, but there's wine and chocolate..." I leaned back into Griffin. "Are we in a fight?"

"I don't know, are we?" Griffin inhaled me, his arms encircling my waist as we stood in the doorway of the cabin, gazing out at his picnic spread.

"It feels like a fight, kind of. You're all tense and silent. But I've never been in a fight because I've never really made it past the BJ on the bathroom floor stage, so I don't really know." I closed my eyes as Griffin trailed his lips down the side of my face and into the crook of my neck, breathing me in. "I did have a guy throw a beer bottle at my head once and call me a heartless prick, but I couldn't even remember his name at the time, so I don't think that counts as a real fight."

"Before I became Alpha, one of the pack wolves told me they were surprised their ass didn't freeze up when I pulled my dick out, but I don't think that was a fight either, because my dick was half out of his ass before I finished shooting my load, and I was already walking away when he said it."

"Wow, you are an asshole," I breathed, tilting my head back to stare into Griffin's eyes. "How about since you've become Alpha? What do the guys you fuck now, say?"

"I haven't fucked any of the pack wolves since I've become Alpha, too complicated, and I warn most guys ahead of time not to try to touch me or talk to me afterward. When I fuck a guy, it's just a fuck, no intimacy."

"Huh." I could feel the tension ease out of Griffin's body as he held me against him tightly, his face buried deep in the side of my neck. "So, this might be a fight then, but we're not sure," I teased, turning around in Griffin's arms.

"You're driving my wolf crazy," he confessed, his honey-gold eyes gleaming darkly.

"Crazy in a good way, or a bad way?"

"I'm trying to go slow for you, Finn. I swear I am, but it's killing me." Griffin exhaled with a sigh of restraint.

"This is you going slow?" I gawked at Griffin in disbelief. "I only met you four days ago, and so far, you chased me into driving off naked in my truck, yanked me out of the bar bathroom in the middle of a blowjob, and dragged me across the bar like a ragdoll in the middle of my shift."

"You took off naked in your truck, I didn't chase you away." Griffin eyed me with dark gold, expressionless eyes.

"True." A familiar knot formed in the pit of my stomach.

"Why did you run off, Finn?" Griffin asked me softly, staying back, giving me my space as we stood, staring at one another.

"Because you bent me over the porch rail and almost fucked my brains out, and I wanted you to," I choked, holding Griffin's gaze intently. "Except, no one has been in my ass since I was 12, and my foster father raped me in his shed, ripping me apart so bad, I needed a fuckload of stitches and couldn't sit down for a month."

"He's a dead man," Griffin whispered so quietly I almost didn't hear him. "I'm gonna rip out his intestines and hang him from them on the door of his shed."

"I don't need you too." My eyes clouded over at the memory of the scared 12-year-old kid I once was. "It's just, you don't know anything about me," I whispered helplessly. "And this is not going slow."

"I'm trying to court you," Griffin groaned in frustration. "I stole the best wine I could find from the lodge's wine cellar. I even went to Portland and bought fancy cheese, salami, and chocolate from some gourmet place, but I have a pack to manage and territory politics to navigate, and if I don't get in your ass soon, I'm going to fucking explode." Griffin's eyes flashed wolfen-gold rimmed with black as he circled me. "You have no fucking idea how slowly I've been going for you, Finn," Griffin exhaled. "I made you a picnic, I put *Ólafur Arnalds* on, I've been trying to do everything right, but these past few days have been eating away at me. My wolf is going nuts, he's so restless and on edge, pushing to break free and claim you as our mate. He's in a panic every time I'm away from you, and he only calms down after I've marked you back up and you at least smell like us again."

"Who's *Ólafur Arnalds?*" Griffin's words washed over me, and thoughts of home, and mine, and safe filled my head.

"He's an Icelandic composer. He used to be a drummer for metal bands and then he started composing classical pieces. That's who's playing in the background." Griffin held my gaze as we stared at each other, neither of us moving.

"It's beautiful, kind of haunting. I don't know that it's seduction music, exactly," I half-laughed, half-choked, as the air between us thickened. "If you really wanted to get the party started, you should have put on *Winter Gordon's* "Dirty Talk.""

"I don't want to fuck you under a strobe light in a club, Finn," Griffin growled. "That's what I'm trying to show you here. You're so much more than a fuck. You're my mate, and I know you feel it too," he declared, advancing on me. "We're two halves of a whole. Tell me you don't feel it and I'll walk away."

"I can't." I closed the space between us, fisting Griffin's T-shirt in my hand and yanking at the button on his jeans as we fell to the floor in a tangle of limbs. I was done with the dance, the back and forth, the promise of his touch. I wanted all of Griffin now, his hands on every inch of my body, his rough cheek against mine, his sweat on my lips.

"I want my mating words, little wolf." Griffin murmured warningly as I pulled his shirt over his head and tugged his jeans down, stripping him bare.

"Fuck the words," I shot back, pulling Griffin on top of me and wrapping my legs around his waist.

"Give me my words, Finn," Griffin whispered, his breath ghosting over my face as he traced a finger through my hairline and down the side of my jawbone. He cupped my chin in his hand, brushing his lips across mine, teasing my mouth open with his tongue and drawing it across my own in a hot, wet, circle. I was utterly seduced. It was the sexiest, most intimate kiss I'd ever had, and I wanted Griffin all over me; I just didn't want to admit he was right, that I felt everything he did.

Griffin peeled my clothes off, one item at a time, his lips whispering across my skin as they brushed over my eyelashes, my nose, my cheekbones, the curve of my throat, my collarbone, my shoulder blades, the length of my arm, each finger on my hand. He traced the faded cigarette burn scars along my ribcage with his tongue, scraping his teeth against my hipbone and across to my bellybutton, erasing every painful touch I'd endured. He brushed his lips across my pubic bone and down the inside of my thighs all the way to my ankles, across the tops of my feet to my toes and then back up again to my dick, which was rock hard and leaking between my legs.

My body was boneless, raw with need, as Griffin ran his tongue along the base of my dick and down to my balls, blowing into the opening of my ass. He spread me open, burying his face between my cheeks and licking me like an ice cream cone until I was loose, wet, and aching, clawing at his arms, begging him to fuck me.

"Not without the words," Griffin growled, lifting dark slitted eyes to meet my gaze.

He leaned over my chest, sucking my bottom lip between his teeth, and I could taste the sweet musk of my ass on his tongue as Griffin pressed his hard, muscled body against mine.

"Give me my mating words, little wolf." Griffin nipped at my lips, my jaw, my ear, his breath hot on my damp skin, his chest pressed against my knees, folding me in half. "Admit you're my mate. Tell me how you feel," Griffin rasped, reaching for a bottle of lube he must have tucked behind the wine on the picnic blanket. He drizzled the lube over my open ass and down the length of his dick, rubbing the tip across my entrance teasingly, as he stared down at me with heat-filled eyes. "I'm not asking you again," Griffin warned. "And I'm not fucking you until you say them."

"Promise me you'll never ask me to submit, that you'll never Alpha me," I panted, my voice thick with my need, as I gazed up at Griffin.

Griffin lowered my knees and pulled one of my legs up over his shoulder, gazing down at me with a mixture of tenderness and amusement.

"I can't not Alpha you, Finn, it's who I am. But I promise you I'll never ask you to submit to me."

"Promise me you won't pull Alpha rank on me," I insisted. "That you'll never take away my free will."

"If I wanted to force myself on you, you'd be on your knees with my dick in your ass and my teeth in your neck, right now," Griffin sighed, his eyes flashing dark gold with exasperation.

"I can't be powerless under you, Griffin."

"Oh Finn," Griffin laughed softly, leaning down, and capturing my mouth in a kiss. "I'm the one who's powerless under you. I would lay down my life for you," he murmured against my lips.

"Fine, but I'm only submitting to you in bed, and only because I want to," I moaned, arching my back, and pushing up toward Griffin hungrily.

Griffin leaned back and pressed his lube-slicked dick against the entrance of my ass, raising his eyebrows as he kneeled between my legs.

"I can wait all night for your words, my sweet little wolf," he taunted, dribbling more lube over my ass, pressing a finger in slowly, until it reached his knuckle. "The question is, can you?" Griffin breathed, adding another finger.

"God, you're infuriating." My body quivered beneath Griffin, my ass tightening around his fingers, skin tingling under his lips. "I could have fucked two different guys in the time it's taking you to shove your dick in my ass! You want the fucking words? Fine!" I yelled at Griffin, lying flushed and aching beneath him. "You're my mate, I feel it with my whole being, even though I don't understand it. My whole body itches when I'm away from you; you're like a godamn STD I can't get rid of. There are your fucking words, now for the love of god, will you please fuck my brains out already!"

"An STD?" Griffin choked on his laughter, his eyes dancing with amusement and darkening with heat, as he slowly pulled his fingers out and eased his dick inside me, sliding all the way in with one deep push.

I could feel Griffin in my throat as he held my leg up over his shoulder, leaning down over me. I thought it would hurt, that it might bring me back to the time I'd tried so hard to forget, but all I felt was safe and loved. Turned on, and hot for Griffin as he held himself still, careful, giving me time to get used to the feel of him inside me.

"You want me to fuck your brains out?" Griffin teased, gently sliding in and out of me with slow, deep strokes as he felt me relax beneath him.

"Yes," I gasped, tilting my hips, inviting him deeper inside me.

"You could have fucked two different guys already?" Griffin growled, sucking my tongue into his mouth, biting down hard. His eyes flashed dark gold as he increased his pace, his gentle strokes turning rougher and harder, as he showed me exactly what he thought of my snarky comment.

Griffin was totally in control, and it was hot as fuck. I gripped his hard muscled ass, digging my nails into his skin, letting him know I could take it as he teased my prostate with every thrust of his hips, owning me, making me his, until we finally came together in a hot, messy burst and Griffin sank his teeth into my neck with a deep guttural roar.

His bite hurt. Fuck, it hurt, but there was so much color all of a sudden, blinding me, it blocked out the pain. It was so bright, yellow, and orange, glowing like the sun and 4th of July fireworks, and I felt snow on my face and smelled pine branches everywhere.

Griffin lifted his head up to meet my gaze, his teeth glistening with drops of my blood, his stomach coated with my semen, and I was overwhelmed with the need to bite him back, mark him, make him mine.

I reached up and grabbed a fistful of his hair, twisting his head to the side as if by instinct, sinking my teeth into his neck with a possession I never knew I had inside me. Griffin's skin beneath my teeth felt so right, the taste of his blood in my mouth natural, and my whole body thrummed with his wolfsong as our mating bond clicked into place.

"I can feel you in my head, and like, everywhere," I breathed, falling back, and staring up at Griffin in awe.

"Mates," he growled, his voice full of satisfaction, his dark gold eyes gleaming with heat and possession.

"But like, I can feel you, feel you," I whispered as my body almost hummed with satisfaction.

"I can feel you, feel you, too," Griffin rubbed his forehead against mine. "Your colors are all blended together like a rainbow, and sparkly like a strobe light," he grinned. "Go figure, my little Disco Queen."

"I do like to dance," I smiled weakly, still in shock. "I thought it would be scary, the whole mating thing, but I feel so warm and safe, like you're literally a part of me now, like the home I never had, but always wished for."

"I am your home now and you are mine," Griffin replied quietly.

"Are you going to stop rubbing yourself all over me now that you've had my ass, or is it just going to get worse?"

"Our scents are going to merge into one." Griffin's whole body was loose with his satisfaction and relief, as he rolled us over onto his back, cradling me against his chest.

"Soooo... You won't need to rub yourself all over me anymore?"

I lifted my head to meet his gleaming, dark yellow eyes.

"Oh, there will be plenty of rubbing, little wolf," Griffin grinned, brushing his lips across mine tenderly.

"When do we get to have the wine and chocolate?" I mumbled sleepily against Griffin's chest, and he laughed in reply, tucking the throw blanket from the couch around me as I drifted off.

10

"Wow, that was some off the charts mating fireworks!" Anya yelled in my ear, bouncing on the bed beside me.

"Huh? Why are you here?" I moaned sleepily. "Is this something in season 3 you haven't gotten to telling me yet?"

"Griff called me over to bring breakfast. He had to go, official Alpha werewolf business, but he wanted to make sure you ate; he said he was pretty sure you can't cook anything besides frozen pizza and toaster waffles," Anya explained as I slowly opened my eyes, still half-asleep.

"Griff left while I was sleeping, the morning after we mated, and sent you here to feed me breakfast?" I narrowed my eyes at Anya, fully awake now, and pissed.

"Yes, but don't be mad, it was an Alpha thing, he had to go," Anya replied hastily as I sat up in bed. "And I already told you about the colors in the pack bonds. We covered that in season one. You're like a big sparkly rainbow and you literally lit up my whole brain when you and Griff merged. It was like, woah, wow! And Griff's colors are so bright and warm now, instead of all, grrr and hot and blazing like a forest fire. He feels so calm and settled. He was so restless before, and he burned. Now he's kind of like a low flame, it's nice."

"You can feel our connection??" I gawked at Anya in horror. "That's so ick, like such a violation!"

"Oh my god, you're so crazy dramatic, will you calm down? It's not like, a creeper peeper thing or anything. No one is spying on you guys. We didn't watch you have sex, and no one knows what you're thinking, it's not like that. It's just, you're pack now," Anya sighed. "Take a minute and just listen and feel. We're with you now and you're with us. It will probably take a bit to get used to, but after a while, you'll be able to distinguish between everyone and you'll know if someone is in trouble or hurting in a major way, but it's subtle, like a background thing. You don't pick up on little everyday emotions except with your own mate."

"Oh my god, I think I can sort of sense you." I closed my eyes and reached for Anya in my head. "You're purplish and silver and feel like a bolt of lightning and smell like an electrical storm." I opened my eyes, staring at Anya in awe. "You're right, it's so weird. It's like, I'm not in your head and I don't know what you're thinking, but I can kind of just feel you in the background, like I could reach for you if I needed you."

"Yes!" Anya clapped her hands, throwing her arms around my neck in excitement. "You're pack now, Finn," she beamed. "Welcome to the family."

"That's so, I mean, I don't know what to say. I've never had any family." I stared at Anya, momentarily at a loss for words. "I feel like I just got adopted, seven years after I aged out of the foster care system," I laughed weakly. "Kind of never thought that was gonna happen..."

"Pack is everything." Anya pulled me into a hug. "Pack is family and safety and love, and once you feel it, you never want to let it go. And this pack is fucking awesome. Griffin's dad was a really good Alpha, and he brought all the ragtag wolves living in this forest together, but Griffin was born to lead this pack. You could feel it instantly, after his father died and he became Alpha."

"So, not all Alphas are the same? I mean, is it possible to get a bad one?"

"No, they're definitely not all the same, and yes, you can get a bad Alpha," Anya snorted. "Half of Griffin's time is taken up dealing with bad Alphas and the fallout to other packs. An Alpha's leadership sets the tone for the rhythm of the entire pack. Griff commands our respect because he's fair and kind, and he never abuses his authority. He connects us together so tightly, when we train, we're like one wolf fighting. He's such a fucking awesome Alpha, and I'm so psyched I'm going to be his second, and you're in our pack now!" Anya practically squealed, squeezing me against her.

"Ow, I think you just broke a rib. You're ridiculously strong, you know." I made a face at Anya. "It's a little emasculating. I'm not sure I love having a best friend who might be able to kick my ass."

"You just admitted I'm your best friend, yay!" Anya squeezed me again.

"Kind of can't breathe," I wheezed, pulling away.

"Your little fireworks mating session last night sparked something in Lillian and she made you French toast and sausages for breakfast. Come eat, they're warming in the oven."

"Where the fuck is Griffin? I'm kind of pissed he's not here." I pulled a pair of boxers on and followed Anya into the kitchen. "This better not be a regular thing now, like, he got to fuck and bite me, so he's cool just taking off and leaving our scents to merge now, or whatever."

"I mean, he does have a lot of shit to deal with right now, and you refusing to submit was making him bonkers, so he probably will get back down to business now that you're mated..." Anya's voice trailed off as I glared at her. "French toast?" she chirped, sliding a casserole dish out of the oven.

"That does look really good," I admitted, still pissed, but

hungry as usual, as I plopped down at the kitchen island.

"So, how did it happen?" Anya asked, dishing up Lillian's French toast and sausage breakfast casserole which looked and smelled completely amazing. "Did Griff just drag you back here after you left the bar and bend you over the kitchen island and bite you?" Anya grinned. "Cause, that was definitely the vibe I was getting off him when he yanked you across the bar last night."

"Not exactly, I mean, there was a picnic with wine and chocolate." I sighed dreamily, remembering waking up to Griffin's lips in my hair after I'd passed out across his chest on the picnic blanket, and the way he scooped me into his lap and fed me chocolate and grapes and then carried me into bed and did things to my body I didn't even know were possible.

"Wine and chocolate, hmm, I'll have to remember that when I'm courting my mate." Anya scrunched up her face like she was making a mental note.

"So, in the wolf world, do you just like, know instantly when someone is your mate?" I asked over a mouthful of French toast.

"Yes, but sometimes it can be buried or blocked, so it's not obvious immediately," Anya replied. "Also, it doesn't kick in until after puberty, so wolves who are mates and grow up in the same pack, like Nate and Cian, will often be really close friends when they're kids but not realize they're mates until after they hit puberty."

"So, if you haven't found your mate by now, they're probably not in your pack and you need to look outside the pack for them?"

"Pretty much," Anya shrugged. "But there's no guarantee you'll find your mate either, that's why it's so special when you do, although it kind of sucks if you meet them after you've already formed a connection with someone."

"Like Molly and Lillian?" I said slowly.

"Yup. The pack has been living with the ripple effects of that shitshow for the last thirty years..."

"What about you? Do you have a type you're looking for?"

"Hmmm, well obviously I'd like to find my mate, but other than that, I like my women soft and sweet, and my men way tougher than I am. If a guy can't pin me down and fuck me with his teeth in my neck, I'm not interested." Anya laughed.

"Hmmm, I know what you mean," I grinned back.

"Ha, I know you do!" Anya snorted.

"Now that he has me, does Griffin even care I'm his mate?" The smile faded from my face as the weight of everything that had happened suddenly sunk in.

"Finn, oh my god, you so don't understand the mate thing. I mean, I don't know how you don't get it, now that you're mated and you must feel the connection, but you're like, literally the most important, living, breathing creature in the world to Griffin now. Of course, he cares that you're his mate."

"The most important, living, breathing creature?" I echoed tentatively.

"The most," Anya sighed, smacking me lightly across the head. "Now, let's go down to the lake, I'm going to teach you how to swim today," she grinned.

"I don't know..." I hedged uneasily, recalling the cold water of the lake filling my lungs and the panic I'd felt before Anya dragged me out.

"Here's the thing," Anya bit her lip. "You live on a lake, and it's kind of a weakness, not knowing how to swim. It puts you at risk."

"And your job is to assess risk and alleviate problems for the pack." I ran my hands through my messy hair in defeat. "This sucks! Is this how it's going to be between us now? Like, we can't just be drinking/dancing buddies anymore? We have to have this whole weird second-in-command-to-the-Alpha dynamic between us?"

"I mean, not exactly, but sort of." Anya gave me a half-hearted grimace of apology. "It's like this, I can't separate who I am and who you are in the pack hierarchy. It's just not possible. But we're still totally bffs and drinking/dancing buddies at the same time."

"Yeah, not really making me feel better," I groaned. "Here's a scenario for you, Griff and I get in a fight, whose side do you take?" I stuck my tongue out at Anya.

"You can't take a side against the Alpha, it doesn't work that way," Anya sighed, rolling her eyes.

"The fuck you can't!" I exclaimed. "I'll be taking plenty of sides against Griffin whenever the fuck I want. You can take orders from him if you want to, but he's not ordering me around!"

"Oh my god, you're so frustrating," Anya moaned. "Griffin doesn't order me around, but if he did give me an order, I would follow it because it would be in the best interest of the pack. My pack, your pack, his pack, it's all one. You'll get it eventually. Why don't you come to the lodge with me today instead of going swimming? I'll introduce you around to everyone. You already know most of the pack from the bar, but you should be introduced formally, and who knows when Griff will get around to doing that since he just left town today."

"Griffin left town?" I stared at Anya in shock. "Without saying good-bye? He just fucked me, bit me, fed me some chocolate and wine, and then left town? He is so fucking dead when I see him again. And he is never getting back in my ass or wrapping his little sunshine and snow-covered pine tree body around me again. He can go curl up around your wolf when he wants to snuggle and jerk himself the fuck off."

"I think I maybe wasn't supposed to tell you that," Anya whispered. "He was going to call you later and explain he had to leave town this morning."

"See? Sides. You're totally taking his side here. Not the role of a gay guy's best friend."

"I'm not taking a side," Anya protested.

"Rule number one if you want to be a gay guy's best girlfriend. You always have to have his back, take his side, even if you witness him blowing his boyfriend's best friend, you figure out how to come to his defense."

"I can totally do that; I'm a spin master, I swear. My brother Ami has cheated so many times and I've always covered for him."

"Hmph," I snorted at Anya, unimpressed. "I thought I was supposed to have like, Spidey senses now, anyway. Why can't I sense where Griff is?"

"Spidey senses?" Anya rolled her eyes. "You mean the mate bond."

"Yeah, all that stuff you said about your parents. Shouldn't I be able to reach out to Griffin telepathically or something? Or at least notice if he's out of town?"

"I don't really know how it works for you since you're not a wolf, but you said you can feel the pack, so if you try reaching for Griffin, you should be able to feel him. You're newly mated, so you won't have a super strong connection yet, that takes years to build, but even if you can't sense Griff right now, he can probably feel you just because he's the Alpha."

"Great, so what you're saying is, Griffin can spy on me, but I can't keep tabs on him?"

"Griff would never spy on you," Anya laughed. "But he should be able to sense if you're in danger or upset about something."

"He totally would spy on me," I snorted, closing my eyes, and searching my head for Griffin. A warmth tugged at me as I reached for his orange, gold thread, but that was it. I don't know what I was expecting, but it was kind of a letdown. "I feel him with me, but I can't tell where he is," I made a face at Anya, stalking out of the kitchen.

"It's not like a shared location on your iPhone," Anya laughed, following me out of the room. "Give it time, you've only been mated one day. You'll figure it out."

"Whatever," I grumbled, as Anya followed me into the bathroom. "FYI, I'm about to strip down and shower."

"I've seen your dick before," Anya smirked, perching on the

toilet seat while I stripped off my clothes and turned the shower on. "Remember, I was up on the bar with you when you did your striptease for the pack."

"Oh god, don't remind me," I groaned, stepping into the shower.

"I know it's all a lot to take in, the whole mating thing, especially since you're not even a wolf," Anya called as I soaped up. "And it sucks you got me instead of Griff this morning, but you'll totally get used to everything, and you know Griff will make it up to you when he gets back." Anya handed me a towel as I turned the water off.

"Hmmm, the sex part of the relationship is not the problem," I snorted, toweling off and padding naked to my bedroom.

"I bet the sex is epic, isn't it?" Anya sighed, following me into my room. "No fair, you get to have amazing sex and you found your mate and I don't even have a date for this weekend."

"It's amazing." I slipped into a pair of lemon-yellow board shorts, and an old, black, *Buffy the Vampire Slayer* T-shirt.

"Ooooh, look at you, not kissing and telling, it's definitely true love," Anya teased.

"I don't know about that," I muttered.

"What do you mean?"

"Nothing," I sighed, definitely not ready to talk about the fact that neither Griffin nor I had said anything about love when we'd fucked and bitten each other last night.

11

"Let's go to my house first." Anya was practically bouncing; she was so excited to officially introduce me to the pack. "My parents are both away with Griffin today, but my sister, Nahla and my brothers, Ami and Ziri will be there since it's Sunday, and they'll be cooking for the pack dinner."

"Pack dinner?" I raised my eyebrow as I climbed onto the back of Anya's ATV and strapped my helmet on.

"The pack always eats together at the lodge on Sundays. It's like a big family dinner and we do it potluck style, so everyone brings something. I made cheesecake brownies last night for it, sooo good!"

"Am I supposed to be there for dinner?" I bit my lip, seriously pissed that Griffin had mated me and abandoned me without even giving me a rundown of anything related to pack life. I was going to fucking kill him when he got back.

"Of course, you're the Alpha's mate, idiot," Anya smacked me on top of my helmet before starting up her ATV, and anything else she said was drowned out by the roar of the engine.

It turned out, my little cabin was smack right in the middle of pack territory, with a network of ATV trails that led directly from my backyard all the way to everyone else. From the direction Anya was pointing, the Pack lodge was literally a hop, skip, and a jump away, and Anya's family cabin was even closer, so it was no wonder she kept showing up at my house every five minutes.

"We're like, next door neighbors," I said, climbing off Anya's ATV.

"Yup." Anya grinned, linking her arm through mine, and pulling me up to her cabin door. Anya's family cabin was a lot bigger than the one Cian gave me, but the design was pretty similar, with a wrap-around porch, wide log frame, and beautiful picture glass windows everywhere, overlooking the forest.

"Guys, look who I brought!" Anya practically sang as she dragged me through the door of her house.

"Blondielocks!" A wolf named Ziri, I recognized from the bar, called out. He was Anya's younger brother and always sat in the corner of the room, surrounded by a protective wall of wolves. "Welcome to the pack!" He practically jumped on me, wrapping his arms around my middle, and pressing his face into the crook of my neck.

Ziri was a couple of inches shorter than me, about 5'10, with a lanky build, and he kind of melted against me, breathing me in with a sigh of contentment. Then another of Anya's brothers, Amastan, who they called Ami, jumped on my back, and Anya's sister, Nahla, slipped behind Ziri, until I was squashed between them in a giant wolf sandwich.

"Wow, um, hi," I mumbled, trying to extricate myself from the group hug.

"He doesn't like to be touched, unless it's sexual," Anya called from across the room where she was helping herself to a bowl of grapes.

"Sorry," Anya's siblings murmured, pulling away from me awkwardly.

"You're seriously hot and everything, but if I touched you

sexually, Griff would castrate me and mount me on a pole in front of the lodge with my balls stuffed in my mouth," Ami winced, backing away.

"What? No, I never said–Anya!" I groaned, throwing Anya a, you-better-get-me-out-of- this-now, look.

"I wasn't telling you to grind up on him, Ami," Anya laughed as I blushed. "I was just trying to tell you guys Finn looked really uncomfortable in your group hug. Maybe give him a week before you climb all over him."

"Got it," Anya's siblings laughed, still eyeing me a little questionably.

"I can't believe you said that," I hissed at Anya, walking over to kick her in the shin.

"They can totally hear you, even if you whisper," Anya laughed. "Wolf ears, remember? Chill out, Blondielocks, everything is fine. My brothers don't think you want to fuck them, even if they have seen you strip on top of the bar at Molly's and go into the bathroom with a stranger for a blowjob."

"Anya!" I yelled, covering my face with my hands. I didn't need a mirror in front of me to know it had turned a deep tomato red.

"Oh my god, I'm totally just fucking with you," Anya laughed, yanking my hands off my burning face. "Ami is the biggest wolfwhore in the entire Northeast, he would never judge you. He can't. He's literally fucked every male species he's come across."

"It's true," Ziri nodded, as Ami grinned and waggled his brows unashamedly. "And Nahla and I are so boring, we enjoy a little excitement in our lives, so no judgement here, just appreciation for livening things up." Ziri flashed a teasing smile at me, bumping his hip against mine as he walked by.

I loved Ziri instantly. His pack bond was a warm thread that hummed through me soothingly, and it was impossible not to love Ami and Nahla too. Ami literally danced with mischief, he reminded me of a sparkler on Fourth of July. And Nahla, beautiful in an understated way, dressed in a loose-fitting sundress, with her long braids twisted together in a rope down her back, was like a cup of tea, warm and comforting with a hint of spice running through her.

"Griffin didn't tell me about the dinner thing today, so I didn't make anything to bring." I bit my lip anxiously as I looked at the collection of covered dishes spread across the countertop in Anya's kitchen.

"No sweat, you can make something now, with us." Nahla smiled, motioning me over.

"But I was going to take him around and introduce him to everyone," Anya pouted.

"He'll feel weird if he doesn't bring something," Nahla scolded her sister.

"He's the Alpha's mate, who cares if he brings anything, he can do whatever he wants." Anya made a face.

"Finn obviously cares." Nahla rolled her eyes at her little sister. "It's true, you definitely don't have to bring anything today if you don't want to," she assured me. "But if you do, I'm happy to help you make something."

"I definitely want to," I replied, making a face back at Anya when she stuck her tongue out at me.

"Boring," Anya sighed. "I'm going to check in at the lodge then. Are you good if I leave you here, Blondielocks? I promise my brothers and sister won't bite you."

"I'm good," I laughed, as Anya walked out the door. "Sooo, Anya said there are seven of you, plus your parents, you don't all live here together, do you?" I looked around the cabin doubtfully.

"No," Nahla laughed. "I live with my mate, Brahk, in the pack lodge, but I like to cook for Sunday dinner here, with my brothers and sister. It's calmer and quieter and gives us special time together."

"That's so nice." I joined Nahla at the sink where she was peeling sweet potatoes.

"Ami, Anya, and I live here with our parents," Ziri chimed in, pulling a tray of sticky pastry oozing with honey and covered in crushed nuts out of the refrigerator.

"Oh my god, that looks amazing," I sighed.

Ziri swiped his finger through the puddle of syrup pooling around the edges of the pastry and stuck it in my mouth.

"Yum," I grinned at him, sucking the rose flavored honey off his finger, and licking my lips.

"Stop flirting with Finn. If I can't have him, you definitely can't," Ami complained to his little brother.

"You can flirt with me too." I winked at Ami, and he laughed in response. "So, if it's just you guys here, where do your other 3 siblings live?"

"Aksil lives in the forest, he's rarely out of wolf form, although our father has been making him spend more time with the pack lately because he's going to take over as pack enforcer when Anya becomes Griffin's second," Nahla explained.

"Which is crazy, because Aksil is totally fucked in the head, not even fully bonded to the pack, and the last wolf we should be sending out to deal with wolf problems..." Ami muttered.

"Leave Aksil alone," Ziri shot Ami a look of reproach, and I was struck again by his warm, soothing vibe.

"Aksil is adopted," Nahla explained." Our parents found him when he was a young wolf, a long time ago, in Morocco, before they came here, or we were born. He was half feral and deeply traumatized, but he's come a long way since then. He's not fully bonded with the pack, so you probably won't feel him in the bond, only my parents and Griffin partially do..." Nahla's voice trailed off. "And the twins live in the pack lodge with me," she added, handing me a cutting board, knife, and the bowl of peeled sweet potatoes.

"And the twins are???"

"Adi and Rahim. They live in the lodge because they're the pack bodyguards. They're amazing fighters, so Griffin wanted them centrally located. He's made a lot of changes since he became Alpha, especially after the attack three years ago, and he's focused a lot on protection and fortification of our pack territory," Ami explained.

"Huh." I took it all in as I chopped the sweet potatoes and arranged them in the clay baking dish Nahla handed me.

"You'll get to know everyone pretty quickly once you move into the lodge, when Griff gets back." Nahla handed me a clove of garlic and bundle of fresh rosemary.

"Move into the lodge? But I already have a house. I mean, Cian gave me his house, sooo..." I looked around at the blank faces staring back at me. "I'm supposed to move into the lodge?" I whispered, my heart sinking.

"It's really nice." Ziri bit his lip at my crestfallen expression.

"You're the Alpha's mate." Nahla looked at me in confusion. "Why wouldn't you want to live in the lodge?"

"I just, I don't know. I mean, I finally have my own house and everything, and I don't really do well around a lot of people, and I don't know anyone there..."

Ziri slipped his arm around my shoulder as my heart rate started to speed up, resting his head against mine gently, steadying me.

"Don't worry about it right now," he said quietly. "Today, you'll cook sweet potatoes with us and break bread with the pack. One thing at a time, okay?"

"Okay," I sighed, my heart rate slowing as Ziri's soothing voice washed over me. "How did you do that? Calm me down?"

Ziri looked like a typical 22-year-old. He was super cute. He had his siblings' same beautiful dark skin and soulful deep brown eyes, short, twisty dreds, and total, I work the boat rentals down on the lake vibe, in his Prana shorts and yellow Moosejaw T-shirt. But there was much more to him, running through his warm comforting bond.

"It's his wolf, he's an empath, the heart of the pack. Ziri's really rare, our treasure," Nahla smiled gently, reaching a hand over to ruffle her brother's hair affectionately.

"So, why don't you live at the lodge?" I asked Ziri.

"Griffin wants him to, but my father won't let him. He doesn't trust anyone besides himself or Ami to guard Ziri."

"Ami?" I asked in surprise, blushing when Ami laughed.

"I'm the secret assassin," he grinned. "You never see me coming."

"Really...?"

I looked Ami over appraisingly, taking in his close-cropped haircut with its cool fade on the sides, loose limbed, wiry build, dressed in well-worn jeans and a black T-shirt, his mischievous vibe crackling through the thread in the pack bond. He looked like the guy you wanted as your wingman on a Saturday night out. Hot enough to attract the guys, but easygoing enough to share.

"You're right, I would never see you coming," I agreed, impressed. "But I feel it now, in your pack bond. What I thought was all mischief and fireworks, is heat and strength coiled at the end of the sparkler ready to spark and burn as soon as you put a match to it."

"You're getting us," Nahla hugged me lightly. "We feel you too, you know."

"You do? What am I like?"

"Fertile," Ziri sighed, with a tinge of longing.

"All the colors of the rainbow covered in glitter," Nahla laughed.

"Strong," Ami said quietly. "You feel like a steel bar that can't be bent."

"Fertile?" I raised my eyebrow at Ziri.

"I can't explain it," he shrugged. "It's just how you feel to me. Like the earth after a storm, when it's all moist and rich, ripe for new growth to shoot up out of the soil."

"Okay, so what do I do with these sweet potatoes?" I laughed awkwardly.

"Whatever you want, it's your dish," Nahla smiled warmly at me. "The great thing about sweet potatoes is they taste amazing no matter what you do with them. You can even eat them raw. You can put garlic, rosemary, and honey on them, or just toss with a little olive oil, salt and pepper..."

"Or brown sugar and butter, my fav," Ami grinned.

"Ami has an impossible sweet tooth," Nahla laughed in exasperation.

"Hmmmm... pineapple pizza and tacos are my favorite food, so, maybe a sweet/salty combo with a little heat?" I drizzled some garlic and cayenne infused olive oil over the sweet potatoes and sprinkled them with fresh rosemary sprigs and generous globs of honey.

"Yum!" Nahla agreed, taking the pan from me, and sliding it into the oven.

"I can put some music on if you want to dance on the table while we wait for them to cook," Ziri flashed me a teasing grin.

"Are you flirting with me, little wolf boy?" I teased Ziri back as he continued to grin at me, all loose and warm.

"Maybe a little," he sighed. "You're really hot, and no one lets me socialize with anyone, like ever. I spend all my time with my family," he groaned, making a face.

"We let you go to the bar with the pack," Ami soothed, slipping an arm around his brother's shoulder.

"Don't pretend to comfort me," Ziri snorted, swatting his brother across the head. "You never let me do anything, the only one worse than you is Aksil. These wolves came here last week, to meet with Griffin, and I was at the lodge when they arrived, visiting Nahla, and Aksil shot out of the woods, burst inside, and sat on me. Like, literally sat his giant, smelly, furry butt on top of me and I couldn't move or barely breathe until they left, and he finally let me up. And it really sucked because one of the wolves smelled soooo good. Wild, kind of. I think he was a Timber Wolf. Were they from Alaska?" Ziri asked Ami. "I feel like he smelled like Alaska, even though I've never been there."

"Yes." Ami frowned at his brother and didn't elaborate.

"You see what I mean?" Ziri sighed. "They never let me talk to anyone."

"Sounds good to me," Ami replied cheerfully.

"Says the guy who's slept with every living creature on the east coast!" Ziri exclaimed, shoving his brother, hard.

12

"Your sweet potatoes came out soooo good, I snuck a taste," Anya confessed, linking her arm through mine as we walked through the woods to the pack lodge together.

"Well, at least that's one thing I don't have to worry about. Thanks for coming back to walk me over."

I leaned my head against Anya's as we walked behind her siblings, carrying our covered dishes to the pack dinner. The whole wolf touching thing was starting to rub off on me, and I was less prickly about it as we walked arm in arm through the woods.

"What are you even worried about? You're the Alpha's mate," Anya laughed. "You have like, guaranteed acceptance by the pack. You're J. Lo, showing up as the surprise guest at a dinner party. Everyone is going to love you, stop stressing."

"I'd hardly say J. Lo," I snorted. "Maybe Justin Timberlake, before he got famous, when he was still a Mouseketeer with Britney and Christina."

"You're such an idiot." Anya laughed, bumping her head against mine.

The pack lodge was beautiful, enormous, majestic. It loomed

in front of us like a Disney log fortress, set in a deep clearing with views from all sides into the forest.

"Griffin's dad and my parents built it when they formed the pack." Anya grinned. "Pretty amazing, huh? Wait until you see the fireplace in the main room. It's insane, its stone chimney stretches all the way up through the house. You're going to love living here, and I'll probably be moving in soon too, so we'll be roommates!"

"Yay," I mumbled, staring at the intimidating lodge in front of me, and fantasizing about murdering Griffin when I finally got ahold of him. Then a warmth spread through me, and I realized I might get my chance sooner than I'd thought.

"Griffin's here," I said in surprise, not sure how I knew, but sensing him inside the lodge.

"Yup," Anya smiled in agreement. "They must have just gotten back, I can feel my parents here too, and they brought a guest with them..." her voice trailed off and she winced as her eyes drifted over my T-shirt. "Your clothing choice is a little awkward, considering the guest, but it's okay." Anya flashed me an overly bright smile. "You're Griffin's mate, it's not like the guest will vamp out on you or anything."

"Vamp out on me? There's a vampire here?" I hissed at Anya in horror, suddenly realizing why she was staring at my *Buffy* T-shirt with a grimace. "You let me come here dressed like this! Why didn't you tell me to change? You're such a bad best friend!"

"I had no idea Vlad would be here," Anya huffed. "Sundays are pack day, not for business. Molly even closes the bar."

"Vlad? Are you for real right now? And it's not even dark out yet, I thought vampires couldn't go out until dark."

"Oh my god, you're so gullible, it almost isn't even funny," Anya snorted. "His name isn't Vlad, for god's sake, it's James, and the elder vampires can all come out during the day, it's only the newbies who burn up in the sun. Now, stop quaking in your little yellow board shorts and come inside."

"I can't." I stood frozen in place on the doorstep of the lodge.

"Everyone knows you're out here; you know. Vampy probably smelled you walking over ten minutes ago. Their sense of smell is even sharper than ours. He won't care about your shirt; I totally shouldn't have said anything. It's so not a big deal, I promise."

"I hate you. You made it sound like this was a whole casual Sunday dinner in the woods. I would have gone home and changed if I knew it was a whole, like, official thing."

"You don't even own nice clothes." Anya rolled her eyes.

"I have a button down and jeans!" I hissed back.

"I don't know why you're whispering; everyone can hear you anyway." Anya sighed. "Do you want to switch shirts with me? I'll take one for the team."

"Like that would be better." I made a face at the skin-tight black bodysuit Anya was wearing, tucked into her jeans.

"I mean, it would probably look good on you," Anya grinned. "Perfect for a little tabletop dancing..."

"Are you guys coming inside or are you just going to stand on the front steps arguing about clothes for the next hour?" a voice called to us in an exasperated tone, and a pretty wolf with dark brown skin, Indian features, pink hair, and a nose ring yanked open the door.

Her eyes widened when she saw my shirt, and I wanted to shrivel up and die. It was so bad; it wasn't even like I was wearing my white *Buffy* T-shirt that just said *Buffy the Vampire Slayer* in black lettering. This one had a picture of Buffy with a stake and everything.

"Nice shirt," the girl grinned. "Should go over well. I'm Fenna." She grabbed my hand, yanking me inside.

"It's her fault," I muttered, motioning to Anya with a sigh of defeat.

"Not surprised." Fenna took my dish of sweet potatoes. "You two are a disastrous combination."

As I followed the wolf into the main room of the lodge, Anya called out happily from behind me,

"My brother Aksil's back too. Yay, you get to meet everyone tonight!"

From the little bit Anya and her siblings had told me about their brother, I was pretty sure Aksil was the wolf standing next to Griffin, in front of the fireplace. He was undeniably beautiful. Tall and broad, with warm, dark brown skin, deep black eyes, multiple piercings running the length of his ears and through his nose, and a closely shaved head covered in tattooed symbols.

The guy next to him, I figured was the vampire guest. He had major, hello, I'm a vampire, vibes. Dressed in jeans and a black T-shirt, with lean, sinewy muscles covered in a swirling mass of symbols tattooed in dark ink around his biceps and down the length of his arms. His short, dark hair was perfectly cut and styled, like he'd just stepped off the runway in Milan, and his midnight blue eyes met my gaze with amusement as he took in my shirt.

He reminded me of a jaguar or snow leopard, something higher up on the food chain than me.

"Interesting shirt, little wolf," he called out to me, quirking a dark brow sardonically.

"Not a wolf," I muttered back, still mortified, but annoyed to hear Griffin's nickname for me out of vampy's mouth.

"Definitely a wolf," he laughed, as the room fell silent, and the wolves all turned to stare at him in confusion. It looked like the whole pack was there, wolves of different ages, races, and genders, milling around the wide-open room with drinks in their hands, or lounging on the couch or oversized chairs grouped around the fireplace.

"Witch-bound, smells like." James wrinkled his nose distastefully at Griffin, nodding in my direction. "Your little wolfmate stinks of magic."

"I told you their noses are even better than ours!" Anya exhaled in awe, sliding up beside me as Griffin's whole face broke out into a wide grin and he strode across the room, oozing with satisfaction.

"I knew it. I fucking knew I smelled wolf in you," Griffin murmured, pressing his lips into my hair and hauling me against his side. "That's why the mating bond clicked in place instantly."

"What are you even talking about, right now?" I gaped at Griffin.

"*You* are a wolf, my little mate." Griffin tilted my face up to meet his, brushing his lips across my mouth with a sigh of content as he breathed me in.

"No, I'm not." I pulled away from Griffin. "And I can't believe you just left me this morning to deal with all this on my own." I waved my arms around at the pack who were all staring at us in wide-eyed fascination. "I wore a *Buffy the Vampire Slayer* T-shirt to our pack dinner with a vampire guest! And I feel like I'm in that episode of *The Crown* where Diana walks into the room with the Royal family for the first time and messes up the whole curtsying order. I don't even know where I'm supposed to sit at the table or who to talk to first, and you should have been the one to introduce me to the pack!" I exclaimed, smacking Griffin in the chest.

"You sit with me," Griffin replied, clearly bewildered by my freak-out, as he pulled me against his side, wrapping his arm around my waist possessively. "Pack, my mate, Finn. Finn, this is your pack," he announced, brushing his lips across the top of my head. "And the vamp is James. He wouldn't normally be joining us for Sunday dinner, but something important came up, so he came back here with me."

"You were bound a long time ago, in your early years, maybe before you even had your first shift," James called out to me after the introduction was over. "Do you remember anything from when you were really young? Any time spent with wolves?" He studied me curiously.

"Or witches!" Anya cried. "Do you remember any witches?"

"No, I don't remember any witches or wolves from my childhood!" I swayed on my feet, suddenly wobbly and raw, twisting in Griffin's arms, trying to get free.

"Hey," Griffin tightened his grip. "It's okay."

"No, it's not," I gasped, struggling to draw a full breath, as a memory I didn't even know I had, ripped through me. It came to me in flashes: snarling wolves pacing around a stone circle, trying desperately to get in. Tall trees with red bark and fertile spongy earth. A woman with long, chestnut hair, chanting. Gleaming, yellow-gold eyes, staring back at me like a reflection.

I wrenched free, running for the door. "It's not okay. I can't breathe," I choked, yanking the door open and stumbling outside, everyone pouring out behind me.

James' voice kept repeating in my ear, *witch-bound, wolf, stinks of magic*, as I doubled over, collapsing to the ground, struggling to draw a full breath.

"Finn's fading fast. He's in shock, Griffin. You have to force his shift."

I knew it was Aksil as soon as he spoke, the rich timber of his voice shooting through me like a bolt of lightning illuminating a midnight black sky. My senses filled with juniper and sandalwood, my skin warmed under the crackling heat filling the air around us, and I could almost taste the promise of an electrical storm on my tongue as the arguing voices continued to rise and fall around me.

"His wolf was taken from him, Aksil. He's witch-bound. What if he never shifts back?" Griffin's voice was thick with panic and anguish. "He's not your mate, he's mine, and I just found him; I can't lose him."

His wolf was taken from him. The words reverberated through me, over and over, the memory of the chestnut-haired, chanting woman flashing through my head again.

"Hold on," my ten-year-old self screamed.

The dirt from the forest floor was rough against my cheek.

Aksil's strong voice rang through the air. "The trauma of facing his loss is shutting Finn down, Griffin. You have to force his shift.

You have to force his shift, or you could lose him forever."

Aksil's words washed over me as a familiar memory flashed through me like a movie I'd seen a thousand times.

I'm ten-years-old. Moving, always moving. No one wants me.

The memory rips through me like a tornado, sucking the air from my lungs, and then I'm suddenly twelve-years-old, back in the shed behind my foster father's house.

My body is so still, laying on the floor of the shed like a carcass. Rotten, festering, split open, left to spoil in the heat. My insides crawl with maggots, feasting on my remains. "Don't look at me," my twelve-year-old self begs the gleaming yellow eyes shining at us deep from within. "Don't smell me." Rot clings to my skin like a million leeches. "Go away wolf. I do not want you anymore." I just want to disappear, to go where no one can see or smell me ever again.

Go away wolf, echoes in my ears, like a song left on repeat, as a silent, bottomless darkness beckons, enveloping me in its inky blanket. I close my eyes to light, my ears to sound, my lungs to breath, giving myself over to the seductive, calming shield the darkness promises, desperate to escape the gleaming yellow eyes that haunt me, the echo of *Go away wolf*, that rings in my ears.

Aksil's thread vibrates against my skin in an almost melody, weaving itself through me in a cloud of juniper and sandalwood as it wraps itself around my body like a steel cable, pulling me back, whispering air into my lungs, refusing to let me go, clinging to me like kudzu.

Then I'm ten again, screaming, hold on, as the chanting woman scoops out my insides. Waking up, my mind a blank canvas, with only my name, Finn, scrawled across its surface in black ink. Moving, always moving, searching for my scent, howling for my song. Twelve, back in the shed, weeping, Go away wolf.

I'm ten and twelve, ten and twelve. *Hold on*, my ten-year-old self screams in terror. *Go away*, my twelve-year-old self weeps, broken. *Don't look at me.*

"Don't look at me," I whisper into the darkness, pulling away from Aksil's steel cable, cutting off the air he breathes into my lungs, as a set of achingly familiar, yellow-gold eyes gleam at me.

"Now! Do it now!" Aksil yells.

Then my head suddenly fills with orange and red, as Griffin's Alpha call tears through me with a deafening roar, returning the air to my lungs like a windstorm, forcing light, bright and sharp into my eyes, every whisper of the forest into my ears.

My bones crack and snap as my fur settles around me like a warm, comforting blanket, my wolfsong pouring out of me in an anguished howl. I sing deep and fierce, into the dusky night, running through the thick pine trees, the soft forest floor beneath the pads of my paws, the wind in my fur, the scent of the sap in my nose, the taste of the cool, moist air on my tongue, singing my wolfsong with Aksil's wolf beside me, till we can sing no more.

13

The dreams are the same every night. They begin with the chanting woman and end with my broken body on the floor of the shed. Nothing from before, nothing after. My mornings echo each other too, like Groundhog Day.

I wake, stretch, uncurl my body from Aksil's wolf, and pad down to the lake to stare at my reflection in the water.

"*Hi*," I say to my wolf, looking down at him, standing tall and proud, the sun shining on his dark grey fur, highlighting his bold black markings.

"*Hi*," he says back.

"*You're still here.*"

"*I am*," he agrees.

"*We can't stay like this forever,*" I remind him.

"*One more day,*" he promises.

"*One more day,*" I echo, except the days are turning into weeks.

"*Don't be mean to Griffin today,*" I sigh, as Griffin approaches, and my wolf tenses, drawing back.

Griffin's wolf is huge, beautiful, his fur, a deep, reddish-brown. Raw power pours out of him, washing over us as he approaches.

My wolf bares his neck to him, and I roll my eyes. He's such a brat, constantly antagonizing Griffin's wolf.

Griffin's wolf's eyes flash angrily at the offer of submission, and he pushes my wolf's head away, nudging him with his snout and brushing his face against his. His eyes are reproachful when he meets our gaze, and my wolf shrugs, pulling away.

It's been a long two weeks of this, a battle of wills, and so far, my stubborn wolf is winning, although I often get the sense Griffin's wolf is waiting him out, rather than giving in, committed to the long hunt.

With Aksil, my wolf is so playful, tackling him from behind and climbing all over him. He trusts Aksil's wolf implicitly, instinctually, which makes his rebuffs so much harder for Griffin's wolf to take. Griffin's wolf is so patient with mine, even though I can tell the constant rejection is wearing on him, especially since he doesn't know where I stand, what I'm thinking.

"*Griffin's our mate,*" I tell my wolf for the millionth time as he turns his back to him, swiping his tail across Griffin's face and sauntering away toward Aksil's black wolf waiting on the edge of the tree line.

"*He's your mate, not mine,*" my wolf reminds me with a snort of derision before taking off through the trees.

I can't pretend I'm not enjoying my time in the forest with Aksil too. It's so joyful, so freeing, running through the trees, nose in the air, breathing in the sweet scent of the pine, leaping over fallen logs, chasing deer and rabbits, scratching my back against the rough bark of the trees. But it's also surreal, almost like I'm outside myself, watching a movie starring my wolf as me, and the battle of wills between us over Griffin is draining us both.

Griffin's wolf sleeps beside us at night now, watching us through narrowed eyes as my wolf curls around Aksil, almost daring Griffin to object, but Griffin doesn't rise to the bait, giving us our space. He's stalking us, quietly, carefully, waiting for his moment.

Our mate bond is gone, it shut down as soon as Griffin forced my shift, and the only wolf I feel in my head is Aksil, steely strong, unwavering, coiled around me like a harness, his juniper, sandalwood scent teasing my senses. His wolf is quiet, solid, ancient. He humors my wolf when he climbs all over him, lets him win their wrestling matches, amused when my wolf triumphantly pins him down. His nips are playful and teasing, his gleaming golden gaze filled with promise, yet he withdraws when Griffin approaches, averting his eyes.

It's all a delicate dance, and as I watch the steps between the three of us, I can't help but feel I'm missing a crucial piece of the choreography.

As I approach the end of my third week in wolf form, Aksil's strong, firm voice pulls me from sleep. "It's time to come back, Finn," he says. "You can be both now. You are wolf and you are Finn, and it is safe to be both."

This is the first time Aksil has shifted out of his wolf since we ran into the forest together. The first time he has spoken to me. It's still night, though dawn is approaching, and Anya, Ziri, and at least a dozen other pack members are standing beside Aksil surrounding me and Griffin.

They must have come in the night. I didn't hear them or smell them, dreaming as usual, lost in the endless loop of the chanting woman and my battered body on the shed floor.

My wolf is confused by Aksil. He is used to Griffin, Anya, and Ziri talking to him in their human forms, trying to coax us back. He doesn't know what to make of it, coming from Aksil, and he stiffens at the betrayal. He doesn't want us to shift back, despite Aksil's promise. He doesn't fully trust me to protect us yet, to keep us safe from witches' spells and men who break little boys.

People hurt Finn; Finn lost his wolf. Finn was not safe. My wolf reminds me as we stare at the people surrounding us. *Wolf is safe, no one hurts us when we're just wolf.*

"I'm not a boy anymore," I remind him. *"And you're not a pup."*

"No, I'm not," my wolf agrees, his implication clear that I am still a child, and he knows best.

"Now, you have to do it now, pull him back, pull him out of his wolf, Griffin." Aksil suddenly shouts, as my wolf seems to make up his mind about something, and the missing piece of choreography clicks into place. My wolf doesn't want me to shift back. He wants me to say good-bye to Finn and stay wolf forever.

Griffin shifts out of his wolf at the same time, kneeling on the ground beside me and wrapping his arms around my body.

"I won't do it," he says softly, burying his face into the crook of my neck. "He'll never forgive me. I won't take his wolf away from him. I can't do it."

"His wolf is taking over, Griffin. Finn will never return to us once the transition is complete." Aksil dropped down to the ground beside Griffin, resting a hand in my fur. "If Finn loses himself to his wolf, he won't come back for either of us," he warns softly.

"I won't take his free will. I promised him I never would." Griffin's tears soak my fur. "I won't take the choice from him."

My wolf stares at me with burning, yellow eyes, and we're suddenly back in the shed again, face to face.

"I'm so much stronger now," I promise him, as we look down at my twelve-year-old body. And then we're in my cabin, the night of my mating, and I can taste Griffin's blood in my mouth, feel my claim on his body, smell my scent on his skin.

"The Alpha is a good choice for you," my wolf says, his voice etched with sadness as he rubs his head against Aksil's steely thread, inhaling his juniper, sandalwood scent.

"He's a good choice for us," I promise, nudging my wolf's head away from Aksil's thread.

When I shift this time, the only color in my head is my own, a muted, iridescent rainbow, like an oil slick on the pavement after a storm. The only roar in my ear, mine, as my bones crack and snap at my command, and I throw myself on top of Griffin, knocking him to the ground.

The air is so crisp, the moon shines through the trees so clearly. Griffin's scent is sharp, the heat of his body, warm beneath me, as I lay stretched out, naked on top of him in the middle of the forest.

He was warm and safe, mine, and mate, and I buried my face into the crook of his neck and just inhaled, as our mate bond clicked back in place and Griffin's orange-gold fire burned bright inside me again.

It seemed like half the pack was standing around us, and everyone wanted to talk to me, but one low growl from Griffin sent them all scattering as he stood up and pulled me into his arms.

"You smell *amazing!*" I cried, rubbing my face across Griffin's neck, and breathing him in deeply. "No wonder you tried to fuck me the first day we met!"

"You stink like Aksil, little wolf," Griffin choked back, wrapping his arms around me so tightly, I could barely breathe.

"Your *smell!*" I exclaimed to Griffin again, as he carried me through the woods and into my cabin. "It's so fucking intense, like wolfnip," I grinned up at him, biting his bottom lip.

"You've been ignoring me for almost three weeks and *now* you suddenly want to fuck me?" Griffin laughed, his voice thick with emotion and relief as he deposited me in the shower beside him.

I wrapped my arms around Griffin's neck as he dumped half a bottle of bodywash over me, lathering me up. "My wolf is kind of a brat."

Griffin made a rude noise in agreement, running soapy hands over every inch of my body, from the top of my head down to the crevices between my toes.

"I must really stink if you won't even talk to me without scrubbing me down first," I teased Griffin, gazing down at him as he squatted down on the shower floor at my feet.

"This is the second time I've had to wash the stink of another man off your body," Griffin growled back at me. "Three weeks, Finn. You retreated into your wolf and took off with Aksil for three weeks. I didn't even know if I'd get you back! Do you know what that felt like? Yes, I'm fucking scrubbing the stink of Aksil's wolf from you before we talk!"

"I'm so sorry." I looked down at Griffin helplessly. "One minute I was standing in the lodge, yelling at you about that scene from *The Crown* and then it was like I was drowning. After James started asking me about my wolf, the breath was just sucked out of me, and I couldn't feel you anymore."

"But you felt Aksil?" Griffin stood up, staring into my eyes as the water streamed down my body, rinsing the soap away.

"Yes." I held Griffin's dark gaze. "I don't know why, but he makes my wolf feel safe."

"Unlike me."

"My wolf will come around."

"I forced your shift, the first time." Griffin turned the water off and pulled me against him. "It felt like such a violation, but I didn't know what else to do. I promised you I would never take away your free will, but I was so scared you were dying, Finn, and I didn't know how else to save you."

"You gave me my wolf back." I buried my face in Griffin's neck. "You gave me my wolf back when I didn't even know he was gone."

"When you disappeared into your wolf, I thought I lost you," Griffin rasped, wrapping a thick, oversize towel around me. "I just found you and then I lost you the day after you became mine."

"My wolf and I have a lot to work out," I confessed, following Griffin into my bedroom, and stretching out on the bed beside him.

"I was so scared I'd never get you back, Finn." Griffin trailed a finger across my lips, staring at me with haunted eyes.

"My wolf didn't want us to shift back. He doesn't completely trust me, and I can't really blame him."

"Do you remember what happened to you?" Griffin asked

gently, brushing his fingers across my face, relearning the shape of my cheek, the curve of my jaw.

"Only the binding." I closed my eyes, recalling the dreams that had plagued me for the last few weeks. "There was a circle of stones, wolves howling, and a woman chanting, I guess, the witch. But I can't remember anything before then, nothing about my pack or where I came from. There's just this horrible, aching feeling when I try to remember, like a limb was ripped off me, and I know that it used to be there, but I can't remember what it felt like to have it."

"That was your pack bond being severed." Griffin pressed his lips into my hair. "When the witch bound you, she cut your ties with your pack. We're going to figure out who you are and where you came from, I promise you."

"You can't promise me that." I looked up at Griffin with wet eyes. "All my life, I thought my parents just abandoned me, Griff, that no one wanted me because I was worthless, but what if that wasn't true? What if I was taken from them, from my family, from my pack? What if they've been looking for me my whole life? And what if I'd kept looking for them, for my wolf, instead of hiding away and burying him inside me?"

"Finn, you were witch-bound, none of this was your fault," Griffin murmured, rolling onto his back, and pulling me into his arms. "You were just a pup when you were bound. James said it might have even happened before your first shift. That might be why you don't remember anything about your wolf."

"But I do remember my wolf now, Griff. I can't remember my pack or my family, or what my life was like, but I remember knowing my wolf before he was bound, and searching for him afterward, even though I didn't understand what I was looking for."

"What do you mean?"

"I peed on the floors of my foster homes, searching for my scent, I howled my wolfsong, singing for him, I growled whenever anyone came near me. It's why no one would keep me, why I kept being moved around, until that day in the shed, when I was 12, and my foster father raped me."

"What happened after that?" Griffin asked softly, his mate bond flashing with pain at the mention of my rape.

"My wolf broke through the binding, and I told him to go away." I lowered my eyes, burning with shame and grief, unable to meet my mate's gaze. "He broke through for me, to help me in the worst moment of my life, Griffin, and I rejected him. I betrayed his trust. I sent him away and I never looked for him again. It's my fault he's been buried away all this time."

"You didn't bury him away, Finn." Griffin tilted my head up to meet his eyes. "He was protecting you."

"I couldn't face the rape." I stared back at Griffin in anguish. "I just wanted to pretend it wasn't real, that it didn't happen, and I thought if I let my wolf see it, witness it, it would be true. I needed it not to be true." I buried my face into Griffin's chest, my shoulders shaking as I finally let out thirteen years of pent-up grief. "I did this to myself, to him, Griff, because of my own fear and weakness."

"That's not how it works." Griffin forced my chin back up. "Even though your wolf reached out to you in your time of need, he was still witch-bound. The only way to break a binding, is to shift, either by force, or free will. But you were too young and too traumatized to understand any of that, baby."

"I still don't understand. You're saying all I had to do to break my binding all this time, was shift into my wolf?"

"Theoretically, yes, but no binding is that simple, and yours was really strong." Griffin brushed his lips across my forehead. "The power of a binding is that it masks your wolf, Finn. Even though he's still with you, you have no idea he's there, and usually no other wolves can sense him either. I think the only reason I was able to force your shift, once James called out the binding, is because you're my mate and my wolf could see your wolf inside you even when I didn't. You couldn't call on your shift because you didn't know you were a wolf."

"Except I did know it in that moment, that day in the shed when I was twelve and he broke through and stared at me! My wolf stared at me with his yellow, gleaming eyes and I told him to go away. That means I could have shifted then and broken the binding all those years ago."

"You were a child, broken, completely traumatized, you had no idea you were bound, what any of it meant. You can't blame yourself, baby." Griffin brushed his lips across mine softly. "Your wolf knows that, and he accepted it to protect you. He retreated because he understood you needed to not be seen in order to heal."

"Maybe he doesn't blame me, but he doesn't quite trust my judgment."

"Which is why he won't accept my wolf as his mate," Griffin said slowly.

"Yes, but he will." I trailed my fingers over Griffin's collarbone and across my mate mark. "He's just working through some stuff."

"Working through some stuff." Griffin repeated, narrowing his eyes.

"He's confused. He doesn't know what he wants right now."

"You mean who he wants."

"He told me you were a good choice before I shifted back, Griff. He knows you're the right choice for us. He just needs some time with your wolf to get used to him."

"He wants Aksil," Griffin said flatly.

"I think it's just that he doesn't know your wolf yet," I protested. "Not like I know you."

"Because the wolf is supposed to choose first, then our human sides fall in line," Griffin sighed, running a hand through his hair. "My wolf chose you, both of you. He could smell your wolf even when I didn't know what it meant, and he wanted you both. But since your wolf was bound, only your human side accepted our mating call."

"I don't understand, are you saying only our human sides are mated? Not our wolves?"

"Not exactly," Griffin growled as his eyes flashed, his wolf clearly unhappy with this line of thought. "You both belong to us; your wolf just hasn't quite accepted it yet."

"You're saying I did the whole thing backwards, because I accepted you before my wolf did? I'm such a train wreck!" I exhaled, wrapping my arms around Griffin's neck. "My wolf will come around; I promise. He's going to love your wolf as much as I love you."

"My wolf will never let Aksil have your wolf; you need to know that," Griffin said softly, his mate bond flaring orange-gold fire in warning. "I'm the Alpha of my pack, Finn, I let you go off with Aksil after I forced your shift because he survived a traumatic experience himself when he was a young pup, and I thought maybe he knew what you needed in that moment, but my wolf will never accept anything more than that between you. I will never except anything else."

"My wolf knows you're our mate," I replied firmly. "He and Aksil's wolf are just friends. That's all it is," I promised, even as my senses filled with juniper and sandalwood, and my wolf sighed in contentment when Aksil's steely thread tightened around us.

"They're more than friends." Griffin tensed. "They're connected somehow."

"It's true our wolves were like one these last few weeks in the woods, but I've only even seen Aksil out of wolf form twice. The first time when I walked into the lodge, and then when I shifted back, and I've never even spoken to him. Whatever weirdness is between our wolves, it's just a wolf thing, I swear, and it will pass."

"There's some connection," Griffin insisted, his voice tight. "Aksil could feel you slipping further into your wolf when I couldn't, that's why he warned me if I didn't force you to shift back, we would lose you."

"But you didn't do it." I pressed my forehead against Griffin's.

"I couldn't." Griffin's voice was thick with emotion. "Even if it meant losing you forever, Finn, I couldn't take your wolf from you again, not when you'd just gotten him back. This whole thing with your wolf and Aksil has been a fucking nightmare, but I couldn't do that to you."

"I know." I brushed my lips across Griffin's. "My wolf knows. You chose me over yourself." We stared at each other with wet, gleaming eyes, my wolf flashing to the surface in a moment of acknowledgment.

"I love you, Finn," Griffin murmured against my mouth, kissing me deeply. "My wolf loves you. I know this whole process has been so hard for you, especially since you didn't even know you were a wolf. But I promise you, I see you and feel you all the way to your core. I know you and I love you."

"I love you too," I admitted, burrowing into Griffin's chest. "I still don't understand any of what's going on, who I actually am, or where I came from, but I know you're my mate, and we'll work it all out."

"Not gonna lie, it's been a rough couple of weeks for me," Griffin laughed weakly. "My wolf wants me to claim you all over again, and he's ready to kill Aksil. We don't have the best relationship as it is. He's never completely bonded to me since I took over as the Pack Alpha."

"What do you mean?"

"Aksil's always been more lone-wolf than pack, even though I know he'd give his life for any of his packmates. Out of all the pack wolves you had to run off with, Aksil is the most complicated one."

"I'm sorry, I wish I had more answers for you." I snuggled deeper into Griffin's chest, wrapping my legs around his. "I know these last few weeks have sucked."

"At least you're willing to admit you love me," Griffin teased, brushing his lips across my head, and wrapping his arms around me tightly.

"Letting myself love you does go against everything inside me," I teased back. "But I do, so there it is."

"Wow, that was so romantic," Griffin laughed, rolling us over onto my back. "Can't say I really expect much more from you though, my prickly wolf." He nipped my neck playfully. "Admitting you love me at all, was like getting down on one knee with a bushel of roses and a string quartet playing in the background."

"Ugh, I hate roses, and I'd never profess my love to you with a string quartet. A little pine tree, maybe, and *Cold Play's* 'Always in My Head' playing in the background, just low enough to hear it with your wolf ears."

"'Always in My Head', huh? I knew you were secretly a romantic," Griffin growled, kissing his way down my body. "I'm going to get you on your knees, holding that pine tree for me one day, baby, and you're going to *sing* "Always in My Head to me," Griffin breathed, burying his face in the wild tangle of my pubic hair.

14

The pack left Griffin and I alone for the next week, and we spent most of the time wrapped around each other in bed or shifting into wolf form and chasing each other around in the woods surrounding the house.

I was a little hesitant to give myself back over to my wolf so soon, afraid he wouldn't let me come back, but Griffin insisted I'd never make any progress with him if I didn't give him my trust, and Griffin's wolf was so arrogant and confident in his claim, he was dying to come back out and face off with my wolf again.

It was amazing and so freeing, shifting on my own, reaching deep inside myself, calling my wolf to me. My whole body came alive as we merged in one fluid movement of fur and bone, my wolfsong thrumming loud and clear through my veins.

My wolf loved running and playing in the forest, and although he bristled at first when Griffin's wolf rubbed up against him, a grudging respect and admiration began to build in him as Griffin's wolf took the lead in our games. His stalking skills were masterful when he led the hunt for deer and rabbits, his playfulness infectious when he teased and chased my wolf through the forest.

Griffin's wolf courted mine, much like Griffin had courted me, dropping dead rabbits at his feet instead of wine and cheese. He rubbed up against him teasingly, challenging him to a race, but slowing down at the last minute so it ended in a tie, like Griffin let our first match end in a draw. My wolf was pretty fast and strong, but Griffin's definitely had a size and strength advantage over me.

Like me, my wolf was a sucker for Griffin's charm, but we still had a long way to go. His frost was slowly starting to thaw, and from the strut in Griffin's wolf's stride, he knew it, but we were far from the finish line. I was way easier than my wolf, and if Griffin's wolf knew what was good for him, he'd slow his strut before my wolf bit him in his arrogant ass.

"I call *Black Sails*," Griffin grinned, slapping me on the ass when I stepped out of the shower. We'd started a little ritual in the evenings after we shifted out of our wolves. Long, hot showers together, T.V. and popcorn on the couch overlooking the lake. Extra butter and salt for me, honey drizzled on Griffin's. I loved learning all the little things about Griffin that I hadn't had a chance to discover yet, although his obsession with dark historical dramas was killing me.

"It's my turn to pick, and I call Mary Tyler Moore," I stuck my tongue out at Griffin as I toweled off and slipped into sweats.

"Baby, I love you, but I can only watch so much of your retro T.V.," Griffin groaned. "I'm sorry, but I'm just more of a blood, death, and destruction kind of a guy."

"I know." I rolled my eyes as I followed Griffin over to the couch. "You like to watch art that imitates your life. I like to escape into the fantasy of what I always wished my life was."

"You always wished you were Mary Tyler Moore?" Griffin teased, stretching out on the couch, and pulling me down into his lap.

"Mary Tyler Moore, any of the Bradys, basically any character from a retro sitcom," I laughed, snuggling against Griffin's chest while he reached for the remote. "Growing up alone, without my family, all I wanted was that 6:00 p.m. family dinner of meatloaf and mashed potatoes in a yellow kitchen with daisy-covered curtains and a dog curled up at my feet, begging for scraps."

"Well, you've got it now, baby." Griffin pressed his lips into my hair and wrapped his arms around my waist. "The Northwoods Pack is one big, noisy, loving family, and you will never eat your meatloaf and mashed potatoes alone again."

"I don't think I've ever even had meat loaf," I laughed, tilting my head back for a kiss. "But now that you've promised it to me, I expect the full dinner, and I want some kind of berry cobbler for dessert too."

"With ice cream on top," Griffin promised, capturing my mouth in a kiss.

We spent the whole week like this, playing in our wolf forms, chilling in front of the T.V., and lazing around in bed, until I woke up to Griffin fighting with someone outside the house, his voice so loud, it was drowning the other one out.

I slipped out of bed and pulled Griffin's sweats on, padding across the house in my bare feet to the front porch.

"I know you just got him back, but it's important, too important to ignore, and you have to go," a familiar voice insisted. I knew the voice from when I was living in the forest in wolf form with Aksil. It was one of the wolves who visited, the one Aksil's wolf's thread shined silver for, Safiya.

"You're Aksil's mother," I said, finally realizing who she was, as I stepped out onto the porch.

Griffin was standing bare-chested in his boxers, leaning against the porch rail with his arms crossed and a black look on his face, anger and tension pouring off him. "You're Aksil's mom," I repeated. "And Griffin's second, and Anya's mom and Ziri's mom." I stared at the beautiful woman standing on my front porch arguing with my mate.

She looked like a slightly older version of Anya, with the same dark skin, although hers had a more reddish bronze hue, and her hair was loose and wild around her face instead of braided like her daughter's. And even though she only looked about ten years older than Anya, she felt ancient.

"Yes, hello. I'm sorry, we never had a chance to officially meet." Safiya smiled warmly, green and gold running through her pack bonds, strong and fierce. She was one wolf I wouldn't want to mess with.

"I'm glad you're on our side," I grinned at her.

"Welcome to the pack," she returned graciously.

"So, what am I interrupting?" I planted a kiss on Griffin's shoulder, slipping under his arm.

"Nothing," Griffin bit out before Safiya could respond. "It's a non-issue because it's not happening," he glowered, pulling me against him tightly and wrapping his arms around my waist.

"How about a cup of coffee?" I offered, as Safiya's eyes flashed with frustration.

"How about you and I have coffee and Safiya gets lost," Griffin grumbled, following me into the house, his hand tucked into the waistband of my sweats.

"Out with it," I ordered once the coffee was brewing and Griffin and Safiya were seated at the kitchen island.

Safiya glanced at Griffin when he didn't respond, almost as if she was surprised he didn't object to my demand. "There have been some rumors brewing about some new trouble up north." Her answer was carefully vague as if she wasn't sure how much she should reveal.

"What kind of trouble?"

"We don't know exactly, that's the problem. That's why James was at the lodge a few weeks ago, the day you..." Safiya's voice broke off awkwardly.

"The day I discovered I was a wolf?" I raised my eyebrow at Safiya in amusement.

"Yes."

"I take it my few weeks of wolfing out came at a bad time?"

"You could say that." Safiya avoided Griffin's eyes as steam practically shot out of his ears.

"Babe." I walked back over to Griffin. "You're wired so tightly right now; I'm just waiting for the bomb to go off."

"I'm not leaving you. End of discussion," Griffin replied tightly, pulling me against his chest and breathing me in. His heart was beating a mile a minute and his pack bond crackled with tension.

"Okay, let's all just take a deep breath." I pressed my lips into Griffin's hair. "I don't really want you to leave me right now either, but can we just hear Safiya out?" I asked, running my fingers through Griffin's hair, and brushing my hands across my mate mark as his heart rate started to slow down.

"There's nothing to hear out. I'm not leaving you, period," Griffin growled, wrapping his arms around me tighter. "Send Badis," he told Safiya gruffly.

"Badis is good for taking care of things." Safiya murmured delicately. "He's not the best at sniffing them out."

"I'm not up on my werewolf code," I sighed. "It's been repressed for a while. Can you just say what you're not saying? And who's Badis?"

"Badis is my mate and the pack enforcer. Let's just say he's really good at enforcing, not so good at negotiating or feeling things out."

"Ahhh...Is there someone else you could send?" I asked Griffin.

"Aksil," Griffin replied slowly, meeting Safiya's cool gaze as something unsaid passed between them.

"Are you officially switching my son over as pack enforcer?" Safiya asked, her eyes carefully blank. She was like the original James Bond, this one.

"Yes, tell Aksil I want him across the border tonight to get a read on what's brewing in Montreal, and send Anya over here later. I'm transitioning her and Aksil over as my second and enforcer today." Griffin's voice was cool as he stared Safiya down.

"Whatever you think is best for the pack," Safiya replied tightly.

"We're done here." Griffin ordered in his Alpha voice, his power sparking orange and red as it washed over Safiya, and she nodded curtly to both of us before walking out.

"That was a little harsh."

"She can fuck off," Griffin growled against my neck. "I've been in complete hell these past few weeks, thinking I'd lost you. There's no fucking way I'm leaving you to go chase down a possible rumor. That's what I have her and Badis for. It's bullshit, sending me for everything. She's used to how my father ran things, and I'm not doing it his fucking way. It weakens the pack, sending the Alpha out to handle everything. It's time for new management. I'm switching Anya and Aksil in tonight."

"Do you want to think about it for a day, make sure you're not just reacting?" I asked tentatively, which was a mistake, because as soon as I reminded Griffin he'd almost lost me, he growled and stood up, pulling me back into our bedroom and showing me exactly what he thought about almost losing me. In fact, he showed me three times, and by the time Anya appeared a few hours later, I was in an orgasmic coma and couldn't muster up more than a wave for her.

"So, my mom really pissed you off, huh?" Anya said cheerfully to Griffin.

"You're my second now," Griffin said. "And Aksil is officially taking over for your father. I told your mom when she was here earlier, and I'm sending Aksil to dig around in the Canada situation. He's leaving tonight."

"Got it, jefe," Anya saluted Griffin. "It will be an adjustment for my parents, but I'm ready. How's Wolfboy?" she nodded over to me. "He speaking in full sentences yet, or still just wandering around, peeing on everything and howling all day and night?"

"I so did not do that," I protested, throwing a pillow at Anya's head.

"You so did," she snorted, ducking the pillow, and leaning

forward to plant a kiss on my cheek. "Tell him, Griff."

"You marked your territory a lot and howled all the time," Griffin agreed, ruffling my hair tenderly and climbing out of bed. "C'mon, A, we've got shit to cover," he yawned, stretching, and pulling on a pair of sweats before he padded out of the bedroom with Anya to go talk Alpha stuff.

I lounged around in bed, marveling at how clearly I could hear Griffin and Anya talking with my enhanced wolf sense.

"I want some answers immediately." Griffin's Alpha voice was full of authority and raw power as he gave Anya her marching orders.

"I'll get whatever James knows out of him. We won't be caught off guard again." Anya promised.

It was like I was right there in the kitchen beside them. And the smell! God, I could smell Griffin so intensely, I just wanted to jump out of bed, climb into his lap and rub myself all over him. I couldn't believe I'd been repressing all these supersonic senses for so long. I could think of a million instances over the years enhanced hearing and sense of smell would have really come in handy.

"Hi," Griffin grinned as I walked into the kitchen, sliding into his lap. "Didn't get enough of me earlier, huh?" His wolf eyes gleamed dark yellow with satisfaction, and he growled low in his throat when I rubbed myself across his lap.

"Give me a break; you guys reek of sex already. There's no way you need to get it on again right now." Anya rolled her eyes. "I mean, I get that you missed your man while you were off roaming the forest with my brother for the last few weeks, but I know Griff, and he's definitely fucked you at least 20 times since you shifted back a week ago, so can we please focus on the business at hand?"

"God, fine. You're such a bossy bitch now that you're officially Griffin's second in command." I stuck my tongue out at Anya, reluctantly sliding out of Griffin's lap and walking over to the fridge to tend to my growling stomach.

"Yeah well, get used to it, Wolfboy." Anya stuck her tongue back out at me. "And FYI, Molly totally gave your job away while you were on your wolfy walkabout."

"She did not!"

"Yup, hired this hot little stray who rolled up in town about a week after you wolfed out. But the chick totally sucks. I mean, don't get me wrong, she's hot as fuck, but she can't make a drink to save her life, and it's totally obvious Molly only hired her to try and make Lillian jealous."

"Huh. Is it working?"

"Ummm, not sure yet. Lillian's been around a long time, I think it's gonna take a lot more than a leggy, freckled, strawberry-blond she-wolf to rile her up."

"You seem to have noticed a lot about this stray who stole my job." I grinned at Anya.

"Yeah well, it's my job to notice things that affect the pack," Anya retorted.

"Uh huh," I laughed, pulling out a casserole someone had dropped off for us. "And exactly what is the effect the strawberry-blond job stealer is having on the pack? Is she distracting the new second in command with her freckles and long legs?"

"Oh, fuck off, Wolfboy."

"Are you two done now?" Griffin demanded. "Because we still have shit to cover," he reminded Anya, and I was really impressed to see her snap to attention and turn her back on our whole exchange without even blinking. Anya totally had the whole second in command thing in the bag.

"Of course." Anya was all business as she turned her attention to Griffin. "Aksil will find out what's going on in Montreal, and I'll follow up with the vamps while you hold down the fort here."

"And I want Adi with Finn whenever he leaves the lodge. We'll move him in tonight, and you'll go to Portland tomorrow, after Finn is settled in," Griffin said.

"Woah, standing right here, and perfectly capable of making

decisions for myself. I'm not moving into the lodge." I slid the delicious looking casserole into the oven to warm for lunch, grabbing a stack of plates out of the cabinet.

"Finn," Griffin sighed, and I could feel the tension and worry radiating off his body as he looked over at me wearily, gearing up for a fight he didn't want to have.

"No way I'm moving to the lodge." I crossed my arms facing Griffin down with a scowl.

"It's safer there, and you're endangering the pack if you don't," Anya said matter-of-factly, in her all business, I'm the second in command now, so shut up and do what I say voice. "It spreads us too thin if we have to have Adi camp out here to watch over you, Finn."

"But no one's been watching over me up until now, so why does it matter? Why do things have to change?" I protested.

"First of all, idiot, I was with you whenever Griffin wasn't, before your wolf-out, and Aksil never let you out of sight when you were in furry mode. You really think Griffin left you unguarded for one minute after he realized you were his mate?" Anya exhaled in exasperation. "Stop being a spoiled little baby and start acting like the Alpha's mate. No one has time for your temper tantrums right now. We have a possible second attack to stave off and shit to figure out, like who the hell you actually are, and why you were witchbound. We haven't even had time to talk about that or have you checked out yet."

"Have me checked out?" I glared at Anya. "What, like by a special wolf doctor?"

"Well, you are a wolf, or have you forgotten already?" Anya glared back.

"Enough." Griffin's voice rang out with authority. "You're moving into the lodge tonight, and I can't fight with you about it right now. I just don't have time, I'm sorry."

"You don't have time to fight with me about a decision that

affects my life?" I replied icily. "Like you didn't have time to tell me you were leaving town for the day, the morning after we mated?"

"Baby, I have to go. I'm sorry." Griffin stood up and walked over to me, pulling my stiff frame against his chest. "I have to brief Aksil before he leaves tonight, and I'll be back to pick you up in a couple of hours. If you pack your stuff, we can bring it with us, if you don't, I'll send someone over to pack it up for you later. Eat some lunch and take it easy. Anya's right, we haven't had you checked out yet and we don't know what's going on with your body. You just went through a forced shift, three weeks completely in wolf form, and we don't know how your body is handling any of it." Griffin pressed his lips into my hair. "I know you're pissed," he murmured, "But I just got you back and I'm not taking any chances of losing you again. I'd rather have you safe and angry at me, then happy and hurt, or even worse, gone."

"You've never experienced me really angry before," I replied, my voice tight. "You may not feel the same way after I move into the lodge tonight."

"As long as you're there, safe and sound, I'll take you in my bed any way I can get you." Griffin forced my chin up to meet his eyes, brushing his lips across my mouth.

"Who said anything about me being in your bed?" I snorted. "You may get me in the lodge, but that doesn't mean I'll be in your bed." I pulled away from Griffin and stalked out of the kitchen slamming the door to my bedroom.

"I love you." Griffin opened the bedroom door and stuck his head in. "I'll see you in a few hours, and you will be in my bed tonight," he growled, his voice low, sexy, and filled with promise.

"When hell freezes over," I yelled back, throwing a pillow at Griffin's head as he walked away.

15

"I get you're pissed at Griff, but we're still bffs, right?" Anya called to me from the kitchen.

"I'm not talking to you for a month," I yelled back. "I warned you about this scenario, and you totally took Griff's side on this."

"I didn't," Anya protested. "I took my own side. I told you pack safety comes before everything and you're pack, so it's all one and the same."

"Benedict Arnold."

"The casserole's done, and it smells amazing..." Anya coaxed.

"Eat it yourself, traitor. I'm not coming out."

"Lillian made it."

"She did?" I opened the door and stuck my head out, breathing in the rich smell of melted cheese, tomatoes, and bacon coming from the kitchen.

"Yup. It's her famous bacon and tomato mac 'n cheese; it's better than sex."

"Maybe the sex you're having," I snorted, padding into the kitchen in my bare feet.

"Oh, rub it in. We all know the sex you're having with Griffin is epic. We can hear and smell you going at it a mile away."

"You cannot!" I gasped in horror.

"Not really, but you're so ridiculously gullible, I can't resist teasing you," Anya laughed. "I mean, even now that you have your wolf back, you're still like, clueless about wolfy things."

"Not exactly my fault, considering I've been witch-bound practically my entire life," I huffed, piling the amazing smelling mac 'n cheese on my plate.

"Aksil thinks it's why you're always hungry and get weak and dizzy when you don't eat," Anya mumbled over a mouthful of the pasta. "He said you've been burning so much energy keeping your wolf repressed."

"Did he say anything else? Like how he knew to make Griffin force my shift, and why I could feel his bond when everyone else disappeared from my head? Or why I took off with him and stayed in the woods with him for weeks?" I asked, fascinated Aksil had been talking to his sister about me.

"Hmm... Not really. Aksil is a wolf of very few words. But he's always been able to sense things other wolves can't. He's my big brother, but I don't really know much about his background," Anya admitted.

"What do you mean?"

"My parents found Aksil a long time ago, like ancient long, when he was a half-starved wolf pup, deeply traumatized and almost completely feral. Adi and Rahim grew up with him in Morocco, but the rest of us were born way later, like a hundred years later, after they came here and formed the pack. I know he's come a long way, which speaks volumes about what kind of state he was in, because half the pack would argue he's still deeply traumatized and half feral now, a century later, sooo..."

"Huh." I ate my mac 'n cheese, which of course, was completely amazing, since Lillian had made it, and I sat with Anya's words, thinking them over. "Maybe Aksil saw himself in me and just knew instinctually what I needed."

"It's possible. He told Griffin he needed to back off and leave you be for the first week after you wolfed out, like he knew you just needed to be left alone with your wolf. That was an epic fight. I thought Griffin was going to kill him. And then he could also tell when you started drifting deeper into your wolf, that's why he tried to get Griffin to force your shift again."

"He doesn't totally trust me, my wolf," I admitted. "That's why he didn't want me to shift back."

"Do you trust him?"

"Yes, although I'm still a little nervous when I shift. We have a few things we still have to work out…"

"I'd say talk to my brother about it, if anyone understands the complexity of dealing with trauma around his wolf, it's Aksil, but I don't think Griff will be letting him anywhere near you for a while… So, good luck with that."

"What do you mean? Griffin can't stop me from talking to Aksil or anyone else, and I'd like to see him try!"

"He wouldn't try and stop you; he doesn't have to. Aksil won't be around much anyway now that he's pack enforcer. Why do you think Griff switched Aksil and my father out all of a sudden? He wants my brother in the wind right now, and as the new pack enforcer, Aksil will have to travel all over the country. It was a bold move."

"I thought Griff was just sending Aksil over to Canada to check out a rumor." My stomach suddenly felt queasy, and I pushed my plate away.

"He is. That's the priority right now, but once we figure out what's going on over there, Aksil will start his real job. Pack enforcer is one of the most important jobs in the pack. Think of it like *The Godfather*. The enforcer is the muscle, the second, the consigliere."

"Great, so you're saying Griff just turned Aksil into Sonny."

"Don't worry, in temperament, my brother is way more Vito than Sonny. He won't get himself killed charging off hot-headed.

He's a strategizer, he'll make a great pack enforcer. He's scary and tough enough to enforce, but smart enough to get the job done without getting himself killed in the process. He's a good choice for the job, even though I think Griff switched him in right now for the wrong reasons."

"To keep him away from me," I said flatly.

"Here's the thing, Finn, you don't smell like Northwoods pack or Griffin when you're in your wolf form."

"Am I supposed to?"

"It means your wolf is unclaimed, which technically makes him up for grabs."

"How can he be unclaimed if Griffin and I are mated?"

"You're kind of in a grey zone until your wolf accepts the claim," Anya shrugged. "Aksil knows that, but he hasn't managed to stay alive for 200 years by being stupid. He's not about to challenge the Alpha for his mate's wolf even if he'd like to. My brother is a really strong, powerful wolf, but you've met Griffin's wolf. He's the pack Alpha, he'd destroy him."

"I'm so confused, what exactly are you saying?"

"Griffin's wolf is ten times more arrogant than Griffin, he's not worried about Aksil, but that doesn't mean Griff wants him around right now, at least not until your wolf accepts his claim and your mating is complete. I've seen this before, but honestly, it's always the other way around, with the wolves recognizing each other as mates and then working to convince the human sides. Once everyone is on the same page, the humans consummate the mating, and the wolf bond clicks into place. You did it completely backwards..."

"So I've been told..." I groaned.

"I mean it is you, so, not really surprising." Anya grinned.

"Thanks." I made a face at Anya. "So where does that leave things with Aksil now? I mean, Griff gave him a really important position in the pack, so he must still be cool with him, despite this whole weird thing with our wolves."

"Hmmm...I don't know. I almost feel like it's some kind of test. Honestly, Aksil's relationship with Griffin and the pack has always been a little dicey. He's pack, but he also isn't. My brother is still partly a nomadic wolf. You must sense how threadbare his bond is to the rest of the pack, like it could snap at any minute. He's never really bonded to Griffin as his Alpha, so Griff knows he has to tread carefully with him."

"What do you mean?"

"I think Griff was hoping Aksil's connection to the pack would strengthen before he put him in such a serious role, but with everything going on right now, I guess he decided to just go for it," Anya shrugged.

"Aksil's bond doesn't feel threadbare to me at all. It's dark and wild, and flashes when I'm not expecting it, like a storm coming out of nowhere on a sunny day. But it's strong, like a steel cable instead of a thread. It doesn't feel like anything could break it to me."

"Huh." Anya stared back at me curiously. "Even my parents admit his bond feels tenuous, like it can't make up its mind if it's going to stay."

"I don't know what to say. Aksil's bond feels like he brought a whole U-Haul, unpacked, and moved in permanently to me. Even planted some trees in the yard for the future."

"You feel roots in his bond?" Anya breathed, staring at me wide-eyed.

"I guess, I mean I haven't really thought about it. I only had one day to experience being a part of the pack before I wolfed out, and when I was with Aksil those few weeks, we were almost like one wolf. Now that I'm back in human form and can feel the pack again, he's the strongest one I feel besides Griffin. He almost runs parallel to my mating bond, and I feel him implanted deeply inside me, like you would have to rip him from the earth to remove him, so yeah, I guess I feel roots in his bond."

"Do yourself and Aksil a favor, and don't tell Griffin that,"

Anya grimaced.

"Don't tell Griffin what?"

"That Aksil's bond runs parallel to your mating bond. Not really something a mate wants to hear, especially the Alpha of the pack. Aksil is already on constant thin ice with Griff because he barely submits, and when he does, Griffin knows it's fake, like he's doing it to show respect, but he totally doesn't have to and could walk away with no problem. If you don't mind, I'd like to keep my brother alive," Anya made a face. "He's a massive pain in the ass and completely fucked up, but I love him anyway and would rather Griffin not rip him to shreds in a jealous rage."

"It's nothing to be jealous about. I'm not saying my bond with Aksil is the same as my mating bond with Griffin, it's different; it just feels equally strong."

"Trust me on this one, Wolfboy, keep it to yourself."

"Whatever," I exhaled. "Let's go get my job back. You totally owe me for taking Griff's side on the whole lodge move-in thing."

"Griff's gonna kick my ass if you go to Molly's now instead of packing up," Anya groaned.

"This is your moment to prove yourself." I crossed my arms, staring Anya down.

"Fine, but I think it might be yours, too." Anya cocked her head in the direction of my porch, and my senses suddenly filled with a familiar sandalwood and juniper scent.

Aksil's chiseled jaw, high cheekbones, deep, soulful black eyes, and beautiful, dark, muscled shoulders and chest filling out his charcoal grey T-shirt, stole my breath when I stepped onto my front porch.

He was so insanely hot, commanding the air around us with his quiet confidence, it wasn't fair, especially since I was still trying to figure out what our connection meant. The last thing I needed was an attraction on top of that, but in my defense, I doubted there was a person on this planet, gay, straight, bi, trans, whatever, who could say they didn't find Aksil attractive.

"I'm leaving tonight."

No greeting. No how are you doing since you shifted back? Kind of weird we lived together as wolves for two weeks and are just now speaking, huh? Just, I'm leaving tonight.

I ran my hand over the porch railing nervously, jabbing myself with a splinter of wood, and wincing as I looked down at my reddening palm.

"Let me see it." Aksil stepped over to me, taking my hand and turning it over in his own.

"It's just a splinter." I shrugged at the dark sliver of wood wedged into my hand, my body tingling at Aksil's touch. "I can handle much worse."

The corner of Aksil's mouth tilted up in a slight smile. "I have zero doubt about what you can handle, Grey."

"Grey, huh?" I teased, knowing I was flirting a little, but unable to stop myself, as Aksil squeezed the flesh of my palm together and worked the splinter out of my hand.

"You were always Grey to me, from the first moment I saw your wolf," Aksil replied, releasing my hand, and holding out the sliver of wood to me.

"Why did my wolf take off with you?"

"You tell me." Aksil was standing so close I could make out every detail in the swirling symbols tattooed all over his shaved head, feel his breath ghosting across my face when he spoke.

"You made him feel safe."

"And you, Grey? Do I make you feel safe?"

"You make me nervous," I admitted, as a shiver washed over me.

"I make your wolf feel safe and you nervous?" Aksil chuckled softly, stepping back from me. "I can work with that," he teased. "Take care of yourself, Grey."

"That's it?" I demanded, as Aksil shifted in a blur of dark fur, and bounded off into the woods.

16

"I tried not to listen in." Anya shot me an apologetic look when I walked back into the cabin.

"I'm sure," I replied drily, rolling my eyes at the innocent look she shot me. "I know you heard every word, but I really don't want to analyze this whole weird thing I have going on with your brother right now. I just want to go get my job back."

"Thank god!" Anya exclaimed, leading the way to my truck. "I don't want to touch that shitshow with a ten-foot pole!"

We spent the truck ride with the windows down and the radio blasting, and when we walked into the bar a half hour later, I laughed at Anya as I took in my little job-stealing she-wolf.

"I hate to break it to you, but not really getting Soft Girl vibes off your little stray over there." I teased.

"So, like I care?" Anya quirked her brow at me.

"Oh please, you care," I snorted. "Just saying, you might need to adjust your whole, I like my sex rough and dirty with men and soft and sweet with girls. I have a feeling your freckle-faced strawberry-blonde over there would pin you down to the ground and sink her teeth into your neck before she'd lie back and let you make sweet tender love to her," I grinned.

"Go fuck yourself, Wolfboy." Anya shoved me, hard. "She's Molly's little chew toy, not mine, and if I were you, I'd be worrying less about who I want to fuck and how I like my sex, and more about getting your job back before you run out of money to buy your ridiculous *Scooby Doo and The Gang* T-shirts."

"This *Scooby* shirt rocks! It's vintage and it has the *Mystery Machine* on it," I huffed, glancing down at my lilac *Scooby Doo* T-shirt. "You're totally jealous you're not wearing it." I shoved Anya back, striding over to the bar.

"Hey Moll, long time no see," I chirped. "Sorry I left you high and dry for a few weeks, but as you might recall, it wasn't really my fault…"

"Whose fault was it? Barbie's?" Molly snorted, rolling her eyes at Anya, obviously unimpressed.

"Hey, don't drag me into this," Anya protested hotly. "I had nothing to do with Wolfboy's little walkabout, and I totally resent being called Barbie. Do you see my beautiful dark skin? No blond Barbie here!"

"Your job is gone, Malibu Ken, or should I call you Shaggy now?" Molly glanced down at my T-shirt. "Or maybe Scooby, since you've recently discovered your inner canine?"

"Hey, I don't think you can say that to me. Isn't that racist or speciesist or something?" I turned to Anya. "You said it wasn't okay to make dog jokes."

"I said canine," Molly smiled sweetly.

"Yeah well, I heard Marcia Brady can't make a drink to save her life," I said.

"She doesn't have to, looking like that." Molly ran her eyes appreciatively over her new bartender as she leaned over the bar to take a customer's drink order.

Even as a gay man, I could agree my replacement was smoking hot. Mid to late 20's, the she-wolf had long, freckle covered legs clad in cut-off jean shorts, wavy strawberry-blond hair, and wide, doe-like green eyes. She was girl-next-door beautiful, and she was also full of shit with her innocent Marcia Brady look.

This she-wolf was anything but soft and sweet. There was an undercurrent of strength and power humming through her that Molly and Anya had obviously missed, but I instantly picked up on. It was strange, suddenly being able to sense things. I still had so much to get used to as a wolf, but I wasn't swayed for a second by this wolf's little innocent act. I loved that for once, I had an advantage over Anya and Molly; as a gay man, I was immune to this girl's charms.

"That's sexual harassment." I rolled my eyes at Molly. "You can't lust after the staff."

"I can do whatever I want, it's my bar. Fuck off, Scooby."

"What do you want?" I sighed. "You want me to make you more muffins? Look at what she's doing? She's not even shaking that drink up. You know how many customers you're going to lose if you keep her around?"

"Zero?" Molly snorted, as Marcia slid the drink across the bar to her customer with a wink, and he practically drooled all over her. "Even if she had no teeth, I wouldn't lose any customers, I'm the only bar in town, genius."

"I'll get Lillian to come and work here with me. She'll cook, and we'll put food on the menu to go with your bucket of pretzels," I burst out in desperation.

"Are you crazy?" Anya mouthed, her eyes widening at my impossible promise.

"You'll get Lillian to work here and cook for the bar?" Molly turned around and stared at me with her hands on her hips.

"Yes," I promised, as Anya kicked me.

"Hey, Strawberry Shortcake, take off. You're fired," Molly called over to the job-stealing she-wolf. "Go get your apron, Malibu Ken, your shift starts in an hour, and Lillian better be here beside you, slinging hash."

"What, like right now, today?" I gaped at Molly, as Anya sighed beside me, and Marcia, totally playing the whole thing up, took her apron off with downcast eyes.

"You just told me you wanted your job back. Are you and Lillian coming to work tonight, or should I tell Marcia she can stay before she starts to cry for nothing?"

"We're coming," I mumbled weakly, as Marcia sent Anya a helpless look before handing me her apron and walking off. "Don't even think about rescuing your puppy right now," I warned Anya, grabbing her arm, and yanking her out of the bar. "We have way bigger problems to deal with."

"You really did fuck yourself over this time," Anya whistled in agreement when we were outside in the parking lot.

"How can I get Lillian to come here tonight?" I muttered to myself, pacing around the lot in circles.

"Tonight isn't your problem, Wolfboy. You could probably get Lillian here for tonight, but I have no idea how you'll get her here on the regular."

"That's it! Anya, you're a genius!" I grabbed Anya and spun her around, planting a wet, sloppy kiss on her mouth. "I don't have to worry about getting Lillian to work here full time right now, I just have to get her here tonight!"

"Whatever you say," Anya replied distractedly, her eyes following a familiar strawberry-blond, freckled, she-wolf across the parking lot as she walked out of the bar.

"Oh, fine! Go bite her and drag her into the woods," I laughed, as Anya's eyes tracked the wolf to her car.

"I do need to speak to her, officially," Anya snapped. "She checked in with Griffin when she first got here, but he was all distracted with your wolf-out, so I need to have a conversation with her and find out why she's here and how long she's planning on being in our territory."

"You do that. I'm going to call the lodge and throw myself at Lillian's mercy."

"Why are you not at the house, packing your stuff?" a familiar voice asked me when I called the lodge.

"How do you know I'm not?" I countered, sticking my tongue out at Griffin through the phone, while watching Anya and fake Marcia across the parking lot.

"We're mates now, remember? And I'm the Alpha of the pack, I can tell where you are through the bond."

"Wow, that's not creepy. I don't remember accepting your share my location request, and how come I can't tell where you are?" I demanded, closing my eyes, and reaching for Griffin's mate bond. It flared orange-red and wrapped around me when I reached for it, filling me with warmth, but no magic pin appeared with a location.

"The bond is too new; I can tell where you are because I'm your Alpha and your mate. But if you need me, you can always reach for me, and I'll come to you."

"Like AAA? I'd rather keep my location on private and just call an Uber if I need a ride, thanks."

"If it makes you feel better, I'll share my location on your phone," Griffin laughed, as my phone dinged with his shared location notification.

"You're such an asshole."

"Babe, I need you to go back to the house and pack your stuff. I'm coming to get you in an hour."

"Well, that should be interesting, since I have to work in an hour."

"I thought Molly fired you."

"I thought you said she couldn't, since I'm pack."

"I mean, you did disappear for almost a month," Griffin replied mildly.

"With good reason," I sputtered.

"Fine. I'll send someone to pack your stuff and I'll pick you up at the bar after work."

"I'll move into the lodge tonight and sleep in your bed on one condition," I countered.

"This should be good," Griffin groaned.

"You get your mom to come work at the bar with me tonight."

"I what?"

"I'll forgive all your macho, Alpha, telling me what to do, stalking my location, and rearranging my life shit, and I'll let you fuck my brains out tonight in your own bed, if you get your mom to come to the bar tonight and cook something for the customers."

"You'll let me fuck the shit out of you?" Griffin growled. "Baby, you'll be begging me to ram my dick in your ass and drill you into my bed by the time I get done with you tonight."

"Fine, whatever, just send Lillian to the bar in an hour with some food."

"Begging. You're going to be begging me to fuck you tonight..." Griffin promised as I hung up the phone.

"She kind of has a Charlie's Angel vibe, doesn't she?" Anya murmured dreamily as she walked back over to me.

"OG or re-boot? Are we talking Farrah, Drew, or Kristen?"

"OG for sure, I'm getting major Cheryl Ladd vibes off her..."

"Ahhh...Kris Munroe, I totally see it. Told you she was badass, pretending to be girl- next-door..."

"Whatever, did you figure out how to get Lillian down here before Molly beats the shit out of you?"

"Sure did," I replied smugly.

"How?"

"Traded my ass for it."

"Of course; you're such a little whore, Wolfboy."

"Um, you're the one trying to leverage your position to get with Kris Munroe."

"Well, it worked. She's coming back in an hour and having a drink with me, so ha!" Anya retorted, pulling me toward the pizza place. "C'mon if you're going to work in an hour, I'd better feed you first. Griff will kick my ass if you're all woozy for his fuckfest tonight."

17

Lillian walked into the bar right as my shift started, and I almost passed out in relief when I noticed the three wolves following her into the kitchen with overflowing bags of food. She showed up and she brought food. I was so keeping my job, at least for tonight.

"Oh my god, you're the best. I love you. I owe you my life," I gushed to Lillian, following her into the kitchen. "It was so nice of you to come here tonight and help me out."

"Griffin ordered me to, not like I could say no," Lillian shrugged, starting to unpack the bags.

"What?" I gasped, totally horrified.

"Oh my god, your face!" Lillian exclaimed, doubling over with laughter. "I totally got you! Griffin told me you're really prickly about the whole Alpha thing, so I just had to say it," she teased, ruffling my hair. "Of course, I came for you tonight. You're my son's mate; you're pack, and we lost you for a few weeks. Welcome back, sweetheart." Lillian brushed a soft kiss across my forehead.

"You mean you would have come if I'd just asked? Griffin didn't have to beg you or anything?"

"Of course not," Lillian laughed.

"Maybe I can re-neg on our deal," I muttered under my breath.

"You made a deal with Griffin to get me here tonight?" Lillian raised her eyebrow.

"Forget it. What are you making?"

"Loaded nachos, wings, and spinach artichoke dip with sourdough bread. That's all Molly's getting out of me, and when we run out, we run out. That's it."

"Oh my god, that sounds amazing. You're amazing! I have to get back out front before Molly notices I'm missing and fires me again."

"I'm prepping everything now, so you can start taking orders in half an hour."

Lillian's food was a huge hit, of course, and I even saw Molly smile a few times when she didn't know I was looking. I also saw Lillian eyeing her out of the corner of her eye whenever she stepped out of the kitchen, which was very interesting and possibly promising for both of them.

"El Jefe's here, so I'm taking off, Wolfboy. Good job on the Lillian thing, totally worth trading your ass for. That spinach dip was fucking insane!" Anya called, blowing me a kiss as Griffin walked into the bar.

"Good luck with Kris tonight," I called back with a grin. Anya had convinced her OG Charlie's Angel to hang with her for the night after she was fired, and from the way Anya was leading her Angel out of the bar with her hand tucked into the belt loop of her jean shorts, it looked like they had hit it off.

"Successful night with my mom?" Griffin grinned wickedly, walking over to me.

"You cheated," I glared at him. "Your mom said she would have come if I'd just asked her myself, and you totally knew that when I made my deal with you."

"Trying to re-neg on the deal, little wolf?" Griffin raised his eyebrow. "Can't say I took you for a deal breaker...." he tskd.

"I don't re-neg on my deals. I'm just saying, you cheated."

"Begging." Griffin reminded me, his eyes going dark honey gold. "You're going to be *begging* me to ram my dick in your ass by the time I'm done with you in *my bed* tonight," he promised.

"Whatever, cheater," I breezed, turning my back on Griffin to finish wiping down the bar.

"See you both tomorrow," Molly called to us when Lillian stepped out of the kitchen.

"Tomorrow?" Lillian raised her eyebrow at me, ignoring Molly.

"Your food went over so well; would you mind trying it out for a week?" I pleaded, giving Lillian my best wolf pup eyes.

"I'll give you every other night this week," Lillian agreed with a small smile.

"Finn's only working every other night too," Griffin growled. "I don't want him at the bar every night."

"You can't dictate my schedule," I glared at Griffin.

"I just did," he retorted, bending down to pick up his mother's bag. "You got that Moll? Finn and my mom are only working every other night."

"Affirmative," Molly called back, as I pinched Griffin's ass, hard.

"You think that's gonna scare me, little wolf?" Griffin laughed as he stood up and we walked out to the truck. "You can dig your claws into me all you want, baby, while I'm owning your ass in my bed tonight."

"Fuck you." I yanked open the truck door and shot Griffin my best death stare as I plopped into the seat.

"Oh, I'll be fucking you, alright," he growled, leaning over, and nipping me on the nose. "Now, be a good wolf and buckle up, we're going home."

"Keep messing with me," I growled back. "And we'll see who's begging who tonight."

When we pulled up in front of the lodge, I suddenly realized I hadn't been back there since my big wolf revelation, and my chest tightened as Griffin turned the truck off.

"You okay?" he asked, reaching for my hand.

"I don't know," I admitted. "It feels weird to be back here."

"C'mon, let's go inside and I'll give you a tour. It's very low-key right now. No big pack dinner with vampire guests staging big reveals," Griffin teased gently, opening my door, and pulling me out.

"I don't know, Griff..."

"Do you trust me?" Griffin asked quietly.

"I think so..."

"I got you, I promise."

"Okay," I sighed, letting Griffin lead me into the pack lodge.

The lodge definitely had a quieter vibe without the whole pack gathered in the main room, and as I looked around, I was struck by how beautiful it was, with its log plank walls, polished wood floors, and wide windows looking out into the surrounding forest.

"Let's go up to our room and take a shower and unwind, and I'll give you a tour in the morning and introduce you around," Griffin murmured, leading me up an incredible curving staircase built from massive logs.

My heart fluttered a little when Griffin said, 'our room', and I nodded in agreement, following him up the staircase and down a beautiful wide hallway lit with wrought iron pine tree wall sconces.

"It feels like a Disney lodge, or what I think a Disney lodge would feel like. I've never actually been to Disney."

"Do you want to go?"

"To Disney? Yeah, I mean who wouldn't? They have a whole Avatar world and Big Thunder Railroad!"

"For someone who's never been there, you sure sound like you know a lot about it," Griffin teased as he opened the door to his bedroom.

I blushed. "I've watched a lot of Disney YouTube videos."

I had to admit, Griffin's bedroom was huge and really inviting. The king-sized log frame bed tucked against the back wall was covered in a forest green quilt with matching oversize pillows, and two wide bay windows faced the lake peeking through the tops of the trees behind the lodge.

"It's pretty swanky." I wandered around the room, running my fingers over a beautiful oak dresser, and ruffling the spines of a stack of books piled on one of the nightstands. "You made room in your closet for me." I smiled, noting the clothes pushed to one side and the empty hangers on the other.

"Our closet," Griffin breathed in my ear, coming up behind me and wrapping his arms around my waist.

"It's beautiful here, Griff, it really is. I just like, started to get used to having my own house though. And I've never owned anything before now, and I already miss it," I confessed, turning around in Griffin's arms, and staring up into his eyes.

"I get it, baby." Griffin led me over to the bed. "We have a lot to figure out. The cabin is still yours. It's not going anywhere, and we'll figure out how to fit it into our lives. It's just, as the pack Alpha, I have to live here, I want you safe, and I don't want to be apart from you. So, for now, while we're still figuring things out, I need you here with me, okay?"

"Like, all the time, or just at night?" I bit my lip as a flutter of anxiety started to build inside me.

"All the time, for now, I guess," Griffin replied, looking at me uncertainly.

"The thing is, I can't like, just stay here in the lodge all day, Griff."

"What do you mean?" Griffin pulled me against his chest, scooting us back against his pillows.

"Well, what do you do all day?"

"I don't know, all kinds of things. I meet with the pack, patrol the grounds. I'm on the phone a lot with other Alphas. One of the biggest parts of managing a pack and territory is keeping apprised of what's going on with the other packs out there, offering counsel, brainstorming with other Alphas about how to deal with problem packs, offering protection to weaker packs who are struggling under poor management," Griffin shrugged. "I guess it's like being the CEO of a company in a way."

"Okay, sounds complicated and very busy. I work in a bar at night, so, my time during the day is my free time to be by myself, hang out with friends, do my own thing. I can't sit in the pack lodge under guard while you Alpha all day."

"Well, as my mate, there will be stuff for you to do too..."

"Like?"

"It depends what kind of role you want to adopt."

"Just spit it out, Griff," I sighed.

"The lodge is like base camp for the pack, the heart and soul. Pack members stop by all through the day to grab a snack, check in, ask for help, offer a hand. Some live here, but a lot don't, so stopping by is their way of staying connected."

"Okay, sounds a little like a bed and breakfast," I winced.

"More like a family home," Griffin laughed weakly, "With a lot of kids."

"And we're the parents?"

"Sort of..."

"Great, so I finally escaped the orphanage and now I'm running one?"

"Baby, it's not like that," Griffin sighed.

"I know, I'm just being a brat. I don't do well with change; in case you haven't noticed. And there's been a lot of change in my life in the last month."

"I know, and I'm sorry to say, there's going to be a lot more change. Safiya and Badis have decided to take some time to themselves, now that I've relieved them of their responsibilities and transitioned their kids into their place. They left this morning on a walkabout and could be gone for months, which will be a lot for the pack to get used to. I'm a little nervous about how everyone is going to take all the changes, and I'm really going to need your help, babe," Griffin admitted. "Everyone loves you and you're so approachable. I think you are really going to tighten the pack's bond no matter what role you choose to take on. Can we just take it one day at a time and figure it out?"

"I'll try." I brushed my lips against Griffin's and snuggled into his chest.

"Good, now I want to show you my amazing steam shower, and then I believe we have some begging to induce." Griffin grinned down at me with a gleam in his eye.

Griffin's steam shower was pretty amazing. His entire master bathroom was seriously impressive, and there may have been some begging on my part as the night progressed. But I still held onto a shred of my dignity, even as Griffin held me spread open over his face, with his tongue shoved so far into my ass, I forgot what my own name was and might have started making animal sounds and thanking every god in the universe for my existence.

"You were begging me like a kid in a candy shop," Griffin crowed the next morning when I opened my eyes to his satisfied grin.

"Go away," I mumbled, rolling back over. My ass was sore from the pounding Griffin gave me last night, and even my dick was still asleep after being sucked and jerked three different times over the course of the night.

"Like a kid in a candy shop," Griffin repeated, slapping my naked ass, and nipping my shoulder. "Please Griffin, fuck me harder, so hard. Oh god, don't ever stop. More, Griff, more..." Griffin breathed in my ear.

"Okay, so I'm a major fucking ass slut, I admit it. I begged for your dick in my ass three separate times last night. Are you happy?" I grumbled. "Now go away, my ass hurts, and my dick feels like it's going to fall off. I'm going back to sleep."

"My mom made blueberry pancakes..." Griffin murmured in

my ear, trailing his lips down my neck. "And I bet I can wake your dick up."

"Oh my god, it's already up. How do you it?" I groaned, rolling over onto my back, still half asleep, but now aroused, just from the feel of Griffin's lips on my neck.

"Good morning, little wolf. It's a major turn on, waking up with you in my bed," Griffin whispered against my skin as he kissed his way down my body, sucking the soft folds of my inner thigh between his teeth.

"Griff," I moaned, running my fingers through his sleep rumpled hair, and sucking in my breath as he swallowed my dick in his mouth. I'm pretty sure the entire pack heard me moaning and yelling Griffin's name as he sucked every last drop of semen out of me.

"Baby, you smell so good," Griffin growled low in his throat, his eyes glowing dark honey gold as he gazed up at me, pushing my legs up to my chest. The air was thick with his scent of arousal and his mate bond crackled with possessiveness and heat.

"You're so sexy when you're hot for me, and I love that I can even smell it now, but you're so not getting back in my ass today," I warned Griffin, sliding my legs down and flipping us over.

"Finn, baby, just the smell of you makes me rock hard," Griffin moaned as I kissed my way down his body, sliding my tongue teasingly around the base of his rock-hard, leaking dick.

"What do you want?" I trailed my tongue up the length of Griffin's dick, brushing my fingers across the opening of his ass.

"You," Griffin groaned, pushing his dick up into my face.

"Who's the one begging now?" I teased wickedly, loving the feel of my strong Alpha writhing beneath me at my mercy.

"Finn, please, I'm gonna fucking explode," Griffin groaned as I drew him into my mouth slowly, scraping my teeth against the length of him and circling my tongue around the tip of his dick.

Griffin pushed himself deep into the back of my throat, fisting his hands in my hair as he held my head down, moaning my name and screaming so loud, there was no way everyone in the lodge didn't hear him as he shot his load down my throat.

"Jesus, babe, maybe I should have just let you have my ass again," I groaned, crawling up Griffin's body and collapsing against his chest. "I think you were just as rough on my throat as you were on my ass last night. I'm not going to be able to walk or talk today," I complained, as Griffin wrapped himself tightly around me.

"I'm sorry," Griffin murmured, not sounding sorry at all, his voice thick with satisfaction and possessiveness.

"Is this like an Alpha thing, where now that you have me in your house, you have to fuck every part of my body so hard, you brand me with your mark or something?" I yawned, snuggling deeper into the crook of Griffin's arms as he ran his fingers down my back and trailed his lips across my head.

"I don't know, maybe. It's all new to me too, you know. I've never had a mate before either. I just love finally having you here in my bed and in the lodge. I guess I do kind of want to fuck you into submission and mark every part of you as mine," Griffin admitted a little sheepishly.

"Just don't start peeing on me or anything," I laughed, lifting my head for a kiss.

"No peeing," Griffin promised. "But I might shoot my load all over you later and rub it in your ass, just warning you," he growled low in his throat, capturing my lower lip between his teeth.

"Babe, you've gotta give me one day before you pound my ass again," I laughed, wriggling out of Griffin's arms.

"How about if I'm really gentle and go slow?" he grinned devilishly as I climbed out of bed.

"We'll talk. Right now, I want some of those pancakes."

18

The pancakes were amazing, and it was actually great to sit and have breakfast with Lillian and some of the other packmates. The table in the lodge dining room was huge, and I thought it would be annoying to be surrounded by so many people because I was used to being on my own with my coffee in the morning, but all the wolves in the pack were so warm and friendly.

Ziri even stopped by to give me a hug and welcome me home, which was so nice. His warm hug was calming, and he was so cute, asking me a million questions about my wolf discovery, and flirting shamelessly with me whenever Griffin wasn't looking our way.

"Uh oh, I think you're about to be recruited." Ziri finally let his arm drop from my shoulder as he pushed his chair away and stood up.

"What do you mean?"

"See that cute little girl heading over here? She's been trying to get me to plan her birthday party for her because her mom is about to pop, but since I turned her down and you're the Alpha's mate, I can tell from her expression she's going to throw herself at your mercy."

"Hey, that's not fair. I don't know anything about kid's parties!" I protested, as Ziri blew me a kiss and took off, and the girl plopped down in his newly vacated seat.

"Hi, I'm Seiko," she smiled.

"Finn," I sighed. No way I was getting out of this. She was ridiculously cute, about eight or nine, with a curtain of straight black hair that fell to her chin, and beautiful, dark, almond shaped eyes. She had me as soon as she sat down.

"Can you help me plan my birthday party?" she asked, not wasting a second.

"Sure," I replied, what else could I say. Not going to start my first day on the job breaking some wolf pup's heart.

"Great! I want a unicorn party with pink glitter decorations, and can we have hot chocolate bombs for the favors?"

"I guess so...?" I gazed across the table at Griffin helplessly. I was totally out of my element and completely clueless as to what a hot chocolate bomb was. Griffin grinned back and saluted me with his mug of coffee before returning to his conversation with a very pregnant wolf who I assumed was Seiko's mother. I could feel her faintly in the pack bonds. Her thread reminded me of water, cool and clean, with a slight undercurrent of exhaustion and frustration.

It was fascinating to watch Griffin in his role as Alpha. The pregnant wolf's tension eased out of her bond as Griffin leaned into her, rubbing his head against hers and murmuring reassurances in her ear. She smiled faintly in reply and leaned back, cradling her swollen belly in her hands with a sigh of relief.

"And can we have streamers and balloons?" Seiko asked me excitedly, drawing my attention back to her.

"Streamers and balloons, got it," I replied, wondering vaguely if I should be making a list.

"Should we go make the invitations now?" Seiko looked at my empty plate pointedly.

"Sure, yes! Let me just clear my place," I replied brightly, hopping up and grabbing my plate.

"I could feel you panicking from across the room," a warm voice teased gently in my ear as I walked away from the table with my plate.

"Oh my god, Nahla, I totally forgot you live here! Thank god," I moaned in relief.

"Do you even know where you're going with that plate?" Nahla laughed, turning me around and giving me a gentle shove in the opposite direction I'd been walking. "The kitchen is over there. So, unless you were going into the greenhouse to leave the plate of syrup for the plants to suck up, I think you want to go this way."

"Griffin still hasn't given me the tour," I complained, following Nahla into a huge kitchen with gleaming granite countertops, hanging copper pots and a massive oak center butcher block. "Woah, this is seriously log cabin chic," I whistled appreciatively. "Even I want to bake something now, and the only thing I've ever made are sweet potatoes and blueberry muffins, and you and Lillian did most of the work both times."

"Nonsense. Those sweet potatoes were all you. And such a shame you never even got to taste them!"

"Don't remind me," I groaned. "I'm kind of trying to block out the last time I was here, with vampy outing me to the whole pack, and me wolfing out and all..."

"It was very dramatic. We enjoyed it," Nahla grinned. "We told you, we don't get a lot of excitement, tucked away in the Northwoods of Maine."

"Glad I could entertain you all." I rolled my eyes at Nahla, rinsing my plate and depositing it in the dishwasher.

"So, you're throwing Seiko's 9th birthday party?" Nahla asked as I leaned against the counter, gazing out at the woods through the windows above the kitchen sink.

"It sure sounds like it, although I have no idea how it happened."

"You're the Alpha's mate, it's your job to help the pack out."

"Okay, but I have no experience with little kids' birthday parties. I mean, if it was a bachelorette party, I'd be the guy. I totally know how to blow up dildo decorations and mix up a pitcher of Sex on the Beach and some Blow Job shots, not sure I know what to do for a kids' party."

"She's a nine-year old girl, isn't that basically the same thing as a gay man?" Nahla teased. "You've got this in the bag."

"Ha ha! So funny." I made a face at Nahla. "But I get where you're going with this. Pink glitter and Ariana Grande, minus the dildoes and alcohol?"

"Bingo."

"Oh my god, I totally do have this," I exclaimed, suddenly excited about planning Seiko's party, as I started to envision the lodge decked out in pink streamers with pitchers of lemonade and a big, frosted unicorn cake. "I have to go talk to Lillian about the cake!"

"Aren't you supposed to be making invitations with Seiko, right now?" Nahla reminded me.

"That's right," I groaned, as Seiko peeked her head into the kitchen, holding a plastic bin overflowing with craft supplies.

"I got all the stuff!" she announced.

An hour later, I was covered in sparkles, had multiple hot glue burns on my hands and pink marker on my cheek, but I was feeling triumphant as I laid the 15th and final completed invitation on top of the stack.

"Nice work, baby," Griffin murmured in my ear, coming up behind me and kissing the top of my head.

"Thanks, I'm definitely feeling in touch with my inner unicorn," I grinned, tilting my head back for a kiss.

"I need to hop on a few calls. Are you okay here if I go work in my office for a little while?"

"Sure, go Alpha away." I tilted my head back again for a second kiss and brushed my nose against Griffin's. "You're really good at it, you know," I murmured against his lips, as my wolf grudgingly agreed with me.

"So are you, at this." Griffin waved a hand at the dining room table, buried in a layer of glitter, tissue paper, and sequins.

"Me and glitter go hand in hand," I laughed, as Griffin brushed his lips across my head before walking off.

"Can we go deliver them now?" Seiko asked, practically bouncing up and down in her seat.

"After we clean up. I don't want to get in trouble for making a mess, my first day living in the lodge," I laughed.

It took multiple wipe downs to get all the glitter off the table and a quick vacuum of the rug underneath before we were ready to head out, but I learned where the supply closet was, and caught sight of a few more rooms in the lodge as we put everything away. I was definitely going to need Griffin to give me a tour later. The place was huge, and more like a resort than a house, which was kind of a perk, because there were plenty of places to hide out in when I did need a little alone time.

"What kind of work do your parents do?" I asked Seiko as we walked out of the lodge hand in hand with her basket of invitations.

"My dad's a pilot and my mom's a kayak guide."

"Wow, that's cool."

"Yeah, my mom leads kayak trips on the lake and down the river, except in the winter when it's all frozen. Then she leads ice fishing trips, and my dad flies tourists in and out in his little plane, and packages and mail and stuff for the pack. He takes me with him sometimes, and he's teaching me to fly. I'm going to be a pilot too when I grow up!"

"Wow, that's awesome! Your parents sound badass."

"I don't think you're supposed to say that word." Seiko's eyes grew wide.

"Probably not," I winced.

I was sooo bad at this kid thing. At least I hadn't said fucking badass...

"So, where are we going to deliver these invites?" I smiled brightly at Seiko.

"All around. Hey, look, there's Adi, I think she's coming with us too."

"The bodyguard, of course she is," I muttered under my breath in annoyance, turning to meet Anya's bodyguard sister.

Adi was gorgeous, with midnight black skin, a shaved head, body that looked like it was chiseled from granite, and a, I can fuck you up before you even have time to blink, look to her. Her skin was luminous, her eyes, dark pools of obsidian, her style, assassin chic. She was wearing loose fitting, black, samurai style pants, a fitted, deep-plum colored tank top that stopped just above her naval, and some type of woven slides. All that was missing was a sword tied to her back; there was no question about her warrior status.

"Wolfboy," she nodded at me. "Pup," she nodded to Seiko.

"Hi Adi, are you coming with us to deliver my invitations?" Seiko chirped.

Adi nodded, standing still as she waited for us to start walking.

"Nice to meet you..." I said awkwardly as Seiko tugged me down the path.

Adi's pack bond felt like a steel bar, with a little of Anya's crackling lightning, but she could have used some of her sister Nahla's warm spice. The only reaction I got from my greeting was a brief nod of acknowledgment as her eyes swept the forest around us.

"Does she ignore everyone, or is it just me?" I asked Seiko, motioning to Adi as we walked through the woods.

"She's the pack bodyguard, silly," Seiko replied.

"She's not allowed to talk to us?" I asked, totally confused as Anya's sister continued to ignore me while we walked down the path.

"She's listening to the forest," Seiko laughed, shaking her head at me as if it was the most obvious thing in the world. "Adi can hear a baby mouse sleeping in a dead tree log all the way down the path."

"But not if she's talking to me..." I said slowly, finally catching on.

"Yup!" Seiko laughed again, obviously finding my cluelessness extremely entertaining. "C'mon, we'll go to Miri's house first. She's my best friend and her mom is going to deliver my mom's baby."

"Miri's mom is the pack midwife?" I asked, remembering Molly had said she'd recently trained her replacement.

"Yeah, and she has a jar of gumdrops she brings with her when she visits to check on my mom and I get to choose whatever color I want."

"She sounds awesome. I love gumdrops."

"She might let you have one. The green ones are the best."

I loved Miri's mom instantly. She was exactly what I thought a wolfpack midwife should be like, which was the opposite of Molly. I don't know how that had ever worked. Her name was Raina. Her skin was a beautiful, burnished bronze, and she had long, wild, dark hair, loosely braided to the side, intricate floral henna tattoos on her hands, and sparkling eyes the color of polished onyx. Green feathered earrings dangled from her ears, and she was wearing a flowered skirt that brushed the tops of her purple suede Birkenstock sandals.

"Finn," she exclaimed warmly, gathering me against her for a tight hug when she answered the door. "So wonderful to finally meet you."

"You too," I replied, slightly dazed by the rainbow, kaleidoscope colors that ran through her pack bond, and the almost musical hum that vibrated through her thread. She made me want to grab her arm and spin around the room until we both collapsed on the floor in a dizzy, joyful, mess.

"I'm having a unicorn birthday and Finn is planning it for me!" Seiko declared, thrusting a glitter dusted, sequin bedazzled, pink tissue paper invitation into Raina's hands.

"Wonderful! Miri will be very excited to come," Raina beamed back at Seiko, holding out a glass jar of gumdrops. "Don't forget your gumdrop."

"Can Finn have one too?" Seiko asked, immediately earning herself a treasured spot in my heart as Raina held out the jar to me with a grin. Seiko was right, green was the best.

It took us over an hour to deliver the rest of the invitations as we walked down the winding dirt road that seemed to stretch for miles along the forest and lake. Most of the pack lived along the private dirt road, with a few houses tucked deeper into the forest, only accessible by ATV, like Anya's house.

It was a nice opportunity to meet more of the pack, and everyone I met was warm and welcoming. But by the time we walked back to the lodge, I was exhausted from all the socializing, and a little nervous Seiko's friends were expecting Beyonce to show up at her party from the way she'd talked it up house to house.

"That was so great! I'm so excited about my party, Finn!" Seiko exclaimed as we walked into the lodge. "Aren't you?"

"So excited," I agreed, flashing a bright smile.

Adi snorted behind me as she took off, the only sound she'd made our whole walk, and I sighed in relief when Seiko ran off to join some other kids too. I was finally alone, and in desperate need of a cup of tea and an hour of mindless T.V. Reality show, mindless, like an MTV dating show or a telenovela.

I took Spanish language classes online and spent six months chatting up the bodega guys in my neighborhood just so I could watch telenovelas without subtitles, which I hate. Although I admit, sometimes I would zone out and just stare at the hot shirtless men singing.

The kitchen was blissfully quiet and empty when I entered, and I found the tea kettle easily, an electric version, plugged in on the counter beside an overflowing basket of assorted teabags. I had to admit, it was homey here, and if I found a tin of tea biscuits or a lemon drizzle pound cake in here too, I might consider staying.

"Earl Grey tea and dark chocolate covered butter cookies," I sighed in content when I spotted the tin of tea biscuits on the other side of the kettle.

"Starting to settle in?"

I turned when I heard Griffin's voice, surprised I hadn't sensed him entering the kitchen with my newly discovered wolf abilities.

"Hey," I smiled, turning the kettle off as it reached a boil, and filling my mug.

"I missed you." Griffin walked over to me, wrapping his arms around my waist.

"Me too." I leaned back against Griffin's chest as he nuzzled my neck.

"How'd it all go today?"

"Fine. Unicorn party planner has been added to my resume," I laughed.

"Thank you for doing that for Seiko. I've been meaning to ask someone to help her out."

"No problem. She's very sweet, and I met more of the pack while delivering invites. Adi followed us around which was kind of annoying because it's not like she talks or anything. I mean, Jesus, she's like a guard at Buckingham Palace. I told like 50 jokes on our walk, and she didn't crack a smile once. That wolf is alllll business. Her sisters are way more fun."

"It's her job to be all business," Griffin murmured against my neck, turning me around and backing me up against the counter. "She's not there to laugh at your jokes, she's there to protect you."

"First of all, in case you haven't noticed, I'm a pretty strong wolf guy, and I can fuck someone up myself. I've been on my own most of life, Griff. You think I survived this long without knowing how to fight? Second," I held up my hand to stop Griffin from interrupting me when he opened his mouth. "Second, what the fuck is this danger you're even worried about? Do you really think I'm not safe on pack land? And isn't this whole town part of your territory?"

"I'm sure you can fuck plenty of people up," Griffin replied, his eyes dark and serious. "And I know all about how strong you are..." His eyes flashed with heat as he ran his hands over my muscled biceps and across my broad chest. "But I can't not protect you, baby. My wolf goes crazy when you're even out of the room, and I wouldn't be able to live with myself if something happened to you. You're my mate, my whole world, the air I breathe. I know it's annoying, having a bodyguard, but it's only when Anya and I aren't with you."

"If you're holding back on me, Griff, it only makes me more vulnerable."

Griffin sighed, pressing his lips to my forehead, and breathing me in. "We think another attack is coming."

"From who? When?"

"That's what I sent Aksil and Anya to find out about. James said their lair is getting pressure from the Montreal vampires and we think they might be coordinating with one of the Canadian wolf packs to stage a joint takeover attempt of our territory and the Portland Lair. I'll know more when Anya and Aksil get back. For now, no one leaves pack land on their own. Everyone is paired up, even to go into town, and the kids aren't allowed to roam the woods without an adult."

"And I'm one of the kids?" I raised an eyebrow at Griffin in exasperation.

"Babe, if you knew what I wanted to do with you, you'd be on your hands and knees thanking me for your escort," Griffin growled.

"What's that supposed to mean?"

"It means, I'd like to tie you to my side and not even let you go to the fucking bathroom without me, forget about leaving the goddamn lodge. You're lucky I haven't locked you in our bedroom and posted a guard at the door."

"Try it, and I swear on my wolf, you'll never get in my ass again," I warned, narrowing my eyes at Griffin, and pushing him off me as I turned to tend to my steeping tea.

"This is me being chill, baby," Griffin sighed, leaning against my back as I fussed over my tea and piled cookies on a plate.

"Assigning a bodyguard to me 24/7, is being chill?" I snorted.

"Beyond chill." Griffin pressed his lips to the back of my neck.

"I want to drink my tea and eat my cookies," I grumbled.

"With a book or in front of the T.V.?" Griffin brushed his lips across my neck, kissing me gently behind my ear.

"T.V., I need a bad dating show or a Spanish soap opera."

"Got it, follow me." Griffin picked up my plate of cookies and led the way out of the kitchen and down the hall, into a cozy little room tucked away under the eaves of the lodge.

"Best kept secret in the lodge," he smiled, setting my plate down on an end table next to an overstuffed forest green chenille couch.

The room was the size of a small den, with a woodburning stove in the corner and a big, old, box style T.V. with wooden legs and actual knobs. The log walls were lined with shelves containing puzzles, vintage boardgames, a tin of marbles and jacks, and an assortment of VHS tapes and DVDs.

"Does that thing even still work?" I asked Griffin, gesturing toward the T.V. as I curled up on the couch.

"Yes, it's totally retrofitted," Griffin laughed, handing me a remote and tucking a thick, dark grey knit blanket around me. "There's a whole home theatre downstairs where most of the pack hangs out, with reclining seats, a popcorn maker, and full video gaming system, which you should totally check out when you want to socialize and have some fun, but if you want to drink your tea in peace and knit while watching *Love Island*, this is the place for you, no one ever comes in here."

"Did I tell you I love you today?" I picked up my mug and took a sip of my warm, soothing tea with a sigh of content.

"I love you too, my little wolf." Griffin kissed me on the forehead. "I'll come back for you in a couple of hours when it's time for dinner."

19

I settled into life at the lodge, much quicker and easier than I thought I would, even growing used to Adi always shadowing me. Lillian was in week eight of working at the bar, and she'd brought another wolf in to help her with the cooking and even added chili and smothered tater tots to the menu. Molly went two days in a row without making a snarky comment to me about my appearance, and her pack bond almost seem to sigh with satisfaction when Lillian was at the bar.

After Anya returned from her vamp meeting and de-briefed Griffin, she and her Charlie's Angel, had become tighter than my ass before Griffin pried it open for the first time, and I couldn't get a peep out of her about the sex, so I knew it was serious.

I was starting to feel settled. Griffin had given me a crash course in everything wolf, from the dangers of silver: it can cage, burn, and poison us, to teaching me how to lockdown the pack bonds when I needed the space: kind of like putting them in a closet and closing the door. They were still there on the other side of the door, but not with me all the time. And I'd even survived my first unicorn birthday party and figured out how to make hot chocolate bomb favors and was now in high demand to plan and host all the wolf pups' parties at the lodge.

The pack wolf doctor, an ancient Chinese wolf named Mei, had thoroughly checked me out and declared me healthy, despite my still blank memory, which she said would probably come back when I was ready for it, whatever that meant. She also confirmed Aksil's theory about my constant need to eat and said that would probably fade now that I was no longer expending so much energy repressing my wolf.

"FYI, that was the most unsatisfying exam I ever had." I made a face at Anya when she poked her head in my room.

"Were you expecting a happy ending?" Anya laughed as I finished getting dressed. "It wasn't an erotic massage; it was a medical exam."

"Eww, gross!" I smacked Anya across the head. "It just would have been nice to have gotten a few more answers from Mei besides, 'all good' and 'you're not ready to remember your past yet.'"

"Oh, chill out. Be grateful she cleared you. You know Griffin would have locked you away for a month, if Mei found the slightest thing wrong with you."

"I'd kill him!" I exclaimed, following Anya out of the room. "Griff has been impossible these last few months since I moved into the lodge as it is. Do you know how annoying it is to have your silent sister shadowing me every second of the day, especially when I'm trying to establish myself in the pack and settle into my role as the Alpha's mate? The other day, I went to visit a wolf at their house, just to check in, cause, I know she's been going through some stuff, and Adi trailed me the whole way there and back."

"Who was the wolf?" Anya raised her brow.

"None of your business! And that's not the point!"

"It cracks me up you've become like the pack therapist, since you're such a train wreck yourself, but I also totally get it, cause you're so non-judgmental and supportive, I can tell you anything."

"I am not a train wreck!" I shoved Anya as we walked out of the lodge and down the path to my cabin, which I'd set up as a sort of annex to the lodge that was my own little territory/fiefdom or as Anya called it, my wellness center.

I'd officially moved into the lodge with Griffin, but there was no way I was giving up my house. Opening it up to the pack had both cemented my position as Griffin's mate and changed the dynamic of my whole relationship with them.

Even though the lodge was still the central gathering spot, my house had become a welcome retreat for many to chill with a cup of coffee away from the masses, do yoga on the porch with me and Ziri, seek advice, or just share their feelings in a more low-key, private setting. I'd learned so much about the pack and everyone's lives and needs in the short time since I set up my little annex, I really felt like I was starting to belong. Now all I had to do was get Griffin to chill on my protective detail.

"Aksil's back," I announced to Griffin, half asleep, sitting up and blinking as I adjusted to my sudden wakeup.

"Yes." Griffin's voice was quiet, almost carefully mild, and his shoulders stiffened at my words as he kept his back to me, gazing out the window into the night. "You felt him cross into our territory?"

"I guess so...." Anya's warning to keep my unusual connection to Aksil's bond a secret, ran through my mind.

Griffin turned to face me, his eyes dark and expressionless. "Do you always feel Aksil so strongly?"

"Um, I don't think so... Why are you being so weird?"

"Our territory spans over 8,000 square miles and Aksil is still 60 miles away."

"Okay..." I wasn't exactly sure where Griffin was going with this, but I had a feeling it wasn't good.

"Aksil is still 60 miles away, yet you felt him when he crossed into pack territory. Do you always feel him while he's off patrolling, even when he's far away?"

"I don't know, and if he's still that far away, why were you staring out the window like he was about to walk up to the house?"

"I'm the Alpha of the pack. I know instantly when another wolf crosses into my territory, especially if it's one of mine, coming home. Do you feel your packmates when you're in town at the bar?"

"I don't know. I don't really think about it. I'm busy working," I replied nervously.

"Do you feel Anya right now?" Griffin pressed.

"No, should I?"

"I sent her to meet with the Portland vampires again late this afternoon, she's on her way back now, and she crossed back into our territory an hour ago. She's less than 30 miles away."

"Okay..."

"You slept through that fine, and you don't sense Anya now, when she's more than half the distance closer than Aksil is, but you woke up the instant he crossed over, and announced he was home."

"Well, I was wrong, obviously, since he's still a gazillion miles away," I shot back, not sure why we were fighting about this, but positive we were, as Griffin's mate bond tightened with anger. "Babe, remember when we couldn't figure out if we were in a fight, the night you made me the picnic, and we mated? This definitely feels like a fight. Why are you mad at me right now?" I asked.

"I'm not mad at you." Griffin stared back at me with dark gold, wolf eyes, still carefully blank.

"Yet, you're not coming over here. You're staying across the room."

"I'm just restless, I've been up since Anya crossed back over, waiting for her to get back."

"Uh huh."

"You should go back to sleep," Griffin said quietly, still not moving from his spot across the room.

"I should go back to sleep. No kiss; no snuggle. Just go back to sleep, Finn. See you in the morning, buddy."

"I didn't call you buddy," Griffin replied, his voice short.

"You might as well have, you dismissed me like I was anyone off the street."

"I'm going for a run, I need to shift," Griffin said tightly.

"You're going on a wolf run, right now, in the middle of this?" I gaped at Griffin.

"There's no this," he replied, already shedding his boxers. "There's nothing going on here. We're not fighting. I'm just going for a run."

I stared at Griffin, speechless, as he strode out of our bedroom naked. I felt him shift as soon as he stepped out of the lodge, his pack bond crackling with tension and restless energy as he ran through the woods, feelings of possessiveness and ownership shooting through our bond as he ran, mate, mate, mate, and mine, mine, mine flooding through me.

"Oh, baby," I sighed, leaning back against the pillows, trying to sort through exactly what had just happened. I guess Anya knew what she was talking about, and I should have just kept it to myself when I felt Aksil cross back into pack territory.

There was no way I was going back to sleep while Griffin was out running through the woods probably plotting Aksil's murder and trying to figure out how he could lock me away forever, so I slipped his sweats and moccasins on and went downstairs to make tea. I was still sitting on the couch in the main room with my mug of tea, long gone cold, when Griffin finally walked back into the lodge with Anya behind him.

"Oh look, Wolfboy waited up for me too? That's so sweet. Why don't you go put a sock on your dick, Griff, and I'll drink tea with granny over here, until you come back."

"Finn's going back to bed," Griffin growled, opening a chest by the door, and pulling out a pair of sweats and a hoody. "I need to talk business with Anya," he told me, barely glancing my way.

"What the fuck is your problem?" I demanded, finally fed up with Griffin's Alpha bullshit.

"This is pack business between me and my second," Griffin bit out. "I don't have time to hold your hand right now."

"You don't have time to hold my hand?" I repeated in shock. "Wow, just when I thought you couldn't possibly be a bigger asshole, you pull the fucking rabbit out of your hat."

"Okay, what did I miss?" Anya demanded, staring back and forth between Griffin and I with wide eyes. "Did the Texan come back and blow you in the bar bathroom again?"

"No, your brother did," Griffin shot back, finally letting the full force of his fury flood his eyes.

"What the fuck are you even talking about right now?" I yelled back at Griffin, as Anya cast me a, 'you idiot look', behind Griffin's back.

"Did you fuck him before or after you discovered your wolf?" Griffin asked, his voice tight with rage.

"Griff, I never did anything sexual with Aksil. I don't know what the fuck you're talking about."

"You slept wrapped around him for weeks in the forest," he growled. "Was the whole thing an act, or were you shifting out of your wolf whenever I wasn't around, and fucking him the whole time?"

"An act? Are you fucking serious?" I exploded. "I was traumatized; you dickwad!" I let the full force of my fury flood my eyes. "You abandoned me the morning after we mated! And then the first time I walk into your lodge, your little vamp friend announces I'm a wolf, and all the pain I'd buried for the last 15 years suddenly came up to the surface and fucking sucked the breath out of me! I thought I was dying; do you understand that?"

"You thought you were dying, experiencing the deepest trauma of your life, and you reached for Aksil, not me," Griffin echoed, his voice barely a whisper.

"I have no idea why I have a connection to Aksil; Griff, I just do," I said wearily. "But I gave you my fucking soul when I let you ram your dick in my ass and bite me after everything I'd been through. I submitted to you, when it went against everything inside me, and you accuse me of betraying you?" I choked, staring at Griffin in disbelief.

"Well, I guess you got a taste for it after me, because if you can sense Aksil when he's 50 miles away, clearly I'm not the only wolf you've been submitting to," Griffin replied, his voice like ice.

"Wow," I breathed, as I felt something break inside me and my wolf flashed to the surface in fury. "Go fuck yourself, Griffin," I whispered. "I'm going home to my own fucking house, and don't you dare send one of your bodyguards with me, or I promise you, you will never see me again."

"Finn, wait, don't go," Anya called after me, as I stripped out of Griffin's sweats and ran out the door, shifting as soon as my feet touched the ground outside.

Griffin let me go without a word, and my wolf was enraged at his betrayal, the months of work we'd put into strengthening the bond between our wolves dissipating like the heat of morning sun burning through an overnight fog.

I shifted back into human form as soon as I reached my porch, grabbing the key I kept under the flowerpot, and opening the door. It was good to be in my cabin, I always felt a sense of peace here. I padded barefoot into my bedroom, numb and in shock from my fight with Griffin as I walked over to my closet to grab a pair of sweats.

I was so out of sorts, trying to understand exactly what had happened between Griffin and I, and working to lock him out of my head, I didn't smell the wolves until they were on top of me, and by then, it was too late to fight them off.

20

"Drink the fucking water and eat the fucking food!"

I opened my eyes, staring back vacantly at the wolf yelling at me. The days had started to blur together since I was taken, and I'd lost track of time, the only clue to my length of captivity, my cracked, bleeding lips and dehydrated state of lethargy.

I'd tried reaching out to Griffin after I was taken, despite how hurt and angry I still was with him. Fight or no fight, I knew he would lose his shit once he realized I was gone. But the cage my abductors put me in seemed to be spellcast with something that blocked the pack bonds. I couldn't feel Griffin or any of the pack when I woke up in it, and I had no clue where I was, other than that we were in the middle of a forest somewhere.

"He thinks it's poisoned," a wolf snapped. His voice was guttural and thickly accented, raw power poured off him as he approached my cage. He was obviously the Alpha of the wolfpack who took me.

"Look, wolf, it's not poisoned. Watch me take a bite and drink a sip."

The Alpha slipped a protective glove on to open the door of my cage. I had learned it was silver the hard way, the bars searing the skin beneath my fur when I shifted into my wolf and threw myself against the door in a pitiful escape attempt.

I bared my teeth at him with what little strength I had left as he picked my water bowl up, and he laughed at my weak threat before taking a sip.

"See, not poisoned," he declared, placing the bowl back down on the floor of the cage. Then he took a bite from the sandwich on the plate and made a show of chewing it down and swallowing it heartily before putting it back into my cage and closing the door.

I lifted my snout up and smelled him. He still smelled like a wolf, so I licked a drop of water from the bowl, and it felt so good on my dry, scratchy throat, and I was still wolf, so I drank some more.

I'd been drifting in and out of dreams and memories since I woke up in the cage after I was taken. Constantly traveling back to when I was ten years old, trapped with the chestnut-haired witch, and I feared anything that might take my wolf away again, even a bowl full of water and a roast beef sandwich.

"That's a good wolf, you're not any use to us if you die before we get started," the Alpha laughed as I drank the water. "We need you alive to get your Alpha here."

My Alpha. The wolf's words brought me back to another time when I was ten, in a cage, just like this, in a back of a van, the familiar memory flashing through me. *"They don't want you anymore,"* the *chestnut-haired woman tells me. "You were a bad wolf, and your pack gave you away. They took your wolf and cast you out. You are Finn now. Only Finn."*

"No." I reached out for Griffin helplessly. It was the same memory that had been haunting me for days, and every time it flashed through me, I searched for Griffin's orange-gold thread, and the feeling of mate, safety, and pack, but it was gone. As my past continued to collide with the present, all I felt was the soul-crushing weight of everyone's rejection, and I drifted away again. Ten and twelve. Ten and twelve. Back with the chestnut-haired woman or trapped in the shed.

I don't know how long I was lost in my dreams before arguing voices pulled me back to the present, but when I opened my eyes, a new dawn was breaking through the trees and I could just make out a large grey wolf, pacing the tree line.

"Do you have someone from my pack here, motherfucker?" he growled low in his throat at the wolves standing guard. I didn't know the voice, but the smell tickled the back of my head, and I lifted my snout to breathe it in.

"Of course we don't have anyone from your pack here," one of the guards growled back at the wolf questioning him. "You think we have time to start shit with your Alpha, right now? Who we have here doesn't concern you, petit garçon. This is not your fight or your coast. We let you pass through here on your way home as a courtesy to your Alpha. Now, get lost and forget you ever smelled anyone here, or you won't make it back to the land of your arbre rouge."

"Who are you?" The wolf pushed into my head insistently, and I didn't understand how or why I could hear him, but I answered him anyway.

"I am wolf. Wolf, wolf, wolf. You smell like the tall trees and the spongy forest from my dreams."

"You smell like pack, wolf," he replied. *"How did you get here? Why is the Levesque pack holding you?"* he asked, as the other wolves warned him to leave again.

"I am hiding. I won't let them take my wolf again." I told him. *"So tired and thirsty, I am going to sleep now. Good-bye wolf who smells like the red trees and the spongy forest from my dreams. Be careful. Don't let them hurt you. Run away and hide before they catch you and put you in a silver cage or glass box no one can break through."*

"The spell on the cage should be partially worn off now, that's probably why the wolf from the Sequoia Pack was able to smell him," the Alpha announced to his packmates, after the grey wolf finally took off through the trees. "Griffin will feel him by tomorrow, but he won't be able to find him for another day, which will drive him crazy.

We're so deep into our territory, it will take him a full day to find his mate even after he figures out we have him. We want him totally off his game, solely focused on his mate's pain and his inability to get to him, then we strike. Tell everyone to get ready."

Griffin. Just the sound of his name filled me with a soul-deep yearning. Then I smelled the red trees again, and a grey, silver thread flashed in my head. It said *grab on, and pack, pack, pack. You are pack. I smell you. I feel you. You are like us. You are a grey wolf from the red forest. I know you. You smell like home.*

Home. I yearned for it for so long, searched for its scent in the wind, and as the Sequoia wolf's thread wrapped around me, the smell of rich, fertile, redwood trees filled my senses. I knew this forest. I smelled like this pack, like the grey wolves I used to run through the tall trees with.

Images suddenly flitted through my mind like an old-fashioned slide projector: a huge timber frame lodge resting high on a mountaintop, a long wooden canoe carved from an ancient redwood tree sitting on the edge of a riverbank. A fishing net lying in a tangle on the hardwood floor of a bedroom, I instantly knew was mine. I could smell the salt from the ocean at the foot of my mountain home, and I rested my head against the Sequoia wolf's thread and drifted back to sleep, the sound of the sea in my ear carrying me away.

A searing pain shocked me awake the next morning, as my captors dripped hot, liquid poison through the bars of my cage, molten silver charring my fur. Raw fire ate away at my flesh, and I thrashed about, flashing my teeth, and clawing desperately at the cage door, which only made things worse, burning the pads of my paws.

There was no escape from the torture, nowhere to hide, as the silver dripped down my back, burning a line from the tip of my spine to the base. The spell around the cage seemed to weaken with each drop of agonizing pain that shot through me, almost as if that was the intention. Griffin's orange-gold thread sparked in my head as he finally broke through, vibrating with unbridled rage at every splash of silver against my fur.

The Levesque Pack continued their torture over the next two days, until most of the fur on my back was gone and all that remained was raw, blistered flesh. Griffin and Aksil's voices were relentless in my head as I drifted in and out of consciousness between my broken twelve- year-old body in the shed, and my present-day wolf, lying in a burnt heap of charred fur on the floor of the cage.

"*Finn!!*" Griffin's voice screamed over and over again, thick with anguish and wrath.

"*Hold onto me.*" Aksil's voice was quiet, calm; his silver-black cable perfectly rigid, a brace, as his rich deep voice resonated through me like a Gregorian chant.

The unrelenting pain kept pulling me back to the shed as Griffin and Aksil's voices continued in my head, and I grabbed onto Aksil's steely cable and pulled it deep inside me, holding onto it like a lifeline.

When the Alpha approached my cage on the third day of my torment, his hands were empty. There was no more liquid silver.

"Time to wake up, wolf," he called, squatting before my cage. "We're going to give your mate a little show," he laughed.

I bared my teeth and snarled at him with what little strength I had left. I could barely lift my head, all the nerve endings in my body cried out in agony from the effort, but whatever he had planned, I wasn't giving in without a fight. I would not return to the shed. I was not Finn anymore, I was wolf, wolf, wolf, strong and fierce.

"Nice teeth," the Alpha grinned, before pushing into my head like a tidal wave.

"Nooooo," my wolf and I howled in unison, the last vestiges of strength I'd been clinging to shattering into a million pieces as the Levesque Alpha forced my shift, ripping me out of my wolf.

"Now that's more like it," the Alpha snarled, dragging my naked, half burnt body out of the cage and dumping me on the ground. "Let's see what your mate thinks about me forcing your shift," he laughed. "I'd have a little fun with you while we wait for him to get here, but burnt meat isn't really to my taste."

"*Finn,*" Griffin roared in my head, his voice thick with agony, clear and sharp, now that I was out of the spellcast cage. "*I'm coming,*" he promised.

"*Stay alive.*" Aksil's voice shot through me like a lightning bolt. "*You can survive whatever they do to you,*" his rich, deep voice promised, as his silvery-black thread pushed up at me from its roots. "*You will heal. Just don't give up, Finn.*"

But I couldn't be Finn. I refused to be Finn, as I lay on the forest floor, naked and burnt, the flesh on my back, open and oozing. Finn was a boy who was not a wolf. Finn was a boy who had lost his wolf. People hurt Finn. They ripped him open.

I wouldn't be Finn again. I was only wolf, wolf, wolf, and I reached inside myself with every ounce of strength I had left and called my wolf back to me in an agonizing, bone crunching, molten flesh shift.

"Holy shit," one of the wolves cried out as my body fought desperately to return to its wolf form. "How is he shifting in his burnt-up state? He shouldn't even still be alive with the amount of silver in him, forget about have the strength to shift."

I didn't have the strength, and as I lay on the ground before the speechless Levesque Pack in a half shifted, grotesque state of burnt flesh and extended claws, the fight finally left me.

"*No, Finn,*" Aksil's deep, warm voice filled my head as his black thread pushed up at me through his roots, breaking through my haze of pain and defeat. "*Stay with us. You can be both, Finn and wolf. Stay with us; Griffin and I are coming; your pack is coming for you.*"

Pack. As soon as Aksil said the words, a low growl became a roar in my head, and I pushed Griffin and Aksil's threads away, closing my ears to the cries of "*Finn, Finn, Finn, and mate,*" as a burst of silver-grey shot through me, and the Sequoia Alpha, my Alpha, filled my head with his call.

I answered him with an anguished howl, singing for everything I had lost, for everyone who was taken from me, who I was taken from. I sang for my Alpha, who called out to me, *"I am coming for you. I am coming."* And I sang for myself, for my wolf who would never hide again.

"Keep holding your position. We don't attack the Northwoods Pack until we have Griffin here," the Levesque Pack Alpha growled into the phone as he stared down at my half-shifted, burnt body, howling on the ground.

And that's when the Sequoia Pack struck. And they were magnificent.

The Levesque pack must have been expecting Griffin and Aksil, or they would have noticed when the Sequoia Pack crossed over into their territory. The Levesque Alpha probably felt the breach and smelled the redwoods, but thought it was just the Sequoia wolf he had granted passage to, still passing through.

They came as one, running through the trees and bursting into the clearing. The Alpha was a huge grey wolf, ancient, so ancient, the blood of centuries running through him as he ripped the wolves apart. And he wasn't just Alpha, he wasn't just my Alpha, he was father, and mine, and home, and family, and pack.

The rest of the Sequoia Pack finished the Levesque wolves off in a blur of claws, teeth, and blood, while my father shifted, dropping to his knees before me.

I pressed my nose into his palm, inhaling deeply as a flood of memories washed over me. *Running through the forest together as wolves, right after my first shift, his voice in my ear as he pointed out all the different species of plants in the forest, the rumble of his laughter as I climbed all over him, trying to pin him down.*

"Hello, my son." My father pressed his forehead gently against mine. "Let me help you with what you started." His voice was rich with love and tenderness as he gently eased his way inside my head, lending me his strength as he guided me through the rest of my shift until I was wolf again. "You're safe now, I promise. We're going to take you home," he said quietly, gathering me into his arms.

I stared back at my father sorrowfully. Home. I dreamed of it for so long, but it felt hollow now, like there was something missing inside me. And then I smelled snow-covered pine branches, and a huge reddish-brown wolf burst through the trees with a black wolf running behind him.

My heart ached with yearning at the sight of Griffin running through the trees, shifting, and coming to a stop in front of us, but I was so confused and tired. I was wolf and I was pack, but I'd never felt so alone and empty.

I crawled back inside myself, burrowing deeper away, as my father cradled me against him, taking care not to touch the raw, burnt flesh on my back.

"Finn!" Griffin lunged forward as the Sequoia Pack surrounded me, growling in warning. "He's my mate," he declared, as my father stood up, holding me against his chest.

My father was so strong, holding me in his arms like I was a mere pup, his raw power pouring out of him as he stared my mate down.

"I feel the mate bond," my father acknowledged, motioning to my packmates to stand down and let Griffin and Aksil approach.

"You're Conall, Alpha of The Sequoia Pack." Griffin stared at my father in confusion.

"Yes, young Griffin of The Northwoods Pack. I knew your father; you look just like him."

"Finn is my mate," Griffin repeated, stepping forward and reaching for me. "He was taken from us, we're his pack."

"He is Sequoia Pack, and he's my son," my father growled back at Griffin, as I burrowed deeper into his chest. "And you," he turned to Aksil, still in wolf form, standing beside Griffin. "I feel your wolf planted deep inside Finn. Your roots are stronger than his mate bond." He assessed Aksil with a dark, questioning gaze as Aksil shifted out of his wolf in a blur of dark fur.

"Yes," Aksil affirmed, staring back at my father with expressionless eyes.

"I feel the mate bond," my father repeated, turning away from Aksil and addressing Griffin. "But his wolf doesn't carry your scent. His wolf hasn't accepted your claim."

"Finn's wolf was bound when we mated, but we're working it out." Griffin's voice was thick with anguish as his thread reached for me, trying to break through the cocoon my pack was weaving around me inside my head.

I grabbed onto Griffin's thread, starting to pull him into the cocoon with me, but as our wolves stared at each other with golden, gleaming eyes, his last words to me back at the lodge, his accusation of betrayal, rang through my head, and I let his orange-gold thread fall from my fingers. Our mate bond was cracked, and I was broken. I didn't want to be Finn; I didn't want to be Griffin's mate. I only wanted to be wolf, and I dug down deeper into myself.

"There are a lot of questions to be answered. I'm taking Finn home. I grant you permission to come into our territory to see my son in a few weeks. Right now, he obviously doesn't want to talk to you, and he needs to go home to his pack to heal," my father told Griffin quietly, holding me tightly against his chest.

"You don't know that." Griffin growled, his eyes flashing Alpha. "You're not taking my mate anywhere," he warned, power and strength radiating off him as he stepped forward.

"Listen carefully, little wolf pup, because I will only say this once," my father warned Griffin. "I have heard great things about you, Alpha of the Northwoods Pack, and I feel your strength," he acknowledged. "I'm sure you will do many important things in the werewolf world, and I look forward to watching you grow up and into your power. But you are just a pup still, and if you think I will let you threaten me and try to take my son from me, you are far more foolish than you look."

"He's my mate!" Griffin exclaimed again, stepping forward. "You have no right to separate us."

"No *right*?" my father echoed; his voice dangerously soft. "A mate is a gift, not a right. You have no right, no ownership here over my son, and while he may have accepted your claim, his wolf has not, and your mate bond is cracked. Right now, Finn has made his choice clear. He's choosing wolf and pack, his pack, not yours. And it will be up to him if he wishes to restore the mate bond."

"Finn!" Griffin called out to me; his voice filled with anguish as my father turned away from him and Aksil, cradling me against his chest.

My wolf stared at me questioningly as Griffin's grief-filled voice rang through the air and his orange-gold thread called out to us, but I closed my eyes in response, burrowing into the cocoon of silver-grey threads my pack was weaving around me.

Griffin's mournful howl filled the air in protest, and I answered him with my own anguished song, but I didn't pull his thread into the pack cocoon even when my wolf yanked Aksil in by his roots as my pack wove its last strand, sealing us in and closing Griffin out.

21

The trip home to Sequoia Pack territory took two days. The pack drove in shifts in a caravan of three Jeeps, stopping only for bathroom breaks. I drifted in and out of the past and present in a dreamlike state, only waking when my father spread salve on my burns and slipped bits of food and sips of water into my mouth.

I was slowly healing, my skin no longer raw and blistered, but the effects of purging the silver from my body was exhausting, and I was empty and aching from being separated from my mate. I longed for Griffin but couldn't find the will to reach out to him. Every time I thought about it, the searing pain of his rejection pierced me, the line between past and present blurred, and I kept drifting back to my ten-year-old self.

My wolf was quiet, watchful, something had shifted between us when I called him back to me after the Alpha ripped me out of him, we were entwined now, no longer separate, and he was curious, rather than oppositional, studying me for my reaction to the orange-gold thread that hovered outside our pack cocoon and the silver-black thread that was firmly wrapped around us.

Then, suddenly, we were home. I felt it deep in my bones as

soon as we crossed into pack territory, and when the caravan slowed at the foot of the mountains, I leapt out of my father's arms and through the open side of the Jeep, inhaling deeply as my paws hit the ground.

I padded slowly through the trees by instinct, not stopping until I was all the way up the mountain. It smelled like home and pack, sweet redwood trees and fresh mountain air. And as I drew closer to my home, I searched for another smell, one that had always meant comfort and warmth, but it wasn't there.

"She's not here anymore," my father said gently, coming up behind me and resting a hand on my head. "But she would be so happy to know you're finally home. All your mother ever wanted for you, Finn, was to be alive and well with your pack."

My head flooded with memories at my father's words, and I shifted, standing naked in front of him, in the clearing where I was taken.

"My life for his." I turned in a slow circle in the dirt, sinking down to my knees. I could see it so clearly now; I couldn't believe I had kept it buried for so long. It was suddenly so bright and fresh in my memory, kneeling on the forest floor where I was taken in front of my house. "I was playing in the woods and then something just felt wrong, so I ran home."

"I was away on pack business," my father said sadly. "Up in the Sierra Nevada mountains dealing with an issue with the other branch of the pack, but I felt it instantly, the moment you were taken, and your mother was killed."

"When I reached the clearing, a woman yanked me inside a circle of stones, and I tried to bite her, I remember that, but once I was inside the circle, it was like I was frozen in place. Then mommy came running out of the house, calling for the pack, but no one could reach me. They tried over and over again, but there was an invisible wall between us."

"The witch was from a very powerful line of witches, and it was an ancient spell, cast to stop a prophecy, there was a lot of power in it," my father said.

"She traded her life for mine, my mother." I wobbled on my feet as I stood up, staring at my father.

"Yes."

"The witch was going to kill me. She said she had to stop the prophecy and mommy offered her life in place of mine. She said, take his wolf if you must, but please spare his life. I offer you my blood in its place."

"Yes, and the witch agreed. But she couldn't take your wolf. You were too strong, and you wouldn't give it up, so she bound you instead and severed your pack ties, using your mother's blood sacrifice to seal it in. When I made it back here, your mother was dead and you were gone," my father whispered, his voice thick with pain and sorrow.

"I think I need to lie down," I murmured weakly, wobbling on my feet. It was too much to take in all at once.

"Come inside. Your burns are mostly healed, but you're still weak. You can shower and eat. We have a lot to discuss, but we'll talk more after you've rested. It's nice to see your face, my son." My father pulled me up, brushing a hand across my cheek, tenderly.

I was a little scared to shower at first, my body still so raw and vulnerable from my ordeal, I didn't know if I could handle anything against my skin, but the warm water was wonderful, and I sat down on the shower floor and just let the hot spray pour over me as I inhaled the smell of the spicy bodywash, letting my mind go blank.

The Sequoia Pack lodge was similar to Griffin's in size and layout, but at least a hundred years older, a timber frame structure instead of logs, tucked high up in the Santa Cruz mountains of California.

I tried not to think of Griffin, Aksil, whose thread thrummed inside me, like an alarm I kept switching to snooze, or any of the pack back in Maine, because as soon as I did, a deep, yawning ache filled me. I still had so much to deal with here, before I could even begin to think about the mess I'd left behind with my mate, my mysterious black wolf who had planted deep roots inside me, and the whole Northwoods Pack, who I'd grown to love and think of as my own.

It was strange being back here in my childhood home. I belonged here, but I didn't, and as I stretched out on my bed, staring up at the star cutouts on my ceiling, I laughed weakly to myself as I took in my bedroom, which had been kept clean and dust free, but otherwise unchanged.

It was hard to believe I'd thought I couldn't swim. Every inch of my room was filled with something from the ocean or rivers surrounding my home. My bedroom walls were covered with fishing nets, canoe paddles and surfing posters, and an elaborate fort was set up in the corner of the room inside an old redwood canoe next to a well-loved surfboard. I'd spent most of my childhood in the water, surfing from age 3.

Memories flooded me as I stared around my room. I was going to be a professional surfer, and a canoe builder like my Yurok grandfather. Just the sight of the surfboard and canoe filled me with a soul-deep yearning. Maybe I almost drowned that day in the lake with Anya because it was the first time I'd been back in the water since I was ten years old, and I wasn't ready to face what I'd lost.

When I came down to dinner, my two brothers and sister were waiting at the table for me. They had all been on the rescue mission to Canada, but I didn't remember much from the trip back to pack territory, so when I saw them at dinner, it was like I was seeing them for the first time in fifteen years. I was the baby of the family. Len was the oldest, ten years above me, then came Collin, five years younger than Len, and Ali, only ten months older than me.

Ali and I were inseparable as kids, I remembered instantly, staring at the beautiful young woman sitting at the table, looking at me with red, shining eyes, trying to keep her tears at bay. We looked like twins with our identical unruly golden blond hair and wide green eyes, and we used to pretend we were, even making up our own secret twin language. We took after our Scottish father, and Len and Collin our Yurok mother, with her dark hair, sharp Native American bone structure and black eyes.

"You look exactly like we expected you to," Collin blurted out. "Just like Ali."

"You got tall," Len added gruffly. "You were always such a little squirt; we never knew if you'd catch up with the rest of us."

"I'm ten years younger than you, of course you were a giant compared to me back then!" I laughed, slipping into the seat beside Len.

It was weird, sitting at the table with my father and siblings, like an awkward guest, yet at the same time, like I belonged there, like I'd never left.

"Do you still love rosemary fries?" Ali asked, passing me a plate piled high with fragrant smelling fried potatoes covered in fresh rosemary.

"Yes, you?" I smiled tentatively at my sister, helping myself to the fries.

"Favorite food," she smiled back.

"You always fought over the last one, whenever your mother made them," my father said, his eyes drinking me in across the table, like he almost couldn't believe I was really there.

"Yes, and you used to make us split it in half." I smiled at the memory.

"We shared everything," Ali choked, reaching across the table, and squeezing my hand.

"I remember." I swallowed the lump in my throat and pushed back my chair, suddenly needing to get away. "I'm gonna get some air for a minute," I mumbled, tripping over my chair as I shoved it away and ran for the door.

The cool mountain air felt good against my skin as I walked

around to the back of the lodge.

"We never stopped looking for you, Finn, I swear," Len said quietly, coming up behind me, and following me over to a circle of chairs around an oversize stone firepit. "We looked for you every day, everywhere we went, scanning the surroundings for a glimpse of your blond hair, your grey wolf. We searched the air for your scent, we sang for you. Collin walked the entire length of the Pacific Northwest Trail last year, still searching for you. Dad made annual trips around the entire world. Ali combed the internet daily. I sniffed every wolf everywhere I went. We never gave up."

"I was in New York, in the Bronx." I sank down into one of the chairs by the firepit as Len's words washed over me, and a dull ache settled in the pit of my stomach. "It's a great place to dump someone if you want them to disappear. The city kind of swallows you up, like a concrete jungle. So many people, so many smells. And I was living on the street for so long, I learned to blend in with the shadows and hide from the world. And then of course, my wolf was bound, so there was that. I'm not surprised you couldn't find me."

"What happened to you after you were taken? Can you, do you want to talk about it?" Len asked tentatively.

"Not really," I flashed a wan smile. "Not gonna lie, it was a suckfest. Probably better I couldn't remember where I came from, what I'd lost, for so long. It might have broken me, you know?" I stared off into the trees. "I think it was easier not knowing, just assuming no one loved me, and I was all alone. At least I didn't have anything to miss, to long for. But it's hard being back," I admitted, staring out into the forest surrounding us. "It's hard seeing you all together, not knowing anything about you, who you've become, and knowing we were once so close."

"I became a Smoke Jumper," Len offered, easing himself into the chair beside me.

"Really? Wow, I remember when you joined the fire department as a volunteer. You were always obsessed with Smoke Jumpers;

pretty cool you became one." I wondered what else I'd missed in my siblings' lives as they grew up without me. "Do you have a mate?"

"Brie, she's from the Sierra Nevada branch of our pack. She's a chef. She has a food truck, Brie's Bites, she runs down on the boardwalk. What about you?" Len asked. "What do you do?"

"Me? I'm a bartender," I laughed, a little embarrassed. "Not as exciting as a Smoke Jumper, but it's kept a roof over my head most of the time these last ten years."

"You've been bartending since you were fifteen?" Len raised an eyebrow at me.

"Yeah, scored a fake I.D., watched a bunch of YouTube videos at the library, hung around and watched bartenders through the windows of bars, and figured out to make a few drinks. After that, I just settled into it pretty well, started making good tips, and realized I could feed myself and keep the rain off my head doing it, so I stayed with it."

"That's amazing. You always were super resourceful. Remember when you were obsessed with Wolverine from the X-men, and you wanted to style your hair like Hugh Jackman's Wolverine? Mom refused to take you to the salon for a haircut, so you cut and styled it yourself, by watching haircutting tutorial videos you took out from the library."

"Oh my god, wow, yes! That was shortly before I was taken..." As the memories washed over me, I was struck again by how much I'd really lost when I was ripped away from my family, my pack.

"What's your mate like? Does he have a food truck like mine?" Len slid his chair closer to me, bumping his knee against mine with an easy smile as he changed the subject. And I suddenly remembered that about him. He was always good at that, at re-directing and changing the mood of the room.

"Griffin? No, definitely no food truck. Although he does make a mean pancake and bacon breakfast," I smiled faintly, recalling the morning after we first met when Griffin fed me, then bent me over the porch rail, and I drove off naked in his brother's truck. "We've had a lot of interesting moments together since we met..." An ache deep inside me, tugged at my mating bond.

"What happened between you guys?" Len asked. "I know you were in shock when we rescued you, but we could all feel you didn't want to go with him. When your mate showed up, you literally retreated inside the pack bonds and pushed your mating bond to the outside."

"You made a cocoon," I said softly. "I didn't even know you could do that. I was just learning to understand the way pack bonds work again, after I discovered my wolf a few months ago, and I don't remember anything like this from when I was a kid. The pack wound themselves around me like a caterpillar spinning a cocoon, until I was wrapped tightly inside, and all I could feel were all of you surrounding me like a shield."

"It's a special technique packs use for traumatized wolves," Len explained. "Not every pack can do it, only a really strong, old Alpha like dad can build a cocoon with the pack bonds. It draws the wolf deep into the center of the pack and pushes everything else out, almost like a giant group hug. The mating bond usually gets drawn in and woven through the cocoon with the rest of the pack, but yours didn't. You pushed it to the outside when we were weaving the cocoon, and I can still feel it there, almost waiting for you."

"It's complicated," I whispered, reaching out for Griffin's bond, and running my fingers over his red gold strings as they hummed for me.

"You let the black wolf into the cocoon. We didn't know what to make of that," Len admitted. "We were pissed at first and started to push him out because we could tell he wasn't your mate, but you dragged him in by his roots when we were almost done weaving, and once we saw you'd planted him inside you, we had to let him finish weaving the cocoon with us. We didn't want to risk further traumatizing you, and it was obvious he made you feel safe by the way you pulled him against you. He's the second string in the cocoon after dad."

"Fuck," I sighed. "Kind of wish you hadn't told me that."

"Who is he?"

"The fuck if I know, my spirit animal?" I exhaled, running my fingers through my hair in frustration.

"You always did love your comic book stories," Len grinned.

"Griffin accused me of betraying him with Aksil, the black wolf in our pack cocoon. That's what caused the fight and set this whole thing in motion," I sighed.

"Did you betray your mate with the black wolf?"

"No! Never."

"But he's something to you," Len murmured thoughtfully.

"I don't even really know him! I don't know how to explain the connection, but when I discovered my wolf, he was the only one I could feel in my head. I spent three weeks with him in the forest in wolf form before I shifted back, and he feels like a part of me, but I don't know why," I admitted. "I love Griffin and I know he's my mate. I don't have any doubt about that. I feel it all the way to my core."

"Huh." Len stared at me with an unreadable expression. "I think dad knows what it all means," he offered. "He said something weird to Aksil when we were leaving with you, the day we found you in Canada. Something about it not being Aksil's planting season. It made no sense, but if anyone would know what's going on with you, dad would."

"Yeah, he told me we have to have some big talk about everything that happened to me and what it all means. I'm kind of dreading it," I admitted. "So much has happened to me in such a short time, I kind of just want to sit and have these moments with all of you right now, you know?"

"Yeah, I know," Len replied softly, bumping his knee against mine.

22

I spent the next week walking in the woods with Ali, breathing in the redwood trees, fishing in the creek with Collin, and sitting with my dad, leaning my head against his shoulder, and staring up at the stars, not needing any words between us.

The pack mostly stayed back, giving me my space, and evenings, I spent around the fire pit behind the lodge with my big brother, Len. We'd made it an unofficial tradition, after that first night when he followed me outside.

"You can't hide from your mate forever, you know," Len teased me gently as I sat, staring into the fire broodingly, my untouched beer going warm in my hand.

I leaned back in my chair. "I feel him pushing at me, but I'm just not ready to talk to him."

"He's ready to talk to you," Len grinned, taking a swig of his beer.

"You can feel him?" I asked, surprised.

"The whole pack can," Len laughed. "He's literally vibrating with frustration, and he feels like he's going to snap at any minute. Everyone's expecting him to throw you over his knee and give you a spanking when he finally gets here." Len's eyes twinkled with mischief.

"I don't know what I'm supposed to do now," I admitted, closing my eyes, and breathing in as Griffin called out to me, like he did every day, his bond pushing at me insistently through the pack cocoon. "I'm physically healed up, so I could go back to The Northwoods Pack, to my mate, but emotionally..." I opened my eyes and met my brother's knowing gaze.

"Your spirit is still wounded," he acknowledged. "But it won't heal on its own."

"I feel so lost," I admitted. "I dreamed of finding my family one day, but I never knew facing what I'd lost would hurt this much. I was going to be a canoe builder, a professional surfer." I half laughed; half choked. "I became a bartender who forgot I even knew how to swim! I forgot who I was. I forgot my wolf. I lost my family, my pack, my path!"

"Your wolf was always with you." Len shook his head at me. "And you didn't lose your family, pack, or path. You walked a different path, and found another family, but your family, your pack, was always here, waiting for your return. It's not the years you lost that's causing your despair, little brother. You're missing half your soul," Len chided, clapping a hand on my shoulder. "You need to let your mate back in, Finn. Don't dwell on the years you lost; think of them as a detour, not a permanent change in your course. You can still build canoes and surf again. You've barely begun your life."

"But everything's different now, I'm different," I choked. "I think the fight for my wolf with the Alpha of the Levesque Pack triggered something inside me. I don't know what exactly, but I was willing to die in that moment rather than give in, Len. I feel like a different wolf now."

"And you don't know if your mate will still want you." Len's eyes were soft with understanding. "You're not keeping your mate away because you're still angry at him, you're afraid he will be angry with you. There will always be ripples in the water, changing the current, little brother," Len said, gently. "And your mate will always love you, want you, even as your spirit shifts. I feel you, deep inside me, and you are the same wolf you have always been, you are still our little Wave Rider," Len smiled, using the Yurok name my grandfather had given me when I was a child. "You are just growing into yourself now, and you will ride the waves again in a new way."

"But what if Griffin doesn't know that wolf?" I whispered back. "What if he's never met him?"

"He's met him. He just may need to be properly introduced." Len ruffled my hair.

Griffin showed up in the middle of the night, toward the end of my second week in the Santa Cruz mountains.

"I don't remember inviting you into my room," I grumped, waking up abruptly to the smell of snow-covered pine branches.

"You're my mate, Finn, I don't need a fucking invitation," Griffin bit out. "You're lucky I didn't just drag you out of bed, throw you over my shoulder, and haul you out of here."

"I'd like to see you try," I snorted.

"Baby," Griffin sighed, walking over to my bed, and sitting down on the edge. "I fucked up. I know I did, and I'll never forgive myself for you getting captured, ever. But I've been dying a slow fucking death without you. I haven't even held you in my arms since you were taken, since you were hurt-" his voice broke off as he stared at me helplessly.

I threw back my blankets and climbed into Griffin's lap, burrowing into his chest as he breathed me in, holding me gently in his arms.

"Is it okay to touch you?" he asked, his eyes wet as he looked over my shoulder at my bare back.

"Yes, I'm almost completely healed," I assured Griffin as he ran his fingers over my skin tenderly. "No scars even, now that my wolf is back. Pretty amazing, considering what I went through." I instantly regretted my words as Griffin's eyes filled with guilt and anguish, tearing up.

"I can't believe I almost lost you," he choked. "Or that I let you run off by yourself. I was just so angry I couldn't think straight. Can you ever forgive me?"

"It wasn't your fault," I murmured, as Griffin leaned me back onto my bed and stretched out over me.

"When I felt your pain and couldn't get to you, a piece of me died, Finn. Then, when I finally found you, half-burnt in your father's arms and he wouldn't let me near you, I almost went out of my mind," Griffin whispered against my mouth, trailing his lips across my face and down my neck. "You are my life's breath, my heart, my soul, I love you so much, my little wolf."

"I love you too," I breathed against Griffin's lips as he brought his mouth back to mine.

"I can barely feel our bond, baby. I can't even take a full breath. Will you please let me back in?" Griffin begged; his eyes naked with grief.

"I didn't sever the mating bond, I don't even know how to do that," I protested.

"It's not severed," Griffin choked. "Don't even say that. It's muffled, like you're behind a padded wall."

"It's the pack cocoon. When my pack found me, they literally wrapped their bonds around me. It looks like a caterpillar cocoon in my head, and I can still see you, crackling orange and red, but you're on the outside of the cocoon," I admitted.

Griffin pulled away from me and sat up. "Where's Aksil's thread?"

"I'm not doing this with you," I replied tightly. "You haven't even apologized for accusing me of fucking him. Or do you still think I did?"

"I don't know," Griffin admitted hoarsely, letting his head drop down between his knees.

"Does it even matter if I tell you again that I never did anything with him?" I sat up and leaned my head against Griffin's.

"I don't know," Griffin repeated, lifting his head up, his eyes wet. "I can feel him inside your head, Finn," he choked. "In your heart. On the edges of our bond."

"Babe," I breathed. "It's not like that. I don't know how to explain what it is to you, but it's not like it is with us. You're my mate. I know it down to my core. I love you and I feel you as a part of me. It's true, I'm connected to Aksil for some reason, but it's different than our connection."

"Yeah, it's different alright, it's stronger," Griffin growled.

"It's not."

"Look me in the eyes and tell me exactly how it feels to you. The truth."

"It's not stronger."

"Tell me how it feels."

"You're not going to like my answer," I whispered, hearing Anya's voice in my ear.

"At least I'll know the truth."

"It feels parallel," I admitted softly.

"Parallel? To our mating bond?"

"I don't know how else to explain it."

"You don't know how else to explain it?" Griffin shoved me back onto the bed and climbed over me. "You're my mate, not his," he rasped, drawing my bottom lip between his teeth.

I fisted my fingers in Griffin's hair, biting him back in a bruising kiss as we wrestled in a tangle of limbs, pulling clothes off, desperate to feel skin against skin, the taste of each other's sweat on our tongues.

We rolled back and forth, each fighting the other to be on top, pinning arms to the bed as we nipped and sucked at skin, palming dicks with sweat-soaked hands, and groaning our need in each other's ears.

Griffin pushed my knees to my chest, spreading the pre-cum from my leaking dick over the opening of my ass and working a finger inside as I writhed beneath him.

"I want you so wet, I slide right in, like your ass was made for my dick," Griffin growled, easing his finger out and searching the bed for his discarded jeans.

"You brought lube? Pretty presumptuous." I nipped at Griffin's shoulder as he leaned over me, pulling a mini bottle of lube out of his jeans' pocket.

"Oh, I was fucking this ass, baby, as soon as I got here, lube or no lube. This is my ass, no one else's." Griffin growled low in his throat, rolling me over onto my stomach.

Okay, so it was going to be this kind of a fuck, I sighed to myself in tender exasperation, as Griffin pulled me up on all fours and shoved his lubed-slicked dick in my ass with a soft groan of satisfaction.

"My ass," Griffin growled again, into the back of my neck, fisting my hair as he drove into me. "My dick." He reached under me, jerking me off hard and fast to the rhythm of his dick driving into my ass, until I shot my load all over his hand while he pumped his out inside me.

"Fuck, Griff, you pounded my ass," I exhaled, collapsing onto the bed in a post orgasmic daze.

"I'm sorry, baby," he murmured, pulling his T-shirt off, and using it to clean us up before he pulled me into his arms. "I didn't hurt your back, did I?" he asked in concern.

"No, I told you, I'm all healed up." I snuggled into Griffin's arms and tucked my head against his chest.

"I couldn't be gentle," Griffin admitted guiltily. "I just needed to make you mine again."

"I mean, I wasn't not yours before you pounded into my ass like a fucking jackhammer," I teased. "I was still your mate, am still your mate. We're just working through stuff..."

"Are we done working through stuff?" Griffin asked quietly, his lips in my hair.

"I don't think so, babe, I'm sorry," I whispered, looking up into Griffin's dark gold wolf eyes.

"I know I fucked up," Griffin said gruffly. "It was my fault you were kidnapped; you were hurt."

"It's not about that, Griff. There's so much I have to figure out about my life now, and what happened to me when I was a kid. I'm just learning my origin story, after 15 years of living in the dark. I'm reunited with my family, and I think I might be part of some larger witch/werewolf prophecy, so there's that too."

"Of course you are," Griffin groaned, pressing his lips to my forehead.

"And there's still the Aksil thing to figure out," I murmured tentatively.

"There's nothing to figure out with him," Griffin growled. "He left the pack anyway."

"What do you mean, he left the pack?" I exclaimed, pulling away from Griffin and sitting up.

"He left. He didn't sever ties, not that he really has any, anyway, and he can come back if he wants to, I didn't kick him out," Griffin replied gruffly. "But he left. Didn't say where he was going or if he'd be back. He just told Ziri he needed a change of scenery and suggested Rahim take over for him as pack enforcer. I gave Rahim the job before I left. He and Anya are holding down the fort until we return."

"Until you return," I said slowly, crossing my arms.

"Until we return," Griffin repeated, narrowing his eyes.

"I don't know what I'm doing for a while, Griff," I said quietly. "I just got my family and pack back and I'm still trying to figure everything out. And you have a territory war going on across the country you have to deal with as Alpha of your pack."

"I'm your family and pack, Finn," Griffin replied, looking stricken.

"So are they, and I just got them back."

"So, what, you're just going to stay here and join The Sequoia Pack?"

"I never left The Sequoia Pack. I was kidnapped, Griffin. This is my pack and my family. I have a father here and brothers and a sister and packmates, just like you do back home. You of all people should understand how that feels, especially having lost Cian. You're an Alpha. Your pack is your family."

"You're my family!" Griffin yelled back, his eyes flashing. "For fuck's sake, Finn, you're my mate. Don't you miss me?" he asked helplessly.

"Of course I miss you. But I didn't just leave my pack and move over to yours when I met you, Griff. I was ripped away from them. Remember what it felt like when Cian severed his pack ties? You said it was horrible, that it left this aching void in all of you. Well, that's how my pack felt when I was taken from them and that's how I felt all these years, I just didn't know what it was."

"That's how I feel with you gone."

"But I'm not gone, I'm just trying to understand who I am and where I come from."

"Can we talk about this tomorrow? I just got you back and I can't fight with you anymore. I just want to hold you and smell you and listen to your heart beat next to mine," Griffin sighed wearily.

"Yes." I crawled back into Griffin's arms and snuggled into his chest, pulling the blankets around us. "I'm yours, I promise. And you don't need to pound my ass into the bed or drag me back home with you to prove it."

"Hmfh," Griffin snorted in disagreement, closing his eyes, and drifting off to sleep.

23

When I woke up the next morning, Griffin was still fast asleep, sprawled on his back beside me, his skin warm, and his hair an adorable mess I couldn't resist running my fingers through. He looked irresistibly sexy and vulnerable at the same time, and my body felt at peace for the first time in weeks, just having him near me.

I brushed my lips across his in a butterfly kiss, waking him gently, as I trailed my lips down his body, rubbing my face through the tangle of hair on his chest and breathing him in deeply. Our scents had started to merge, and I could smell myself, rich and fertile with a hint of the sea mixed in with his snowy, pine forest smell.

Griffin chuckled softly as I continued to rub my face down his body, pushing my nose into every crevice, digging my forehead into his skin as I pushed against him. I wanted to roll in him like a pile of leaves, until all I could smell was my scent on his body.

"What's so funny?" I demanded, raising my face up to meet Griffin's gaze as his shoulders shook with laughter.

"You're marking me," he grinned, tangling his fingers in my hair, and pulling me back up his body.

"I guess I am," I grinned back.

"Good morning." Griffin ran his fingers across my face, tracing the outline of my jaw. "It's nice to see your face in the morning light, I've missed it."

"I've missed yours." I copied Griffin's movements, tracing his jaw in time with his fingers as they trailed across my face.

"So, this is your childhood room, huh? Where the formation of the mysterious Finn began. Where are the Britney posters and the disco ball?" Griffin teased, looking around my room. "It looks more like my room than what I would have thought yours would be like," he laughed.

"I was ten when I was last here." I swatted Griffin's head, rolling off him and curling into his side. "I wasn't in my Britney disco ball phase yet."

"Do you remember everything now?" Griffin laced his fingers through mine, bringing my hand to his lips. "From before you were taken and after?"

"Yeah, I remember everything now," I sighed. "All the happy times I had here with my family and pack. It was a good life, Griff, filled with love and joy. I remember my mom the clearest. I can even still smell her scent, she smelled like the ocean. She was from a Pacific coastal pack here in Northern California, before she mated my father and joined the Sequoia Pack."

"She was Yurok Pack," Griffin breathed, staring at me in awe. "I can smell it in you now, the redwoods mixed with the ocean. Holy shit, Finn, you're fucking werewolf royalty, descended from the two most powerful packs on the West Coast."

"Yeah." I laughed faintly. "And I didn't even know I was a wolf. I was pumping Anya for werewolf history, when it turns out, I'm descended from the longest line of wolves in existence. I guess that's why the witch couldn't strip my wolf from me when she tried. That's why she bound it instead, and even the binding didn't take right away."

"What do you mean?"

"After the witch bound my wolf, I kept searching for him, I still knew he was in there, even though I couldn't feel him, so she added another layer to the spell. She convinced me my family and pack had cast me out and taken my wolf from me because I was bad and unwanted. I think that was the final layer of the spell I really had to break through."

"I'm so sorry for everything you've gone through, baby," Griffin murmured. "I couldn't imagine losing my family, my pack, my wolf; it's who I am."

"It's weird, because I was so young when I was taken, I grew up without my wolf or my pack, so it's like re-learning how to walk or talk, almost," I admitted.

"I can feel your strength pouring into you; it's like you're a different person, a different wolf, now that you know who you actually are," Griffin mused, staring at me thoughtfully. "And you've never marked me up like that before."

"Yeah, I feel different," I admitted. "More confident and grounded now that I know who I am and where I come from, but I'm still me," I added reassuringly, biting my lip as I met Griffin's thoughtful gaze.

"Of course you're still you." Griffin's eyes widened in surprise. "Did you think it would bother me?" he asked. "Did you think I wouldn't be happy for you?" his voice caught, thick with hurt.

"I didn't know," I confessed, choking up. "I've gone through so many changes since we mated, first discovering my wolf, now my pack, it's a lot to digest, for both of us."

"It is, but I want to be a part of it, to help you with it, please don't shut me out," Griffin said quietly.

"I stopped looking for my wolf, Griff." I buried my head against Griffin's chest. "I just gave up; I gave up and I lost fifteen years of my life. What if I did this to myself?" I asked him, lifting wet eyes up to meet his gaze.

"You didn't give up, Finn. That was your wolf protecting you.

I told you that after you found him again, back in Maine," Griffin reminded me softly. "Your wolf is so strong, Finn. He resisted being stripped from you by witchcraft and he sacrificed himself to protect your spirit. He let you bury him away all this time, so you didn't lose yourself to the trauma of being raped as a child. He stayed underground so you could heal."

"You're saying I didn't repress him, he stayed hidden on his own?" I asked, confused.

"I don't think it was James calling out your wolf that made you face him," Griffin said softly. "I think that was just the trigger; I think you were finally ready after we mated."

"You mean after I gave you my ass."

"I mean, not literally," Griffin laughed. "But I think when you offered yourself to me, you were telling your wolf you were okay, you were strong enough to face everything now."

"When did you become the fucking Dr. Phil of the werewolf world?" I stared back at Griffin with my heart in my eyes.

"Hey, I've always been deep, you've just never noticed because all you've ever cared about was getting in my pants," Griffin scoffed.

"Me?" I exclaimed. "You tried to fuck me over the porch railing the morning after we met!"

"You tried to fuck me in the bar parking lot the next day in front of half my pack," Griffin returned smugly. "And you were all over my dick the moment you met me, don't even try and deny it. I could smell your lust across the driveway when I stepped in front of your truck."

"I did want to lick you as soon as I saw you," I admitted with a sigh.

"All over my dick," Griffin repeated with a tender growl, rolling over on top of me to show me exactly how much he wanted my dick right back.

No one looked surprised when Griffin came down to breakfast with me an hour later, so my family must have heard him pounding my ass all night and into the morning. They all welcomed him, and seemed genuinely curious to get to know him, not just because he was my mate, but because he'd built quite a reputation for himself as the Alpha of the Northwoods Pack.

"How's the pack?" my father asked Griffin as we dug into our Huevos Racheros. Everyone in the Sequoia Pack took turns cooking the pack meals, and my sister, Ali, made the best Mexican food, so I knew she was on today as soon as I took a bite of my eggs.

"They're fine. We had a little scuffle I had to attend to when you left. That's why it took me a little longer than I expected to come here, but it's handled," Griffin replied over a mouthful of his eggs.

"What's going on over there, another power grab coming in from Canada?" my brother Collin asked.

"Yeah, it was a small pack out of Quebec. They were looking to expand their territory and figured they'd try and push us out instead of fighting one of the other Canadian packs, since we're pretty small but hold such a big territory. We knew an attack was coming, and were getting ready for the fight, we just didn't know which pack it was, and hadn't anticipated them grabbing Finn." Griffin's eyes were dark with self-recrimination.

"You knew an attack was coming and you left your mate unguarded?" my father asked Griffin quietly.

"Yes," Griffin admitted, holding my father's gaze.

"That's not exactly what happened," I sighed, slipping an arm around Griffin's shoulders as I felt his guilt and misery seeping out of his mate bond. "He had me under suffocating guard 24/7, but we got into a fight in the middle of the night when I was at home with him in the lodge, and I took off on my own. That's when they grabbed me."

"You let him leave on his own?" my father asked Griffin incredulously.

"Must have been some fight," my brother Len muttered under his breath.

"You let your anger take precedence over my son's safety." My father eyed Griffin with an unreadable expression.

"Yes," Griffin admitted, still holding my father's gaze. "I went after Finn shortly after he left, but it was too late. They'd already grabbed him. I will regret letting him leave unescorted for the rest of my life."

"For the record, before you torture Griffin any further over this, I threatened him and told him he'd never see me again if he sent anyone with me when I left."

"It doesn't matter, Finn. I'm your mate and your Alpha, and I never should have left you unprotected for a second. I bear the responsibility for what happened, and I accept it," Griffin broke in, his voice thick with grief.

"You make it sound so simple, so black and white, but it wasn't," I protested, taking Griffin's hand.

"You're very young, Griffin." My father said. "I think you learned a valuable lesson from what happened with Finn, and I hope you will never allow your youthful pride and arrogance to endanger another one of your packmates again, but you still have a lot of growing up to do before you are ready to be my son's mate."

"Dad," I sputtered, choking on my juice as Griffin stiffened beside me. "We're already mates. I may not be up on all my wolfy stuff, but I know that's not something you can take back. We're mated, marks and all." I pulled down my T-shirt to expose my mating mark.

"I'm aware he claimed you with his bite, and I heard enough of his visit last night to know you've consummated your mating, my little pup. But sex and a bite do not make someone worthy of being your mate," my father replied, in what'd I'd come to recognize as his deadly serious Alpha voice.

"Oh my god, I want to die," I whispered to my sister Ali, my face heating up. "Kill me now, dad just said he heard me having sex." I covered my face, hiding against Ali's shoulder.

"The whole lodge did." Ali patted my head. "But it sounded really hot, so you must be a good match."

"I know I'm not worthy of Finn," Griffin broke in, his voice tight with guilt and sorrow. "But I love him deeply, he's my mate, and I pledge my life I will spend every day trying to be worthy of him."

"You failed the first test, I'm not leaving him in your hands on a chance you'll pass the next one," my father replied. "I told you in Canada, I think you have a lot of potential, but you also have a lot of growing to do, young wolf. You came into your Alpha role young and unseasoned, and you'll make a lot of mistakes along the way as you figure things out. All Alphas do. I'm just not going to let my son get hurt along the way."

"I went after him. I did. I knew I shouldn't have let him go alone after he left," Griffin protested miserably.

"But you did let him go. You chose your young, foolish pride over my son and he was kidnapped and almost killed."

"Yes," Griffin rasped.

"They put him in a cage and burnt him with silver!" my father roared, slamming his fist down on the table.

"I know." Griffin's voice broke as he lowered his head to the table in shame and sorrow.

"Next time you want to put your pride or jealousy before my son's safety, you remember the sight of his burnt skin, the smell of his charred fur in the air," my father bit out, his voice tight with rage.

"It's imprinted on my memory already," Griffin choked, lifting red, anguished eyes up to meet my father's burning gaze. "The smell fills my dreams at night."

"You have no idea, the tests that lie before you with my son as your mate. I will rip the mating bond out of him myself and burn your mark from his body, if you do not give me your pledge as an Alpha on the lives of your pack that you will never put yourself before my son again, no matter the circumstance."

"I give you my pledge." Griffin dropped to his knees without hesitation, baring his neck to my father.

"I accept your pledge as his mate, but not as his Alpha. He stays in my pack for now," my father announced before turning and walking out of the room.

"Now you see why I don't have a mate, or even a fucking boyfriend or girlfriend," Ali exhaled. "I'm too scared to bring anyone onto pack land, forget about home for dinner."

"I'm sorry," I whispered to Griffin, still reeling from my father's speech.

"Don't you dare apologize," he choked, pulling me against him and burying his face against my neck. "Everything your father said is true. I did put my pride before you, and I failed you as a mate, but also as your Alpha."

24

"The witches, wolves, and vampires came here from Europe with the colonists to settle the land." My father's rich, deep voice filled the room.

"When you said you wanted to talk to us, I didn't know you were going to tell us a bedtime story," I teased, sprawling out on the couch beside Griffin. My father had left us alone for most of the week to reconnect, but he'd finally summoned us to his study for a serious talk.

"This is way more important than a bedtime story," my father chided, his gaze fixed and serious. "Pay attention, both of you."

"Sorry." I sat up respectfully.

"The witches, wolves, and vampires were seeking the same thing as the colonists," my father continued. "They wanted freedom from the ruling packs, covens, and lairs. They wanted to live unfettered, out of reach of the controlling arms of the European supernatural monarchy. And the monarchy allowed it, because they were few and far between, scrappy little groups without much power to speak of, and no threat to their rule. But as time passed, the ones who came here found others who had come before them. Native

American witches, wolves, and vampires who had lived on the land long before they arrived, and others from Africa, Latin America, India, Asia, and the Middle East. They merged their packs, covens, and lairs, increasing their power."

"And I'm guessing the monarchy in Europe didn't like that?" I asked.

"No, they didn't," my father said.

"But it was more complex than that," Griffin broke in. "My father talked to me about it a lot before he died, preparing me to take over as Alpha. The thing the monarchy feared the most was the harmony that was forming between the witches and wolves here in the U.S."

"What do you mean?" I asked.

"Each group has always had a unique weakness, perhaps nature's way of balancing out the supernatural population," my father explained. "For vampires, it's sunlight, only the elders can walk in the daylight, and they lose many of their newborns to the sun. For the witches, it's the vampires. Something in their blood calls out to them, and they are vampires most favored prey."

"What about the wolves? What's our weakness?" I asked.

"Fertility," my father replied softly, his voice tinged with sadness. "A female wolf only has a 10-year fertility cycle every hundred years, starting at age 25, and if they shift even once during their pregnancy, they lose their pup."

"Did you and mom lose pups before we were born? Is that why me, Ali, and the boys are so young?"

"Yes." My father's eyes clouded over as he drifted away, momentarily lost in a memory of long ago. "Female wolves were lucky if they had one pup every hundred years until we struck a deal with the witches. It was something they were never willing to do in Europe. We offered protection from the vampires in exchange for potions that suppressed a female wolf's shift during pregnancy."

"So, the wolves and witches formed an alliance, and the

European rulers didn't like that?" I asked.

"The ruling families in Europe feared an alliance between any of the groups more than anything, because as individual groups we didn't have enough power to declare independence, but if even two groups united, they would be strong enough to completely sever ties."

"But then the wolves and witches suddenly started fighting," Griffin added. "My father said while he could never quite prove it, he was positive the strife that was sowing between them was coming from Europe."

"Yes," my father agreed. "There were rumors of betrayals, potions that didn't work, pups who were lost, vampire attacks on covens that were left unprotected, until the witches and wolves became as divided again as they were in the rest of the world."

"Does this have something to do with why I was kidnapped, and this prophecy thing you mentioned when we first got back here?" I asked nervously.

"Yes," my father replied. "About a hundred years after the alliance between the witches and wolves was dissolved, rumors of a prophecy started floating around. The rumors stated that a witch and wolf would be born with entwined destinies, and they would come together and reunite the two sides."

"A witch and a wolf?" I echoed. "Wait, I think Anya mentioned this story to me."

"Everyone knows this prophecy, we grew up on it, like a wolf fairy tale. Are you saying Finn is the wolf from the prophecy?" Griffin demanded, his eyes narrowing.

"There are those who believe he is," my father allowed.

"That's why I was kidnapped and dumped in the Bronx; witchbound?" I exclaimed. "To keep me from fulfilling some prophecy with a witch?"

"The prophecy states the witch and wolf are born as mates," Griffin said flatly, staring my father down.

"There are many versions and interpretations of the story,"

my father replied carefully. "The relationship between the wolf and witch, isn't clear. What the prophecy states clearly, is what they will do together. That is what the monarchy fears, that they will unite the witches and wolves, or even worse, find a way to bring all three sides together."

"I've heard the story say the witch is also part wolf, born to a witch mother and wolf father." Griffin held my father's gaze.

"Yes," my father agreed, his face blank.

"Okay, what am I missing here," I broke in, staring back and forth between my father and Griffin as the air crackled with tension and Griffin's eyes began to darken with awareness.

"No fucking way!" Griffin suddenly exploded, shaking his head at my father.

"We don't know anything for sure," my father said quietly.

"Except werewolves and witches don't mix. Hybrids are immune to the Alpha bond, so they can't really ever become a part of a pack," Griffin bit out, his eyes dark with rage.

"Is anyone going to tell me what you guys are talking about?" I demanded. "I feel like a five-year-old kid whose parents are spelling out all the bad words in the middle of a fight."

"Aksil is the witch from the prophecy," Griffin spat, his eyes flashing wolf gold with barely restrained fury.

"But Aksil is a wolf," I said slowly.

"He's a hybrid. That's why he's never completely bonded to the pack. He's immune to the Alpha bond. Safiya and Badis found him as a young, feral, wolf pup, alone without a pack. Something must have happened to his parents, and he was left all alone to fend for himself because he didn't belong to a coven or a pack."

"I don't understand," I said, as Griffin gazed at me with haunted eyes.

"He must have known who you were the moment he felt you in the pack, and he planted roots. He planted roots in your bond, and you let him," Griffin choked.

"I didn't know," I whispered helplessly.

"You knew!" Griffin roared back in anguish. "You recognized him in your heart, and you pulled him inside you!"

"Of course I didn't know! I still don't even know what you're fully talking about right now!" I protested.

"These are the tests I warned you of, young Alpha. And you gave me your pledge on the lives of your pack. My son before yourself, always," my father reminded Griffin with a low growl.

"I love your son with my entire soul, and I will always put his life before mine, but I can't even look at him right now," Griffin choked, turning, and leaving the room.

I rose to go after Griffin and my father placed a hand on my shoulder. "Give him a few minutes," he suggested gently.

"Is he right? Did I betray him? Did I plant Aksil inside me, knowing I had some pre-destined connection to him?" I whispered to my father in horror, sinking down onto the couch beside him. "I'm so confused, what is Griffin even accusing me of exactly?"

"There are some who interpret the prophecy as the witch and wolf being mates," my father explained. "The actual language of the prophecy is two souls born as one. Some interpreted that to mean twins, and for a while, it was said that the rulers were searching for any twins born to a wolf and witch pair. No one actually knows the full meaning of the prophecy, or who the destined pair are."

"So, I might not even be a part of this prophecy?" I exclaimed. "I might have been kidnapped and witch-bound for fifteen years out of a case of mistaken identity?"

"The witch who came for you was certain you are the one, that's all I know. That, and you do have a strange connection to a wolf who can't seem to fully bond to his pack," my father added gently. "He was the first string you reached for after me when I started weaving your cocoon."

"So, you're telling me Griffin has every right to hate me, and I basically have cheated on him, even though I didn't even realize it?"

"Oh Finn, my son, you are a pawn in an ancient war."

"How do the vampires play into all this? It was a vampire who sniffed my wolf out of me."

"The vampires hate the witches, they resent the call of their blood, and the last thing they want is for them to align with the wolves against them."

"So, how come it was a witch who came after me and not a vampire?"

"The vampires here have been searching for the prophecy pair as long as the ruling parties in Europe, the monarchy just discovered you first and sent a witch to dispose of you. If the vampires had found you first, you wouldn't still be alive."

"Why do you think the witch let me live?" I asked my father softly, wincing as my mate bond flared with Griffin's pain.

"The witches have been saving wolves' babies for centuries with their potions, I think it was more instinctual for the witch to spare your life, than to take it, especially when your mother offered her blood in exchange," my father replied quietly.

"I still don't really understand all of this," I admitted.

"We've had enough revelations for one night. Why don't you go find your mate."

"I don't know what to say to him," I confessed.

"He's a young Alpha, trying to manage his pack and a threat to his mate claim, Finn. There's so much power, strength, and need to dominate running through him right now, this kind of challenge to his authority, to his mate bond, it's a lot to take. And you are a young, traumatized wolf, who was cut off from your pack, only recently reunited with your wolf. There are going to be missteps along the way for both of you. Griffin is just scared of losing you and angry because Aksil planted roots before your mating bond has even had a chance to grow any roots of its own."

"That's my fault." I was stricken as the full weight of what I'd done to Griffin sunk in. "When I was in the cage and the Levesque

Pack was burning me with silver, it triggered trauma from my past, and it was like I was twelve years old again," I choked. "I latched onto Aksil's thread and pulled it deep inside me."

"Oh, my son, my little wolf." My father pulled me into his arms, holding me tightly against him. "I'm so sorry I failed to protect you. I combed the earth for you, coast to coast, after you were taken, continent to continent, but the concealing spell was too powerful. I couldn't smell a trace of your wolf anywhere."

"People hurt me dad, after the witch took me. They burned me and locked me away. A man raped me," I cried against my father's chest, finally letting all my pain out.

"Give it to me," my father whispered back. "Let your pack carry it for you, my brave, strong wolf. Give us your pain, let us carry it now. You've carried it long enough."

My father slipped into my head gently, walking back through my memories, through all the years I spent on the street alone, back to the shed where I was raped, to the dark closets I was locked in, the cigarette burns along my rib cage, the moment the witch bound my wolf with my mother's blood and severed my pack ties.

Howling a song of grief and rage, he spread my memories out through the pack, and the air filled with my pack's mournful answering cry as they each took one to carry for me. My father saved the memory of my most recent kidnapping and torture for Griffin, and his deep, heart-wrenching howl was the loudest of all, as my father passed it to him.

"You don't have to say anything to him now," my father said quietly.

"You didn't have to do that to Griffin."

"He needed to see his own culpability," my father replied, his voice tight. "Next time he wants to blame you for Aksil's roots, he can remember it was his pride that put you in that cage and almost cost you your life and be grateful you had Aksil to latch onto."

I found Griffin sitting outside, staring into the forest.

"I can't believe I let you go off by yourself that night. I can't believe I put my arrogance and jealousy before your safety," Griffin whispered, holding his head in his hands.

"I'm coming home with you tomorrow." I walked over to Griffin, sliding into his lap, and wrapping my arms around his waist.

"Everything that happened to you was my fault," Griffin choked, pulling me against his chest tightly and pressing his lips into my hair.

"It wasn't." I lifted my head to meet Griffin's wet eyes. "I'm sorry your mate is a part of an ancient prophecy. You must have really sucky luck or fucked up karma to get stuck with me."

"Fuck Aksil." Griffin brushed his lips across mine. "You're my mate, not his, and the prophecy can go fuck itself."

25

"So, should I call you Prophecy Boy now? Or Two Mates?" Anya threw her arms around me and hugged me tightly.

"Really????" I rolled my eyes at Anya and brought my coffee cup up to my face to inhale the steam before taking a sip. We got back to Maine late the night before, and I still wasn't fully awake.

"Too soon to make prophecy jokes? Or was it the two mates comment?" Anya raised her eyebrow.

"Why don't you ask Griffin?" I snorted.

"I'm not insane! You think I'd make jokes to Griffin about the prophecy? I'm already afraid he's going to gut me just for being related to Aksil! I was afraid to even make eye contact with Griffin when he briefed me on your situation."

"Do you even care that I was kidnapped, tortured, and reunited with my family and lost wolf pack all within the last few weeks?"

"Of course I care, Wolfboy, but it's the kind of drama I've come to expect from you... I was almost killed by Kris Munroe, and have you asked me about that?" Anya huffed.

"Griff told me she tried to slit your throat when the Levesque wolves ambushed the pack. You totally deserved that one. I saw her coming a million miles away, but you just had to live out your Charlie's Angels fantasy..."

"I mean, it was kind of worth it..." Anya grinned. "She totally lived up to the hype in bed."

"Of course she did, idiot! She was a legit undercover agent, a mole, a secret assassin."

"And here you go with the drama..."

"Did she or did she not, fuck your brains out and then try to slit your throat when you weren't looking?"

"Well, when you put it like that..." Anya huffed.

"Griff told me you took her out in two moves..."

"Yeah, she was better in bed then in battle." Anya grinned.

"Did Molly give my job away again while I was being kidnapped?"

"No, but only because no one applied. I'm pretty sure she stuck her stupid napkin sign on the door again, though."

"What the fuck? That woman has no sense of loyalty."

"None," Anya agreed. "Plus, Lillian stopped coming in while you were gone. Griffin made her stay at the lodge under lock and key after the last attack, so Molly's pissed about that."

"So, you don't think I'll have to barter to get my job back this time, or you do?"

"I mean, I doubt she's going to just hand it back over..."

"God, she's such a bitch!"

"Why are the beds in your pack lodge more comfortable than ours?" my sister Ali called out, yawning as she padded into the kitchen.

"Holy shit, Wolfboy, you have a fucking twin?" Anya gaped at Ali.

"She's 10 months older actually..."

"She's you with tits and a better ass! I mean, she's wearing fucking Bat Girl Underoos! I'm pretty sure I've seen you in that same outfit."

"You have not! Those were Wolverine boxers. And my sister's ass is not better than mine!"

"Um, standing right here. You know I can totally hear you, right?" Ali huffed. "Even if I didn't have supersonic wolf hearing, I'd have to be deaf not to hear you talking about me right in front of my face."

"She said supersonic! Oh my god, you say supersonic, like all the time. Twins for sure."

"Is she having a seizure?" Ali asked me as Anya continued to gape at her.

"No, I'm not having a fucking seizure, but I see you have your brother's smart mouth to go with his fashion sense."

"Wow, she's a real charmer, huh?" my sister laughed, snagging a piece of bacon off my plate. "Where'd you find her, the DMV?"

"That was actually kind of funny," Anya grinned at Ali. "Wait until you meet his boss at the bar. That wolf, you'd definitely find at the DMV."

"FYI, you're so not fucking my sister," I warned Anya. "She can do way better than a wolf who fell for Kris Munroe's little act."

"You fucked Kris Munroe? I would have totally gone for Sabrina Duncan." Ali shook her head at Anya, perching her Underoo clad ass on the edge of the kitchen table beside me, and stealing the rest of the bacon off my plate.

"So, what are you doing here anyway, Batgirl? Just in town for a little visit?" Anya narrowed her eyes at my sister suspiciously.

"Sure, something like that." Ali grinned back at her.

"My father sent her. He doesn't trust Griffin to protect me," I sighed. "You can imagine how well that conversation went over with Griff."

"He doesn't trust the Alpha of the pack to protect his mate, but he trusts Superhero Barbie?" Anya stared at me in shock.

"I'm the Sequoia Pack enforcer, sweet cheeks." Ali smiled sweetly at Anya, baring her teeth.

"Will wonders never cease..." Anya murmured, baring her own teeth back at Ali.

"Okay, so if you bitches are done with your little dick measuring contest, I'd like to go get my job back."

"This should be good," Anya rolled her eyes as I stood up. "Go get dressed, Wolfboy, I'll be waiting by the door."

"I've got him, you can go do your thing." Ali smiled sweetly at Anya, her eyes flashing wolf.

"Listen, little girl, I get that you think you're hot shit and everything, in your superhero Underoos, but Finn is under my protection here. He's in my pack and he's my responsibility," Anya said hotly.

"Actually, he's in my pack. He answers to our father, who is his Alpha, not Griffin, who let him get kidnapped," Ali snarled. "And he's under my protection, not yours, *little pup*. Why don't you go get your blanky and finger paints and go back to pre-school? How old are you anyway, fourteen?"

"Twenty-three, and I'm the Alpha's second, so you can fuck the fuck off," Anya snapped back at Ali, turning questioning eyes to me. "You're not in our pack anymore?" she asked quietly. "I can still feel you in the pack bonds, though."

"He's still your Alpha's mate." Ali gentled her tone. "So, he's still connected to you and the pack, but Griffin isn't his Alpha anymore. You guys fucked up. Your Alpha fucked up, and we're not taking any chances with one of our own. We lost him once and we're not losing him again."

"You're right," Anya agreed, her voice small and thick with regret. "We did fail you, Finn." She met my gaze with anguished eyes. "I'm so sorry."

"Enough with all the drama. No one failed me. I'm a big boy, I made my own decision to take off, and I threatened Griff not to send anyone with me. I take full responsibility for my own kidnapping. Can we just move on and go get my job back before Molly gives it away to another Canadian spy?"

"Is Molly the bitch who belongs in the DMV?" Ali asked with a grin, breaking up the tension that had settled over us.

"She sure is, and I don't think the DMV would even hire her," I sighed, heading off to my room to get battle ready.

"What the fuck are you wearing?" Anya gawked at me when I came back downstairs.

"Moll's always giving me shit about my clothes, so I thought I'd dress a little more professionally this time. What's wrong with my outfit?"

"I mean, I don't even know where to start, but there's no way I'm missing this shitshow. Batgirl can escort you in your truck if she wants, but I'm following behind for this."

"Al, back me up here. I look professional, right?" I turned to my sister as she walked in the room. She'd traded her Underoos for a pair of low riding cut off jean shorts and one of my *Buffy* t-shirts, which she'd knotted in front to reveal a perfectly chiseled set of abs and a pierced belly button with a gold arrow sticking through it.

"Sure, baby brother," my sister grinned, taking in my white button-down shirt and khaki shorts. "The dress shoes are a nice touch too." She stifled a laugh.

"They're Griffs, I don't own anything besides Vans and Chucks," I groaned helplessly. "Do I look like I raided my daddy's closet?"

"No comment," Anya muttered, looking mildly horrified.

When we pulled up to the bar, I could see Molly inside. It was almost noon, and she was starting to open up.

"Thanks, but I'm good. I've got all the Bibles I need, sir." Molly called to me when I walked into the bar.

"What?"

"You're a Bible salesman now, right? Only reason I can think of you'd be dressed like that, unless you've become a Jehovah's Witness, maybe? Very nice fellas, they come by once a year with pamphlets. Way better manners than you have, so if you are a Jehovah's Witness now, you may want to work on your snark. No one likes anyone proselytizing to them with an attitude."

"I was trying to be professional!" I sputtered.

"In shorts and tuxedo shoes?" Molly raised her eyebrows.

"They're tuxedo shoes?" I groaned. "I thought they looked awfully shiny."

"Karyn and Toby had a black-tie wedding last year. Griffin bought them for his tux. I helped Lillian find them for him."

"Okay, fine. So, I don't own any professional clothes, but this isn't an office, it's a dive bar in rural Maine. It's not like there's a dress code here or anything!"

"I see you also brought a whole entourage with you this time, are you planning a Coyote Ugly routine for the bar?" Molly swept her eyes over Ali and Anya, lurking behind me.

"This is my sister, Ali. You may have heard I was kidnapped, tortured, and then reunited with my wolf pack and family..." my voice trailed off as Molly continued to stare at me, unimpressed.

"Did you at least bring any muffins this time, or just the tuxedo shoes and the backup dancers?" she asked, totally ignoring my little speech.

"I forgot them in the car..." I said meekly, running back outside to the truck to quickly change into the clothes I saw Ali stuff in the back on our way out.

"I need you to go down the street and buy some muffins from the café," I told my sister breathlessly, stripping down to my underwear in the bar parking lot and changing into the orange and pink striped board shorts and turquoise t-shirt my sister had grabbed for me.

"I probably could have gone with a different shirt choice." Ali laughed, giving me an 'oh well' shrug as I glanced down at my shirt and winced. *Wow Look At Me Adulting All Over The Place* was printed across the front in hot pink.

I stuffed my feet back into Griffin's tuxedo shoes with a sigh of defeat.

"You couldn't have brought me sneakers at least?"

"Be happy I brought you clothes at all. You were the one who went to beg for your job back looking like a serial killer."

"It was a button-down and khakis!" I yelled back.

"Khaki shorts," my sister corrected. "With tuxedo shoes..."

"Why are you still standing here? You were supposed to get me muffins for her."

"Not to interrupt or anything, but I thought Molly hates muffins," Anya broke in, taking my new outfit in with amusement as I turned to face her.

"That's right, she does hate muffins," I exhaled. "God, she's such a fucking bitch!"

"How about a pizza? It's almost lunchtime," my sister suggested, glancing at the pizza place across the street.

"Good idea. Plus, I'm still hungry. You ate all my bacon," I complained, elbowing my sister as we crossed the street with Anya trailing behind us.

"Are you going to follow us all day? Because it's a little creepy," Ali called back to Anya.

"Will you stop," I sighed, smacking my sister across the head, and linking my arm through Anya's. "She's my bff/bodyguard/drinking and dancing buddy. Leave her alone."

"She drinks while guarding you?" Ali shook her head in disgust.

"Griffin was there!" Anya protested as we walked into the pizza place.

"Oh, now I feel better," Ali snorted. "Griffin, the mate who let my brother get kidnapped..."

"Give it a rest," I sighed, when Anya winced. "The whole pack is already drowning in guilt over the whole thing. I can feel them wallowing in it, so just let it go, Al, okay?"

"Sure," she chirped in a suspiciously agreeable manner.

I ordered three different pizzas, not knowing what Molly liked. One pineapple, my personal favorite, one sausage and onions, because c'mon, it's sausage and onions, who doesn't like that? And a bacon and American cheese, cause, yum! I could eat that all day.

"Those are some weird pizzas," Anya whispered to Ali as we walked back to the bar.

"No, they're not," she scoffed. "What do you eat on your pizza?"

"Pepperoni, and I'm pretty sure Molly eats hers plain..."

"Plain? Who only eats plain pizza? That's like cereal without milk or ice cream without toppings!" I exclaimed.

"Not really," Anya muttered as we walked back into the bar.

"Took you a long time to get your muffins out of the car," Molly yelled as I walked back in.

"I did even better, I brought you lunch!" I beamed, setting my three pizzas down on the bar triumphantly.

"Huh." Molly looked at the pizzas suspiciously.

"Hungry?" I asked hopefully.

"I could eat," Molly grudgingly allowed, sweeping her eyes over my new outfit with a shake of her head.

"What is it with you and the shoes?" she sighed. "You're either not wearing any or you have something ridiculous on, like Griffin's slippers and now his tuxedo shoes."

"Pizza?" I spread the boxes across the bar, opening them up with a flourish.

"What on earth is on them?" Molly gawked, backing away in horror.

"Pineapple, sausage and onion, and bacon and American cheese..." my voice trailed off at her look of distaste.

"Who puts American cheese and bacon on a pizza? It's not a burger," Molly exclaimed. "And pineapple? If I wanted pineapple, I'd make myself a Piña Colada."

"I give up." I plopped down at the bar, helping myself to a slice of pineapple pizza. "Maybe I'll try selling Bibles, apparently, I have the outfit for it."

"You'll never find anyone around here who can tend bar like Finn, and you know it," Anya told Molly, grabbing a slice of bacon and American pizza. "He's New York City good. You're lucky you snagged him in the first place. Everyone loves him. His fucking dirty martinis are the shit, and who else are you going to get to strip on the bar top and entertain the customers after a long night?"

"Does that taste like a cheeseburger?" Molly asked Anya, ignoring her little speech, and watching her take a bite of her slice of pizza with interest.

"It kind of does, actually, but it's even better," Anya marveled. "Who would have thunk it, Wolfboy, your bizzarro pizza combo rocks! I'd fuck with this any day."

"Give me a slice," Molly growled, grabbing a piece of pizza out of the box, and taking a bite. "Tastes like what you crave after a night of long drinking," she mused as she chewed. "Get Lillian to come back and make this for the bar and you can have your job back." Molly grabbed the box of bacon pizza and walked off into the kitchen.

"Huh, and I would have thought the pineapple one would have swayed her for sure," Ali said, grabbing another pineapple slice.

"I don't think anyone on this coast eats pineapple pizza," I mumbled. "I never met anyone in New York who did. I should have known just from my pizza tastes that I was from California. That, and I never felt like I could find a good burrito anywhere."

"You definitely dress like you're straight off the Venice Beach boardwalk, no NYC vibes coming off of you," Anya wrinkled her nose. "Do you even own any black?"

"Maybe?" I shrugged.

"So, this was fun, what are we doing next?" Ali asked after we'd finished the pineapple pizza and moved onto the sausage and onion.

"Now we have to convince Lillian to come back to work at the bar with me and make cheeseburger pizza," I sighed, stuffing the empty pizza boxes into the trash behind the bar and leading the way out.

26

Aksil was waiting for me when we got back to the lodge. I sensed him inside as soon as we pulled up.

"Aksil's back," I told my sister.

"Oooh, your dark and stormy prophecy mate, I wonder what he wants," Ali chirped.

"Wow, great pep talk, I'm totally not ten times more nervous now," I groaned, climbing out of the truck.

"At least you're not still wearing your serial killer clothes," Ali choked on a laugh as I reluctantly stepped out of the truck and walked up to the lodge.

"Oh my god, the shoes," I hissed at Ali, feeling a full-blown panic attack start to come on.

"Kick them off," she hissed back, pushing me behind her.

I kicked Griffin's tuxedo shoes off and into the bushes as the door to the lodge swung open and my breath was suddenly sucked out of me.

Fuck, fuckety, fuck. The air was thick and moist with the promise of a coming storm, my skin burned from the lightning crackling around us, and I was momentarily paralyzed as Aksil's juniper and sandalwood scent washed over me. This was so not good.

"Shit, fuck, shit," I muttered, as the tall, dark, insanely hot wolf dressed in a fitted white T-shirt and jeans, stood in the lodge doorway drinking me in.

"So, you're the witch/wolf from the prophecy, huh? I'm Ali, your destined other half's sister," Ali grinned at Aksil, walking up to him and holding out her hand.

"Ah, the Sequoia Pack enforcer." Aksil breathed in deeply, taking Ali's hand. "Redwoods, with a slight hint of the ocean."

"So I've been told," Ali laughed. "Your other half is hiding behind me, in case you were wondering." She tossed me a, you're such a moron look over her shoulder before she walked into the lodge.

"Shall we walk?" Aksil asked, his dark eyes never leaving my face.

"Sure," I croaked. I'd meant it to come out breezily, but for some reason, my voice sounded strangled, like I was choking on a frog, and I blushed as we turned to walk into the woods.

We walked for a little in silence, stopping when the lodge was out of sight.

"I don't think it was supposed to happen this way." Aksil turned to face me as we made our way into the forest.

"What do you mean?"

"I believe we are the prophecy pair; we both feel it, but I don't think we were supposed to meet like this, at this time." Aksil's eyes drifted over my face and down the length of my body, before coming back up to meet my gaze.

"Well, nothing's really followed a normal trajectory for me so far, so you're probably right," I grimaced. "I've been kept from my wolf for the last fifteen years and just re-united with my family and pack, so my whole life is out of whack." I stared into the forest. "I didn't even know what I was missing until we crossed into Sequoia

Pack territory. The smell was so powerful, it hit me like a punch to the gut, and I suddenly knew I was home."

"You miss it."

"Yes," I admitted. "I just got it back and then I had to leave it behind again, so soon. But having Ali here helps."

"That's why your father sent her with you, to give you a piece of home to keep by your side."

"I thought he sent her for my protection," I laughed, suddenly realizing Aksil was right.

"Your father knows Griffin is perfectly capable of protecting his mate. He sent your sister with you, so you'd have a piece of your pack."

"Do you feel like you're a part of this pack? Does it hurt, not really being bonded to the pack? Is it lonely?"

"Not anymore." Aksil stepped forward, so close, I could feel his warm breath against my face.

"I don't know what our connection means, but Griffin is my mate," I whispered, lost in the dark heat of Aksil's gaze. "I love him."

"I know," he whispered back. "I feel it in you."

I stepped back from Aksil as my heart sped up and my balls swelled, heavy and aching below my swollen dick. "Maybe we're two parts of a whole like the prophecy says, but like siblings," I rasped.

"That must be it," Aksil agreed, his voice thick with amusement and heat, as he inhaled the scent of my arousal swirling around us.

"Or you were right earlier." I swallowed the lump in my throat, backing further away from Aksil as I willed my heart to slow down and my dick to shrivel up. "We weren't meant to meet yet. The prophecy is probably something that's supposed to come into effect in like two hundred years or something."

"I never said we weren't supposed to meet yet," Aksil corrected softly. "I believe we were supposed to meet earlier, little wolf."

"Earlier, like before me and Griffin?" My heart sank at Aksil's implication.

"I dreamed of you for a century before you came here, Grey, before you were even born. I saw your green eyes and felt your thread, pink and gold and shimmery, teasing and tugging at me, but I never knew what it meant, until I felt you cross over onto pack territory, the day you arrived at Cian's house."

"You're saying we were supposed to meet first, before me and Griffin?"

"Does it matter, either way?" Aksil asked, his voice weary. "You came here, mated Griffin, found your wolf, and here we are. This is all how it's supposed to play out now."

"But what about the prophecy? What if we're still supposed to unite the two sides?"

"Then I guess we will one day, little wolf," Aksil smiled faintly. "Today, I came to say good-bye."

"You can't leave the pack," I choked. "Your family loves you. The pack loves you."

"The pack loves me?" Aksil echoed; his eyes unreadable. "The whole pack?"

"Yes."

Aksil's bond flared and sparked inside me.

"I'm not leaving the pack, Grey, I'm just not staying here right now. It's a little too crowded, don't you think?"

"You don't have to leave," I protested, feeling Aksil's dark thread tug at me. "You can stay, and we'll figure it out. You were here first, this is your home, your pack, your family. Please don't leave because of me."

"You're so young, Finn." Aksil smiled at me faintly, his tone rueful. "I've waited a century to meet the grey wolf behind the green eyes in my dreams. I can wait another hundred years to see how it all plays out if I have to."

"You don't have to leave," I repeated, taking Aksil's hand. "If we are the prophecy pair, having my wolf bound for fifteen years may have altered our entwined destinies, but we're still connected. We're still a part of each other." It was the truth I'd been hiding from ever since we first met.

"My wolf is old and tired, Grey," Aksil ran his thumb over my palm gently. "He knows you belong to us, but he's willing to wait because he also knows no good will come from trying to claim someone who still loves another. I tried that once and it was a long twenty years." Aksil flashed a wan smile.

"So, this is good-bye, for now?" I held Aksil's dark gaze, feeling his thread loosen inside me.

"Yes, Grey, we are letting you go for now," Aksil whispered, reaching a hand to my face and trailing calloused fingertips across my lips. "For now, little wolf," he repeated, shifting in a lightning-fast blur, and bounding off into the forest.

A month passed, and Anya and Ali were still wrestling for control over me, but it was entertaining, and I got to hang with my two best girls all day, so I didn't interfere. Griffin, on the other hand, had a massive dick up his ass, and it wasn't mine, so I was pissed.

We barely saw each other outside the bedroom at night. And when we did, Griffin avoided me. He sat on the other side of the table during pack meals, busying himself with conversation amongst the pack, and rarely came into the bar to see me at night. I missed him desperately, and when I saw him teasing his packmates and touching them affectionately, it only hurt more.

Griffin was open, warm, kind, and loving with the pack, settling disputes in a firm but fair way, always softening his verdict with a touch or reassuring remark. He commanded the pack's respect because he gave them his, and I was getting sick and tired of him disrespecting me.

"Out with it!" I finally demanded, when I woke up for the third night in a row to find Griffin standing at our bedroom window staring out into the night. "You fuck me so hard each night, I can barely move the next day, but you don't stay in bed with me. You've barely slept a whole night in bed with me since we've been back here, and you don't touch me anymore unless you're marking me up and fucking me into the mattress. What the hell is going on with you, Griff?"

"I'm trying," Griffin said quietly.

"You're trying what? To push me away, to punish me for being a part of a prophecy I have no control over, to cheat us out of our time together?"

"Is that how you see it?" Griffin asked softly. "This is our time together until Aksil comes back, and everything after is his? He may not be around, Finn, but I still feel him inside your head. He's still part of the pack in his weird, semi-detached way, and I know he's out there somewhere, just waiting until the right time to swoop in and claim you so you two can run off and fulfill your fucking prophecy together."

"Babe," I sighed wearily. "Is that what's going on with you? You stand at the window brooding every night thinking about what's going to happen if Aksil decides to come back? I've got news for you; I'd run away with the mailman at this point. You've stopped running in the woods with me, you won't sit next to me at dinner or stop by the bar anymore. You're completely shutting me out, and it's total bullshit."

"You're telling me you don't think about it?" Griffin demanded.

"We don't even know what the stupid prophecy means. It's a fairytale, and just because someone decided I was the prophecy wolf and kidnapped me, doesn't make it true. I haven't talked to Aksil since he said good-bye to me last month. I think about you, not the prophecy."

"You think about me?"

"Yes. I wonder why the man I love, the wolf I'm mated to, barely seems to want to be around me anymore. I think about how when you fuck me now, it feels like you're trying to prove something, and I cry sometimes, after you leave in the morning, and I'm alone in bed with the feel of your cum in my ass and the cold sheets where you used to lie wrapped around me."

"You cry after I leave in the morning?" Griffin's voice caught and he turned around to gaze at me with haunted, yellow-wolf eyes.

"Do you even still love me?" I asked softly.

"More than anything," Griffin choked.

"Then why are you doing this to me? To us?"

"Every time I look at you, Finn, I see the future, us getting closer, until we're bonded so tightly together, you can barely tell where our bond begins and ends, we are one wolf, like Anya's parents."

"And that's a bad thing?"

"It is if you choose Aksil over me for your fucking prophecy one day. It will destroy me, Finn. I know that sounds weak when I'm supposed to be strong. But when I look at you, I feel so vulnerable, like you could break me with a single word, with your choice. Our wolves have gotten closer, but your wolf still doesn't carry my scent. What if Aksil is your destiny and you sever our mate bond for him?"

"I've already chosen you, Griff. You're my mate, and my wolf accepts that, scent, or no scent. I don't care about the prophecy. If Aksil and I are destined to bring the wolves and witches together, we'll do it, but that has nothing to do with us, baby."

"I feel so upside down. I don't know if it's because your father took you out of my pack, or the threat of Aksil's claim, or both, but I feel like I did when we first met, before I claimed you as my mate, and it's driving me and my wolf insane," Griffin admitted helplessly, sinking down to his knees on the floor.

"There's something I also haven't told you," I confessed, climbing out of bed, and walking over to Griffin.

"Great," Griffin sighed wearily, as I sank down on the floor beside him.

"I've just needed to sit with it by myself for a little bit first."

"Okay."

"But it might also be part of what's pushing you over the edge."

"Just an FYI, if you tell me Aksil blew you in the forest before he left, I'm gonna fucking lose my shit," Griffin croaked.

"You're the only wolf who's ever blown me in the forest," I teased gently, brushing my fingers through Griffin's hair.

"The only wolf?" Griffin growled.

"My teenage years were filled with blowjobs in the woods," I grinned at Griffin as his mate bond flared with jealousy. "Behind the horse stables at Van Cortlandt, down by the train tracks in the Bronx, and behind every rock and bush in Central Park, baby."

"You better tell me what you've been keeping from me, quick, because I'm about to stuff my dick down your throat," Griffin growled warningly.

"I'd much rather suck your dick than have this conversation, baby, but I've been putting it off long enough." I slid into Griffin's lap and wound my arms around his waist. We'd been through so much already with the prophecy revelation, I hadn't wanted to spring another big thing on Griffin, especially since I'd barely processed the news myself, and there was no easy way to break it to him.

"Just spit it out, babe," Griffin sighed, as I took a deep breath, procrastinating.

"I'm a natural born Alpha, and I'm in line to take over the Sequoia Pack," I finally told Griffin the news I'd been holding in since my father had broken it to me last month, back in California.

"Of course you are." Griffin's face was carefully blank.

"My father said we're not the first Alphas of our own packs to mate, and he's not planning on stepping down for at least another century, so it doesn't really matter right now..."

"It doesn't matter?" Griffin echoed, staring at me in disbelief. "It doesn't matter that you'll have to choose to stay with me and my pack or go off with Aksil and be Alpha of your own pack? Pretty sure it matters, Finn, and you're just choosing to be blind if you pretend it doesn't."

"Griff, I didn't ask to be a part of some ancient werewolf/witch prophecy, and I can't even think about becoming Alpha of my own pack. I just got my wolf back after 15 years, and I'm trying to understand who I am. But the one thing I have no doubts about, is us. We'll figure this whole mess out together."

"I'm done figuring shit out," Griffin growled, flipping me over and pulling me up onto my knees.

"So, we're back to this again?" I sighed, as Griffin spit onto his fingers and spread my ass open roughly. "Babe, for fuck's sake," I exhaled, my ass straining against Griffin's fingers as he started to push them inside me.

"I need my dick inside you, right now," Griffin growled hoarsely.

"You are not fucking me dry with the amount of possessive wolf crazy I feel pouring out of your mating bond, baby," I warned Griffin, rolling out from under him.

"I'm sorry, you're right." Griffin scooped me up and threw me over his shoulder, grabbing a bottle lube off the dresser and carrying me back across the room and over to the window.

"You're mine, Finn," Griffin growled in my ear, pushing the screen out and leaning me over the sill, hanging me halfway out with my ass in the air. "Say it," he growled, kneeling behind me.

"Always," I panted, gripping the windowsill tightly, my dick, rock-hard against my stomach, as Griffin gripped my ass between his hands roughly.

Griffin rubbed his scruff-covered face across my cheeks, nipping the soft flesh between his teeth and squeezing my ass as he spread me open, burying his nose inside me with a soft groan of relief. His breath was so hot against my skin, the moist heat of his mouth like hot velvet as he blew teasingly inside me, I was lost beneath him. His tongue glided in slow circles over the crinkles of my ass, as he inhaled my musky scent, rubbing his nose and chin from the top of my crack down to my balls, hanging heavy and swollen with need.

"You belong to me and only me," Griffin growled into my ass, flattening his tongue out and pressing it against me until I was dripping wet with saliva and need, writhing under his hot, wet tongue and the promise of him inside me.

"I'm yours," I moaned, in total submission.

The blood rushed to my head as Griffin bent me further out the window, pouring half the bottle of lube over his dick before shoving himself inside me and sinking his teeth into my shoulder with a wild growl.

I was so wet, open, and aching, from Griffin's tongue in my ass, his lube-slicked dick slid in and out of me like hot silk as he fucked me desperately, holding me in place against him with his hands on my hips and his teeth sunk firmly into my neck. It was feral and hot as fuck, and I couldn't hold out any longer as my orgasm finally ripped out of me, and Griffin filled my ass with his release in perfect harmony.

"That was some serious, Alpha, hear me roar, I own you shit, right there," I laughed weakly as Griffin pulled me back against his chest, sinking to the floor with me in his lap.

"Was it finding out I'm an Alpha too, that made you drag me across the room and dangle me halfway out the window while you fucked me like a feral wolf?"

"Hmmm...I don't know, maybe?" Griffin admitted with a yawn, pressing his lips to the top of my head.

"At least you didn't run away from me afterward," I sighed. "So that's an improvement."

"No more running away and leaving you alone in an empty bed with cold sheets in the morning." Griffin tucked me under his chin, wrapping his arms around me tightly. "I was a bastard for doing that to you and I'm so sorry. I can't promise I'm going to stop fucking the shit out of your ass every night, but I will be there to love you properly afterward."

Griffin refused to put the screen back in our bedroom window, so I had a feeling there was more window sex in my future, not that I objected. It was crazy hot, kind of like I was in a scene from *Game of Thrones* during the whole thing, and who doesn't want to be fucked *Game of Thrones* style, so there was that... But there was still an underlying tension in our bond that I was determined to flush out, while keeping my ass intact.

27

"What's a good romantic getaway theme?" I asked Anya and Ali as we lay stretched out on my dock with our sleeves pushed up and our faces tilted toward the sun. Summer was over, and we were solidly into fall, but Maine was usually cold by the end of October, like fires in the fireplace and break out the down jackets cold, so we were taking full of advantage of the unseasonably warm day to sun ourselves on my dock.

"What do you mean, a romantic getaway theme?" Anya wrinkled her face in confusion.

"God, you are literally the most unromantic wolf I've ever known," I sighed. "She is, right?" I turned to my sister to back me up.

"Um... I mean, I've only known her a few months, but yeah, I don't really get romantic vibes off her, sorry." Ali shot Anya a grimace of apology before pulling her shirt off and rolling over to sun her back.

"I'm romantic," Anya sputtered.

"Okay, name something romantic you've done for someone," I laughed.

"I wrote down the thing you told me Griff did for you with the wine and chocolates," Anya protested.

"Uh huh, but did you make a picnic for anyone, yourself?"

"No, of course not, why would I? I'm saving that for my mate."

"Ahhh, so you're saving all your romance for when you find your mate." I rolled my eyes. "Good luck with that. They'll probably be so disgusted by your unromantic attitude; they'll take off before you have a chance to claim them."

"Are you kidding me right now? Before you mated Griffin, the farthest you'd ever gotten in a relationship was being blown in the bathroom of the bar during your first night at work!" Anya yelled back.

"It's not about that, it's about the romance that lives in your soul. I have a very romantic soul."

"Yet, you're asking us for advice on how to romance your mate," Anya snorted.

"You know who's romantic?" Ali murmured. "Rahim. You should ask him for tips."

"Rahim?!!!" Anya and I exclaimed in unison, sitting up at the same time to gawk at Ali.

Rahim, the male version of his twin sister, Adi, was scarier and even less talkative than her, if that was possible. Equally hot, with a matching shaved head, flawless, midnight dark skin, and his twin's warrior fashion sense. I think he'd said a total of five words to me since we'd met.

"Are you fucking my brother?" Anya asked Ali.

"No... I've just noticed he's a romantic person, that's all. I'm very observant," Ali retorted smugly. "It's what makes me a great pack enforcer. That, and my super, badass martial arts skills."

"Yeah, yeah, whatever, we all know you're the fucking Karate Kid," Anya muttered, still pissed my sister had destroyed her in a fight when they sparred last month. Her smackdown had also seemed to kill whatever sexual interest Anya had initially displayed in my sister, and Ali wasn't interested in her either, so that was one drama I didn't have to worry about.

"Um, try, JeeJa Yanin. I'd destroy the Karate Kid," Ali snorted.

"Can we get back on topic," I sighed, not even wanting to go near the thought of Ali and Rahim.

"What's the goal here?" Ali asked, rolling over onto her stomach. "Is this like a put a spark back into your sex life romantic thing you're looking to set up, or a soothe my man's ego over the fact that I have a secret second mate who I'm supposed to save the world with one day?"

"The second one, definitely," I groaned. "If I light any more sparks in my sex life, I'll never be able to walk again."

"Griff's still fucking you like it's mating season and you're his brood mare, huh?" Anya clucked her tongue at me sympathetically.

"Fuck off, Ms. I haven't gotten laid since my undercover agent tried to slit my throat after she ate me out."

"I'm being cautious!" Anya yelled.

"You need to get back on that horse, sweet cheeks," Ali laughed. "Maybe come back with Finn and I next month when we go to California. We've got some hot, single wolves in the Sequoia Pack who would happily sink their teeth into your fur." Ali winked at Anya.

"Once again, off topic!" I yelled.

"How about a night here? Away from the lodge and the pack. Just the two of you, where it all started?" Anya suggested.

"You are a secret romantic!" I exclaimed, throwing my arms around Anya. "That's perfect. It's exactly what we need. I'm going to invite Griff back here tonight."

"Sorry to burst your bubble, but the vamps are coming tonight for a big meeting. How about tomorrow?" Anya suggested.

"I'm working tomorrow," I sighed. "Until 2:00 a.m. I swear, all anyone does in this Podunk town is drink. What's the whole vamp meeting about, anyway?"

"I don't know. You going to wear your *Buffy* shirt again?" Anya teased.

"Maybe, James totally deserves it after he outed my wolf to me without even prepping me first. I mean, who just does that to a guy, anyway? He totally could have broken it to me gently and maybe spared me a three-week wolf out!"

"Set it up for tonight anyway. You can bring Griff over after the meeting, that is, if your house is free, and you're not holding Finn's 'circle time,'" Anya laughed, referring to the monthly sleepover I'd started hosting here for pack wolves who wanted a night away from their lives to decompress.

"Nothing on the calendar for tonight." I stuck my tongue out at Anya. "The place is mine."

Griffin hadn't mentioned his meeting with the Portland vampires tonight, but I suspected it was more brainstorming about the situation brewing in Canada. We still didn't know if there was a larger force behind the attacks on the pack, but Griffin and my father both believed they weren't isolated incidents, and we all suspected it was somehow related to the prophecy and what lay ahead. What exactly that meant, no one seemed to know. But everyone agreed a war was looming, and the witches, wolves, and vampires were all antsy.

After Anya left to get ready for the meeting, Ali stayed behind and helped me prep the house for my romantic night, and it came together so perfectly, even she was impressed, and it took a lot to impress my sister.

"You're really pulling out all the stops tonight, huh?" Ali whistled as we walked back through the woods to the lodge.

"We've been through so much in such a short time, we've barely had time to savor our relationship, and when we mated, I didn't even know who I was. It almost feels like we need to start fresh, mate again with all our cards on the table."

"Now that's romantic!" Ali smiled, linking her arm through mine as we walked into the lodge.

"Ali, I thought I smelled my favorite little redwood wolf," James, the vamp called out to my sister, when we stepped inside.

"I'm Sequoia Pack, not Redwood," Ali called back in annoyance.

"Yes, so you always remind me, but you smell of the redwoods, my sweet little wolf, so I'll always think of you that way."

"You know James, the vamp?" I hissed at my sister as James walked over to us.

"We've had each other's backs a few times over the years when our interests aligned," Ali replied, meeting James's gaze as he stepped out of the study.

"That's certainly one way of putting it," James grinned back, flashing Ali a fang wickedly.

"Oh my god, have you fucked him?" I whispered to my sister, grabbing her arm, and pulling her toward the staircase.

"Get off." Ali pulled away in annoyance. "Stop dragging me out of the room like a 13-year-old girl you're trying to keep away from the hot, bad boy with the motorcycle and leather jacket. I'm the Sequoia Pack enforcer, for fuck's sake, Finn. I can handle my own shit."

"Yeah well, I'm your brother, and it's my job to keep you away from guys like that," I hissed back at my sister.

"Why am I always the boy on the bike, brothers warn their sisters away from?" James sighed with mock hurt. "You wound me, little wolf. Your sister and I go way back, and I assure you, my intentions, though maybe not entirely honorable, have never been harmful toward her."

"That's just great! He all but announced to the room, he wants to seduce you!" I exclaimed, reaching for my sister's arm again.

"Yank my arm again, little brother, and I'll lay you out," Ali hissed at me.

"Don't make me go Alpha on you," I hissed back.

"Please, I'd like to see you try. You're not Alpha yet," she snorted, staring me down.

"As entertaining as this little show is, we need to get back down to business," Griffin interrupted, stepping into the main room behind James.

"Please do," I breezed. "We were just passing through."

"Perhaps Ali should sit in on the meeting," James suggested. "It does concern the Sequoia Pack too, in a roundabout way."

"No," Griffin replied tightly. "I'll call The Sequoia Pack's Alpha and give him a follow up report when we're done. This is Northwoods Pack business only, and the Sequoia Enforcer is only here as a courtesy to my mate's father," he growled. "She stays out of my pack business."

"How interesting..." James murmured, holding Ali's gaze.

My sister's pack bond bristled and sparked angrily at Griffin's words, but her expression and body language remained serene as she stared back at them.

"As you wish," Ali smiled sweetly, linking her arm through mine, and turning her back to Griffin and James to walk up the stairs with me.

"Okay, so I know that was a little rude of Griffin," I began, following my sister into her room.

"You think I give a shit what your mate says to me?" Ali snorted. "I'll find out exactly what the fuck that meeting is about, and *I'll* be giving our father the full fucking report, not him," she scoffed.

"What are you doing?" I asked as my sister stripped down and started yanking clothes out of the closet. "You're not leaving, are you?"

"Finn, I know you've been out of my life for a long time, but you really need to get a fucking clue about me. I don't run away from shit, ever. I fuck shit up. You understand? I'm a closer, and I'm not afraid of anyone, especially your little Alpha boy who thinks he's hot shit when he's barely out of diapers."

"Al, that's not fair. Griffin is a great Alpha, even dad thinks so, and dad is like the Alpha Supreme."

"Alpha Supreme, huh?" Ali smiled at me affectionately. "Dad

is the Alpha Supreme, and you're right, I could go easier on Griffin. I've been watching him these past few months and he is a really good Alpha. He's fair, smart, industrious, kind, and totally badass. All great traits for an Alpha. But he's also really green and brash, Finn, and I know you can't see it, partly because he's your mate, and partly because you didn't grow up in a pack, so you don't understand."

"What do you mean, I don't understand?" I demanded.

"Big balls are great, but sagacity is just as important. Dad has both in spades, he's sagacious and fearless, and that's what makes him the Alpha Supreme. I don't doubt Griffin will get there one day himself, just like I don't doubt his love for you, but this prophecy would test even dad, and I don't trust Griffin when it comes to protecting you or placing your best interests before his own."

"That's not fair," I protested.

"He only sees you as his mate right now, Finn, not a separate individual, not the future Alpha of the Sequoia Pack, and our interests don't align. My only interest is keeping you safe. His is keeping you for himself."

"Al," I sighed, not really sure how to respond.

"I'm not saying I'm some wise guru, Finn, I fuck up all the time too. I'm just as young and green as Griffin, but I'm not the Alpha of a pack trying to hold onto a massive territory with a brand-new mate caught up in an ancient prophecy that threatens my mate bond. I'm a good pack enforcer because I know I'm not infallible. I seek dad's counsel, I listen to him, and I trust his judgement above everything else, and that's why I'm telling you this, not because I'm pretending to be wiser than Griffin, but because I know dad is, and he's the only wolf I trust right now to truly put you first, Finn."

"I don't understand what you're trying to say, Al."

"I'm saying, if Griffin wants to keep me out of his fucking secret meeting, that's his right as the Alpha of his pack, but I'm going to find out what the fuck the meeting was about because it's my job to protect the future Alpha of my pack, and I don't think our interests align." Ali slipped into a pair of skintight low riding leather pants and a sheer camisole that skimmed the top of her belly button right above her piercing.

"You're going to fuck the meeting details out of the vamp," I groaned, as my sister slipped her feet into 4-inch stilettos and flipped her head upside down to tousle her blond waves a few times.

"Such a wise little grasshopper, you are." Ali winked, blowing me a kiss as she sauntered out of the bedroom with a tube of red lipstick and a compact in her hand.

"Fuck Anya's Canadian Kris Munroe, my sister is a legit, OG Charlie's Angel," I sighed, following Ali downstairs.

"Need a ride somewhere?" James asked, stepping out of Griffin's office as if on cue, just as my sister reached the bottom step of the staircase. His voice was thick with heat, and his eyes dark with intent, as they drank Ali in.

"I was thinking of going into Portland for the night," Ali smiled back innocently. "Are you heading back there?"

"On my bike." James grinned wickedly at me. "Don't worry, little brother, I'll give her my helmet."

"Oh, fuck off," I sighed, heading into Griffin's office to pull him away for the romantic night I'd planned for the two of us back at my house.

28

"So, you just felt like sleeping in your old bed tonight?" Griffin asked as we walked into my cabin.

"Something like that," I murmured, taking Griffin's hand, and leading him into the bedroom.

"What's all this?" Griffin came to a stop in the doorway of the room.

"This is my version of the bushel of roses and string quartet," I whispered, slipping my arms around Griffin's waist, and pressing my lips into the back of his neck.

I had scattered pine needles across the floor of my bedroom and laid out a picnic on the bed with a bottle of Fireball, a pizza, a snow globe with a snow-covered pine tree in the center, a box of chocolates, and Cian's letter.

"This is us, babe, this is our story. You and me and our crazy adventure." I took Griffin's hand, leading him over to the bed. "This is us first meeting, you feeding me frozen pizza when I was about to pass out. Us, after I got trashed on Fireball and tried to blow you in the bar parking lot, the picnic you made for me the night we claimed each other. How I see and smell you, pine needles and snow-covered trees in the forest."

"I love it." Griffin's eyes were wet as he took the whole scene in.

"I love you so much, Griff. I need us to move past the whole prophecy thing. I need us to just be us again. Can you do that? Can you just be us with me, baby? Can you trust us again, can you trust me?" I asked Griffin, going down on one knee before him and pulling out a small vial from my pocket.

"Yes," Griffin choked, his dark eyes gleaming wolfen gold.

"I brought you dirt from my forest floor back home. I collected it after we had that storm when you were there with me, but I've been waiting for the right time to give it to you," I said softly, as Griffin sat on the edge of the bed in front of me.

"Things were so tense when we first got back, babe, and I feel like they're better now, but we're not all the way there yet, and I don't feel like we're going to get there if I just keep waiting for it to happen," I admitted. "I brought the dirt home for you so you would always have something to remind you of me when you're feeling doubtful or scared about us. You said I smell like dirt after a storm, the fertile earth that calls out to your wolf," I whispered, handing Griffin the vial. "I'm giving this to you as my mating pledge. I'm giving your wolf the essence of me, the fertile ground that calls out to him, and I'm inviting you to plant your roots deep in my soil, Griff. Plant them and trust me to keep them safe."

"Finn, I'm ready to. I'm so ready, and I accept your pledge and I give you mine back." Griffin wrapped his fingers around the vial of dirt and pulled me up into his lap. "I love you so much and I'm ready to move forward and just be us. I'm going to plant my mating bond so deeply inside you, you won't know where you start and end without me," he promised, kissing me deeply.

"The night we mated, you seduced me; now it's my turn." I brushed my lips against Griffin's teasingly and pushed him onto his back.

"Seduce away," Griffin grinned up at me, his eyes dancing with a mixture of heat and amusement.

"You don't think I can!" I peeled Griffin's jeans down slowly, trailing my fingers along the waistband of his underwear.

"Let's just say, you lack a certain patience," Griffin choked on a laugh as I tugged his underwear the rest of the way off and tossed his jeans to the floor.

"I do not!" I sputtered, yanking Griffin's shirt over his head.

"Always in a rush to unwrap the present, eat the cupcake before you've even tasted the frosting," Griffin grinned up at me as I stretched out over his naked body.

"Oh, I'm gonna taste the frosting." I nipped at Griffin's chin as I kissed my way down his body. "And you're going to be begging me to eat the fucking cupcake," I promised, drawing the tip of Griffin's rock-hard dick into my mouth.

"Taste away," Griffin breathed, as I trailed my tongue up and down his length teasingly, cupping his balls in my hand and running my finger over the crack of his ass. "I love a good appetizer before the main course."

"Appetizer, my ass," I swallowed Griffin's dick into my mouth, sucking it hard and sloppy, like I knew he loved it. "You're going to be begging me for the main course before I'm done," I warned as I came up for air, staring into Griffin's dark, slitted eyes in satisfaction.

"You're the main course, little wolf," Griffin chuckled, his voice raspy and thick with heat as he yanked me up his body and flipped us over in a lightning-fast blur.

"I'm the one doing the seducing," I pouted, nipping at Griffin's lip as he pinned me beneath him.

"Consider me seduced," he grinned, nipping me back and sliding his hand up my shirt.

"I barely even tasted the frosting!" I sucked in my breath as Griffin brushed his fingertips across my ribcage and up to my nipples.

"You swallowed the cupcake after one taste," he tskd, shaking his head and brushing his lips across mine. "So impatient, little wolf," he chuckled, drawing my tongue into his mouth slowly.

"I was just getting started," I moaned into Griffin's mouth as he peeled my shirt over my head.

"*I'm* just getting started," Griffin corrected, rolling me over onto my stomach and pulling my jeans and underwear down.

Griffin dipped his head into the hollow of my back, brushing his face against my tailbone and down the sides of my hips, carefully avoiding contact with my ass, as I arched my body up, begging him to spread my cheeks and stuff his tongue inside me.

"I haven't even started on the frosting." Griffin laughed wickedly. "Why would I taste the cupcake?"

"You said I was the main course," I moaned into the pillow, my whole body tingling with need as Griffin trailed his lips up the outside of my thighs, to the curve of my hip, all the way to the top of my shoulder blade, outlining my body, as I writhed, boneless beneath him.

"It's a seven-course tasting menu," Griffin breathed in my ear, rolling me back over.

"I'll be dead before the 3rd course." I gazed up at Griffin, knowing my eyes were dark gold with my need.

"Good thing we're still on the first course, then," Griffin whispered, blowing softly in my ear as he trailed his lips down the side of my face, across my chin and down to the base of my throat.

Griffin's lips were like warm silk, whispering across my skin as he traced a path from my collarbone to my shoulder blades, outlining the front of my body, like he did the back. He slid his tongue down across my hipbone, planting soft kisses down the length of my legs, across my ankles and back up to the inside of my thighs, stopping just before he reached my rock-hard, aching dick and swollen balls.

"I had a plan," I moaned, closing my eyes as Griffin kissed his way back up my body and stretched out over me, wrapping my legs around his back.

"Before you stuffed the whole cupcake in your mouth?" Griffin teased, rolling us over onto his back, and reaching for the bottle of lube I'd strategically placed on the bed.

"Yes." I opened my eyes, meeting Griffin's dark, slitted gaze as he pulled me up into a sitting position, dribbling lube over both our dicks.

"Tell me about this plan." Griffin gipped my waist, lifting me up and sliding me back down onto his lube-slicked dick with one, slow, push.

"I can't remember it anymore," I moaned, as Griffin gripped my dick in his right hand and placed his left on the small of my back, guiding me up and down on top of him in time with his slow, teasing strokes.

"Were you on top, riding me like this?" Griffin breathed, bringing the hand on my back up to my head and fisting it my hair as he pulled my head down for a bruising kiss.

"Maybe," I moaned into Griffin's mouth, as he stroked my leaking dick harder and faster.

"So close, and only on the second course," Griffin breathed into my mouth, slowing his strokes down and releasing his grip on my dick just as my orgasm started to build.

"I hate you," I gasped as Griffin slid out of me and rolled over onto his side, pulling my back against his chest like a spoon.

"You love me, little wolf," he murmured in my ear, hooking my leg over his arm, and sliding back into my ass. "You love me, and I love you," Griffin whispered against my neck, holding me tightly against him as he slid in and out of me. "You are my life's breath, Finn, my heart and soul," he breathed, turning my face to his and capturing my lips in a kiss.

Griffin was so warm and strong against my back, holding my leg over his arm and cradling me against his chest, I never wanted him to let me go. He trailed kisses across my shoulder and whispered love words in my ear, hitting my prostate with every thrust, until I was so close to my orgasm, I could barely breathe.

When my toes started to curl, I threw my head back against Griffin's shoulder, begging him to finish me off with everything he had.

"Look who made it to the 3rd course alive," Griffin laughed softly in my ear as he thrust into my clenching, over-sensitized ass one final time, sinking his teeth into my shoulder with a low growl as we came together, and he filled my ass with his release.

"Barely," I grumbled, as Griffin slid out of me and grabbed his discarded T-shirt to clean us up. "You love torturing me." I stuck my tongue out at Griffin as he finished wiping us off and pulled me into his arms.

"I do," he agreed, tucking me against his chest and pressing his lips into my hair.

"I could have seduced you; you know." I tilted my head back to stare into Griffin's eyes. "If you'd given me the chance."

"Baby, I'm seduced just by the sight of you," Griffin assured me, brushing his lips across mine. "One kiss, and I'm wrecked. That's all it takes," he whispered, trailing his lips softly across my face.

"To new beginnings." I brushed my fingers across my mate mark on Griffin's neck.

"To new beginnings," Griffin echoed, wrapping his arms around me tightly and burying his face in my hair.

I loved being back in my house, alone with Griffin again. He made a fire in the living room fireplace for us, and we curled up on the couch under a blanket, feeding each other cold pizza and chocolate, and licking drops of Fireball off each other's lips.

The spicy, cinnamon taste brought back the memories of that hot night in the bar parking lot, and we climbed all over each other, tipsy and horny and laughing like teenagers as we jerked each other off sloppily, grinding our dicks together with sweaty palms and collapsing in each other's arms afterward with a groan of contentment.

"God, that felt like I was sixteen again," Griffin laughed,

adjusting me in his lap as he stretched back out on the couch and pulled the blanket back over us.

"I know, remember how good a simple handjob felt back then?" I groaned in agreement.

"Like heaven," Griffin breathed into my hair.

"When did we get so greedy? I'm only twenty-five, and you're still a few years away from thirty, and it's all ass, all the time. I used to be grateful for a fucking blowjob. I never expected to get in anyone's ass on the regular, and fuck if anyone was getting in mine."

"I was greedy for your ass the second I smelled you," Griffin growled low in his throat, scraping his teeth against my jaw. "And I didn't just want in, I wanted to split you apart," he confessed. "I wanted to fuck you so hard, you would feel my dick buried in your ass for a week afterward."

"News flash, babe, that hasn't changed," I snorted.

"I know," Griffin groaned. "I just want to fucking own you. The thought of anyone even thinking about your ass makes me crazy, forget about anyone else fucking it."

"Let's have sleepovers here, once a month. Can we do that?" I lifted my head up to meet Griffin's eyes. "Just us, making out on the couch like teenagers in front of the fire. Reminding each other how good it feels just to lie wrapped up together and feel our dicks pressing against each other's stomachs. I feel grateful to have that, baby. I just want to feel grateful for that."

"Definitely," Griffin agreed, kissing me softly. "I can't think of anything I'd love more than a make-out session with you on the couch in front of the fire here on a Friday night. The taste of Fireball on your lips and the feel of you squirming in my lap with your dick pressing against me, just begging to be touched. I want a lifetime of these nights here with you, baby."

"You've got them," I promised with a sigh of contentment, curling up against Griffin's chest and closing my eyes.

The morning was bittersweet, even though we spent it in bed, fucking slowly and tenderly, then showering together and going at it again out on the porch after breakfast. Griffin finally got to bend me over the porch rail and own my ass, like he'd tried to do the morning after we'd first met, but it was all over too soon, and I was sad leaving as we cleaned everything up and locked the house.

"We'll be back here together soon, baby," Griffin promised when he saw my face fall as I locked the door.

"I know," I sighed. "And I get why it's important we live at the lodge with everyone. I just miss being alone with you like this, too."

"The whole pack loves you; you know. They come to you as much as they come to me now, and what you've done with your house, making it into a refuge for everyone, it's pretty amazing. I've never felt the pack so tight and cohesive before." Griffin scooped me up in his arms.

"What are you doing with me?" I laughed, wrapping my arms around Griffin's neck, loving that my big strong wolf could pick up all 6 ft, 180 lbs. of me like I was nothing.

"I'm carrying you to the car, like I should have carried you over the threshold of the lodge on your first night." Griffin brushed his lips across mine. "We've had so many rough starts, Finn, I just want to do everything right this time."

"We're getting it right, baby," I promised, kissing Griffin softly as he deposited me gently in the seat of my truck.

29

It took a little longer to get back to the lodge, taking the road instead of the trails, but I didn't mind the drive. It was nice, just sitting in the truck with Griffin, the smell of our scents blending, and the sex we'd had that morning swirling around us.

Griffin had Alpha calls to make and a meeting with Anya and Rahim, so we went our separate ways when we got back to the lodge, and I wandered upstairs to find Ali and hear about her secret agent night with the vamp.

"So, how was the hot night with the vamp? You didn't let him bite you, I hope," I teased, walking into Ali's room, and stopping short in confusion. "Why are you packing? Did something happen back home?"

"Dad is on his way," Ali replied, her voice tight. "And I already packed you. Your stuff is by the door in your room."

"Why is dad coming?" I asked slowly. "And why did you pack me too? What happened at home? Are Len and Collin okay? The pack?"

"Nothing happened at home. The pack is fine. The boys are fine," Ali replied, still not looking at me as she finished shoving her clothes in her bag and zipped it up.

"Why is dad coming here? Al, tell me what happened."

Ali finally met my gaze. "They put a bounty out on Aksil, Finn."

"Who did? What do you mean?"

"The vamps, but Griffin sanctioned it."

"No, he didn't. He wouldn't do that, Al. Even with the prophecy shit, Aksil is still a part of his pack. He's Safiya and Badis's son. Anya, Ziri, Nahla and the twins' brother. Griffin wouldn't do that!" I tugged on Aksil's bond unconsciously, my chest tightening up.

"He did. The vamps came to him about the prophecy rumors, said they heard it was you and Aksil, and Griffin gave them Aksil. We leave as soon as dad gets here." Ali said grimly.

"But I don't understand." I sank down to the floor. "Griffin said he was ready to start fresh, to be us, to plant roots, to let the prophecy go, to trust us, to trust me," I choked, lifting wet eyes up to stare at my sister. "We made out like teenagers on the couch in front of the fire, it was going to be a regular thing, we were starting a tradition. He fucked me like I was the only one who mattered, like he had nothing to prove to Aksil or the prophecy," I cried, my heart breaking as Ali knelt beside me and gathered me in her arms. "He wouldn't do that to me, Al. He wouldn't lie to me like that."

"Maybe he wasn't lying, Finn. Maybe, he felt like this was his chance to start over. Maybe, with the threat of Aksil out of the way, Griffin could trust you and the mate bond again," Ali whispered, holding me tight.

"But that means everything between us last night was a lie," I choked, feeling Griffin reach out to me as our mate bond flared with my despair.

"Yes," Ali agreed sadly.

"I gave him my soul, Al. I trusted him with everything. I invited him to plant roots deep inside me, forever roots. I pledged forever to him."

"Oh Finn," Ali sighed, as Griffin called my name in alarm,

running up the stairs.

"What's wrong? Are you okay?" Griffin demanded, running into the room, and reaching out for me, as our mate bond thrummed with my grief.

"Get off me," I roared, rising, and pushing Griffin back with all my strength and slamming him against the door. I could feel my Alpha power thrumming through my veins as I stared him down coldly.

"Finn, what the fuck?" Griffin yelled, staring back at me in bewilderment.

"You sanctioned a hit on Aksil? On one your own?" I demanded, still hoping deep down it wasn't true.

"That's not what happened." Griffin's eyes filled with anguish. "The vamps in Europe have been searching for the witch and wolf mate pair for centuries. They more than any other group are dedicated to stopping the prophecy. James came to me to warn me you and Aksil had been identified as the prophecy pair. He said the vampires didn't want to risk the wrath of the Sequoia Pack's Alpha by coming after his son, or make an enemy out of me, by killing my mate. He came to warn me there was a bounty on Aksil. Anya was there, ask her. She knows about the threat to Aksil, so do her parents."

"But you didn't tell me." I stared at Griffin in disbelief. "You knew the entire vampire world had just put a target on Aksil and you came to me last night, letting me talk about trust and starting fresh and planting roots, and you didn't say anything, knowing there was a chance Aksil was going to be killed. Is that why you agreed so easily, because you figured Aksil would be dead soon anyway, so it wouldn't matter?" I choked.

"No," Griffin whispered. "I didn't tell you because I didn't want to feel your pain at the thought of something happening to your other mate. I didn't tell you because for once, I just wanted it to be about us, and there was nothing you could do about it anyway.

There's nothing any of us can do."

"He gave me his pledge as an Alpha, Finn," my father said quietly from behind Griffin as he walked in the door. "To always put your safety first, above himself and all others."

"I put you first, Finn," Griffin choked. "I let James walk out of the lodge after telling me the vampires were going after Aksil because I was putting you first, before the pack, before me, before everyone. I was protecting you!" Griffin growled desperately.

"They gave you their word, they won't come after my son?" my father demanded.

"Yes, James gave me his word they won't touch Finn."

"Because you gave him permission to kill Aksil?" I asked Griffin in horror.

"I didn't give him permission, but I didn't do anything to put a stop to it," Griffin admitted, his voice thick with anguish.

My world went black at Griffin's admission, and I reached deep inside myself, tearing into my pack cocoon, and pushing Griffin's orange-gold threads to the outside, weaving my own threads around myself like a shell.

"What are you doing?" Ali asked me, wincing, as she felt me break up the Sequoia Pack cocoon and push her to the outside next to Griffin.

"He's building his own cocoon," my father murmured in wonder.

"But how?" Ali gasped. "It took the entire pack to build that cocoon around him."

"He's coming into his Alpha," my father said, with a mixture of pride and sorrow. "The true power of an Alpha lies in his connection to his pack, son," he cautioned me. "If you wall yourself in too deeply, you will cut yourself off from the heart and soul of your core."

"I'm not severing any ties with anyone," I replied quietly. "But I'm not a child anymore either. I don't need to be hidden away in a cave, like a pup you're protecting from predators. I don't need to be cocooned inside my father's pack, and I'm not standing aside, while my pack suffers from poor leadership. I am an Alpha, a leader of wolves." My voice deepened as I stood tall, staring my father down.

"You're challenging dad for Alpha of the pack?" Ali gaped at me. "Are you insane?"

"He's not challenging your father." Griffin stared at me in shock. "He's challenging me for Alpha of the Northwoods Pack."

"You can't choose your mate over one of your pack. When you chose to protect me, you essentially chose yourself over pack. I challenge you for leadership of this pack and I pledge to the entire pack to always put them before myself, even if it means sacrificing my mate."

"Don't you mean mates?" Griffin replied tightly, his body thrumming with power. "Isn't that what this is really about? You protecting your mate? You, protecting Aksil?" he demanded.

"He challenged your position," my father broke in, as the air crackled between Griffin and I, our Alpha power brushing up against each other and sparking with our rage. "It goes to the pack. Alphas, call your pack," he commanded quietly, his voice rich and deep with ancient authority.

Griffin and I locked eyes as we reached deep inside ourselves, almost in harmony, calling the pack into our hearts. Our grief, anger, and love washed through us, crackling through our mate bond as we sang for the pack.

Visions of Safiya and Badis running through the mountains in Morocco flashed before my eyes. Aksil's silver black thread sparked and crackled, Rahim's thoughtful gaze bored through me, Seiko's smile lit up my head, Ziri's energy washed over me like a soothing balm, and Lillian and Anya's threads vibrated with warmth, as the pack's answering song rippled through us in a kaleidoscope of lights, scents, and emotions.

The pack sang their wolfsong back to us in a slideshow of memories. Griffin, bloody from battle, eyes glazed with pain, expression fierce, me, surrounded by wolves in a circle around my firepit, face soft with understanding. They passed their memories to us as my father had passed mine to his pack. They poured them into our mating bond as Griffin and I spun our individual cocoons, pulling us in as one final string, which wrapped around the entirety of the pack cocoon, sealing everyone in place, and burying Aksil deep in the center.

"They chose you both," my father declared quietly.

"And you pulled Aksil in, even though he was never really bonded to us before." Griffin stared back at me in shock. "He was never completely pack, but you managed to pull him into our core."

"The pack forgives you," I replied quietly, feeling the calm, relief, and love of the pack wash over us.

"But you don't."

"I love you, Griff," I sighed wearily. "You're my mate and my co-Alpha of this pack, but right now, they are my only priority. I'm calling a meeting with the vampires, and I'm telling them Aksil's off limits. If they come after him, they come after the Northwoods Pack and the Sequoia Pack, and I'm calling in our allies on both sides. Dad, is the Sequoia Pack with me?"

"You're pack, son, we're always with you," my father replied firmly, clapping his hand on my shoulder.

Griffin stared at me, his eyes expressionless, as I grabbed the bag Ali had packed for me and followed my father and sister out of the room. None of us spoke as we left the lodge and headed for my truck. The weight of everything that had just happened, settling on our shoulders as I drove back to my cabin.

When we reached the cabin, Ali grabbed our bags and brought them inside, leaving my father and I alone on the porch to talk.

"Did you know?" I asked my father as we stood on my porch, staring out at the lake.

"That you would re-shape the Northwoods Pack around Aksil and become co-Alpha of your mate's pack, while still keeping a thread connecting yourself to your home pack? No, I didn't even know it was possible." My father laughed faintly. "There's so much about this whole prophecy we still don't understand, son, especially with all the twists and turns it's had to adapt to, from you being kidnapped and cut off from your pack to the resulting trauma which repressed your natural Alpha for so long." My father's voice was thoughtful as he mulled everything over.

"Why did you come here when Ali called you? What did she say to you that made you feel like you needed to come?"

"I was already on my way," my father laughed gently. "I felt a storm coming and knew you'd need me here when it arrived."

"Do you think Griffin hates me?" I whispered, turning to face my father. "Do you think he wishes Cian never sent me here, that he'd never met me or mated me?"

"Is that how you feel?" my father asked softly.

"No, of course not."

"Then why should he?"

"I'm like the mate from hell!" I exclaimed. "I'm caught up in an ancient prophecy. I have another possible mate waiting in the wings for me to fulfill some crazy prophecy with who just happens to have been a fringy member of Griffin's pack. Then, if that wasn't bad enough, I challenged Griffin's authority as Alpha and tried to steal his pack from him!"

"First of all, the fact that his pack still chose him and accepted him as their Alpha speaks volumes about their love and respect for Griffin, and he knows that. They chose you both because they recognized you both as their Alpha. They answered both your calls. That's pretty amazing." My father stared back at me with pride. "I knew you were special when you were born. I could feel your strength humming through you even as a baby, and when you refused to give up your wolf against a centuries old witch at just ten years old, I knew if we ever managed to find you again, and bring you back into the pack, you would be an incredible force to be reckoned with. I just always assumed you'd be leading our pack, not building a pack of your own."

"I didn't build my own pack," I protested. "I staged a coup! I don't know how Griffin is ever going to forgive me or how we're supposed to lead this pack together. This pack is his birthright, and I came in like the bastard son of the king's maid and stole it from him!" I exclaimed miserably.

"You're no bastard son of a maid," my father growled back at me. "You're Alpha royalty, and you did build this pack. You built it when you called them to you, and Aksil is the first member you brought in. He lies at the center of your pack, connecting everyone else together. I can feel him deeply rooted in the core of your pack, and I suspect, he is just the beginning of the wolves you will draw in, my son."

"What do you think it all means, dad? Me becoming co-Alpha of Griffin's pack, the prophecy, Aksil's relationship to everything?"

"There is so much ahead of you we still don't understand, my young pup," my father sighed. "But what you just did, essentially building a pack with Aksil and calling Griffin and his pack to merge with you, leaves little doubt in my mind you are the wolf from the prophecy. Only time will tell now what that means and what the relationship between you Aksil will become."

"I don't know what to say to Griffin," I admitted. "I felt like we were finally in a good place this morning, before I found out about the bounty on Aksil. I felt so hopeful for us and so in love with him."

"And now?"

"I'm still in love with him."

"But no longer hopeful?"

"Unsure, I guess. Like, I don't know where we stand with each other anymore."

"Because you feel betrayed by him, or because you feel like you betrayed him when you called his pack to you?"

"A little of both, I guess," I replied honestly.

"Then you're in the right place to move ahead." My father clapped a firm hand on my shoulder. "Accepting responsibility for your own complicity, is the first step in healing any rifts. If the witch, werewolf, and vampire worlds could have each just accepted their part in the rifts that started dividing them so many centuries ago, we wouldn't be in the mess we're in today. Perhaps, your new fresh generation can close the wound that has been open and bleeding for over 200 years. A witch and a wolf just built a pack together and called another to merge with them. I saw great potential in Griffin as a leader of wolves when I met him. Together, maybe you can do the impossible, unite the three sides, stop the wars, and begin a new era of peace."

"Wow, no pressure, huh, dad? That's kind of a tall order for a couple of gay werewolves in their 20s, don't you think?"

"Don't forget you've got an almost 200-year-old werewolf/witch hybrid in your pack too, and his parents, if they ever return from their walkabout..." my father laughed, kissing me affectionately on the top of my head.

"Oh my god, Safiya and Badis," I groaned, searching the pack bonds for their threads, faint, but ancient and steely. "I can only imagine what they think of me, coming in from nowhere and stealing the pack they founded!"

"They answered your call, so clearly they think you're up for the task," my father assured me. "Safiya and Badis are as old as I am, true nomadic wolves who only settled with Colm out of a sense of loyalty and friendship to him. They will always be loyal to your pack because their children are a part of it, but their souls are wild and yearn to be free."

"What are you saying exactly?"

"They left because they knew they weren't needed anymore. They'll always come if you call them, if they're needed, but their souls are nomadic, and they will always choose to roam free as long as they can."

"I still have so much to learn about the wolf world, don't I?" I leaned my head against my father's hand.

"One day at a time." My father patted my head. "Come inside, son, don't you have a meeting to set up?"

30

I smelled Griffin before I saw him, walking through the forest, and a deep ache tugged at my mate bond as he walked up to the porch.

"Hey." His eyes were guarded and uncertain as they met my gaze.

"Hey."

I ached to throw myself in Griffin's arms and turn the clock back to this morning when we were standing in this same spot, wrapped in each other's arms in a post orgasmic haze after he'd fucked me senseless over the railing.

"So, are we in a fight?" Griffin attempted a wan smile.

"It kind of feels like one, but I don't really know..." I smiled back tentatively. "Never been in a relationship before this, and the last fight I had ended up with me hanging half out the window, being fucked *Game of Thrones* style..."

"*Game of Thrones* style, huh?" Griffin raised an eyebrow at me. "That sounds pretty hot."

"It was. Although, being bent over the porch railing this morning was pretty hot too, and the sex last night was in a whole different league."

"So, what you're saying is, I'm really good at the sex part of our relationship, but I suck at everything else?" Griffin half-laughed, half-choked, staring at me with anguish-filled eyes.

"You suck at everything else? I'm the one who sucks at this whole mate/relationship thing," I choked back. "I'm like a giant suckfest, relationship killer!" I stared back at Griffin miserably. "I tried to steal your pack from you."

"You did steal my pack from me." Griffin laughed weakly. "You built a pack with Aksil and called mine in to merge with you, but surprise, they brought me with them, so here I am, third wheeling it with you and Aksil at your big vampire meeting."

"Is that how you see it?" I asked softly, feeling our mate bond spark with Griffin's grief and anger.

"Is there a different way I should see it?"

"I asked you to come here for the meeting. You could see us as co-leaders of one pack, as mates, lovers, best friends. We felt like that this morning, like we could do anything together, like we made each other stronger, better wolves."

"It just feels like I always choose you before everyone and everything, even risking my relationship with my pack, and you always choose him," Griffin replied hoarsely.

"I chose Aksil as pack, not as my mate," I choked. "I've been trying to explain to you since the beginning that my connection to him is different from ours. I don't feel him as my mate, baby. I'm standing up for him because he belongs with us. He's been a lone wolf for almost 200 years with no Alpha, living on the fringe of your pack for the last 40 years and roaming the earth lost and half feral for a hundred years before that."

"You can't pretend he's just another wolf in the pack, Finn."

"There's so much I don't understand about the prophecy or what's ahead of us, Griff, but I know how much I love you and how lost and empty I feel without you," I replied helplessly.

"Do you?" Griffin asked, his eyes raw with pain.

"My father said the first step to healing any rift is owning your own complicity. I own mine, Griff. I know I've fucked up with you time and time again. Do you own yours? Do you want to move forward with me and stand up to the vampires to protect one of our own? Do you want to present a united front to the world, two Alphas, leading a formidable pack who won't back down to their threats? I'm terrified of the idea, but I want it more than anything, to lead our pack together." My eyes flashed wolf, and my mate bond thrummed with my love and need, as I reached out to Griffin.

"I told James they could kill Aksil if they left you alone." Griffin sank down to his knees on the porch before me. "I didn't know what else to do."

"I know," I sighed, dropping down in front of Griffin. "The pack forgave you because Aksil was never completely pack. He never accepted you as his Alpha and they understood the choice you made, even if it broke their hearts."

"Do you understand?" Griffin searched my eyes for the truth.

"I don't know. I just became an Alpha. The one thing I'm certain of is I'll be fucking up many times myself. We're young and green, Griff, and brash and arrogant, but we love our pack, and we love each other. That has to count for something."

"It counts for everything. It's the most important thing," my father's voice broke in behind us. "The wisdom and prudence will come with time. The vamps are here. It's decision time, young Alphas. Are you together or divided?"

"Together," Griffin said firmly, pulling me up with him. "Let's go tell the vamps to fuck off."

They arrived together, in a sleek black car, three vampires, exiting as one, walking into the house.

"I knew things were going to get interesting up here in the

woods of our little state when you became Alpha, Griffin," James said, strolling into the house with his entourage. "But I must admit, even I didn't expect this. Three Alphas controlling one scrappy pack and 8,000 square miles of territory, aligned by blood with the most powerful werewolf packs on the West Coast. Will wonders never cease..."

"Three Alphas?" I echoed in confusion.

"Motherfucker. That fucking, witch/wolf motherfucker," Griffin swore under his breath as Aksil stepped into the room.

"Three Alphas," Aksil confirmed, walking over to stand at my side like it was the most natural thing in the world and not a complete mindfuck.

"Aligned with the Sequoia and Yurok Packs," my father confirmed behind us.

"So, where do we go from here, I wonder?" James asked, taking a seat in the leather chair by the fireplace.

"You can fuck off and leave Aksil alone for starters," I said hotly, still trying to process James' revelation that I had somehow made Aksil an Alpha of our pack too when I pulled him inside the core of it. Fuck James and his goddamn, motherfucking revelations.

"James knows I rather enjoy the little bounties the vampires put on my head, Grey. That's not something we need to waste our breath debating, is it James? We have far more pressing issues here at hand," Aksil murmured, brushing his fingers across mine as he crowded next to me. "You know the takeover attempts from Canada are not just aimed at our pack. They're after your lair too."

I could feel Griffin's mate bond spark with anger, as Aksil coolly assumed his Alpha role, but he remained tightly in control as he returned James' dispassionate stare, presenting the united front I'd asked him to.

"You guys need to stand the fuck down," Griffin spoke up. "As Aksil just said, we have a turf war on our hands that's much more pressing. Your little frenemies from Europe are making their way north through Canada and picking up mercenary wolves along the way to do their dirty work for them, and it's just a matter of time before they attack your lair next."

"Yes, we do have more time sensitive matters to address at the moment," James agreed thoughtfully. "But rest assured, the witch problem will come up again as we draw closer to the finish line," he murmured, flashing a fang in warning.

"I look forward to it," Aksil murmured back, his eyes flashing a deep amber as his wolf pushed against the surface. "I always enjoy our little sparring matches, so."

"We've sparred over the centuries when your identity was just a rumor, witch. Now that it's confirmed, our next match won't be for sport."

"How exciting," Aksil smiled back darkly. "Something to look forward to."

"If we're not going to kill the witch today, we might as well bring the baby wolf up to speed on everything, since we came all the way out here to the fucking woods and they don't even have the decency to feed us dinner," one of the vamps from James's entourage broke in drily.

He looked Hispanic, with dark olive skin, molten deep brown eyes, and an oh so fuckable vibe that had me sweating him, even standing beside Griffin and Aksil. What was my problem? Did I have to have the hots for everyone?

"Dinner? We can totally feed you dinner," I offered, mortified at my lacking Alpha host skills. I had called the meeting and I didn't even think about serving refreshments. "We'll order pizza!" I chirped brightly, growing more embarrassed by the minute as James's mouth quirked in amusement and his hotter than shit comrade threw his head back and roared with laughter.

"Pizza, how charming." James grinned wickedly. "Are you offering Santi, the delivery man as dessert?"

"Um, no...?" my voice trailed off as James continued to grin, and Aksil's bond literally shook with mirth.

"They're not allowed to feed on pack territory," Griffin said softly, taking my hand.

"But pizza is a great idea. I'm starving." Aksil flashed his teeth at James and Santi as he took my other hand.

Wow, was I totally fucked. I was standing between my current mate and pre-destined prophecy partner, facing down a posse of ancient vampires I'd summoned to my house for a meeting as a brand-new Alpha, and I'd just offered them pizza when they wanted blood. I totally sucked at this whole Alpha thing. I sucked so bad; I needed a T-shirt that said *Worst Alpha Ever* on it.

"The sauce is red at least..." I said weakly, and Aksil choked on a laugh as Griffin groaned quietly beside me. "You can do the rest of the talking now," I whispered to Griffin, walking over to the couch to sit down across from James.

"I'll have Anya bring over a few bottles of blood with the pizzas," Griffin said smoothly, taking a seat beside me and spreading his legs so there was no room left on the couch for Aksil.

"Let's begin." Aksil perched on the edge of the couch arm next to me, as Griffin reached out to Anya through the pack bonds. "I know Finn originally called this meeting to discuss the bounty on me, but since we've already put that matter aside for now, shall we get to the real matter at hand? Your bloodsucking friends in Canada trying to stage a takeover of your territory?"

"You mean the Canadian wolves trying to take over yours?" James replied coolly.

"When I was there, all the buzz I heard was about the big vamp in town coming for your little brother again," Aksil taunted. "Apparently, he's still rather annoyed Griffin rescued your brother from the Sinclair Pack three years ago and gave him back to you before he was able to get his hands on him."

"Enough," Griffin broke in quietly. "The bottom line is, we know the French-Canadian vampires want to take over Portland

and the Montreal Pack wants to take our territory, and they're both being backed by Europe. The Montreal wolves have been sitting back watching how we've handled the attacks from the smaller Canadian packs, and they've been learning from the mistakes those packs made. When Aksil was there gathering intel a few months ago, he said they're strong, they've been bringing in wolves from Europe, and they have a good chance of taking us as we stand now. As James and his crew know, the situation with the vampires is pretty similar. They're being backed by France and even though they lost the negotiating piece they were trying to get their hands on when we rescued James's brother, they're still ready and planning an attack. So, if we're done fucking around and making threats about shit that's all hypothetical anyway, let's talk about how we're going to defend our territories and crush this takeover attempt."

"We bring the witches in," I announced.

"I'd hand The French-Canadian vampires my territory on a silver fucking platter, first, wolf," James replied coldly, his eyes bleeding red and his fangs dropping down.

"Whatever your beef with the witches is, it can't be worse than mine," I exhaled. "They killed my mother in front of me, bound my wolf, severed my pack ties and dumped me halfway across the country to fend for myself at ten years old."

"They held my brother prisoner and tortured him for a century, before the Canadian wolves bartered for him to be used as a pawn in their negotiations with the Montreal vampires," James snarled, his fangs out and his eyes burning red with a century of rage.

"And I returned him to you when I discovered him three years ago in my counterattack against the Sinclair pack. So, do my mate, and the co-Alpha of this pack, a fucking courtesy, and listen to what he has to say," Griffin bit out, his eyes flashing wolf.

"I called this meeting for a different reason tonight, so, I'll admit I'm not completely prepared to hash all of this out right now without being fully caught up," I began. "But, I believe, from my own history with the witches, that there are two main factions operating here, the old guard and the new, and you, as part of the old guard, are playing right into their hands."

"Are you three supposed to be the new guard?" James asked coolly. "Because your Alpha witch is as old as me."

"Yes, he is. But Aksil also has the benefit of being both old guard and new, since he has just become an Alpha to a wolf pack, like myself."

"So, what are you saying, exactly?" Santi asked.

"I'm saying, the ruling European monarchy has feared U.S. independence since the three groups came out here, it's why they're always stoking the fires, sowing seeds of discontent between our three groups."

"That may be true, but the origins of the divide don't matter, we're long past that now, little wolf," James bit out, his eyes flashing with fury.

"Why, because we gave the ruling parties exactly what they wanted? Okay, so now let's take it back. Aksil is in the perfect position to reach out to the witches because he has a foot in both worlds. He can ask them to join our fight and we can defeat the wolves and vampires coming at us from Canada."

"Unite the witches and wolves?" James sputtered in disbelief. "Why do you think we want to kill Aksil? That's the last fucking thing we want, to give the witches more power and alliance against us!"

"He's talking about a union, but not one between the witches and wolves," my father broke in, striding over to sit down beside James.

"Think of what we could accomplish, with all three groups united, not just in this instance, against the Canadian wolves and vampires fucking with us, but in general, what it would mean for our overall autonomy here," I said.

"You're talking about a revolution. The colonists going against the monarchy. The Monarchy will see that as a declaration of war," my father warned.

"Don't you think they've already thrown the gauntlet down?" I asked my father quietly, holding his gaze. "I don't know about the rest of you." I looked around the room. "But I'm sick of the old guard dictating my life to me, and I don't need a fucking prophecy to make me stand up and fight back. They're ruling over us from Europe, while pretending to grant us autonomy. That's probably why they're backing the Canadians now."

"It wouldn't be the first time they've backed a group to make a point," my father allowed.

"So, maybe after Griffin defeated the Sinclair Pack and rescued James's brother, the Wolf Council in Europe saw the potential for his power to grow and felt threatened," I said. "And when you got your brother back, James, the European vampires had nothing left to hold over your lair. Your brother was the bargaining chip they were hoping to get a hold of to keep you in line. Am I right?" I challenged James who stared back at me coolly, not offering a reply. "I bet the witches are just as fed up with being used as pawns. Why do you think they kidnapped and tortured your brother?" I demanded, as all three vampires stared at me through narrowed eyes. "I would guess the order came from across the sea, to keep you in line. I say, fuck this takeover attempt from Canada and fuck the old guard pulling all the strings from Europe and using us as puppets to get their work done for them. Let's make our own path, united and standing independent when we're done."

"And who's going to lead this mighty revolution? You, a 25-year-old kid, one day into your reign?" James laughed softly.

"We're going to lead it together. Three Alphas, united as one," Griffin replied, taking my hand as Aksil as reached for my other one.

"What is the proposal?" the third vampire who'd arrived with James asked quietly. He only looked about nineteen or twenty, but he felt ancient, and there was a deep sadness mixed with a quiet rage that radiated off him. He looked Southeast Asian, with a slight, tightly muscled build, delicate bone structure, and bottomless dark eyes. He was beautiful, with a predatory stillness that reminded me of a tiger poised to strike.

"Tai," James sighed.

"It is my mate who the witches tortured and kept from me for a century. I say if we consider the proposal or not," Tai replied, the ice in his voice leaving no room for argument.

"Raffi is your mate, he's James's brother, he's my best friend. We all claim him as ours. We all burn to avenge him. We all want to heal him, to bring him back to us, the way he was before he was taken. We listen to the wolf pups and their witch/wolf, and we decide together if we join with them," Santi declared, flashing his fangs at James and Tai.

When Anya and Ali showed up at that moment with the pizzas and blood, I was relieved to have an excuse to get up. The tension in the room was worse than when Griffin realized Aksil was my future prophecy mate, and I didn't know it was possible anything could feel worse than that moment.

"Ah, sweet blood," James murmured, his eyes drinking Ali in as she set the bottles down on the table beside the pizza, and it was obvious he wasn't referring to the thick red blood in the bottles. "Who knew the redwood trees of the California forests could smell so sweet, so rich, so fertile," he murmured, brushing his hand across Ali's as he accepted the bottle she offered.

"You know that's our dad, standing behind you about to rip your head off?" I reminded James cheerfully, as I grabbed a slice of bacon and American cheese pizza out of the box. Thank god for Ali and Anya, they knew exactly what I needed tonight.

"I have only the deepest respect and regard for your daughter," James murmured to my father, backing away with a flicker of a smile.

"I can smell you on her," my father growled.

"Dad!" Ali exclaimed, blushing bright red.

"Now you know how I felt that morning at breakfast," I said to Ali smugly, over a mouthful of my pizza.

"At least it was just family there," Ali hissed, trying to hide behind me as James grinned at her wickedly across the room.

"Your sister is so, fucking James," Anya whispered as we huddled over the pizza boxes together, chomping down and watching the sparks fly between Ali and James like it was the season premiere of *The Bachelorette*.

"I would like to hear the proposal now," Tai said wearily from across the room, and I realized I fucked up some Alpha etiquette shit again. Like, I probably wasn't supposed to be scarfing bacon pizza down right now and gossiping about my sister with my best friend in the middle of a serious werewolf/vampire meeting. Griffin and Aksil hadn't moved from the couch or touched the pizza. I was sooo bad at this.

"Right, the proposal." I wiped pizza grease from my fingers and mouth and walked back over to the couch. I didn't actually have a plan, since I'd called the meeting just to get the vamps to take the bounty off Aksil.

Anytime either of you want to step in... I said to Aksil and Griffin in my head, smiling brightly at the vampires and clearing my throat, stalling for time as I settled myself between Griffin and Aksil on the couch.

"I will reach out to the witches," Aksil offered. "Finn is right, as both a witch and wolf, I have certain relationships with them..."

"I'll bet you do," Griffin muttered under his breath.

We're three Alphas, presenting one united front, I reminded Griffin in our head, kicking him in the shin.

"There's a witch I know in New York, who just started her own coven. She's young, but very powerful, and has a lot of sway with the other East Coast covens. I'll reach out to her and see if she's open to a meeting," Aksil said.

"We will meet with the witches on our territory. You have two days to set it up," Tai declared, standing up to leave.

"We said we'd decide together," Santi said mildly.

"No, you said we'd decide together. I'm the one who feels Raffi's pain, every minute of the day, not you," Tai spat. "I have decided we will meet with the witches, and I will decide if we join with them."

"The latitude I give you for my brother," James sighed, shaking his head as he followed Tai and Santi out the door. "Call me after the meeting is set, little wolf. Big wolf, always a pleasure," he nodded to my father. "Witch wolf, we'll have our day soon," he flashed a fang at Aksil. "Alpha," he nodded respectfully at Griffin.

31

"How come I'm little wolf, and you're Alpha?" I exclaimed to Griffin in indignation after the vampires left.

"He saved James's brother. You'll never get the same respect he gives Griffin," Anya said breezily, grabbing another slice of pizza. "If no one else is going to eat any of this, I am. I'm starving after the emotional rollercoaster you three put me through earlier, calling the pack, then re-shaping the pack. I feel hungover from that shitshow. It was like being at the bar with Finn every time he goes to beg Molly for his job back. You know she's going to give it to him in the end, but the hoops he has to jump through to get there, yeesh! I didn't know if I was about to get blown by a Texan in the bathroom, or if I was going to have to bake muffins there for a minute!"

"You don't have a dick, remember? How are you supposed to get blown?" I rolled my eyes at Anya, and then blushed when I remembered my dad was still in the room with us. "Forget you heard any of that," I muttered, avoiding his eyes.

"I think it's time to take a walk," my father said. "All three of you."

"Fuck, I always get my ass handed to me on these walks," I muttered, grabbing a slice of pizza as I followed my father out the door.

"He's not even my father, why do I have to go?" Griffin complained as he trailed behind Aksil and I.

"I may be his future son-in-law one day, so I'm going..." Aksil flashed Griffin a wicked grin from beside me.

"The fuck you will," Griffin growled at Aksil.

"Like I need you antagonizing Griff right now," I groaned to Aksil "I'm literally about to get schooled by the Alpha Supreme my first day on the job, a little support would be nice."

"You did great in there." Griffin took my hand. "You kicked ass, seriously. That was some awesome fucking strategizing, babe. Some serious Alpha shit, coming up with that witch plan."

"First day on the job, Grey, and you got the vamps to agree to a meeting with the witches." Aksil whistled in admiration.

"If you boys are done stroking my son, I'd like to have a word," my father broke in drily.

"Sir, yes, sir," Griffin replied, literally snapping to attention.

I rolled my eyes. "Really? This isn't the fucking Marines, Griff, he's not your drill sergeant."

"Yeah? Well, he's definitely my commanding officer," Griffin hissed back.

"You can't think like that if we're going against them," I sighed.

"We're fighting your father?"

"How long are you planning on letting this go on?" my father asked Aksil in annoyance, as he stood back, quietly laughing at us.

"The general would like a word, boys," Aksil grinned, his eyes dancing with amusement.

"He's not our general!" I exclaimed, turning around to face my father.

"No, I'm not," my father agreed, taking me in. "I'm your father and I'm three centuries older than you. I actually know this old guard you're planning on going up against, would you care to seek my counsel on anything?"

"Sir, yes, sir," I replied weakly, shrinking back under my father's glare.

"Hah, who's kowtowing to the drill sergeant now?" Griffin whispered.

"First of all, you have two separate objectives right now," my father began, fixing me, Griffin, and Aksil with his Alpha stare. "Your first objective is to protect your pack from your Canadian threat, putting it down, once and for all."

"Yes," Griffin agreed. "One hundred percent."

"You'll take care of that in a day," my father said dismissively. "Once you coordinate your attack with the vampires, with or without the witches, you'll go in and take Montreal."

"Yes," Griffin and Aksil agreed while I digested my father's statement.

"Just like that, we'll go in and wipe out the Montreal Pack and Lair?" I asked in shock.

"We have no other choice." Griffin took my hand. "If the witches join us, we attack the Montreal Coven as well and take the whole city."

"It will be your launching point for sending your message," my father stated, looking at each of us pointedly. "Do you understand that? Everything you do from that point on decides your course."

"If we claim the city and expand our territories, we're declaring war on Europe. But if we go back home and form our own councils, we're sending a different message," I said slowly.

"You're taking a stand, defending your territory, and declaring a degree of autonomy, but not outright war," my father said softly. "And if you are really going to try to bring the wolves, witches, and vampires here together for more than just this skirmish with Canada, you need to form a council with a representative from each group," my father declared. "There will be zero room for error in this, boys."

"I agree, and I vote your father assembles the council," Aksil said to me. "We'll need an elder from each group on it to advise us, and he'll know the best wolves, witches, and vampires for the job."

"When you say advise... You mean give advice, not tell us what to do, right?" I asked Aksil uneasily.

"God, you're like a fucking toddler resisting his nap, sometimes," Aksil exploded, grabbing my face between his hands. "You are one of the strongest wolves I've ever come across, Grey, and your scent makes my blood boil from a mile away, but if you keep forging ahead blindly with the arrogance and pride of a two-year-old who won't accept his father's help tying his shoelaces before he goes running down the street, you will trip and fall. And I need you to live long enough for me to finally find out what you taste like, do you understand me?" Aksil growled low in his throat, his face so close to mine, I could feel his breath ghosting over my lips and smell the scent of his arousal as it swirled around us, mixing with my own.

I wanted to step back. My mate bond was vibrating with Griffin's rage at Aksil's claim, but I was momentarily frozen, lost in the heat and promise in Aksil's eyes, and the myriad of conflicting emotions swirling through me.

"This isn't going to work," Griffin snarled at my father, his eyes gleaming wolf gold and his claws fully extended. "I'm going to rip him apart."

"You're not." my father placed a steadying hand on Griffin's shoulder. "You're going to lead your pack with your other two Alphas, because you made a promise to your pack to always put them before yourself, and you gave me your vow as an Alpha, that you will put Finn above yourself as well. I will form your war council, Aksil will call the witches, and we will all meet at the vampires' Lair in Portland in two days."

"I don't know if I can," Griffin admitted, his eyes sweeping over me as I stepped back from Aksil.

"It's just sex, Griffin; lust," my father sighed. "He's not mated to him, you are. Even if they are the wolf and witch from the prophecy, you're Finn's mate. You need to start believing in that. Aksil isn't going to be the first wolf sniffing around your mate, and he won't be the only one Finn sniffs back, either. So, let them fuck it out of their system, or accept there's going to be sexual tension between the three of you for a while, and move on to focusing on this revolution you're planning."

"Fuck it out of their system?" Griffin half-shifted, his claws extending as he advanced on Aksil. "I'll kill him before he ever learns what Finn tastes like."

I'd had about enough of this shit. I stepped between Griffin and Aksil.

"I'm canceling the prophecy; don't you get it?" I yelled at Griffin. "None of it matters anymore. I'm literally leading a fucking revolution right now, so I don't have to choose between you two in the future. But if you threaten to kill Aksil again, you'll have to go through me," I warned.

"And you!" I turned to Aksil, shoving him against a tree. "You want to taste me? Here I am."

My father led Griffin away, and Aksil and I were alone together in the forest as I brushed my lips against his roughly. "Mystery solved. This is what I taste like, now you can stop wondering and find someone else to fuck."

Aksil didn't move as I brushed my lips against his, his black thread inside me silent and paralyzingly still, until I started to pull back, and he pounced, flipping us around, and pressing me against the tree so hard, every ridge of the bark dug into my back.

When Aksil's lips touched mine, my whole head went blank. He was the sap in the tree, sticking to my body, merging with me as his lips fused against my mouth and his tongue wrapped around mine like hot velvet.

"I could take you right now, against this tree and you'd let me,"

Aksil whispered, his eyes never leaving my face as I let him see the full force of my longing and confusion naked in my eyes.

"Maybe," I whispered, even as a part of my heart broke at my admission.

"But I won't." Aksil brushed his lips across mine. "I won't because you're not ready to let him go yet. And once I make you mine, Grey, I will share you with no other. You will only feel me inside you for the rest of your life, you will only crave my lips on your body, my tongue in your mouth, my cock in your ass, my hand on your dick, rough and strong, the way you like it," Aksil whispered into my mouth, his hand brushing my swollen dick straining against my jeans. "And I can wait for you because I'm not a child, and I don't care what you look like when Griffin wraps his lips around your dick or fucks you into the mattress at night so hard, you can barely walk the next day. I don't care, because I now know what you're going to look like spread out underneath me. I see it on your face right now, and that image will keep me warm until you're mine, even if I have to wait another hundred years." Aksil stepped back from me, his eyes wolfen gold and filled with a promise I felt down to my soul.

I worked to regulate my breathing and will my dick down as Aksil walked away, collapsing to the ground once he was out of sight. Fuck this nightmare! And fuck this fucking prophecy!

I loved Griffin with my whole soul. This attraction to Aksil was going to be the death of me. Why did he have to be so crazy hot? And why was I such a slut that I totally wanted him to fuck me against the tree even when I knew it was wrong and I'd regret it? I seriously had to get my shit together or I was never going to be able to lead my pack, keep my mate, and plan a revolution.

"*I love you. Nothing happened, I promise.*" I reached out to Griffin through our mate bond, wrapping my threads around him and sending him thoughts of love and mate. "*I think we all just need a couple of nights away from each other to re-charge and present a* united front to the vampires. I'm sleeping in my house alone until the meeting. Don't freak out."

"Please come home," Griffin begged me, wrapping his own threads around me, and pulling me in tighter.

"Not now, not before our big war meeting. We need to be united as the three Alphas of The Northwoods Pack, Griff. If I come home now, you're going to spend the next two days fucking me senseless and marking me up. Walking into that meeting reeking of you and wearing your teeth marks like jewelry isn't going to unite us or make us stronger."

"But you walking in, smelling like Aksil is?" Griffin demanded.

"I'm going to walk in smelling like me, baby. Me, the third Alpha of the pack, not a fucktoy two wolves are fighting over. I won't tolerate being treated like anything less than your equal, Griff. I'm co-Alpha of this pack and my father is right, the territorial bullshit over me has to end or we can't fight the real fight to protect our pack."

"You're not fucking him, Finn," Griffin growled at me as our mating bond flared. *"Not now, not in a hundred fucking years."*

"*Okay*," I said, because there really wasn't any other answer I could give right now.

"*Okay?*" Griffin repeated.

"Yes. I love you, Griff. I just need these next two days to myself. I'll see you at the meeting. I'm riding with Ali."

"You're bringing Ali?"

"I know she's kind of only on loan to our pack, but I think we all have our own seconds. Anya belongs to you. Ali is mine for now, and even though Rahim is our pack enforcer, he'll probably stand as Aksil's."

"I guess you're right. Griffin agreed thoughtfully. "Okay, I'll see you at the vamps', and Finn?"

"Yeah?"

"You're not a fucktoy I'm fighting over. You're my life's breath, my heart and soul, my mate. I love you."

"I love you too," I sighed. "So much, Griff, I wish you could feel it."

"I do. I feel it," he sighed back. "And I trust you. I'm just gonna trust you to figure it out in your own way. I have to."

"Thank you." I closed my eyes, leaning against the tree as Griffin drifted out of my head, and I just sat with all my feelings swirling inside me.

32

The witches arrived at the vampires' lair the same time we did, almost as if we'd choreographed it, six wolves: three Alphas and their seconds, and six witches, all striding up the driveway to the massive fortress looking house perched on a hill overlooking the ocean.

"Papi, that ass, it just gets better every time!" one of the witches whistled at Aksil, his dark brown eyes drinking Aksil in appreciatively while he flashed him a teasing grin. The witch looked about 30, and felt young too, not like the vampire Tai, who looked 19, but you could tell was probably three hundred. The witch was model thin, with lithe muscles, beautiful olive skin and thick Latin charm. His dark loose curls fell over his sparkling black eyes, and he literally oozed sex. He was the guy who could charm a married woman out of her pants in front of her husband, or in this case, my maybe future mate out of his in front of me.

I could smell Aksil respond to the witch's flirtatious grin, and when he brushed his hand across Aksil's ass, my eyes flashed deep wolf gold and my claws start to extract. I took deep breaths, getting my wolf under control as Griffin sighed in annoyance behind me at my obvious jealousy.

"Ah, and this must be your prophecy mate, the baby wolf. My, what big teeth you have," the witch grinned at me teasingly as I growled low in my throat, and Aksil began shaking with silent laughter beside me.

"Well, this should be interesting, you've only fucked Aksil a few times, wait until he meets Kai, weren't they together for 20 years?" one of the other witches piped up. She had the same beautiful black eyes and warm honey bronze skin as the witch hitting on Aksil. They also smelled the same, kind of like Rahim and Adi, and I instantly thought, twins, as she looped an arm around the witch, pulling him against her.

"Stop teasing the wolves," a third witch broke in. She was spectacular, with pale skin, almost completely covered in freckles. Her fiery red hair was in long boxer braids, and she was dressed in baggy ripped jeans, a black, cropped, Adidas hoody, and pink suede Timberland boots with black laces. Massive gold hoop earrings swung from her ears, and she had a thick as fuck New York accent.

"I'm Fiona, you can call me Fi." She held out a hand, snapping a piece of gum in her mouth. "The player scoping your witchy wolf out, is Mati, and his twin sis, is my girlfriend, Ana. The shifty looking motherfucker over there is my baby brother, Jack." Fiona pointed to a skinny skate rat in baggy Dickies and scuffed Vans, wearing a *Dropkick Murphys* ball cap pulled low over his face. "And the other two are Marcel and Paddy." Fiona motioned to a cute black kid, who looked about 20, with a wild fro, dressed in Parisian streetwear, and a hot as shit, thick, burly 20-something kid with black hair, freckles and blue eyes, a personal weakness for me. He looked like he'd just gotten done playing rugby and was about to walk into an Irish pub for a pint.

Fuck, I hoped Griffin couldn't smell my hard on for this witch right now. I was already in trouble for being jealous over Aksil. What was my problem?? Why did I literally want to fuck everyone?

"I think that about covers it. If any of you bitches try and grab my woman's ass, like Mati did with Aksil, I'll bury you six feet under the ground. Other than that, if you want to give me the rundown on your crew, I say, let's do this shit and get inside."

Wow, I was in love, like actually in love with this witch. She was so fucking beautiful and badass, and that accent! It totally brought me back to the Bronx.

"I'm Finn, this is my mate and the other Alpha of our pack, Griffin, his second, Anya. You already know Aksil, that's our enforcer, Rahim, and this is my sister, Ali," I replied, waving my hand around to each person as I introduced them to the witches.

"And just so we're clear, you fuckers can grab Aksil's ass as much as you want, but anyone touches Finn, and I'll rip your head off," Griffin broke in, flashing a wolfy mouthful of teeth at the witches in warning.

"Nice! Now that we've all marked our territory, let's go fuck with some vamps!" Fiona flashed us all an evil smile before ringing the doorbell.

"Ahh... The children have arrived," a female vampire called out in a melodic voice, holding the door open for us. "Would you like some refreshment? Lemonade and cookies perhaps?" she purred, leading us into an elegant drawing room with red silk wallpaper and deep blue velvet couches.

"Some wine, I think, Miranda, and a cheese plate for our guests, please," James broke in smoothly, rising from an overstuffed leather chair by the fireplace.

Such a better host, I sighed to myself, looking at the sideboard with an inviting array of Scotch, crystal glasses, and silver dishes of warm, fragrant nuts. I so needed to get a setup like that at my house for meetings. Or did we already have one at the lodge, I wondered, totally drifting away, and forcing myself to re-focus on the expectant faces before me.

"My son, Finn, Alpha of the Northwoods Pack." My father's

voice boomed out an introduction before I could say anything. He must have arrived with the Council. "His mate and co-Alpha Griffin, and the third Alpha, who I think everyone already knows, Aksil. Finn, Griffin, Aksil, this is the advisory council I assembled for you," my father rose from the chair opposite James and waved his hand over to the couch.

I knew instantly, the witch sitting in the center next to the female vampire, was Kai, Aksil's ex Ana had mentioned outside. I could feel the heat between him and Aksil from across the room.

Fuck, he was beautiful. He looked like a Hawaiian sea god, with his gorgeous Japanese bone structure and beautiful, loose-limbed body. He lounged on the couch barefoot, in jeans and a white silk button down shirt open halfway to his chest, with a fucking shell necklace around his neck. I was so jealous; I couldn't even look at him.

"Allow me to introduce Kai, from Hawaii, Madelaine, from Louisiana, and Tate from the Yupik Pack in Alaska." My father introduced his council to us.

They were an interesting mix, my father's advisory council. Madelaine oozed ancient vampire. Sex, charm, and danger seeping from the pores of her beautiful, ebony black skin. She looked about thirty, going on five hundred, like the rest of the council, dressed in a black silk jumpsuit with five-inch, red bottom stilettos on her feet. Tate was Alaska all day. Probably a fur trader a million years ago. Long, slightly tangled brown hair fell to his shoulders, he barely grunted a greeting, and I was pretty sure he was wearing deer hide pants.

I introduced our seconds and the witches, James graciously poured us all a drink, and we got down to business.

"Thank you all for coming. I wanted us to meet because I think we share a common oppressor, and I want to do something about it," I began, conscious of the tension radiating off Tai from across the room, and the way the young witches had all grouped together uneasily in response. "I know there's bad blood between all three of our groups for varying reasons, but as far as I know, none of the witches, wolves, or vampires in this room have sought to harm one another, and we should not hold each other responsible for the crimes of others."

"We agree, and we came to this meeting because we're sick of carrying the burden of ancient feuds and being used as pawns in a war between the wolves and vampires," Fiona chimed in. "I started my own coven in N.Y. because I wanted to stay out of all the politics, but the ruling covens in Europe have been fucking with us big time too, mostly by turning the vamps against us. We'll help you crush the fuckers coming at you from Canada, but if we join your fight, we want your word you're in it to win it. We're not going against the old guard unless we know you've got our backs until the end. The only way we all come out of this still standing is if we're united as one group."

"I want to know who ordered Raffi's kidnapping," Tai spoke up quietly. "The wolves say it came from Europe. I want proof, and if it did, I'll burn down the castle myself."

"Everyone in this room has their reasons for being here," I said, looking around at the tense faces. "But what Fiona just said is the most important. We have to stop fighting each other and unite against the real enemy. From what I've been told, the old guard in Europe has been controlling all the wolf packs, witch covens, and vampire lairs in the U.S. to some extent since we got here, dictating the rules of engagement to everyone, and doling out punishment with consequences that stretch out into the next century, because the ultimate thing they won't tolerate from us is power. Am I right?" I looked around the room at everyone as heads nodded in agreement.

"They're coming after our pack because we control such a large territory," Griffin broke in. "They want to break up James's lair, because he won't heel at their command, and as Fiona just said, the witches here are being forced to carry out the monarchy's dirty work. They've been sowing discord and using our three groups as puppets for over a century, pitting us against each other to keep us weak. The question is, who wants to put a stop to it?"

"I've been kidnapped twice, and apparently born into a prophecy specifically to end this shit, so, I don't know about you guys, but I'm fucking ready to rise up!" I exclaimed.

"The prophecy states you and Aksil will bring the witches and wolves together, it says nothing of uniting the three sides," James said coolly, looking unmoved by my passionate speech.

"The prophecy can say whatever the fuck it wants," I retorted. "Maybe I was born to unite the witches and wolves, but I never follow directions properly, and my mate can attest to the fact that I tend to do things backwards," I laughed weakly, as Griffin grimaced in agreement. I guess things were still a little too tender between us for any jokes about our mate bond.

"We asked Finn's father to assemble an advisory council, and I invited the witches here, because we want to talk about creating our own ruling councils, taking a stand together, and uniting all three sides, not just the wolves and witches," Aksil's deep voice broke in.

"The last big uprising against the ruling families was 300 years ago," Madelaine said thoughtfully. "It was led by a scrappy pack of Scottish wolves who broke off and came here."

"Your father was the Alpha who led the uprising and migration," Aksil told me quietly.

"Okay, so now I feel a little stupid about my he's not our general comments yesterday," I whispered back.

"It was bloody, but a general success I'd say, since most of us who joined the fight are still here 300 years later," Kai added.

"We're not going to destroy them, we'll never be as powerful as they are, even banded together," Griffin said thoughtfully. "The key is to squash the takeovers they're inciting here, on our turf, and show enough of a united front to get them to back off and leave us alone."

"Without making them feel threatened," James added softly. "If we make them feel threatened, they will wipe us all out, population be dammed."

"What do you mean?" I asked.

"He means, the monarchy has left us alone for the most part because the ultimate enemy is the human world, and they want to keep their supernatural numbers up," my father explained. "If they wipe out all the witches, wolves, and vampires in the U.S., they leave themselves vulnerable. Right now, they can still call on us if we're needed. We're living separately but still a part of their world. But if they decide we're more of a threat than an asset, they'll come at us with everything they have."

"Is that why they took your brother?" Fiona asked James. "You pushed back too hard on something, and they retaliated to show you you're dispensable?"

"Something like that, although they framed it a bit differently," James murmured. "They refused me any aid in getting him back."

"To punish you for what?" Aksil asked.

"Not giving me up. The monarchy has been after me for centuries for reasons better left unsaid," a vamp announced, striding into the room. "So, the ruling family took our other brother as punishment instead. I've said it was them all along and I offered myself in Raffi's place over and over again, but they claimed no knowledge of his whereabouts."

I heard the vampire who entered the room speaking, but it was as if I was in a fog, all I could smell was Griffin. Griffin on him. I could smell my mate all over him. Satisfaction radiated off the vampire as he gazed at my mate with a possessive predatory heat, the intimate gleam of someone who knew the taste and smell of him well and looked forward to sampling his charms again.

Then, all I could hear was the roar in my head that ripped through me, yanking my wolf to the surface without warning, as I shifted and lunged for the vampire with a wild snarl, and Griffin tackled me from behind.

"Wow, a bit extreme, Griff, don't you think?" James said drily. "Parading your old lover in front of your mate one day after he's become an Alpha? That's akin to marching a human into the room with a brand-new vampire and telling them they can't have a taste. But, nicely done, at least it clears up the question of who the baby wolf belongs to for now. Simon, get lost, we don't have time for any games right now."

I struggled to pull my wolf back as Griffin kept me pinned to the floor beneath him, but I could still smell the vamp's desire for my mate lingering in the room, mixed in with the scent of Griffin on his body, and my wolf was solely focused on ripping him apart.

"Feel better now?" Aksil murmured to Griffin, shoving him off me and wrapping his arms around my snarling, wild wolf. "That was childish and selfish. Finn's a one-day old Alpha. He's barely holding onto his control by a thread as it is, and you shove your old boyfriend in his face, stinking of you? God, you're such a fucking jealous baby, Griff."

"I told him to stay away," Griffin protested, as Fiona broke in angrily.

"Aksil's right, Griffin. We don't have time for this shit. Finn could have killed the vamp, and then what? How are we supposed to lead a revolution together if two of the three Alphas in charge of the wolves are having a fucking lover's spat? Jesus, Mary, and Joseph, grow the fuck up," Fiona snapped, pissed.

"No need to overdramatize the whole thing. Simon is 500 years older than the wolf pup; he was in no danger. And Griffin didn't call him in to make his little mate jealous, I did. I am also the one who requested Kai join the council for the same reason," the vampire Madelaine broke in, striding over to us as I breathed in and out, wrestling for control back over my wolf. "You can release him, Aksil," she said, crouching down on the floor beside me. "You and Aksil are the wolf and witch pair from the prophecy. I've dreamed of you both many times over the last century, wondering if you'd find each other and fulfill the prophecy, and what that would mean for the vampires. But the dreams changed recently, and I had to see for myself if they were true."

I shifted back, finally gaining control of my wolf, and stood up naked in front of the ancient vampire, shooting Griffin a death stare that stopped him in his tracks when he moved toward me.

"I'm getting really sick of everyone fucking with me because of this godamn prophecy," I growled, panting as I fought to maintain control over my wolf.

Madelaine shrugged in response, clearly not giving a shit about what a one-day old Alpha had to say about her little game. "As I was saying," she continued smoothly. "Fate has intervened, and the three of you are intertwined now. The prophecy is no longer just about you and Aksil. You have chosen Griffin as your mate and your wolf instinctively sought to defend his claim on Griffin, not Aksil. You were able to hold onto control of your wolf, despite the jealous feelings we could all smell Kai bring out in you, but you could not contain him when Simon entered the room. Your wolf has answered the question the three of you have been asking. He may still want Aksil's wolf, but he accepts your claim on Griffin as your mate. Now, you have to accept his answer and lead this revolution as the three unified Alphas of the Northwoods Pack."

"You have your work cut out for you," Kai added, slipping his shirt off and offering it to me. "You will need to choose your ambassadors wisely, select the right witch, wolf, and vampire to begin your outreach campaign to all the packs, covens, and lairs in the U.S. We will make a list of who you should approach from each group about forming governing councils."

"So, everyone's on board?" I asked, staring around the room at the witches and vampires, as I buttoned Kai's shirt up, which thankfully, was just long enough to cover my junk and most of my ass, returning a shred of my dignity to me. Simon had left the room, which helped me rein my wolf back in a little, but it was still awkward standing in front of everyone in just a shirt.

"I want the name of who ordered Raffi's kidnapping," Tai repeated his earlier demand. "We're not doing a fucking thing with the witches until then."

"I am your liege, and I control this lair," James reminded Tai in a mild voice, with a hint of warning at the end. "I decide when and if we join this fight."

"I will not stand with the witches without the name," Tai replied defiantly.

"You will do whatever my brother tells you to do, or he will kill you," a vampire said softly from the doorway. "The fact that James has allowed you to live this long is a testament to the depth of his love for me, but I would not test him further," the vampire, who I assumed was Raffi, advised, leaning against the doorframe.

He shared certain physical characteristics with James, the same black hair, thick, dark brows, the slant of his cheekbones. But that's where the resemblance ended. James exuded power and control. He had a stealthy, terrifying, predator vibe that caused the hair to stand up on my arms in his presence. His brother was an empty shell, eyes vacant with acceptance, body limp with defeat, voice weary and devoid of emotion.

"We will join for the Canada battle, and we'll wait for the name to proceed with the rest," James declared, ignoring his brother's speech from the doorway.

"We're not backing you for the Canada fight, if you won't commit to going the distance with us," Fiona said flatly. "We have no beef with the Montreal coven right now, but if we back your fight and wipe them out and you don't stand with us, the European witches will come at us with everything they've got. No fucking way, we're risking our necks for nothing."

"I will back your coven," Madelaine said, shooting James a cool stare. "And one of my own will sit on the Vampire Council. My lair is ready to take a stand."

"Then it's decided," Aksil said. "Fiona's coven and James's lair will join us for the Montreal fight, and if James decides he's out after that, Madelaine is guaranteeing her backing with the vampires."

"We'll attack in three days. We want to move fast, before they suspect anything and have time to prepare," Griffin said.

"Agreed," James nodded. "War meeting tomorrow night?"

"Pack lodge, 7:00 p.m." Griffin nodded back.

"We'll be there," Fiona agreed.

"Tate and I have some battle suggestions, so we'll join the meeting as well," my father added.

"Kai and I will be in touch." Madelaine blew me a kiss, as I bent over to retrieve my shredded clothes and sneakers and headed for the doorway.

"Are you okay?" Aksil asked as I followed Ali to my truck, stiff backed, still keeping my distance from Griffin.

"Peachy," I replied, keeping my back to Aksil and Griffin as I hopped into my truck beside Ali, who slid into the driver's seat.

33

"That was a dirty trick, right?" I asked my sister for the third time, grabbing the super chunk peanut butter out of her hand and dipping my half of her jumbo Hershey bar into the jar.

"Definitely," Ali agreed yet again, one hand on the wheel of my truck, the other reaching for the peanut butter.

"By the way, worst freak out food ever. We need some jumbo burritos or something," I complained.

"It's my emergency period stash. I don't keep burritos in my go bag."

"But you keep a massive jar of super chunk and a jumbo chocolate bar in it?" I laughed.

"You have no idea what it's like to be a hormonal bloody wreck. You need to have peanut butter and chocolate on hand for periods. And be happy I also keep a pair of sweats in there or your naked ass would still be sticking to the seat of this truck since you shred your clothes with your little psycho wolf shift."

"I can't believe some ancient vampire set me up to have a jealous, Alpha wolf-out in front of everyone, just to see if I would pick Griffin or Aksil as my mate!"

"Hmmm," Ali agreed over a mouthful of chocolate and peanut butter.

"Was it bad? It was bad, wasn't it? I'm so mortified," I wailed. "My first big Alpha meeting and I totally humiliate myself by trying to kill one of the hosts because he smelled like Griffin!"

"Uh huh." Ali avoided my eyes as she stared straight ahead at the road.

"He totally smelled like Griffin; I didn't fucking imagine that, right?" I demanded. "It wasn't just that he was eyeballing my wolf like an ice cream cone, he fucking smelled like him!" I growled. "Why the fuck did he smell like him?"

"I was kind of wondering when you were going to ask that question," Ali sighed.

"I'm going to kill Griffin! That hypocritical motherfucker!" I roared. "He's been up my ass non-stop over Aksil, while he's been secretly banging some vamp?"

"I mean, maybe find out for sure before you totally freak out on him..." Ali grimaced as we pulled into my driveway and Griffin stepped out in front of the truck.

"How did he beat us back here? We left first and we didn't even stop for burritos!"

"I'm sure he knows all the backroads. This is his pack territory. I was using Google maps to get us back," Ali snorted.

"He smelled like you!" I opened the truck door and yelled out to Griffin. "Why the fuck did he smell like you, Griff?"

"I went to see him last night," Griffin sighed, walking over to me, and pulling me into his arms and against his chest.

I pulled away from Griffin, shooting him a look of death. "You went to see him?"

Griffin winced. "It's not what you think, babe, I promise you. I didn't do anything with him, and I didn't go there with the intention to either."

"I'm gonna go for a run after that tense little night, let you two talk." Ali stripped out of her clothes and shifted, running off into the forest.

"So, why did you go there?" I demanded as Griffin followed me into the house.

"I was a mess these last two days," Griffin admitted, running his fingers through his hair in frustration. "You challenged me for the pack, dared Aksil to kiss you, and told me you wanted time apart all in the same day. I just needed to get away and clear my head. I went to Portland for a drink and ended up running into Simon. He invited me back to the house, and I didn't want to be alone, so I went."

"You didn't want to be alone," I repeated, plopping down on the couch.

"No, I didn't want to be alone, Finn. I didn't want to go back to the lodge and try to sleep alone in my bed again, wondering what you did with Aksil in the woods after I left with your father yesterday, and why you didn't come back home to me."

"Okay," I said quietly. "Did you also want to get back at me a little, maybe hook up with an old boyfriend to get even for whatever I might have done with Aksil in the woods? And don't even try to deny Simon is an ex, because the way he looked at you said it all. And he's not some guy you coldly fucked once and walked away from either. His body language alone left no doubt to the entire room that he's fucked every single part of you, and you loved every minute of it."

"Yes, he's an ex, no I wasn't planning on hooking up with him and I didn't," Griffin replied quietly. "But did it feel good to know I was wanted? Yes," Griffin admitted, sitting down on the couch beside me.

"And so, what, he smelled like you this morning because you stopped by the night before?" I raised my eyebrows.

"I stayed over," Griffin admitted. "I fell asleep, and I stayed over."

"Did you sleep in his arms?"

"No."
"Same bed?"
"Not exactly."
"Not exactly?"
"Same couch."
"Same couch?"
"We fell asleep watching a movie."
"Huh. How romantic."
"Did you kiss Aksil in the woods?"
"Yes."
"I fucking knew it," Griffin swore.
"Did you kiss Simon?"
"No."
"Did you want to?"
"Yes."

"To get back at me, or because you wanted to hook up with him?"

"Both, maybe? I don't know," Griffin exhaled. "I don't want to be with him, if that's what you're asking. I only want you, Finn. You're my mate. But I was pissed at you and I think I did want to feel like I was wanted by someone at least."

"I want you," I whispered. "I know my connection to Aksil is fucked up, but I want you, Griff. I love you. You're my mate and I would have killed Simon just for smelling like you if you hadn't tackled me," I admitted.

"That's how I've felt about Aksil since the beginning."

"I'm so sorry," I choked, taking Griffin's hand.

"Your wolf chose me," Griffin whispered, pulling me into his lap. "You were annoyed when Mati grabbed Aksil's ass, and you were jealous of Kai, but you fucking went wolf-shit crazy when Simon walked into the room smelling like me," Griffin grinned, brushing his nose against mine.

"You're my mate, no one else gets to touch you," I growled,

nipping at Griffin's lip. "No one else gets to smell like you," I whispered against his mouth, kissing him deeply.

"I know it was fucked up, smelling me on him like that, especially when you're a brand-new Alpha with so little control," Griffin said quietly. "But Madelaine, forcing your wolf to choose like that, I think I needed it, Finn, whether I realized it or not. I know I said I was okay, and I trusted you, but I needed to see your wolf views me as his mate. I needed to see it and feel it after everything that's happened between us."

"I get it, I really do now. I think I needed to see someone laying a claim to you to understand what it feels like," I whispered, curling up in Griffin's chest.

"So, you think Madelaine is right? The three of us are part of the prophecy now?" Griffin asked quietly.

"Yes. I can't really explain it, but the three of us feel entwined now. I don't know what lies ahead, or what the journey is going to look like, but you, me, and Aksil are going to unite the three sides, I feel certain of that."

"Are you ready for the battle ahead of us? Because there will be casualties, Finn, and part of being an Alpha is accepting that weight and bearing it for those who are left behind."

"That's why you're mad at Cian," I said slowly.

"It was my job to bear the brunt of his loss," Griffin choked. "But he wouldn't let me. He took off without giving me a chance to help him through it."

"I see it now." I trailed my fingers across Griffin's face, tracing the worry lines etched into his skin. "You carry so much for the pack. It's what Anya was trying to tell me when we first met. It's not just your warrior skills that make you such an amazing Alpha, you protect the pack physically, but you also carry their emotional burdens as well. You really are incredible, Griffin. I'm sorry I haven't told you that, and I hope you can forgive me for asking your pack to choose between us."

"You earned the right when you stood up for Aksil. I fucked up when I put you before him. You were right when you said I don't get to choose between my pack members, and even though Aksil wasn't fully bonded to my pack, he was still a part of it, and I should have figured out a way to protect him without endangering you."

"I'm not ready for a battle. I can't imagine losing any of the pack, but I want to unite the three sides, and I'm willing to do whatever it takes, including learning how to be a good Alpha from you."

"You already are a great Alpha, Finn. That's why the pack answered your call. All three of us bring such different things to the role," Griffin admitted.

"I never meant to bring Aksil in as an Alpha when I challenged you for the pack, Griff. I swear, I would never have done that to you intentionally, and I have no idea how it even happened."

"The pack pulled him in," Griffin sighed. "It actually makes perfect sense. He's been with them since the beginning, when my father first formed the pack with his parents, before I was even born. He came here with Safiya, Badis, and my father. This whole thing is so much bigger than us and my jealousy over Aksil's connection to you, Finn, and it's time I stop focusing on Aksil, and address the needs of the pack and the werewolf world in general."

"What do you mean?"

"The division between the witches, wolves, and vampires has been hurting us all since it began. But even worse, is our lack of leadership. Part of what takes up so much of my time, is trying to help other packs who suffer from poor leadership, or power-hungry Alphas abusing their role, and the witches and vampires have the same problem. All three groups need their own councils, we need real accountability and leadership here in the U.S. Then we can stand independent from Europe and work toward uniting all three sides."

"How do we do that?"

"We work together." Griffin pressed his lips into my hair. "I'll never accept Aksil's claim on you, but I will accept him as the third Alpha of this pack. He's been with them since the beginning, and he deserves to lead them as much as I do."

"How about me?" I tilted my head back to meet Griffin's eyes.

"The pack fell in love with you the moment you climbed onto the bar at Molly's," Griffin teased, ducking to the side when I swatted him.

"Ha ha."

"Seriously Finn, I meant what I said earlier, you earned the right to lead this pack when you stood up for Aksil. The pack knows you would put each and every one of them first, and they love you for it. Look what you've done with your house, opening it up to everyone, turning it into a wellness center, a safe space to seek council and support."

"I think I finally know why Cian gave me this place."

"You mean other than a means to torment me and keep us apart?" Griffin teased gently.

"I think it's supposed to be a sanctuary for wolves who have lost their way, and I'm supposed to build it."

"You mean what you're doing with it for the pack?"

"No, I mean a real haven, a place for lost wolves outside our pack to seek sanctuary, heal, start fresh, find a new path."

"You mean wolves like Cian?" Griffin's eyes flashed with pain. "Wolves whose pack let them down, wolves seeking a new home."

"Wolves who have lost their way, for whatever reason," I said gently. "You didn't let Cian down, Griff. He never gave you a chance, but regardless, he is lost and hurting, and from what you've told me, there are countless wolves out there on the run, alone and feeling helpless. I want to create a safe space for them, whether they use the time here to heal and move on or stay and join our pack."

"It's a great idea, your wolf sanctuary. It's a wonderful way to honor Nate, and whether Cian ever comes back to our pack or not, he would love you using this house to help lost and wounded wolves.

In fact, I think you have your first guest." Griffin scented the air, and we both breathed in deeply as a truck rattled up the drive and came to a stop in front of the cabin.

About the Author

Ariel Ellman received her BA in English Literature from Drew University. A native New Yorker, she now resides in New Jersey with her husband and five children. She has been writing since she was a little girl. This is her fifth novel. She loves to hear from her readers. Visit her Facebook page for excerpts from her books and info on upcoming releases. You can contact her at: www.goodreads.com/arielellman or www.facebook.com/thesweetspotbook.

Acknowledgments

Thank you to all the people in my life who supported and encouraged me throughout the process of bringing this series to print, my husband Damon, my brother-in-law Jeff, my sister Victoria, my five wonderful children, Elijah, Jonah, Gavi, Chava, and Zahara. A huge thanks to my editor, Vinessa, who pushed me not to give up on this book until it was out there in the world, and to all the amazing writers in my workshop, whose critique and encouragement made the final version of this story what it is today! A big thank you to my book designer Dan for his amazing covers and great book layout, and to my son Gavi for getting it all started! I am deeply grateful to be surrounded by so many wonderful, talented people!

The Northwoods Pack Saga continues with

WolfStruck

Book Two in
The Northwoods Pack Series
out now!

Made in the USA
Columbia, SC
30 September 2025